02/14

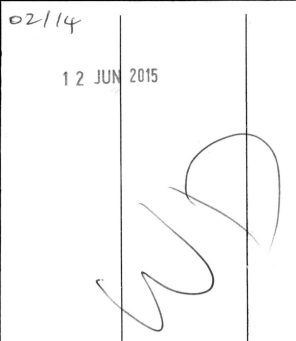

Published in Great Britain 2014
by Mills & Boon, an imprint of Harlequin (UK) Limited,
Eton House, 18-24 Paradise Road, Richmond, Surrey, TW9 1SR

AUSTRALIAN QUINNS © 2014 Harlequin Books S.A.

The Mighty Quinns: Brody, The Mighty Quinns: Teague and *The Mighty Quinns: Callum* were first published in Great Britain by Harlequin (UK) Limited.

The Mighty Quinns: Brody © 2009 Peggy A. Hoffmann
The Mighty Quinns: Teague © 2009 Peggy A. Hoffmann
The Mighty Quinns: Callum © 2009 Peggy A. Hoffmann

ISBN: 978 0 263 91173 2
eBook ISBN: 978 1 472 04468 6

05-0214

Harlequin (UK) Limited's policy is to use papers that are natural, renewable and recyclable products and made from wood grown in sustainable forests. The logging and manufacturing processes conform to the legal environmental regulations of the country of origin.

Printed and bound in Spain
by Blackprint CPI, Barcelona

THE MIGHTY QUINNS: BRODY

BY
KATE HOFFMANN

Kate Hoffmann has been writing for Mills & Boon for fifteen years and has published nearly sixty books, including Mills & Boon® Blaze® books, novellas and even the occasional historical. When she isn't writing, she is involved in various musical and theatrical activities in her small Wisconsin community. She enjoys sleeping late, drinking coffee and eating bonbons. She lives with her two cats, Tally and Chloe, and her computer, which shall remain nameless.

For Sarah Mayberry, fellow author and gentle reader,
who took the time to make sure this book
had "no worries."

Prologue

Queensland, Australia—January, 1994

"HOW CAN A ROCK be magic?" Callum asked, standing at the base of the huge boulder. "It's just a bloody big rock."

"Look around you, dipstick," Teague shouted from the top of the rock. "Do you see any other rocks like this around here? Gramps said it's here because it *is* magic. You stand on top of this rock and make a wish and it comes true. Aborigines brought it here and they know a lot of magic."

"I think Gramps had a few kangaroos loose in the paddock." Callum chuckled. "I wouldn't believe everything he said."

Brody stepped up to the rock. "He did not. And I'm telling Dad you said that. It's not nice to speak ill of the dead."

"He told us there was treasure buried out here, too," Callum said. "He even told me he dug for it when he was a boy. Who would bury treasure out here?"

Brody punched Callum in the shoulder. "Give me a leg up," he said.

"No, we have to get back. Mum will have supper ready."

"I want to climb it," Brody insisted. It was hard enough always being last in line, but he hated it when Callum tried to be the boss. At least Teague liked to explore and have adventures. He treated Brody as if they were the very same age, not eighteen months apart. Callum was always the careful one, warning them off when things got too dangerous. Three years older than Brody and he might have well been forty, Brody thought.

"You'll fall and crack your noggin open," Callum warned. "And I'll get the blame, just like I always get the blame for every bad thing you morons do."

"Cal, help him up," Teague said. "It's not that high. And I'll hang on to him."

"You don't have to hang on to me," Brody said. "I'm not a baby."

Reluctantly, Callum wove his fingers together and bent down. Brody put his foot into his older brother's hands and a few moments later, Teague had dragged him to the top of the rock. "Wow," Brody said. "This is high. I bet I can see all of Queensland from here."

"You've climbed to the top of the windmills. They're much higher," Callum said as he scrambled up behind him. "And you can't see Brisbane from them. And Brisbane *is* in Queensland."

"Make a wish," Teague said. "We'll see if it works."

"I have to think," Brody said. He wanted so many things. A computer, video games, a dirt bike. But there was something he wanted more than anything. He'd never told his brothers because he knew they'd laugh. After all, there wasn't much chance he'd ever get off the station.

"Come on," Teague said. "Say it. It won't come true unless you shout it out loud."

"I want to be a footballer," Brody yelled. "I want to go to a real school and play on a real team. I want to be famous and everyone will know my name. And I want to be on the telly." To Brody's surprise, his brothers didn't laugh. In fact, they seemed to think his wish was a good one.

"That's a big wish," Callum said soberly.

"My turn," Teague said. "I know exactly what I want. I want an airplane. Or a helicopter. I want to learn how to fly. Then I can go anywhere I want, just like that. I could even fly over the ocean and see America or Africa or the South Pole."

"You could take me to my football games," Brody said.

Teague reached out and ruffled Brody's hair. "I could. But only if you give me free tickets." He stared over at Callum. "What about you?"

"I know what I want," Callum said.

"You have to say it."

Callum sat down, draping his arms over his knees as he took in the view. "How do you think this rock really got here?"

"I think it's a meteor," Brody said, sitting down beside him. "It dropped out of the sky."

Callum ran his hand over the smooth surface of the rock. "Maybe the Aborigines did move it here. Maybe it was like Stonehenge. You know, that place in England with all the rocks."

"And I think a giant prehistoric bird took a crap and it fossilized," Teague teased as he joined them. They all laughed, lying back on the rock and staring up at the cloudless sky.

Brody wrinkled his nose. "How can bird poop be magic, Teague?"

"Maybe it came from a magic bird." His brother gave him a sideways glance. "All right. It's a meteor. Or an asteroid. From another universe. Come on, Cal, you have to make your wish now."

Callum drew a deep breath. "I wish that someday I could have a place like this."

"You want a rock?" Brody asked.

"No, dickhead. A station. As big as Kerry Creek. Bigger, even. And I'd raise the best cattle in all of Queensland."

"Why would you want to live on a station?" Brody asked.

"'Cause I like it here," Callum replied.

Brody shook his head. His older brother had no imagination. Station life was horribly dull, the same thing day after day. There was never anything interesting to do. All the good stuff happened in cities like Brisbane and Sydney. Callum could have the station and Teague could have his plane. Brody knew his dream was the best.

"Dad told me he brought Mum out here when he asked her to marry him," Callum said, sitting up to scan the horizon.

Teague and Brody glanced at each other, then looked away silently. Brody wasn't sure why Callum had brought the subject up. Their parents hadn't been getting along for nearly a year now. When they weren't arguing, they were avoiding each other. Dinner was usually a shouting match or an endless meal marked by dead silence.

"I want to change my wish," Brody murmured,

sitting up beside Callum. "I wish that Mum and Dad wouldn't fight anymore. I wish they'd be like they used to be." He drew a deep breath, fighting back the tears that pressed at the corners of his eyes. "Remember when they used to kiss? When Dad would hug her so hard, she'd laugh? And they'd turn on the radio and dance around the kitchen?"

"Yeah." Teague braced his elbows behind him. "I remember that."

The first ten years of Brody's life had been spent in what he'd believed was a happy family. But then he began to be more aware of his mother's unhappiness and of his father's frustration. She hated life on the station and his father didn't know any other life *but* the station.

Callum grabbed Brody's hand and then Teague's and pressed all their hands together. "Wish it," he said, dragging them closer. "Close your eyes and wish it really hard and it will happen."

"I thought you didn't believe in the rock," Teague said.

"Do it!" Callum said. "Now."

They all closed their eyes and focused on the one wish. But somehow, Brody knew this wish didn't depend on the rock or the combined powers of the three Quinn brothers. It was up to their parents to make it come true.

When he opened his eyes, he found his brothers staring at him. Brody forced a smile, but it did nothing to relieve his fears. Something bad was going to happen, he could feel it.

He rolled over onto his stomach and slid down the side of the rock, dropping to the dusty ground with a soft thud. His horse was tethered nearby and he grabbed the reins and swung up into the saddle. As he watched his brothers jump down, Brody couldn't help but wonder whether the rock had heard them. It was just a rock. And though it didn't belong where it was, there probably wasn't anything special about it.

Pulling hard on the reins, he kicked his horse in the flanks and took off at a gallop. If his mother left the station, then he was going with her. She'd need someone to take care of her, and Brody had always been able to make her smile. She'd once whispered to him that he was her favorite. If that was true, then it was his duty to leave the station. He felt the tears tumbling from his eyes and drying on his cheeks as the wind rushed by.

The breeze caught the brim of his stockman's hat and it flew off, the string catching around his neck. Brody closed his eyes and gave the horse control over their destination. Maybe the horse wouldn't go home. Maybe it would just keep galloping, running to a place where life wasn't quite so confusing.

1

Queensland, Australia—June, 2009

HIS BODY ACHED, from the throbbing in his head to the deep, dull pain in his knee. The various twinges in between—his back, his right elbow, the fingers of his left hand—felt worse than usual. Brody Quinn wondered if he'd always wake up with a reminder of the motorcycle accident that had ruined his future or, if someday, all the pain would magically be gone.

Hell, he'd just turned twenty-six and he felt like an old man. Reaching up, he rubbed his forehead, certain of only one thing—he'd spent the previous night sitting on his arse at the Spotted Dog getting himself drunk.

The sound of an Elvis Presley tune drifted through the air and Brody knew exactly where he'd slept it off— the Bilbarra jail. The town's police chief, Angus Embley, was a huge fan of Presley, willing to debate the King's singular place in the world of music with any bloke who dared to argue the point. Right now, Elvis was only exacerbating Brody's headache.

"Angus!" he shouted. "Can you turn down the music?"

Since he'd returned home to his family's cattle station in Queensland, he'd grown rather fond of the accommodations at the local jail. Though he usually ended up behind bars for some silly reason, it saved him the long drive home or sleeping it off in his SUV. "Angus!"

"He's not here. He went out to get some breakfast."

Brody rolled over to look into the adjoining cell, startled to hear a female voice. As he rubbed his bleary eyes, he focused on a slender woman standing just a few feet away, dressed in a pretty, flowered blouse and blue jeans. Her delicate fingers were wrapped around the bars that separated them, her dark eyes intently fixed on his.

"Christ," he muttered, flopping back onto the bed. Now he'd really hit bottom, Brody mused, throwing his arm over his eyes. Getting royally pissed was one thing, but hallucinating a female prisoner was another. He was still drunk.

He closed his eyes, but the image of her swirled in his brain. Odd that he'd conjured up this particular apparition. She didn't really fit his standard of beauty. He usually preferred blue-eyed blondes with large breasts and shapely backsides and long, long legs.

This woman was slim, with deep mahogany hair that fell in a riot of curls around her face and shoulders. By his calculations, she might come up to his chin at best. And her features were...odd. Her lips were almost too lush and her cheekbones too high. And her skin was so pale and perfect that he had to wonder if she ever spent a day in the sun.

"You don't have to be embarrassed. A lot of people talk in their sleep."

Brody sat up. She had an American accent. His fantasy women never had American accents. "What?"

She stared at him from across the cell. "It was mostly just mumbling. And some snoring. And you did mention someone named Nessa."

"Vanessa," he murmured, scanning her features again. She wasn't wearing a bit of makeup, yet she looked as if she'd just stepped out of the pages of one of those fashion magazines Vanessa always had on hand. She had that fresh-scrubbed, innocent, girl-next-door look about her. Natural. Clean. He wondered if she smelled as good as she looked.

Since returning home, there hadn't been a single woman who'd piqued his interest—until now. Though she could be anywhere between sixteen and thirty, Brody reckoned if she was younger than eighteen, she wouldn't be sitting in a jail cell. It was probably safe to lust after her.

"You definitely said Nessa," she insisted. "I remember. I thought it was an odd name."

"It's short for Vanessa. She's a model and that's what they call her." Nessa was so famous, she didn't need a last name, kind of like Madonna or Sting.

"She's your girlfriend?"

"Yes." He drew a sharp breath, then cleared his throat. "No. Ex-girlfriend."

"Sorry," she said with an apologetic shrug. "I didn't mean to stir up bad memories."

"No bad memories," Brody replied, noting the hint of defensiveness in his voice. What the hell did he care what this woman thought of him—or the girls he'd dated? He swung his legs off the edge of the bed, then raked his hands through his hair. "I know why *I'm* here. What are *you* doing in a cell?"

"Just a small misunderstanding," she said, forcing a smile.

"Angus doesn't lock people up for small misunderstandings," Brody countered, pushing to his feet. "Especially not women." He crossed to stand in front of her, wrapping his fingers around the bars just above hers. "What did you do?"

"Dine and dash," she said.

"What?"

Her eyes dropped and a pretty blush stained her cheeks. "I—I skipped out on my bill at the diner down the street. And a few other meals in a few other towns. I guess my life of crime finally caught up with me. The owner called the cops and I'm in here until I find a way to work it off."

He pressed his forehead into the bars, hoping the cool iron would soothe the ache in his head. "Why don't you just pay for what you ate?"

"I would have, but I didn't have any cash. I left an IOU. And I said I'd come back and pay as soon as I found work. I guess that wasn't good enough."

Brody let his hands slide down until he was touching her, if only to prove that she was real and that he wasn't dreaming. "What happened to all your money?" he asked, fixing his attention on her face as he ran his fingers over hers. It seemed natural to touch her, even though she was a complete stranger. Oddly, she didn't seem to mind.

Her breath caught and then she sighed. "It's all gone. Desperate times call for desperate measures. I'm not a dishonest person. I was just really, really hungry."

She had the most beautiful mouth he'd ever seen, her

lips soft and full…perfect for— He fought the urge to pull her closer and take a quick taste, just to see if she'd be…different. "What's your name?"

"Payton," she murmured.

"Payton," he repeated, leaning back to take in details of her body. "Is that your last name or your first?"

"Payton Harwell," she said.

"And you're American?"

"I am."

"And you're in jail," he said, stating the obvious.

She laughed softly and nodded as she glanced around. "It appears I am. At least for a while. Angus told me as soon as he finds a way for me to work off my debt, he'll let me out. I told him I could wash dishes at the diner, but the owner doesn't want me back there. I guess jobs are in short supply around here."

Brody's gaze drifted back to her face—he was oddly fascinated by her features. Had he seen her at a party or in a nightclub in Fremantle, he probably wouldn't have given her a second glance. But given time to appreciate her attributes, he couldn't seem to find a single flaw worth mentioning.

"Quinn!"

Brody glanced over his shoulder and watched as Angus strolled in, his freshly pressed uniform already rumpled after just a few hours of work. "Are you sober yet?"

"You didn't have to lock me up," Brody said, letting go of the bars.

"Brody Quinn, you started a brawl, you broke a mirror and you threw a bleedin' drink in my face, after insulting my taste in music. You didn't give me a choice." Angus braced his hands on his hips. "There'll be a fine. I figure a couple hundred should do it. And you're gonna have to pay for Buddy's mirror." Angus scratched his chin. "And I want a promise you're gonna behave yourself from now on and respect the law. Your brother's here, so pay the fine and you can go."

"Teague is here?" Brody asked.

"No, Callum is waiting. He's not so chuffed he had to make a trip into town."

"I could have driven myself home," Brody said.

"Your buddy Billy tried to take your keys last night. That's what started the fight. He flushed the keys, so Callum brought your spare." Angus reached down and unlocked the cell. "Next time you kick up a stink, I'm holding you for a week. That's a promise."

Brody turned back and looked at Payton. "You can let her out. I'll pay her fine, too."

"First you have to settle up with Miss Shelly over at the coffeeshop and then you have to find this young lady a job. Then, I'll let you pay her fine. Until you do all that, she's gonna be a guest for a bit longer."

"It's all right," Payton said in a cheerful voice. "I'm okay here. I've got a nice place to sleep and regular meals."

Brody frowned as he shook his head. It just didn't feel right leaving her locked up, even if she did want to stay. "Suit yourself," he said, rubbing at the ache in his head.

Payton gave him a little wave, but it didn't ease his qualms. Who was she? And what had brought her to Bilbarra? There were a lot of questions running through his mind without any reasonable answers.

He walked with Angus through the front office

toward the door. "Let her out, Angus," he said in a low voice. "I'll fix any mess she's made."

"I think she wants to stay for a while. I'm not sure she has anywhere else to go. I figure, I'll find her a job and at least she'll eat." He cleared his throat. "Besides, she doesn't complain about my music. She actually likes Elvis. Smart girl."

When they reached the front porch of the police station, Brody found his eldest brother, Callum, sitting in an old wooden chair, his feet propped up on the porch railing, his felt stockman's hat pulled low over his eyes.

Brody sat down next to him, bracing his elbows on his knees. "Go ahead. Get it over with. Chuck a spaz and we'll call it a day."

Callum shoved his hat back and glanced at his little brother. "Jaysus, Brody, this is the third time this month. You keep this up, you might as well live here and save yourself the trouble driving the two hours into town every weekend. At least I wouldn't worry about how you're getting home."

"It won't happen again," Brody mumbled.

"I can't spare the time. And petrol doesn't come cheap. And it's not like I don't have enough on my mind with this whole land mess boiling up again."

Callum had been a grouch for the past month, ever since Harry Fraser had filed papers in court to contest what had to be the longest-running land dispute in the history of Australia. Harry ran the neighboring station and the Frasers and the Quinns had been feuding for close to a hundred years, mostly over a strip of land that lay between the stations—land with the most productive water bore within a couple hundred kilometers.

Ownership of the property had passed back and forth over the years, dependant on the judge who heard the case. It was now the Quinns' property to lose.

"He's lost the last three times he tried. He hasn't been able to find any decent proof of his claim. What makes you think that will change now?"

"I'm still going to have to hire a bloody solicitor and they don't come cheap." Callum sighed. "And then this genealogy woman just shows up on the doorstep yesterday morning and expects me to spend all my time telling stories about our family history."

"I said I was sorry."

"You're turning into a fair wanker, you are. You could find something better to do with yourself. Like lending a hand on the station. We could use your help mustering now that Teague's practice is starting to take off. He's been taking calls almost every day. And when he's home, he spends his time doing paperwork."

"I haven't decided on a plan," Brody muttered. "But it bloody well doesn't include stockman's work. Now, can I have my keys? I've got some things to do."

"Buddy doesn't want you back at the Spotted Dog. You're going to have to find yourself another place to get pissed—" Callum paused "—or you could give up the coldies. It would save you some money."

Brody's brother Teague had been back on Kerry Creek for about a year after working as an equine vet near Brisbane. He'd taken up with Doc Daley's practice in Bilbarra, planning to buy him out so that the old man could retire. He'd saved enough in Brisbane to purchase a plane, making it possible to move about the outback quickly and efficiently.

Callum's income came directly from working Kerry Creek, the Quinn family's fifty-thousand-acre cattle station. Part of the profits went to their parents, now living in Sydney, where their mother taught school and their father had started a small landscaping business in his retirement.

And Brody, who'd once boasted a rather impressive bank account, was now unemployed, his million-dollar contract gone, many of his investments liquidated and his savings dwindling every day. He could survive another three or four years, if he lived frugally. But after that, he needed to find a decent job. Something that didn't involve kicking a football between two goalposts.

When Brody had left the station as a teenager, there'd been no other choice. He'd hated station life almost as much as his mother had. And though he'd wanted to stay with his brothers, his mother needed someone to go with her, to watch out for her. It had been a way to realize his dream of a pro-football career and he'd grabbed the chance. If it hadn't been for the accident, he'd still be living in Fremantle, enjoying his life and breaking every last scoring record for his team.

One stupid mistake and it had ended. He'd torn up his knee and spent the last year in rehab, trying to get back to form. He'd played in three games earlier in the season before the club dropped him. No new contract, no second chance, just a polite fare-thee-well.

"I'm sorry you're not doing what you want to do," Callum said, reaching out and putting his hand on Brody's shoulder. "Sometimes life is just crap. But you pick yourself up and you get on with it. And you stop being such a dickhead."

Brody gave his brother a shove, then stood up. "Give it a rest. If I needed a mother, I'd move back to Sydney and live with the one I already have." Brody grabbed his keys from Callum's hand then jogged down the front steps and out into the dusty street. "I'll catch you later."

As he walked down the main street of Bilbarra, his thoughts returned to the woman sitting in Angus's cell. "Payton," he whispered. He hadn't been attracted to any woman since Vanessa had walked out on him a year ago, frustrated by his dark moods and eager to find a bloke with a better future and a bigger bank account.

But Payton Harwell didn't know him, or football. All she cared about was a place to sleep and her next meal. And he certainly had the means to provide that.

PAYTON SIPPED at the bottle of orange juice that Angus had brought for her breakfast. She'd finished the egg sandwich first, then gobbled down the beans and bacon, enough nutrition to last her the entire day. Sooner or later, Angus would let her out and then she'd be back to scraping by for her meals. It was best to eat while she could.

She glanced over at the adjoining cell. It had been pleasant to have some company for a time, she mused. Actually, more than pleasant when the fellow prisoner was as handsome and fascinating as Brody Quinn. Payton rubbed the spot where their hands had touched, remembering the sensation that had raced through her at the contact.

She'd been in Australia for a month now and this had been the first real conversation she'd allowed herself.

She'd told him her name, but not much else. In truth, since her arrival, Payton had spent most of her time trying to figure out exactly who she was, now that she wasn't what she was supposed to be.

Until a month ago, her life had always been neatly laid out in front of her—the best schools, carefully chosen activities, the right friends, exotic vacations. As she grew older, a top-notch education and a careful search for an appropriate husband. Finally, a wonderful wedding to a successful man that her parents adored. It had been exactly the path her mother had followed, a step-by-step guide to happiness.

Payton had taken on the role of the dutiful daughter, doing all she could to please her parents and never once rebelling against their authority. Even when they'd insisted she stop riding at age seventeen after breaking her arm in a fall, Payton had agreed. She'd loved her horse, and riding had given her a wonderful sense of freedom. But she'd simply assumed that her parents knew best. If she'd had a rebellious streak, it hadn't shown itself—until a month ago. And then, it had erupted like a dormant volcano.

When it came to the moment to say "I do," Payton had turned and run. For the first time in her life, she'd made a decision for herself. Though she was twenty-five years old, her perfect life up to that point had never prepared her to deal with self-doubt. Running had been her only option.

She'd met Sam her first day at Columbia. He was the man her mother had always told her about, the man who could give her everything she'd ever want or need. He was handsome and smart, four years older, and from a wealthy

East Coast family. Her father, the scion of a banking empire, approved of his finances, and her mother, a third-generation socialite, approved of his bloodlines. And it wasn't as if there hadn't been an attraction between them. There had been...in the beginning.

An image flashed in her mind. How easily she'd forgotten Sam. All she wanted to think about now was this stranger who had touched her, this man with the penetrating gaze and the dangerous smile. A tiny thrill raced through her at the memory of his eyes raking the length of her body.

Payton leaned her head back against the concrete wall of the cell. Brody Quinn was incredibly sexy. Any woman would be attracted to a man like that. She allowed herself to speculate. Shirt on, shirt off. Completely naked and—without the bars between them, she wondered just how far she would have gone. A kiss, a quick grope, maybe more?

Payton sighed. Maybe her attraction to Brody wasn't an early midlife crisis. Maybe she was experiencing some sort of sexual schizophrenia caused by all the stress she'd been under. She'd never thought a whole lot about sex until recently. It had never been that important.

But suddenly, she found herself thinking about passion and desire, about what it truly meant to connect on a physical level with a man. Wasn't it normal for her to worry if Sam was the last man she'd ever sleep with? Shouldn't he want to touch her and make her moan with pleasure? Shouldn't sexual attraction be just as important as love and mutual respect?

There hadn't been that many men in her life—a grand total of four—so she hadn't much experience on which to rely. Two boys in high school, one in college after she and Sam had broken up for a time, and then Sam. She knew sex was supposed to be exciting and it had been, up until Sam had started working twelve- to fourteen-hour days. Suddenly, intimacy had become just another job for him, an obligation, like the bouquet of flowers he brought her every Friday evening.

In the weeks before the wedding, her mother had assured her it would all even out over time. There were meant to be highs and lows in a marriage. It kept things interesting. And heaven knows, she'd said, sex wasn't everything. She and Payton's father kept separate bedrooms and they got along just fine.

Until that moment, Payton had always assumed the arrangement was because her father snored, but once she realized her parents no longer needed each other in that way, she began to question her assumptions about a happy marriage. She wondered if her own marriage might end up more a convenient arrangement than a lifelong passion.

From that point on, Payton began to look at Sam in a different way. Every touch, every kiss, was more evidence that the passion between them was waning. Worse, she began to doubt herself. Perhaps she was just incapable of keeping a man sexually interested. Maybe it was genetic.

But that crazy attraction hadn't been missing with Brody Quinn. There had been an excitement between them, a delicious anticipation that she hadn't felt in a very long time. Her heart beat faster at the thought of him, and her breathing suddenly grew shallow. He'd been attracted to her, too, that much was obvious.

She thought back to the night before her wedding, a night spent pacing her room at the resort in Fiji. Every instinct told her to call it all off—or at least delay until she had her head on straight. But she knew what an embarrassment it would be to her parents, how upset they'd be. As an only child, so much had always been expected of her, and she'd done her best to make her parents proud. But wasn't there a point in life where she had to think about herself first?

It had taken her until the very last minute to decide to run. She'd been walking across the terrace on her father's arm, the ocean breezes ruffling her silk dress as family and friends waited on the beach. Her father had kissed her cheek and handed her over to Sam. Yet when she'd looked into Sam's eyes, Payton knew she couldn't go any further.

She tried to push the memory aside, taking another sip of orange juice as she fought back the tears that threatened. She'd run straight back to the room and grabbed her passport and a single bag. Five minutes later, she was on her way to the airport, still dressed in her white gown, ready to take the first flight off Fiji to anywhere in the world.

But a new charge on her credit card might betray her. So she'd exchanged her honeymoon ticket to Sydney for a ticket to Brisbane, assured that the airlines would keep her plans confidential. She had a visa, so it had been no problem entering the country. And once she was there, it had been even easier to lose herself.

Unfortunately, even following a strict budget, the cash she'd had with her had only gone so far. She'd heard from a woman in Brisbane that there were often jobs available for foreigners at some of the cattle and sheep stations in Queensland. They offered room and board and a decent wage—and for Payton, a place to hide out until she could bear facing her family again.

Perhaps it wouldn't be so difficult to go back, she mused. She could call her parents and explain the pressure she'd been under. Perhaps Sam might even forgive her. She drew a ragged breath. But would that stop these feelings of doubt?

Her mind flashed an image of Brody Quinn again and warmth snaked through her veins. He was dangerously handsome, his body lean and muscular, probably toned more by hard work than hours in the gym. His skin was burnished brown by the sun and his rumpled hair was streaked with blond.

But it was his eyes that she found fascinating. They were an odd color—part green, part gold—and ringed with impossibly long lashes. He didn't say much, but when he spoke, she found his accent entirely too charming. And when he looked at her, she had to wonder what he was thinking. Had he been undressing her in his head? Had he been thinking about more than just touching and kissing?

Had Angus not let him out, Payton wondered whether they might have acted on the attraction. In truth, he'd made her feel something she'd never felt before. He'd made her feel like a real woman, alive with desire and passion, not just a naive girl playing at womanhood.

Payton felt a tiny sting of regret that she hadn't accepted his offer of help. She could have used a friend in the outback, someone to show her the ropes, maybe help her find a job. Though her abilities were rather limited, she had spent the last year perfecting her skills as a gourmet cook. She could teach piano and French and Italian. She'd been an excellent rider, winning medals in dressage and show jumping. Surely there was something she could do for an honest wage.

Payton crawled off the bed and walked over to the spot where Brody had stood. She'd make a vow, here and now. From this moment forward, she'd act on her instincts. If she saw something she wanted, she'd go after it. She'd stop planning and start doing. And maybe, once she'd figured out just who she was, away from her parents and Sam, she could get on with the rest of her life.

"You finished with your breakfast?" Angus sauntered into the room, his keys jangling from a ring on his belt. He unlocked the cell door and opened it then stepped inside to collect the tray.

"Thank you," Payton said. "It was good."

He nodded. "Answer a question for me?"

Payton knew she'd have to explain at some point. What was she doing stranded in the middle of the Australian outback without a penny to her name? And what had made her think she could walk out of a restaurant without paying. "Sure. Fire away."

Angus's brow furrowed. "Have you ever been to Graceland?"

"Graceland?" The question didn't take her by surprise considering the police chief's taste in music. "No. But I hear it's supposed to be very nice. I once saw Priscilla Presley in New York, though."

"Priscilla?"

"Yes, I think she was there for Fashion Week. She was hailing a cab on Madison Avenue."

"Well, I'll be buggered! Priscilla Presley. That's almost as good as seeing Elvis." He nodded. "It's always been my dream to visit Graceland. Most folks would go to Disney World or Hollywood or one of those big tall buildings they have in New York City. Me, I'd head straight to Graceland." With a sigh, he stepped out of the cell. "Your debt has been settled, Miss Harwell. You're free to go."

"I am?" She didn't really want to leave. Not before she'd figured out her next move. But then, she had vowed to stop planning and start doing. "Who paid it?"

Angus nodded toward the door. "He's waitin' out front. You'll have to square up with him."

Frowning, Payton grabbed her bag and stuffed her belongings inside, then glanced around the cell to make sure she had everything. Whoever her mysterious benefactor was, she'd find a way to pay him back.

When she reached the porch, she saw a familiar figure waiting for her, dressed in the same faded jeans and wrinkled T-shirt he'd worn earlier. She allowed herself a tiny smile. "Are you the one who—"

Brody grabbed her bag from her hand and slung it over his shoulder. "No need to thank me," he interrupted, motioning toward the dirty Land Rover parked in front of the police station. "We criminals have to stick together, eh?"

Payton walked slowly down the steps, glancing over her shoulder to find him staring at her backside. She reached for the door of the truck, but he rested his hand on hers. "That's the driver's side, sweetheart," he said.

"Sorry," Payton murmured, the heat from his touch

sending a tingle up her arm. He followed her around to the passenger side and helped her in, resting his hand on the small of her back as she climbed up into her seat.

When he slid in behind the wheel, he looked over at her. "Where to?"

"I—I don't know," she said.

"You don't know?"

"I don't have anywhere to go."

"You're giving up your life of crime?" His dark brow arched. "You must have somewhere to go. Everyone is going somewhere."

"Not me," Payton said. "Since I'm out of cash, I can't afford to go anywhere. I need to find a job."

He nodded, then grinned. "All right. Well, I think I know a place that might need some help. As long as you're willing to work hard. What can you do?"

"Anything."

"The local brothel likes to hire talented girls. I could take you over there."

She laughed softly when she saw the smile curling his lips. He had a way of speaking, his accent broad and his voice deep, that made it hard to tell when he was teasing. "Very funny."

"You think I'm kidding? Bilbarra has a legal house of ill repute. And it stays quite busy since women are in short supply in the outback. You could make a decent wage if you were so inclined."

"I'm better with horses than I am with men," Payton said.

"Horses? Well, that sounds promising." He turned the SUV around and headed out of town on the dusty main street. As they drove, the landscape became dry and desolate, an endless vista of…nothing. This was the outback, Payton mused. And she was driving right into the middle of it with a complete stranger. "Where are we going?"

"To my place," he said.

She swallowed hard. So much for acting on instinct. "Your—your place?" Had she just made the biggest mistake of her life? He could drive them out into the middle of nowhere, chain her up and keep her as his sex slave for years and no one would ever know. But then Angus had seen them leave together and if Angus trusted this man with her safety, maybe she could, too. The idea of serving as Brody's sex slave rolled around in her mind for a moment before she shook herself. The thought was intriguing. In truth, any thought that involved Brody's naked body seemed to stick in her head.

"It's my family's place," he explained. "We have a cattle station and we raise horses, too."

"Horses!" she cried. "I'm good with horses. I can groom them and muck out the stalls and feed them…."

"Good," he said. "Then I'm sure we'll have a spot for you." He reached above the visor and pulled out a CD, then popped it into the player in the dash.

Payton watched the countryside pass as they bumped along the dirt roads. Compared to the beautiful scenery on the coast with its lush greenery and ocean views, the outback was a harsh and unforgiving environment. Only occasionally did she see signs of human habitation—a distant house or a windmill on the horizon.

When she wasn't staring out the window, Payton attempted a careful study of the man beside her. He kept his eyes fixed on the road ahead, humming along with the AC/DC songs as he navigated around bumps and potholes.

After an hour of bouncing over rutted roads, the orange juice Payton had gulped down for breakfast had worked its way through her body. "Will it be much farther?" she asked.

"Another half hour," he said.

"Is there a gas station coming up? Maybe a convenience store? Anyplace with a ladies' room?"

Brody pulled the truck to a stop, then pointed out the window. "There's a nice little shrub over there. For privacy." He shrugged. "There isn't a ladies' room between here and the station."

Reluctantly, Payton opened the door. "Don't watch," she said.

"I won't. And if a giant lizard comes wandering by, you just scoot back to the truck flat out."

Payton closed the door. "I can wait."

"The road only gets bumpier," he warned. "I'll keep an eye peeled. If I see anything approaching, I'll hit the horn."

Payton hopped out of the truck and walked gingerly through the scrub to the closest bush. It looked more like tumbleweed than a living plant, but it provided enough cover for her modesty.

She was a long way from home, a long way from marble bathrooms with gold-plated fixtures and expensive French towels. But for the first time in her life, she was in charge of her own destiny. She no longer had to please her parents, or anyone else for that matter. And though she didn't know where she'd be tomorrow or what she'd doing next week, Payton didn't care. Right now, life was one big adventure. And her traveling companion made the adventure a whole lot more interesting.

BRODY LEANED BACK against the front fender of the Land Rover as he stared out at the horizon, taking a long drink from a bottle of water he'd pulled from the Esky in the backseat. He'd been living in the civilized part of Oz for so long that he'd forgotten just how desolate the outback was.

He and his mother had left when he was fourteen. And though he'd returned for his school holidays, he was always anxious to leave again. Now, here he was, back where he started.

He heard footsteps in the gravel at the edge of the road and he turned around as Payton approached, bracing his elbows on the hood of the SUV. "Feel better?"

"Much," she said. She turned slowly, taking in the view. "It's beautiful in a rugged, bleak kind of way. You can breathe out here. The air is so clean."

"Yeah, we have plenty of clean air in Queensland. And we're a big producer of dust. Mozzies and blowies, too." She gave him an odd look. "Mosquitoes and blow flies." He offered her the bottle of water. "And where do you come from?"

She took a long drink of water, then smiled. "The East Coast. Connecticut."

"Is that near New York?"

She nodded. "Yes. Very near. My father works in Manhattan. I went to college at Columbia."

"So you're smart, then?" Smart and beautiful. A deadly combination and one he hadn't really appreciated until now. He'd never considered a brilliant mind an important part of sexual attraction. But as much as he wanted to touch her and kiss her, he also wanted to talk to her. Who was this woman? What was she doing here with him?

"I did my master's thesis on the history of anatomical study in seventeenth-century Dutch artists. I'm not sure how smart that makes me." She glanced around. "Especially out here. Unless you have an art museum filled with the works of Vermeer and Rembrandt."

"We do," he teased. "It's right behind the stables. Doesn't get a lot of visitors, though." Brody drank the last of the water. "So how does a sheila like you end up skint in a place like Bilbarra?"

"Skint?"

"No money."

"Broke," she said. "Flat broke. Probably because I didn't have a lot to start with." She paused. "I'm just a poor grad student trying to see a bit of the world."

"There's not a lot to see in the outback," he said.

"You don't think the scenery out here is spectacular?" Payton asked, pointing to a low range of hills in the distance. "It's wild, untamed. Dangerous. I like that. Don't you?"

He stared down at her face, taking in the simple perfection of her features. "It's gotten a lot nicer since you arrived."

Her eyes met his and Brody held his breath, wondering just how far he could go. He wanted to kiss her. Hell, he'd wanted to kiss her from the moment he'd first seen her. He leaned in, hoping for a sign that she shared the attraction. Her eyes dropped to his mouth and her lips parted slightly. It was all he needed.

Bracing his hands on either side of her body, he pressed her back into the side of the SUV and brought his mouth down on hers. Her lips were soft and cool and fit perfectly with his.

Brody's tongue traced the crease between them before she opened and let him taste her. At first, he thought she might end it all quickly, but then, Payton reached up and ran her fingers through the hair at his nape, sending a shiver through his body and a flood of warmth to his crotch.

The kiss turned intense, fierce and filled with need. God, she was incredible, he thought as his hands skimmed down her arms, then clutched at the hem of her shirt. It had been a while since he'd touched a woman, but he hadn't remembered it being this good. He smoothed his palms beneath her shirt, up her torso to cup her breast. Payton arched toward him, a tiny sigh slipping from her throat.

Brody had seduced his fair share of women, but he'd always tempered his attraction with an underlying suspicion. What did they really want from him? Were they merely interested in bedding a famous footballer? Or did they imagine themselves catching a husband who had the money to provide a fancy lifestyle?

There were no worries with Payton. To her, he was just the guy who'd bailed her out of jail and found her a job. He could let down his guard, at least for a little while. In truth, for the first time in his adult life, he could enjoy a woman without any inhibitions.

When he finally drew back, he found her face flushed and her lips damp. "We should probably go," he said, certain that there would be much more to come. Once he got her to the station, she'd be there for a time. He could afford to seduce her properly.

Her eyes fluttered open and she drew a deep breath. "Yes," she said softly. "Yes, we should."

Brody reached around her and opened the door. But before she could crawl back inside, he stole another kiss, lingering over her lips until he was satisfied that they'd both had enough. He liked kissing her. She had a mouth that was made for that particular pastime.

They drove on for another ten minutes before they spoke again. She cleared her throat and Brody turned to look at her, noting the pretty blush that stained her cheeks. "What?" he asked.

"Nothing," she said.

"You have something you want to say?"

She shook her head. "No."

"Do you regret what just happened?"

She drew another breath and then twisted to face him. "I hope you don't think I just go around kissing strangers, because I don't. It's just that I…" Payton paused. "No, I don't regret it. It was…nice."

"Onya," he replied, satisfied with "nice." Next time it happened, it would be better than nice. Brody grinned. There would be a next time. And a time after that…

"Onya?"

"Good onya," Brody corrected. "Ah…good for you."

"Right, good for me," she said, nodding. "I mean, on me. Good on me."

"No, it doesn't work that way." He grinned.

She smiled and shrugged. "Then, good onya. On you."

"No worries, then?" he said, knowing full well that his kiss was more than welcome.

"No worries," she replied.

Brody chuckled. "And feel free to perv on me whenever you like. Because I wouldn't mind if that happened again. Between us. But I should warn you off on the other blokes."

"Blokes?"

"It's mostly men on the station. There's just our cook and housekeeper, Mary. You'll be the only other woman. The boys on Kerry Creek are root rats of the first order, so keep a watch out for them. They go through women like water." All of a sudden Brody regretted his decision to bring Payton out to the station. He should have flown them both straight back to Fremantle, to his comfortable apartment with the big soft bed and the river views.

Though Callum and Teague weren't quite as bad as the rest of the jackaroos, his brothers wouldn't be immune to Payton's beauty. Women were in short supply in the bush and Brody intended to keep her all to himself. He'd have to find a way to make that clear to his brothers before they got any ideas about seducing her.

"Root rats," she said. "I suppose I could guess at the meaning of that." She sighed. "Are there a lot of root rats where we're going?"

"Yeah," Brody said. "But if any bloke cracks on you, just speak up. I'll sort him out."

"If any guy comes on to me, you'll punch his lights out?"

"That too," Brody said, chuckling. "Don't worry, you'll be safe. I'll watch out for you."

She'd be safe from the other blokes, but could he

guarantee she'd be safe from him? Right now, his thoughts weren't so much focused on protecting her as they were on seducing her. And he couldn't help but wonder what was going through her pretty head.

2

"WILL YOU EXCUSE US for a moment?"

Payton nodded, sitting primly on the edge of her chair as Brody and his brother Callum stepped out of the cluttered office. They didn't go far and their whispered discussion in the hallway soon became loud enough for her to hear.

"And who was whinging about all the work to be done just a few hours ago?" Brody accused. "She claims she knows horses and isn't above mucking out the stables. If she takes care of that, then you've got more help mustering."

"You met her in the jail," Callum shot back. "That might give you a clue to her character."

"She's just down on her luck," Brody said. "She needs a job. I'll vouch for her. If you catch her stealing, I'll haul her back to Bilbarra without a word."

"And what about you?" Callum asked. "If I give her a job, what are you going to do? Just lay about the house all day feeling sorry for yourself?"

"I reckon I'll give you a hand," Brody said. "I've got nothing better to do."

There was a long silence and she heard a curse, though she wasn't sure who it came from. A moment later, the two brothers reappeared in the door. "Brody tells me you're good with horses. You'll be expected to put in a full day."

"I really need this job. I'll work hard, I promise," Payton said. It was the truth, though she didn't want to sound too desperate. This station was the perfect place for her, a good spot to stay until she figured out her next step. She'd have a place to sleep and three decent meals a day. She'd have a job to occupy her time. And then there was Brody. "You won't regret this."

"All right. You can stay in the south bunkhouse," Callum said. "It's got a proper dunny and shower. But you'll have to share it with Gemma."

"Who's Gemma?" Brody asked, frowning.

"The genealogist," Callum explained. "Gemma Moynihan. She's from Ireland, doing some sort of research on the Quinn family. I told her she could stay until she finished her work here."

"No worries," Payton said, adopting the local language. "The bunkhouse will be great."

"All right," Callum said. "You'll start in the stables and you'll lend a hand in the kitchen when Mary needs help. You slack off and you'll earn yourself a ride back to Bilbarra. You work hard and I'll pay you a fair wage."

Payton nodded, relieved that he'd agreed to Brody's plan. It was the first real job she'd ever held and she was determined not to mess up. Her new life began here and now and Payton couldn't help but be a bit excited at the prospect.

Callum glanced at his brother. "Brody will show you around and get you settled. If you have any questions, ask him."

The elder Quinn brother strode out of the office and Brody followed after him. "I'll give her a day. Two at the outside," Payton heard Callum say.

When Brody returned, she pasted a smile on her face. "He's wrong. I'll work hard."

Brody reached out and took her hand, turning it over so he could examine her palm. Running his thumb over the soft skin, he slowly smiled. "You'll need a pair of gloves," he said. "And a proper hat."

Payton laced her fingers through his and gave his hand a squeeze. "Thank you for this. I won't disappoint you."

He hooked his finger beneath her chin, forcing her gaze up to his. At first, she hoped he might kiss her again, but then he must have thought better of it. "No worries. I can't imagine that ever happening."

"No worries," she repeated.

Brody picked up her bag and motioned her toward the door. "Come on. I'll show you what's what. We'll see the homestead first. Maybe Mary will make us a bite."

As they walked through the beautifully furnished room that Brody called the parlor, Payton's attention was caught by a huge oil painting hanging over the fireplace. She walked up to examine it more closely. "This is a beautiful portrait," she said.

"We call him the old man," Brody explained as he stepped up beside her. "His name is Crevan Quinn. He was the first Quinn in Australia. Came on a convict ship when he was nineteen."

"He was a convict?"

Brody nodded. "A bit of a thief, a pickpocket they

say. He had the portrait painted for his seventieth birthday, in the late 1800s. Went all the way to Sydney to sit for it. And then he died the day after it was finished. It's hung in this house ever since. His only son was my great-great-grandfather."

"Backler. I've never heard of the artist," she said. "It's quite lovely."

Brody gave her a dubious look.

"The technique," she said. "The layering of color." She stared at the subject, a man with wild white hair, huge muttonchops and a fierce expression.

"Good thing his looks don't run in the family," Brody said.

"His penchant for crime does," Payton teased.

With that, Brody grabbed her around the waist and gently pushed her back against the mantel. His hand cupped her cheek and he looked down into her eyes. Payton held her breath, caught by the desire in his gaze.

"And where would you be right now if it weren't for my criminal activities?"

"Or mine," she countered. "I'd be without a job and with no prospects for finding one."

"I think that deserves a kiss, don't you?"

"I suppose I could spare one. But don't get greedy."

She pushed up onto her toes and kissed him, not waiting for Brody to make the first move. She liked the taste of him, the way his hands felt on her body. His touch made her feel alive, as if she was doing something far too dangerous for her own good. It was exhilarating and frightening all at once.

Payton looped her fingers in the waistband of his jeans and pulled his hips against hers. He groaned softly as the kiss deepened and their bodies melted into each other. Her hands slipped beneath his T-shirt and she ran her nails up his spine and back down again.

She'd never been so aggressive with a man, but with Brody, all her inhibitions seemed to fall away. There were no rules when she kissed him. Here in Australia, she'd live every day as if it were her last, with no regrets and nothing left undone.

Suddenly, he pushed himself away from her. He sucked in a sharp breath and Payton could see he was trying to regain his self-control. She glanced down and noticed the bulge in the front of his jeans. His reaction pleased her.

"Later," he assured her. He picked up her bag, then grabbed her hand and pulled her along to the front door of the house.

They ran into a man jogging up the front steps and he stopped and pulled off his hat, glancing back and forth between Payton and Brody, before noticing their linked hands. "Hello," he said.

"Teague, this is Payton Harwell. Payton, this is my brother Teague."

He held out his hand and Payton was forced to let go of Brody's to shake it. "Pleasure," he said with a wide grin.

"She's going to be working with the horses," Brody said.

"Good onya," Teague replied. "That's where I'll be working for the next few days. You have much experience with stock ponies?"

Payton shook her head, grateful for the welcome but worried that she might not prove herself useful. "No.

But I've been around horses since I was six or seven. Show jumpers. But horses are horses. They all have four legs and a tail, right?"

Teague chuckled, as if pleased with her little joke. "Yeah. They usually do. So I guess I can't give you any of our three-legged ponies."

Payton's eyes went wide.

"Crocs," Teague said, a serious expression on his face. "They'll eat the legs right off a pony if you let them. One leg we can deal with. But a two-legged stock pony just doesn't work."

"Oh, no," Payton said. "That's horrible. Can't you—"

"Don't be a dipstick, Teague." Brody shook his head.

An older woman appeared at the screen door. "Doc Daley is on the phone," she said to Teague, motioning him inside. "Says it's an emergency and he's tied up in surgery this afternoon."

Teague frowned, shaking his head. "Probably another croc attack," he said. "Another three-legged pony. Mary, have you met Brody's new friend?"

The woman stepped out onto the porch, a smile twitching at the corners of her mouth. She wiped her hands on her apron, then smoothed a strand of gray hair from her temple. "Well, now. It is a pleasure to meet you, dear. I'm Mary Hastings. No matter what these Quinn boys tell you, I'm the one in charge here."

Payton shook her outstretched hand. "Payton Harwell."

"Ah, an American. We seem to be attracting an interesting group of ladies. First, an Irish lass and now a Yank. If you need anything, you come to me, dear. We girls have to stick together." She leaned forward and lowered her voice. "And don't believe a word about those three-legged ponies. These boys get too cheeky."

Teague grabbed Mary around the waist and planted a kiss on her cheek. "And don't you love it? Don't worry, Mary, you're still my girl."

Brody took Payton's hand and led her off the porch. "Come on, I'll show you the bunkhouse."

"It was a pleasure meeting you," Payton said, waving at Teague and Mary.

"See ya later, Payton," Teague called.

"When you're settled, you come back to the kitchen for tea," Mary called.

They walked together to the south bunkhouse, a low building set near a small grove of trees and a neatly tilled vegetable garden. "That's Mary's garden," he said. "You might want to avoid walking by when she's working. She'll have you pulling weeds all day long."

"She's nice," Payton said.

"After my mum left the station, my dad hired her. She's kept the house running."

"Are your parents divorced?"

He shook his head. "Nope. They're living together in Sydney. But there was a time when they were separated, my dad here and Mum in the city. Station life is hard, especially for women."

Payton gave him a sideways glance, wondering if he was warning her off. She was just looking for a job. She didn't intend to spend the rest of her life in the Australian outback. "I can imagine," she replied.

Brody opened the front door of the bunkhouse, then stepped back to let her enter. Payton found the interior simple but clean. In one corner of the room, several overstuffed chairs were gathered around a small iron stove. There was a scarred desk beneath one of the windows and a dry sink beneath another, complete with bowl and pitcher. An old wardrobe stood near the backdoor. Each of the three walls held a bunk bed, crudely constructed of rough planks and a pair of mattresses. One of the lower bunks was made up with a colorful quilt and two pillows.

"That must be where the genealogy lady is sleeping," Brody said. "Bedding is in the chest at the end of the bunk. The dunny is out back, through that door."

"The dunny."

"The toilet. There's a shower back there, too." He walked over to the wardrobe and rummaged through the contents until he found a pair of gloves and an old felt hat, like the one his brother Teague wore.

Brody set the hat on her head and handed her the gloves. "There you go," he said, tugging on the brim. "Pretty spiffy."

"I'd like to get to work," she said.

"You don't have to. It's your first day. Take some time and settle in. We'll have some lunch."

"No, I'm ready to start," she insisted, well aware that she'd have to prove herself to Callum.

"You're not really dressed properly. We'll need to find you something to wear."

"I don't really have anything else along," Payton said, glancing down at the peasant blouse and jeans she'd bought in Brisbane. "Just a few dresses. This will have to do for now. I'll find something later."

"All right," he said with a shrug. "Let's go."

They walked out of the bunkhouse and through the

dusty yard. The station was almost like a small village. Brody pointed out each paddock and barn and shed, telling her what function it served. There were two more bunkhouses for the stockmen and a small cottage for the head stockman.

The stables consisted of a long building with stalls along one side and tack, feed and supplies stored on the opposite side. "We breed stock ponies here, so we keep a lot of mares. We break the ponies and then sell them to stations all around Queensland. Kerry Creek ponies fetch a good price."

Payton pulled on her gloves and braced her hands on her hips. "All right. Well, I'd better jump right in." She spotted a pitchfork in a corner and grabbed it. "I guess I'll see you later."

He seemed to be a bit surprised that she was blowing him off so quickly. Though Payton found him wildly attractive, she needed to keep this job and first impressions would count. If she had to ignore her desires for a few hours, it was a small price to pay.

"We eat dinner at six this time of year. I'll come and fetch you."

"That's all right," Payton said. "I'll find my way."

He turned and walked out of the stable. Payton folded her hands over the end of the pitchfork and watched his retreat. Her girlfriends had always told her how hot Sam was and she'd never quite understood what they meant. Sam was handsome, but Brody Quinn was hot. He oozed masculinity from every pore.

She tried to imagine him without the T-shirt, without the jeans, without any clothes at all. A shiver skittered down her spine and she felt her pulse quicken. Sleeping with the boss was never a good thing. But was Brody her boss or was Callum?

Payton made a mental note to find out as soon as she could. For now, she had a bed and free meals and something to occupy her time—along with a man who made her heart race and her body tingle. What more did she need?

LIKE EVERYONE ELSE at Kerry Creek, Brody had worked the station from the time he'd been able to walk. He'd started in the garden with his mother, then moved to the stables and on to working with the stock as soon as he could ride. But he'd spent most of his teen years in the city, and once he'd signed his first pro contract, he'd made only occasional visits to Queensland, stopping in before a holiday spent surfing or diving on the Great Barrier Reef.

His brothers teased him, insisting that city life had made him soft. Maybe it had. But now that he was living on the station again, it was all coming back to him. He'd spent the afternoon repairing fences with the newest jackaroo, a kid named Davey Thompson, who'd wandered in a few months before to join his older brother, Skip, on the station.

Davey had kept up a constant stream of chatter, moving from women to music to cars and back again. One thing was quite clear. He was glad to have moved up in the pecking order, his stable job handed off to Payton, who was now the lowest in seniority.

"That new girl, she's a pretty sheila," he said as he picked up a roll of barbed wire. "She has nice hair. All long and curly."

"You just steer clear of her," Brody warned.

"What? She's your girl?"

"As far as you're concerned, yes," Brody said. "She's my girl."

"No worries," Davey replied with a grin. "But does she have a sister? If she does, I wouldn't mind an introduction."

They worked until sunset, hauling their gear with quad bikes rather than on horseback. Since his father had left the station to join his mother in Sydney four years ago, Callum had taken steps to modernize the operation and his ideas had made the work at least a bit more enjoyable.

Brody and Davey unloaded the gear from the ATVs, then headed to the big house for dinner. Mary fed everyone at the large table in the kitchen, preparing the heartiest meal at the end of the workday. Brody took time to wash up at the outdoor sink before going inside.

He'd expected to see Payton there, waiting for him, but she wasn't seated at the table. The other new arrival was the genealogist from Ireland. He'd expected some gray-haired lady with sensible shoes and little reading glasses perched on her nose. Instead, he found himself smiling at a woman almost as beautiful as Payton.

"Gemma Moynihan," she said in a lilting Irish accent. "And you must be Brody. I can see the family resemblance."

"Gemma," Brody repeated. He glanced over at his brother Callum, only to find him staring at them both, a tense expression on his face. It was easy to see why Cal had been on edge. His oldest brother had always been obsessed with the station. But the choice to work or to spend time with Gemma the genealogist was probably causing him to seriously question his work ethic.

"Have you met Payton?" Brody asked, suppressing a grin.

"Yes, I have," Gemma said.

"Is she coming in to eat?"

"I don't know. She was lying in her bunk when I left. She looked knackered."

"Maybe I should take her something," Brody suggested, stepping away from the table.

This brought amused glances from the rest of the stockmen, but Brody didn't care. He grabbed a plate and loaded it with beef and potatoes, covering the entire meal with a portion of gravy. Grabbing utensils and a couple of beers, he headed out to the ladies' bunkhouse.

He found Payton curled up on her bunk sound asleep. He set the meal on the floor beside the bed, then pulled up a chair, straddling it. Reaching out, Brody brushed a strand of hair from her eyes. Her lashes fluttered and she gazed up at him.

"Morning," he said.

Payton pushed up on her elbow looking worried. "Is it morning already?"

He laughed. "No. I brought you some dinner. Are you all right?"

She sat up, wincing as she moved. "Yes. I'm fine. I'm just not used to shoveling horse poop for four hours." She groaned, rubbing her shoulder. "I was just going to lie down for a minute, and I must have fallen asleep."

"Come here," Brody said, swinging the chair around and patting the seat.

When she was seated, he handed her the plate, then stepped behind her and began to massage her sore shoulders. "Oh, that's nice," she said, tipping her head back and closing her eyes. Her silky curls fell across his hands. "Right there."

He rubbed a little harder at her nape, brushing her hair over her shoulder. "Here?"

"Mmm," she said.

"Eat your dinner before it gets cold."

She glanced down at the plate, then scooped up a forkful of beef and potatoes. "This is good," she said as she chewed. "I didn't realize how hungry I was. Don't you want some?"

"You eat," he said. "I'll go back and get another plate."

She reached down and grabbed a bottle of beer, then attempted to twist off the cap. When she couldn't, she handed it to him. "What did you do today?"

"Repaired fences," Brody said.

"What time does work start in the morning?"

"The stockmen are usually up at dawn. But you could probably sleep later, if you like. The stables aren't going anywhere."

"No, I'll get up with everyone else."

"I don't reckon Cal expects you to put in stockman's hours."

"What else is there to do except work and eat and sleep?" Payton asked.

Brody bent over her shoulder and sent her a devilish grin. "I can think of a few things," he whispered.

She filled a fork with food, then held it up to him, and he took a bite of her dinner. "Other than that, what do you do with your free time?"

"We're five hours from the nearest movie theater in Brisbane, but we've got DVDs to watch. Cal favors westerns, I like gangster movies and Teague prefers science fiction." He paused. "We've got a pool," he added. "Sometimes we go swimming when the weather is warm."

"I didn't see a pool."

"It's not a swimming pool, more like a watering hole. And Cal put in a hot tub out back. That's nice now that the nights are a bit cooler."

"Oh, that sounds like heaven," she said.

"Finish your supper and we'll go for a dip."

"I don't have a swimsuit."

"You won't need one," Brody said.

"I'm sure that will create a good impression," she replied.

To his surprise, she finished the entire plate in ten short minutes, then drank her beer and his. Through it all, she asked questions about the station and he did his best to answer. She'd just assumed he'd worked the station his whole life, and he wasn't going to tell her differently, at least not yet.

He had his secrets, but Payton Harwell had her own. When he asked for details about her life in the States, she always gave him some airy-fairy answer. After fifteen minutes of questioning, he realized he didn't know much more than he'd learned on their ride to the station. But the more beer she drank, the more forthcoming she became.

"Let's go," he said, anxious to spend some time in a location more conducive to seduction. "The hot water will make you feel better."

"Later," she said. "I just want to lie down for a bit."

She crawled back into her bunk and patted the spot beside her. "Just for a minute. Then we'll go."

Brody crawled into the tiny bunk, and he had to wrap his arms around her just to keep from falling on the floor. He smoothed his hands over her hair and she looked up at him and smiled. "Who are you, Payton Harwell?" he murmured.

"I don't know," she said with a soft sigh. "If you figure it out, be sure to fill me in."

He bent closer and kissed her, this time allowing himself to relax and enjoy the experience. His hands roamed over her body, slipping beneath the waistband of her jeans to cup her backside. Brody pulled her beneath him, his shaft growing harder as the kiss deepened.

His hips pressed into hers and he slowly began to move, creating a delicious friction. He remembered the first time he'd done this with a girl and the rather surprising results. But thankfully, he'd managed to acquire a bit more self-control over the years. Still, the feel of her beneath him, her leg pulled up alongside his, teased at that control. Brody knew Gemma might be back at any second, but he didn't care.

Payton slipped her hand beneath the hem of his shirt. She smoothed her palms up his chest, then trailed her fingertips down his belly. He groaned softly when she slid her hand lower, across the front of his jeans, then back again. Somehow, it all seemed more intense, more pleasurable, with clothing between them and the chance of discovery.

He pulled her shirt over her shoulder, exposing a delicious curve of flesh. Pressing his mouth to the base of her neck, he slowly worked his way down, to the tops of her breasts, left exposed by her lacy bra.

He slid lower along her body, his lips teasing at her nipple through the lace and satin. Payton furrowed her fingers through his hair and he sucked gently, until she moaned in response.

He fought the urge to strip off all their clothes, knowing they didn't have much privacy in a shared bunkhouse. Perhaps Gemma would be occupied with Callum for the rest of the evening. Maybe she'd choose to spend the night in his bed instead of her own. But their privacy was cut short when he heard the front door open.

"Sorry," Gemma called. "I'll come back later."

When the door closed behind Gemma, he drew back and looked into Payton's eyes. She forced a smile. "Maybe you should go," she said.

"Maybe you should come with me," he suggested. He curled up against her, nuzzling his face into the curve of her neck. "I have a very large bed in my room. And a strong lock on the door. We won't be disturbed."

"We won't get any sleep, either," Payton said.

"That's the point, isn't it?"

She sighed softly and he waited for her decision. But after a minute or two, Brody realized that she'd fallen asleep. Her breathing had grown soft and even and the arm resting on his hip had gone limp.

He bit back a curse, then pressed a kiss to her forehead. She stirred for a moment, her eyes fluttering. "I'm going to go. You need your sleep. I'll see you in the morning."

"Morning," she sighed.

Reluctantly, he untangled himself from her embrace, rolled off the bed and tugged his shirt down. He turned to look at Payton, her dark hair fanned out over the pillow, her hand curled over her face.

If he wasn't such a gentleman, he'd pick her up, carry her to his bedroom and make love to her all night long. But he had time. And when it happened, they'd both be awake and completely aware of what they were doing. It would be good between them. Maybe better than it had ever been with any other woman.

For that, Brody was willing to wait.

PAYTON GRABBED the hoof pick, then pushed the horse up against the side of the stall with her shoulder. Lifting the gelding's front leg, she held its hoof between her thighs and began to clean out the debris between the frog and the bars.

Unlike the horses she rode for show, the horses on the station didn't spend much time in the stable. They were brought in after a day's work and then quickly groomed and sent out to a large paddock where they were fed. The ground was dry and the stable kept clean, so there was no need for a farrier and horseshoes.

The Kerry Creek horses were a sturdy lot, most gentle and accommodating—the furthest thing from the pampered, high-spirited show horses she'd learned to ride. Brody had informed her that the stockmen were responsible for the daily care of their own mounts, but she was expected to care for the remainder in the paddock and the stables—nearly forty by her count.

These included mares that were in foal and the colts who were yet to be broken, along with at least ten extra stock ponies. She'd also spend part of each day in the tack room, keeping the stockmen's saddles and bridles in good working order. And with what time was left over, she'd turn her attention to mixing feed and keeping the stables tidy.

The dry season was the busiest of all on a cattle station. The stockmen were getting ready to bring the cattle in for the yearly mustering, setting off to the far corners of the station to gather the herd, sometimes staying out three or four days. The new calves would be examined, vaccinated, tagged and branded with the *K* that signified Kerry Creek station.

The horses that were part of the breeding operation were pastured closer to the homestead where they could be watched closely and brought inside as their time grew near. Foals that were dropped outside could be easy prey for dingoes.

"You look like you know what you're doing."

Payton glanced up to see Brody's brother Teague standing just outside the stall, his shoulder braced against a post, his arms crossed over his chest. Like Brody and Callum, he was gorgeous. But unlike Brody, he didn't send shivers of desire coursing through her body, nor did she spend hours thinking about kissing him.

She shoved the sleeves of her oversize work shirt above her elbows, then nodded. "It's a whole different kind of horse," she said with a smile. "They have a wonderful temperament."

"That's the way we breed them and train them," he said. "And for stamina and strength and agility. They need to be able to last all day long. Sometimes all week."

Payton continued her work. "What are the bloodlines?"

"Originally thoroughbreds and Arabians with some Welsh mountain and Timor pony thrown in."

"When do they foal?"

"They tend to start in September and go through the first of the year. Usually right after mustering ends, we start in with foaling."

"Davey said the colt in the next stall has been sold. He's beautiful."

"He's going to be trained as a show horse. Some of our horses are used for polocrosse. And some for camp-drafting."

Payton set the horse's hoof onto the concrete floor and straightened, brushing her hair out of her eyes. "What's that?"

"Besides Aussie-rules football, polocrosse and campdrafting are the only native Aussie sports. Polo-crosse is a mix of polo, lacrosse and netball. And I reckon campdrafting is kind of like your rodeo riding. The horse and rider cut a calf from the herd, then they have to maneuver it around a series of posts."

"I'd like to see that," she said.

"I'll take you sometime," Teague promised. "There's a campdrafting event in Muttaburra in August if you're still around."

"I'd like to try it."

"Then I'll teach you."

"Teach her what?"

Brody appeared at his brother's side. He was dressed in traditional stockman's attire, a work shirt, canvas jacket, jeans. He wore a felt hat on his head and his hands were clad in well-worn leather gloves. She hadn't seen him since the previous evening and she'd forgotten just how beautiful he was.

"Hey, little brother. Where have you been?"

"I went out with Davey to fix the windmill in the high pasture."

Teague clapped his brother on the back. "Good to see you putting in an honest day's work." He touched the brim of his hat and nodded at Payton. "I've got a call. I'll see you later, Payton. Maybe you can give me a hand tomorrow morning. I've got vaccinations to do on the yearlings."

"Sure," Payton said. "I'd be happy to help."

He nodded again. "I think I'll like having you here." Teague turned to Brody, arching an eyebrow and examining him critically. "Have you had all your shots?"

Payton watched Brody's jaw grow tense. As the youngest brother, he probably had to put up with a greater share of the teasing. "Don't mind Teague," Brody said as his brother turned and walked away. "He has a bad habit of yabbering to anyone who'll listen."

"So, is Teague in charge of the horse-breeding operation?"

"When he's around. He's a vet."

"A veterinarian? Really?"

Brody nodded. "He's usually flying from station to station. He spends a few days at home, then takes off again. He's the brilliant one in the family."

"He's nice," Payton murmured. She met Brody's gaze and her breath stopped in her throat. It was all there, the desire, the need and even a tiny hint of jealousy. She drew a ragged breath as he crossed the short distance between them to pull her into his arms.

Payton had tried to put all of this out of her head. From the moment she woke up that morning she'd been waiting to touch him, to taste him. It had been eight hours of sheer torture and now she felt the tension in her body release as their mouths met.

The more she saw of him, the more difficult it was to resist him. And yet, that didn't frighten or confuse her. She didn't need to figure out the consequences of her every action and reaction. She could kiss Brody and that was all it was, a kiss. It felt good to cast aside her penchant for planning and just go with the flow.

But how long could that last? How long before a simple fling turned into something more complicated? Her feelings for him were already so intense, her desire undeniable. She'd promised herself that she'd be guided by her instincts, and every instinct told her to enjoy their time together. They didn't need to make promises to each other. This was enough.

He cupped her face in his palms and drew her deeply into the kiss, as if desperate to possess her. Payton was stunned at how easy it was to stoke his need. There was no hesitation, nothing she held back. Though she barely knew Brody, she felt a connection with him that she'd never shared with a man before.

He pulled her out of the stall, his hands tight around her waist. Stumbling back, they fell into a pile of straw, their mouths still frantically searching for the perfect manifestation of their need. He tossed his hat aside, then tugged off his gloves, his hands immediately moving to cup her backside. Though Payton knew their privacy in the stable wasn't certain, she didn't care. All that mattered was his touch, his fingers tearing at her shirt until he exposed the curve of her shoulder.

His teeth grazed her skin and Payton tipped her head back, inviting him to take more. There were moments when she acted on instinct, as if this woman had always been buried deep inside her and was just waiting to get out. And then, at other times, she felt like a teenager, fumbling her way though her first sexual experience.

He excited her and frightened her all at once. And yet, she pushed aside her fears, rushing headlong into her desire, aching to experience release. Payton tugged at his jacket, pulling it over his arms until she could unbutton his shirt.

"Too many clothes," she murmured as she brushed aside the shirt and placed a kiss in the center of his chest. He was so magnificent, she mused, his skin deeply tanned and his body finely muscled. Her lips found one of his nipples and she circled it with her tongue.

Brody ran his fingers through her hair, sighing her name softly as if urging her on. Slowly, Payton worked her way lower, trailing kisses over his abdomen. But before she could go farther, she heard the clip-clop of hooves on the concrete floor of the stable.

She looked up to find Callum standing just inside the stable door, his horse's reins dangling from his fingers. With a soft cry, Payton scrambled to her feet, brushing the straw from her clothes and trying to adjust her shirt. Callum arched a brow as he looked down at Brody. "I can come back later," he said slowly.

Brody shook his head, cursing. "No. Feel free. We were just…talking."

"Oh, is that what they call it?" Callum asked. He pulled his horse along until he stopped in front of Payton. "Is my brother bothering you? If he is, you can just tell him to leave."

Callum was always so serious that Payton couldn't tell if he was angry or just teasing. She gave him an apologetic smile. "It—it won't happen again," she said. "I'm sorry."

Callum reached up and plucked a piece of straw from her hair and handed it to her, a grin quirking at the corners of his mouth. Payton felt her cheeks warm and she took the reins from his hand. "I'll take care of your horse," she mumbled.

Tugging at the bit, she pulled the horse along the length of the stable, hoping to get as far away from the two brothers as possible. She would not keep this job for long if she continued to show such a blatant disrespect for her employer.

And she needed this job! She wasn't ready to go home. The thought of facing her family and Sam was just too much for her right now. Here, on the station, she felt useful, which made her far happier than she'd been in a very long time.

But was it the work that made her happy or was it her growing infatuation with Brody Quinn? She'd be deluding herself if she ignored his part in this. Glancing back, she caught sight of Callum and Brody, deep in conversation, Callum gesturing with his gloved hands and Brody watching him with an indolent expression.

She barely knew the Quinn brothers, but the family dynamics were quite evident. Callum was the caretaker, the responsible brother whose only focus was the success of the station. Teague was the charmer, the smart, funny one with the ready smile and witty conversation.

And Brody...well, he was a little more difficult to define. He seemed to be the rebel of the family, a bit of an outsider. Payton couldn't understand why he stayed on the station when it was so obvious that it wasn't his favorite place to be.

She tied Callum's horse up to a nearby post and began to remove the saddle. When she straightened from unbuckling the cinch, she found Brody standing behind her. He gently turned her around to face him, then bent lower and kissed her.

"Sorry about that," he said, reaching out to smooth his hand over her hair.

"We can't do that again," she said, looking up at him. "I need this job, Brody."

"You're not going to lose your job," he said. "Cal doesn't care. He's so preoccupied with Gemma, he doesn't have time to worry about us."

"*I* care." Turning back to Callum's mount, she pulled the saddle off and set it on a bale of straw. "I like working here. And I need to pay you back for taking care of my debts."

"Cal can't complain about what you do when you're finished working, can he?"

"No," she said, setting the saddle pad on top of the saddle. "I guess not."

"All right, then. We'll just have to confine ourselves to the hours before breakfast and after dinner. And we're going to have to find a place that offers some privacy." He grabbed the saddle and hoisted it over his shoulder. "Why don't you let me take care of Cal's horse and you can finish what you were doing earlier. Then we'll go eat."

"You don't have to help me."

"Yes I do," Brody said. "Because the sooner you finish, the sooner I'll have you all to myself."

Perhaps he was right. As long as she finished her work, Callum couldn't begrudge her evenings spent with Brody. "Okay."

Her second day of work had been as exhausting as her first. But the prospect of spending time alone with Brody gave her a sudden surge of energy. She'd fallen asleep in his arms last night then woken up to an empty bed. She wasn't about to do that two nights in a row. "It's a date."

"Good." He grabbed the blanket and headed toward the tack room.

Payton watched him, smiling to herself. There was something so attractive about a man who actually worked for a living, a man who used his body the way it was meant to be used—for hard labor…and seduction. Brody was dirty and sweaty, yet she wanted him more than she'd ever wanted a man in her life.

3

BRODY DROPPED the phone into the cradle, then pushed back in Callum's desk chair, linking his hands behind his head. He hadn't bothered to pick up his messages on his mobile phone since reception in Bilbarra and at the station was nonexistent. But remotely checking the voice mail of his home phone at his apartment in Fremantle had brought an interesting development.

Cursing softly, he closed his eyes, a tightly held breath escaping his chest. When he'd left Fremantle, the team doctors had assured him there was no chance he would ever play football again. But now, a doctor in Los Angeles had developed a surgery that offered a way to reconstruct his bum knee.

Why now, why after he'd resigned himself to his fate? Why even tempt him with the possibility of regaining everything he'd lost? Brody knew it would be a long shot at best. And even if the surgery was successful, there'd be months, maybe a year or two, of rehab. Was he really willing to put in the time, just for another chance to play?

He didn't really have a choice. Brody had never been cut out for station life. The problem was he didn't have any options beyond football and stockman's work. He could invest in a business before he retired, but he wasn't sure what he wanted to buy. Or he could go to university and learn something new, but he was too old to go back to being a student.

"You never were one to plan ahead," he muttered to himself.

"Hey, dinner is on the table," Callum said, poking his head in the door. "Best be quick or Davey'll snag the seat next to your girl."

"She isn't my girl," Brody said, running his hand through his hair.

Callum shrugged. "I'm sure the boys will be happy to hear that. They've been carrying on like pork chops since she and Gemma arrived."

"All right, she *is* my girl. For now. And I expect that pretty Irish thing won't be spending much time with the boys, either. I see the way you stare at her. Explain to me again what she's doing here?"

"Research," Callum said. "She's working for some distant relative of ours on a family history. I guess one branch of the family left Ireland for the States and another branch came here. She's been going over all the old records for the station."

"What does that have to do with family history?" Brody asked.

"I don't know." He drew a deep breath. "I don't really care. As long as it keeps her here."

"Maybe she really fancies Teague. He's always been the looker in the family."

"Teague's got something else going," Callum murmured. "I was up early this morning and I saw him come in just before sunrise. There's not an available woman, besides Gemma, Payton and Mary, within fifty kilometers of this station, but he sure looked well satisfied."

"Maybe he's clearing the cobwebs at the brothel, or with a married lady," Brody said.

Callum shook his head. "Teague wouldn't do that. He's too bloody honorable. And why would he when he can usually have any woman he wants?" Callum paused. "I'm just worried he—"

"What?" Brody asked.

"I heard Hayley Fraser's back on her grandfather's station. Teague's always been a bit jelly kneed when it comes to her. First love and all that."

"Marrying Teague off to Hayley would solve all your problems." Brody teased. "The Frasers would be family, and family don't sue family." He pushed away from the desk. "If that's who he's messing with, he should be encouraged, don't you think?"

Callum cursed softly. "And maybe Fraser is using his granddaughter to mess with us," he shot back. "Did you ever consider that? Maybe he thinks if he can't get the land in court, he'll get it another way."

"How?"

"I don't know. Blackmail. Extortion. Fraser will go after that land any way he can. I just hope Teague doesn't get caught in the crossfire."

"Come on, Cal, you're talking crazy now. This feud has gone on for so long that nobody can see straight."

"I'm not going to surrender to Harry Fraser," Cal said. "That land belongs to the Quinns and we're not going to lose it while I'm in charge." He nodded his head. "Come on, dinner is ready. Mary won't wait."

Brody stared after him, then slowly stood. There were times when Brody wondered how Cal handled all the pressures of running the station. So many people depended on him. His parents took a share of the station income. Then there were the stockmen who expected to be paid. Teague's practice wouldn't make decent money for a few years, so he traded vet services for room and board. And now Brody was sponging off Callum. From now on, he'd make a better effort to pull his own weight.

The kitchen was already noisy when Brody walked in, filled with the usual dinner guests—the stockmen, Teague and Mary, and now Gemma and Payton.

With women at the table, the conversation had become much more civilized. Brody dislodged one of the jackaroos from the chair next to Payton, then sat down beside her. Unlike the majority of the men, Brody unfolded his serviette and placed it on his lap instead of stuffing it down the front of his shirt.

"What exactly is a B and S?" Gemma asked.

"Bachelors and Spinsters Ball," Teague explained as he grabbed a piece of bread and slathered it with butter. "All the unmarried people get together for a weekend of silliness. If you're not an Aussie, I don't think I'd recommend it. Foreigners might not have the fortitude to survive the weekend."

"But it sounds like fun," Payton said, leaning forward and bracing her elbows on the table. "I always loved balls and dances and cotill—" She stopped short, as if she'd suddenly revealed too much. Forcing a smile, she continued, "Is it formal or semiformal?"

"Tell her, Teague," Brody insisted, chuckling to

himself. Though Payton hadn't said much, she had revealed something of value this time out. She'd either enjoyed a high-class upbringing or she was a professional princess. He'd never known a single person who'd been to a real ball.

"It's not really a ball, the way you're thinking," Teague explained. "And by silliness, I mean debauchery."

"It's more like a big outdoor party," Callum explained.

Teague nodded. "There's music and drinking and... well, the whole idea is to get pissed, have a good time and hopefully enjoy a shag at the end of the night."

Gemma and Payton looked at each other, shocked expressions on their faces. "Have sex?" Payton asked.

Teague nodded. "Yeah, I guess that's the point. Lots of blokes bring their swag along for just that purpose. Life gets real lonely in the outback."

"What is swag?" Gemma asked. "Money? Do you pay for sex?"

"It's a sleeping roll," Brody explained. "Camping gear. Believe me, you don't want to go to the B and S. It gets feral."

"Filthy is a better word for it," Mary said as she set a bowl of peas next to Brody. She took her spot at the far end of the table. "If you don't want to get dirty or pawed, I wouldn't recommend it. And the loos are disgusting."

"I heard they're going to do something about that," Callum commented. "The organizers reckon they'll get a better class of sheilas if they guarantee clean toilets. They're going to hire someone to keep them tidy."

"I remember last year, Jack made his own loo with

a milk crate and a dunny seat," Teague said. "All the girls were wild for it. He'd let 'em use it, then try to charm them out of their grundies. Such a player, our Jack."

The lanky stockman shook his head, his long hair falling into his eyes. "I won't be able to compete with trailer toilets," Jack said glumly.

"It might be fun," Payton said. She turned to Gemma. "What do you think? When in Australia, do as the Aussies do?"

Gemma laughed. "We'd have to get something nice to wear."

"I have dresses," Payton said. "I need work clothes. I can't wear Davey's castoffs forever. Not that I don't appreciate the loan," she said, giving the kid a warm smile.

"I have to fly to Brisbane in a few days. I could take you shopping," Teague offered.

"Hang on there," Callum interrupted. "Gemma and Payton are not going to Bachelors and Spinsters."

"We won't participate," Gemma said. "We'll just go to…observe. Think of it as sightseeing. Or anthropological research."

"If you want to see the real sights of Australia, I'll take you," Teague said. "Queensland is beautiful from the air."

"There's an idea," Callum said. "You'd be much safer in a plane piloted by our brother than at Bachelors and Spinsters."

Brody slipped his hand beneath the table and smoothed his palm along Payton's thigh. "We could always send Mary to the ball. It's about time she got off this station and had a bit of fun. There are plenty of blokes who'd fancy a dance with our Mary."

The older woman's cheeks turned bright red and she hushed the laughter around the table. "Maybe I will," she said, giving them all a haughty expression. "I'd venture to say I could outdance all you boys."

The rest of the dinner conversation focused on the sights that every visitor in Australia needed to see, the Bachelors and Spinsters forgotten. Everyone at the table had an opinion about the finest tourist sights, both in and outside of Queensland. By the time they'd finished dessert, Teague had a long list, starting with a trip to Brisbane.

As Mary began to clear the table, Brody pushed back, then slid Payton's chair out for her. The rest of the hands looked at him in disbelief. "What are you all gawking at? Some of us here have good manners," Brody said.

The men quickly scrambled to their feet and rushed to Gemma's chair, but Callum waved them off. In truth, Brody's actions had nothing to do with manners. He wanted Payton all to himself and the faster that happened the better. But she seemed determined to keep him waiting.

"I'm going to help Mary clean up," she said, taking his plate and hers.

"Go along with you now. I have all the help I can handle," Mary said. "Davey promised to lend a hand."

Brody squeezed her elbow and pulled her along, out the backdoor to the porch that ran the width of the house. He found a dark corner and pushed her back against the house, then kissed her long and hard, his hands trapping her arms on either side of her head, his hips pressing into hers.

"I've been wanting to do that since I sat down next to you." He groaned.

Payton clutched the front of his shirt, then pushed up onto her toes and kissed him back. "Me, too," she said breathlessly. "I know where we can go. Someplace private."

This time, she pulled *him* along. They headed toward the stables, now dark and silent. When they got inside, Payton fumbled around in the gloom. "There's a flashlight here somewhere."

Brody grabbed it from a shelf above her head and flipped it on, holding it under his chin. "It's called a torch," he said.

Payton held out her hand and he gave it to her. They made their way down the length of the stable to an empty stall. She slid the door open and stepped inside. To Brody's surprise, she'd laid blankets over a mound of straw and arranged a few bales for seating.

"You did this?"

Payton nodded. "When you left to take the phone call. I figured we wouldn't have any privacy in the bunkhouse with Gemma there."

"And what do you plan to do with me once you've lured me inside?" he teased.

"I think we should get to know each other a little better," she said. She caught the front of his shirt and pulled him toward her. "There's so much I don't know about you. So many questions I have to ask."

"You want to talk?"

She nodded.

"I don't know anything about you," he said, smiling down at her. "Tell me something. Anything"

"My birthday is August tenth," she said. "I'm going to be twenty-six."

"Something more interesting," he demanded, his breath warm against her mouth.

"I broke my arm when I fell off my horse. I was seventeen. I had to have surgery." She pointed to her elbow. "I have a scar."

He ran his fingers through her hair and she closed her eyes and tipped her head back. "Something more intimate," he urged, pressing his lips to her throat.

"I lost my virginity in a stable. The Grand Prix in 2001. A month before I broke my arm. I was seduced by a Brazilian stable hand with the most beautiful blue eyes."

"Funny," Brody replied. "I lost mine in the back of my mother's car after footy practice. I was fifteen and she was older. Eighteen, if I recall."

Payton worked at the buttons of his shirt and when they were all undone, she looked up at him. "What else?"

Brody chuckled. "I think we can leave the questions until later."

"So you know what you're doing?" she whispered.

Somehow, he found her question incredibly intriguing. "Yes," he replied as she slid his shirt over his shoulders. "I know exactly what I'm doing. Do you?"

She nodded. "Close the door."

Brody moved to do as she asked, then froze. Hell, he didn't know what he was doing. He hadn't even bothered to bring along protection. "Sorry," he said, turning to face her. "Wait here. I'll be right back."

He tugged his shirt back on, then took the torch from her hand. He jogged back to the house and when he got to the kitchen, he found Mary sitting alone at the table, reading a magazine and sipping a cup of coffee.

"Back so soon?" she asked.

"It's a little chilly out. I need to get a jacket for Payton. Wouldn't want her to catch a cold."

"You're a gentleman," she said, glancing up. "And I hope you'll use a condom. Safe sex and all."

Brody stopped short. Mary had slipped into the role of mother to Callum and Teague after their own mother had moved off the station. And now that Brody had returned, she'd welcomed him as a surrogate son and was equally as protective. "Yes, I won't forget that. Not that it's any of your business."

After retrieving the condoms and a jacket from his room, Brody jogged back out to the stables. He found Payton standing at the stable door waiting.

"What was so impor—" She stopped when he held up the string of three condoms. "Oh. Well, that's probably a good idea."

He drew her into his arms and they stumbled toward the stall. After they stepped inside, Payton pulled the door closed. The light from the torch, when reflected off the walls of the stable, was just enough to see by. Suddenly, he felt nervous, just as he had the first time he'd been with a girl.

This was silly. There had been plenty of women in his life since then. But none of them had ever affected him the way Payton did. Was it because she was still a stranger? That couldn't be it. Or was it because she seemed more exotic, different from the women he usually took to his bed?

She was well educated, he knew that much about her. Though she chose to work in a stable, Brody suspected that she'd probably never done a hard day's work in her life before arriving at the station. And there was the sense that Payton Harwell was the kind of woman who wouldn't give a guy like him a second glance out in the real world. She was seriously out of his league.

So why was she here, trying to seduce him? What did she really want from him beyond having a shag? Brody stood in front of her and cupped her cheek in his hand. Was it just an undeniable sexual attraction they shared? Or was it more?

He'd find some of his answers in her touch, in the feel of her body. And the rest, he'd leave for later. Spanning her waist with his hands, he pulled her body against his, then reached down and drew her leg up along his hip.

Her breath caught in her throat as he stared down into her eyes. Burying her fingers in his hair, she fixed her gaze on his mouth. "Well, then," she murmured, "I guess we're both ready now."

PAYTON ARCHED against the stable wall, reveling in the feel of Brody's hands on her body. It was so simple to want him. She didn't even think before falling into his arms. Maybe there was something in the water here in Australia. Or maybe it was just the man, Payton mused.

Something had changed inside her. For such a long time, she'd tiptoed through life, afraid to make a mistake, fearful that she might disappoint her parents. She'd been their only child, her difficult birth the cause of her mother's inability to have another baby. So there'd been a lot of pressure for her to be perfect.

But from the moment she'd hopped on that flight in Fiji, she'd felt a burden lift from her shoulders. Her parents would never forgive her, so there was no use trying to appease them. She could be whoever she wanted to be now. And she wanted to be wild and passionate, a woman who took chances and lived life.

She looked up into Brody's eyes. This was what she wanted, and not just his gorgeous face or his beautiful body, his penetrating gaze or his playful smile. He was what a real man was supposed to be—strong, confident and just a little bit dangerous. His muscles were hard and his hands rough.

Was that what she'd been looking for? Payton wondered. A man who had the power to possess her completely? Except for that very first time, she'd never made love outside the confines of a bedroom. But here she was, in a stable again, anxious to shed her clothes and feel him move inside her.

Here, everything seemed so much more real, more intense. She didn't feel sheltered and protected anymore. Instead, she'd become wild and uninhibited, like this land and the people around her, taking pleasure in the simplicity of everyday life—and everyday desires. This was her chance to start again. The ties to her past were gradually fraying.

Drawing a deep breath, Payton kissed him, this time making certain he understood her need. She slowly let her leg drop down along his hip, until she stood squarely in front of him. Then she tore at the buttons of his shirt.

He was as anxious as she was to get rid of the garment and a moment later, it lay on the straw at their feet. Payton ran her trembling hands from his shoulders to his belly and back up again. Then, she leaned forward and pressed a kiss to his warm skin, just below his shoulder.

What began gently gradually turned desperate. With every kiss, every caress, Payton wanted him more. He found the hem of her shirt and tugged it up, the fabric bunched in his fists as his hips pinned hers against the side of the stall. Slowly, Brody sank lower until his mouth was on her bare belly.

Payton's fingers furrowed through his hair and his lips trailed higher. He pulled at the lacy bra she wore and when his mouth captured her nipple, Payton cried out in surprise. A wave of sensation washed over her and for a moment, she wasn't sure she could stand.

Holding her tight, Brody tumbled them onto the blankets, pulling her on top of him. His fingers worked at the elastic that held her hair in check, freeing it to fall like a curtain around them both, and then he yanked her shirt over her head.

Payton sat up, straddling his hips, and ran her hand through her hair. Reaching behind her, she unhooked her bra and shrugged out of it. A tiny smile played at the corners of her mouth as she saw his expression shift.

"God, you are beautiful," he murmured, smoothing a hand over her shoulder to cup her breast. He rubbed her nipple to a hard peak and Payton closed her eyes. She didn't want to wait any longer. He could seduce her slowly some other time. Right now, she needed to satisfy a craving deep inside of her.

Payton pushed to her feet, standing over him, her gaze fixed on his. She kicked off her shoes, then slowly shimmied out of her jeans. There wasn't any hesitation or any insecurity. She knew exactly the effect she had on him.

She reached out for him and pulled him up beside

her. Her fingers worked at his belt and then his zipper and when he was standing in just his boxers, Payton let out a soft sigh. "That's better," she said.

He reached out and wrapped his arm around her waist, pulling her against his body. Brody's mouth came down on hers, his kiss deep and demanding. His hands skimmed over her. He knew exactly where to touch to make her ache with desire.

They fell back onto the blankets, Brody rolling her beneath him until his body was stretched out over hers, his hips cradled between her thighs. The delicious sensation of his weight sent a shiver through her limbs.

There were a lot of things Brody said that Payton didn't quite understand. They came from different worlds, and yet their desire for each other needed no translation. Her pulse racing, his hands searching, the anticipation growing between them until it was almost too much to bear.

As he moved above her, his shaft hard between them, Payton remembered her first time and the strange mix of fear and desire and excitement she'd felt. It was like that now with Brody, as if she were just a teenager, still in possession of her virginity.

She sensed this experience wouldn't be like anything she'd ever had before. He was different. But even more important, she was different. Something inside her had changed the moment she'd run away from her wedding. And it was time to see exactly what it was.

However, Brody seemed intent on taking his time. He smoothed his hands over her bare skin, sending shivers of sensation coursing through her body. His lips drifted lower until he drew her nipple into his mouth again.

Payton couldn't take it anymore. Holding him close, she rolled on top of him. Then she straddled his hips, feeling the hard ridge of his cock between them.

"We can do it that way, too." He grinned.

She reached for the condoms lying on the blanket next to them. His erection pressed out against the cotton fabric of his boxers, but she didn't take the time to pull them off. The need to feel him inside her had overwhelmed any thought of seduction.

After tugging the waistband down, she sheathed him, then drew her panties aside. A moment later, Payton slowly sank down on top of him, closing her eyes and holding her breath until he'd buried himself completely. She'd never taken control like this, but she knew exactly what she wanted and how it would feel.

Liberated, she thought as she slowly released her breath. Sex had always been an obligation with Sam, but now it was a basic need, a desire so strong that she'd lost any sense of propriety.

When she opened her eyes again, he was staring at her, passion burning in his gaze. "Don't move," he warned.

"I have to move," she replied with a slow smile. "That's the way it works. At least where I come from." She rose on her knees, then slowly lowered herself again.

"Oh, God, this is not going to last long if you can't follow directions."

Payton leaned forward and kissed him softly. "What is it they say? Just lie back and think of queen and country?"

Brody grabbed her hips and held her still. "Australia is a constitutional democracy," he said.

"I don't care," Payton replied as she rocked forward, ignoring his plea. "We can discuss politics later."

What began slowly and purposefully soon dissolved into a frantic need to satisfy. Brody wasn't as close as he claimed and drove into her again and again, their bodies straining.

Payton felt the beginnings of her release grow inside her, the urge to surrender more intense than she'd ever experienced in the past. She closed her eyes and focused on the feel of him, the wonderful sensations that their coupling created in her body.

His hand touched her face and he drew her down again until their lips and tongues met. It was the kiss that sent her spiraling over the edge. The orgasm came as a complete surprise at first and then Payton was forced to let go, to surrender to the powerful shudders and spasms. She collapsed on top of him, and a moment later Brody found his own release, driving deep inside her, his body tense and then trembling.

They lay together for a long time, gasping for breath, neither one of them speaking. Payton wasn't sure what to say. Thanks were probably in order, considering she'd never experienced an orgasm so powerful. But then, this was only their first attempt. What would subsequent seductions bring?

"That's never happened before."

He gently pushed against her shoulders until their eyes could meet. "You're kidding, right?"

She felt a warm blush creep up her cheeks. If she was liberated enough to make love to a man she barely knew, then she should be able to express her desires. "I mean, it's happened, but not in that way."

He stared at her, a perplexed expression on his face. "Well, that's good, then."

"Yes," she said, smiling. "Maybe we could do it again?"

Brody chuckled. "I think we might have to wait just a bit."

"A bit? What is that in Australian? Because in American that means a minute at the most." She reached down and ran her fingers along his still-rigid shaft, pulling the condom off along the way.

Brody groaned as he clenched his teeth. "A minute. Maybe two." His breath caught in his throat. "Maybe less, if you're very gentle."

BRODY WASN'T SURE of the time. It was late. After midnight. He and Payton had chosen conversation over sex and she was curled up against him, her leg thrown over his hips and her cheek resting on his outstretched arm.

The batteries on the first torch had faded, but Brody had run out and gotten another. For now, they relaxed in complete darkness. Though he loved to look at her, he was just as content to communicate through touch. Her body was made for his hands, her skin so soft and her curves like a landscape to explore.

"We'd probably be more comfortable in my bed," he said, smoothing his hand over her tangled hair.

"We can't," she said.

"Why? There's nothing wrong with what we're doing."

"I know. I'm not ashamed. It's just…"

"What?"

"I'm an employee here and I should probably try to behave myself." She pushed up and grabbed the torch, then shined it on his face. "Besides, this is much more exciting, don't you think?"

"Exciting, maybe." Brody chuckled, holding up his hand. "But not nearly as comfortable." He rolled to his side and pulled a piece of straw from the blanket beneath him.

She sat up beside him and brushed her hair over her shoulder. With a lazy caress, she smoothed her hand over his belly. "When I saw you in the cell next to me, I thought about what you'd look like without your clothes."

Brody gasped, a laugh slipping from his lips. "Really?"

She nodded. "You look different than what I imagined."

"Different bad or different good?"

"Good," she said. Her fingers drifted lower, running along the length of his thigh. He watched, surprised at how such an innocent action could so easily stir his desire. He loved the feel of her hands on his body. As far as he was concerned, she could take whatever she wanted from him. He was willing and quite able to satisfy whatever need might arise.

Her fingers paused when she reached his knee and Brody sucked in a sharp breath. He knew it was ugly. The scars were still sharply defined, to the eye and to the touch. "What happened?" she asked.

He didn't want to tell the story again, especially not to her. It had been a foolish mistake that had changed the entire course of his life. But then, that course had led to her, hadn't it?

"I tore up my knee in a motorcycle accident," he said. "It's not nearly as bad as it looks. It happened a long time ago. I barely even think about it anymore." At least that was the truth, he mused.

She bent over him, her hair tickling his thigh, then pressed her lips to the scar. "There. All better."

Brody chuckled softly. "Yes. That does make things feel much better."

She pushed up on her hands and knees and crawled on top of him. In the soft light from the torch, Payton looked like some ancient goddess, her perfect skin gleaming like marble. He could imagine how a woman like her could drive men into battle for her favors. He was already lost and he'd only known her a few days.

"Any other interesting scars?"

"What exactly are you looking for? Defects?"

She picked up the torch again and shined the light on the tattoo on his right biceps. "What is this?" She rubbed her fingers over the inked skin.

"Nothing, really. Just something tribal."

"I have a tattoo," she said.

Brody pushed up on his elbow, stunned by the admission. "Where?"

She pointed to her ankle and he took the torch from her and held it there. "I don't see anything."

"There. It's that red dot right there."

"That's not a tattoo, that's a freckle."

"No, it was supposed to be a tattoo. But I chickened out after just a few seconds."

"Because it hurt?"

"No. Because I was afraid of what my parents might say. And my—" She smiled. "My boyfriend." She shook her head. "There were a lot of things I thought about doing and then never followed through on. Spontaneity was not something that was encouraged by my family."

"Tell me about this boyfriend," he said.

"That was a long time ago."

"What would they think of you now, lying here naked in a stable with me?"

"They'd probably have me committed."

Brody reached out and picked up her hand, then pressed it to his lips. "I wouldn't let them take you," he said. "You'd be safe with me."

A winsome smiled touched her lips. "I'm not sure *safe* is the right word."

Brody leaned forward and pulled her into a long, lingering kiss. "Will you spend the night with me?" he whispered.

"Here?"

"Wherever you want. Here is good."

"Gemma is probably going to wonder where I am."

"I think Callum is keeping her occupied," Brody assured her.

"The same way you're keeping me occupied?"

He shook his head. "I expect my brother has his own talents. He's—" Brody stopped short when a sound from outside the stall caught his attention. He reached over and switched off the torch, then pressed a finger to Payton's lips.

"What is it?" she whispered.

"Someone is out there."

The sound of horse's hooves on concrete echoed through the silence and Brody got to his feet and moved to the door of the stall. A moment later a light flicked on in the tack room, illuminating the interior of the stable enough to see who had intruded.

Payton stepped to his side, wrapped in one of the wool blankets, and peered out through the bars on the top edge of the stable door. "Who is it?"

"Teague," Brody whispered.

"What's he doing?"

"I think he's saddling his horse."

"Where is he going to ride in the dark?"

"Hell if I know," Brody said. He might guess where his brother was going. Hayley Fraser was back on Wallaroo Station. One plus one equaled two.

Brody thought about what Callum had said earlier. Family loyalty aside, whatever Teague was up to was his business and no one else's. Just like what went on between Payton and him didn't involve his brothers. They were adults now, and they made their own choices. "He's probably riding out to check on the herd," Brody said.

"Alone?"

"Yeah. Why not?"

They listened until the stable was once again silent, the light from the tack room left burning by his brother. Then Brody turned and tugged the blanket off of her. She squirmed playfully as he ran his free hand from her belly to her breast. "We're alone again," he said.

"We should get some sleep," Payton murmured.

Brody groaned as he kissed his way to her nipple. Teasing it to a peak with his tongue, he tried to convince her that sleep was the last thing on his mind. But when she ran her fingers through his hair and pulled his gaze up to hers, he realized just how tired she was. Her eyelids fluttered and she bit back a yawn.

"You're right," he said. "We both have to work tomorrow." Why the hell had he decided to bring her here? Brody wondered. If she hadn't taken this job, then they'd be free to do exactly what they wanted with their time. He should have bought them both a ticket to

Fremantle and they could have spent a week in his apartment. Or he could have found some private getaway where they'd be waited on hand and foot.

Instead, he'd brought her to the station, where they had to sneak around and hide in a horse stall to find some privacy. "You know, the weekend is coming up. You don't have to work on the weekend."

"What? Do you send the horses off to a spa on Saturday and Sunday?" she inquired with a raised brow. "They still need to be fed and groomed."

"But someone else can do that," Brody said.

"It's my job," she replied.

He drew a deep breath and sighed. "There has to be some benefit to sleeping with the owner's brother, don't you think?"

She slipped from his embrace and began to collect her clothes, scattered over the straw-covered floor. "There are a lot of benefits. But I'm not sure unlimited vacation time is one of them."

Brody wrapped his arms around her waist and pulled her back against him. "But aren't you interested in seeing some of Australia while you're here? Isn't that why you came? I'm sure Callum can get one of the jackaroos to take your job for a while."

She shook her head. "Not now. Maybe after I've worked here longer."

Brody understood her worry. After all, when he met her, she'd been reduced to petty crime just to survive. Here, she had a place to sleep, three meals a day and a paycheck at the end of each week. Security trumped great sex, at least for now.

"All right." He took Payton's clothes from her hands

and grudgingly helped her dress. Though she'd removed her clothes as quickly as possible, Brody didn't rush putting them back on, taking the chance to touch her one last time. When he finished, he pulled his jeans on, before slipping his bare feet into his boots. He didn't want to bother with the rest, tossing the remaining clothes over his arm.

"Come on, I'll walk you back to the bunkhouse."

Payton shook her head. "No. Wait here for a few minutes. I can walk back on my own." She pushed up onto her toes and gave him a sweet, lingering kiss. "I'll see you tomorrow," she whispered.

"Abso-bloody-lutely." He captured her mouth again with a deep and possessive kiss of his own.

"All right," she said, running her hands over his bare chest. "Tomorrow."

She turned and hurried out of the stable. Brody watched her as she disappeared into the dark. They'd only known each other for a few days, but he'd already twisted his life around hers. Living on the station had become almost tolerable and working the stock just a way to mark time until he could be with her again.

Brody knew the fascination would probably fade. It always had in the past with other women. There was something about Payton, though, that made him believe it might be different this time.

But was it her with her sweet smile and gentle touch? Or was it him? Had he finally let go of his former life and begun to look forward to what the future held?

4

A BEAD OF PERSPIRATION fell into Payton's eye and she straightened and brushed her arm over her damp forehead. Her back ached from the day's work—mucking out the stables and moving bales of straw into the freshly cleaned stalls. Setting the pitchfork against the rough wooden wall, she stretched her hands above her head and twisted to work the kinks out of her back.

"A dip in the hot tub would soothe those sore muscles," Teague said.

"Sounds good," Payton replied. "Maybe after dinner."

He stared at her for a long moment. "You know, you don't have to work quite so hard. Callum is already impressed. You do twice as much work as all of the jackaroos who've had the job before you."

"What exactly is a jackaroo?"

"Just another name for a stockman. Technically, you're a jillaroo since you're of the female variety."

She smiled. "I like that. I have a title. Maybe I should get some business cards printed. Payton Harwell, Jillaroo."

"Really, I'm serious. No one is going to fire you. And if you're trying to impress Brody, don't bother. He's never been one to enjoy station work."

"Why is that?"

Teague shrugged. "From the moment he could express an opinion, he wanted off the station. He's more like our mum than our dad. He finds it sheer drudgery."

"So, why does he stay?"

"I expect because you're here. Before you came, he spent most of his time in Bilbarra."

"No, I mean, why did he stay as an adult?"

"He didn't. He left the same time our mum did. Moved with her to Sydney when he was fourteen. After that, he only spent holidays here. He hasn't told you this?"

Payton shook her head. "We haven't really talked about our pasts. I guess we've been focusing on the present." She pulled off her gloves, then sat down on a nearby bale of straw. "So he's just here visiting?"

"He's been back for a while. Since his accident—"

"His motorcycle accident?"

Teague nodded. "Since his accident, he hasn't been able to play and he got dropped by his club."

"Club?"

"He hasn't told you much at all," Teague said. "Football club. He was a professional footballer. Aussie rules. He played for a club in Fremantle for the past five years. But he tore up his knee in the accident."

"I've seen the scar," she murmured. "He just brushed it off like it had happened years ago."

"He was in the hospital for a month and in a cast for six. He's lucky to be alive."

"I wonder why he didn't tell me?"

"He doesn't like to talk about it. The accident ended his career. Just when he was starting to play really well, too. And I suppose he thought it didn't make any difference." He sat down beside her. "Does it?"

"No. The scar doesn't bother me. Why would it? It's just that—" She shook her head.

"What?"

"I guess we don't know each other very well. At least not in that sense."

Teague shrugged. "Believe me, it isn't any easier when you know everything about each other. Maybe you and Brody are better off. Less...baggage?"

"Maybe." What Teague said might be true. She and Sam had known each other for years and the passion between them had faded to nothing more than a dull glow. But with Brody, there was fire, flames shooting up into the sky every time their bodies came together. Maybe all the things she didn't know just kept it more exciting.

"I'm flying into Brisbane day after tomorrow. Do you and Gemma want to ride along? You'd mentioned you wanted to shop."

"I have to work," she said.

"We'll be back before dark. I can't land on the station after sunset. And I'm sure some of the guys will take over your duties for a day."

"I don't have any money."

"Payday is Friday," Teague countered. "And I'd be happy to loan you a dollar or two if you're short."

"I couldn't ask you to do that."

"Hey, I think you're a trustworthy sort."

"Then you haven't heard of my criminal past," she said, laughing. "I met your bother in jail."

"Callum mentioned something about that. I guess we've all done things in the past that we wished we could change." He stood, then held out his hand to help her up. "Can I ask you something? From a woman's point of view?"

"Sure," she said.

"Do you think it's possible to forgive past mistakes? I mean, if things get royally stuffed up, is it possible to begin again?"

"I don't know," Payton said. She'd wondered the same thing. "I'm not sure you can ever go back and fix the mistakes you've made. You can just go forward and promise not to make them again."

He nodded, then smiled. "Yeah, I see what you mean." He drew a deep breath. "Listen, if it's all right with you, can we vaccinate those yearlings next week? I've got somewhere I need to be."

"I'm not going anywhere," she said. "Except to Brisbane, if you still plan to take us."

"That I do," he said as he strolled out of the stable. Brody passed him as he wandered in with his horse. Glancing back over his shoulder, he sent his brother an irritated frown, then turned to Payton. "What did he want?"

"He just stopped by to say hello," she said. "We were going to vaccinate the yearlings, but then something else came up." She slipped her gloves on. "He's going to fly Gemma and me to Brisbane on Saturday."

"And what are you and Gemma going to do in Brisbane?"

"Shop. I need to buy some work clothes," she said, glancing down at Davey's jeans and shirt. "And maybe we'll have some lunch and get a pedicure and a manicure. I'd like to get my hair cut, too. I feel like I need a change. This hair just gets in the way."

Brody rested his hands on her shoulders and dropped

a quick kiss on her lips. "But I like the way you look right now." He rubbed a stray strand between his fingers. "And I'm fond of your hair."

Pulling her against him, he kissed her again, this time more passionately. A shiver skittered through her body and she felt her desire warm. It didn't take much to make her want to pull him into a stall and tear off their clothes. "We could go to Brisbane together," he suggested. "Maybe spend the day at the beach instead. Do some surfing."

"It's really a girls' day out," she said. "I'm sure you can get along without me for a day, can't you?"

"I don't know," he teased.

"We'll spend the evening together. I'll be back before dark. Teague said he can't land once it's dark."

"Which means he'll probably find a way to keep you both in Brisbane for the night," he said cynically.

She shook her head. "I don't think so. I think Teague has something else going on."

"Why is that?"

"He asked my advice. Something about starting over again."

Brody sucked in a sharp breath. "Oh, hell. That can only mean one thing. Hayley Fraser. I figured that's where he was off to last night. Callum is going to be mad as a meat-ax."

A giggle slipped from Payton's lips.

"What?" Brody asked.

"How could a meat-ax get angry? And what is a meat-ax?"

"I don't know. What would you say?"

"Mad as a…wet hen?" She laughed. "All right. Yours is much better."

"Wet hen," he muttered. "That's just lame. Who would be afraid of a wet hen?"

"Why will Callum be angry?"

"There's a lot of history between our family and the Frasers. It has to do with a piece of land that Hayley's grandfather claims my great-grandfather stole from the Frasers. We've been fighting about it for years."

"A family feud. Like the Hatfields and McCoys." She paused. "The Montagues and Capulets."

"Yeah, I think Teague and Hayley fancied themselves Romeo and Juliet back when they were teenagers. They were obsessed with each other, to the point where my mum and dad thought they might run away and get married. Then Teague went off to university and a few months later, Hayley ran away. After that, he never mentioned her name again."

"What happened?"

Brody shrugged. "I don't know. Teague doesn't talk about it. He was really messed up for a while."

"So if they're Romeo and Juliet, who are we?" she asked. "Bonnie and Clyde?"

He grinned. "I loved that movie. And we did meet in jail."

"They died in the end of the movie. Riddled with bullets, I think."

"So you're expecting a happy ending for us? I can't think of a movie that ended happily. *Casablanca.* No, that one really didn't—how about—no, that one ended badly, too."

"*Breakfast at Tiffany's,*" she murmured. A happy ending? Payton hadn't thought about the future at all. It was silly to think that she and Brody would share anything beyond her time in Australia. "Life isn't a movie. It's not…perfect." She reached out and took the reins of his horse. "And I have work to do."

"Time for a break," he said. He circled her waist with his hands and lifted her until she could swing her leg over his horse, then handed her a small canvas bag. "Come on. Let's go for a ride."

Brody hooked his foot in the stirrup and settled behind her, taking the reins from her hands and slipping his arm around her waist.

"I haven't been on a horse in years," she said. "Where are we going?"

"I fancy a swim. And there's dinner in that sack."

"I don't have a suit."

"Then you can sit on the shore and watch for crocs."

He gave the horse a kick and guided it out of the stable. They rode in silence past the outbuildings and toward a small grove of trees in the distance. The sun was low in the late-afternoon sky but the air was still warm. Winter in Queensland was more like summer in Maine—the nights cool, sometimes chilly, and the days comfortably warm.

"Won't the water be cold?"

"The pond is pretty shallow," he said.

"Are there really alligators?"

"No. We don't have alligators, we don't have crocodiles, either. They're not common in this part of Queensland. Teague was just being cheeky with you." He paused. "Although, I suppose they could wander in here without us really knowing."

"Snakes, crocodiles, spiders. It's kind of easy to get hurt here."

He nuzzled his face into her neck. "I'll protect you."

"Who will protect you?"

They reached the pond a few minutes later. It wasn't like any pond Payton had ever seen. The water was brown, like the soil around it, and a pipe led from the pond to a nearby windmill. She studied the shoreline, searching for anything that moved. "How long can a crocodile hold its breath?"

"An hour, maybe more," Brody said. "The salt-water crocs are the bad ones. Freshwater crocs aren't nearly as nasty. And if they were here, they'd be on the shore, warming themselves in the sun."

He slid off the horse, then helped her down, before wrapping the reins around a nearby branch. Taking her hand, Brody led her to the edge of the water. Then he slowly began to remove his clothes.

"I really wish you wouldn't go in," she said.

"I've been swimming in this pond since I was a kid. Believe me, it's safe."

"And I think I'll just watch for a while," she said.

He kicked off his boots and socks, then slipped his jeans over his hips. A moment later, he was naked. Payton held her breath as she watched him walk to the water. He really was a beautiful man, every muscle in his body perfectly toned.

Desire raced through her body and her fingers clenched at the thought of touching him. Suddenly, crocodiles didn't seem like such a big deal. Not compared to swimming naked with Brody. As he sank into the water, Payton removed her jacket and dropped it to the ground. A moment later, she pulled off her shoes.

"My parents used to take me to the beach when we

went on vacation," she said. "And they'd never let me go in the water."

"Why not?"

"My mother was afraid of sharks. And my father was afraid I'd drown, even though I'd taken swimming lessons for years." Payton shook her head. "They spent so much energy protecting me from alligators that weren't there."

"Crocodiles," he said.

When she skimmed her jeans down over her thighs, he smiled. And when she was left in just her underwear, he slowly stood. She walked to the water's edge. "Take it all off," he said softly.

Payton drew a ragged breath. They'd been naked together last night, in the shadows of the stable. But it felt just a little bit naughty out in the open. Still, her desire for him was strange and powerful, a force she didn't want to deny.

The water was cold on her skin and she groaned as it slowly moved up her body. Then, holding her breath, she slipped beneath the surface and popped up in front of him. "It's freezing!" she cried.

He pulled her into his arms. "You'll be warm soon," he said, letting his hands drift over her body.

"I've never done this before. I've always thought it would be fun to swim naked, but I've never had the opportunity." As he wrapped her legs around his hips, she leaned back, letting her hair fan out in the water. "It feels nice on my sore muscles."

"You work too hard."

"That's what Teague was telling me," she said as she floated on the surface of the pond.

"And what else was Teague telling you?" Brody asked, an edge to his inquiry.

"Nothing." She didn't want to tell Brody that she'd had an interesting conversation with his older brother, that he'd told her things Brody hadn't bothered to mention. Even now, as she looked into his eyes, Payton saw him differently.

He wasn't just an object of her desire anymore. He was a man with a real life, a life that hadn't gone exactly as planned. But then, her life wasn't exactly a fairy-tale, either. Payton smiled.

She felt his eyes on her naked body and a moment later his hands smoothed over her breasts and down her belly. The sensation was like nothing she'd ever felt before. His touch was warm yet cold, fleeting yet so stirring. Every sensation seemed magnified by the water, her skin slick and prickled with goose bumps.

When he touched her between the legs, a tiny moan slipped from her throat. His caress was so light, so skilled that Payton felt the rise of her need almost immediately. Her eyes still closed, she gave herself over to the feeling. The water lapped around her body, her skin chilly in the late-afternoon air.

She still couldn't understand how easy it was with Brody. She wanted him and he wanted her. They satisfied each other in the most basic way, driven purely by sexual desire. And yet, there was an intimacy growing between them, a trust that seemed strengthened by their passion.

He slipped a finger inside her and she felt herself losing control. And then, a heartbeat later, Payton dissolved into spasms of pleasure. She arched back as the orgasm rocked her body and for a moment, she sank beneath the surface.

But then Brody grabbed her and pulled her up against his chest. Payton coughed and sputtered. She wrapped her arms around his neck, her heart slamming. Another shudder shook her body and he held her tight.

"Are you all right?" Brody asked, brushing the wet hair away from her face.

She nodded, wiping the water from her eyes. Then she began to giggle and couldn't seem to stop. The things Brody did to her were scandalous—she felt wicked when she was with him. Payton kissed him hard. "I think you're more dangerous than the crocodiles. But what a wonderful way to go."

THERE WERE TIMES—though not many—when Brody truly did appreciate the beauty of the outback. He stared up at the inky-black sky, picking out the constellations that he recognized as the moon slowly rose. "Look," he said, pointing to a shooting star. "Quick, make a wish." He drew Payton closer, his arm wrapped around her shoulders. "Got it?"

She nodded as she lay beside him on his bedroll. "The stars are different here."

He pointed into the darkness. "There's the Southern Cross. And the Milky Way."

"No Big Dipper. Or Orion."

"We have Orion," he said. "In the summer. Orion is upside down here. Standing on his head." He rolled onto his side to face her. "It's not much, but it's all the station has to offer for entertainment."

"The swim and the sunset and the stars were perfect," Payton said softly.

"Better than all those balls and cotillions you used to go to?"

"Much better," she said, turning to face him. "And I didn't go to that many balls. Well, maybe I did. But my mother was into those kinds of things. High society and all that. Her one goal in life was to find me a good husband."

"And now you're here in low society with me."

She shook her head. "I'm exactly where I want to be."

"And how long will you be here?" Brody asked, twirling a strand of her hair around his finger.

"I hadn't thought about it. I came in on a tourist visa, so I have three months." She shook her head. "I like it here. I'm not leaving anytime soon."

He drew a deep breath. "Don't you think about going home? To your family and friends?"

She turned her attention back to the stars and Brody sensed she was avoiding his question. She seemed to be reluctant to talk about what had brought her to Oz. He suspected she wasn't just a student touring the country. If she came from a wealthy family, what was she doing working for slave wages on a cattle station? And why had she run out of money so quickly?

"You don't belong here," he said.

"I don't have anyplace else to be right now," Payton replied.

"I don't believe that. What are you running away from, Payton?"

"Nothing," she said. She glanced over at him. "Really. Nothing."

"Talk to me," Brody said, suddenly desperate to know more. Sooner or later, the sex wouldn't be enough. And if there was nothing else to hold her here, to keep her in Australia, she'd leave.

"There's nothing to say," she insisted. "And what difference does it make, anyway?"

He'd always been realistic about his relationships with women. He'd been an enthusiastic lover, romantic when the time called for it, and supportive if required. But he'd never surrendered his heart, never allowed himself to get too close.

Yet the intimacies he'd shared with Payton made him want more. He needed to know who she was and where she came from. He longed to know how she felt about him. Why was she here and how long would she stay? "Fine," he muttered. "And I suppose I shouldn't be surprised if I wake up one day and you've just moved on."

"I wouldn't do that," she said. "I'd say goodbye."

"Well, that's nice to know." Brody couldn't keep the sarcasm from his tone. He pushed to his feet and walked over to the edge of the pond, the moonlight gleaming on the water. He grabbed a small pebble and threw it into the pond, hearing the *plunk* before the ripples glimmered in the dark.

He closed his eyes when he felt her hand on his back. "I don't understand what you want," she said.

"I don't know what I want." He turned and pulled her into his embrace. How could he answer that? All he knew was he didn't want to hold anything back. He wanted honesty and openness and complete surrender. But then, he hadn't been honest with her. Perhaps that's where it would have to start.

The problem with his story was it really didn't make him look good. He hadn't planned well for his future, he'd bet everything on a successful football career. And then, in one incredible act of stupidity, he'd blown it all.

"We should go back," he said. "It's starting to get really cold and I don't want to you catch a chill."

He rolled up his swag and retied it onto the back of his saddle, then took her hand and led her over to his horse.

She looked up at him and forced a smile. "Thank you for bringing me here. It was fun."

Grasping her waist, Brody helped her up into the saddle. After he mounted, he turned the horse toward the house. Payton leaned back against him and he turned his face into her damp hair, inhaling her scent.

"Stay with me," he said.

"I'm not going to leave."

"I mean tonight. Stay with me tonight."

"Not tonight," she said.

"I want you with me," he said. "I don't like sneaking around. We're not doing anything wrong, why do you act as if we are?"

"Because it's just between us right now," she said. "Nothing can mess it up if it's just us. I've known you for three days, Brody. We should at least try to take a few things slowly, don't you think?"

This was exactly why he couldn't be friends with a woman. He didn't understand the reasoning. It was all right to have sex in the stable, but not in his bed. Everyone on the station knew what was going on between them, but pretending that nothing was happening made more sense.

Arguing with her wouldn't help, he mused. If he

wanted more from her, then he'd just have to wait until she was ready to give him more. When they reached the bunkhouse, he helped her down and gave her a quick kiss. "I'll see you tomorrow," he murmured.

She nodded. "Tomorrow."

He turned away and led his horse toward the stable. As he passed by the house, he saw Callum sitting on the back porch, a beer in his hand, his feet kicked up on the railing. "Where were you?" Callum asked.

"I went for a swim with Payton," Brody said. He swung off his horse and wrapped the reins around the post at the bottom of the steps. "Do you have another one of those?"

Callum reached down and picked up a bottle. "You have to go fetch the next round," he said.

Brody twisted off the cap, then sat down in the chair beside Callum's. He took a long drink of the beer and belched.

"Nice," Callum said. "A bit more choke and you would have started."

"Thank you," Brody muttered.

"Funny how you're on your best behavior around Payton and then you revert to typical Brody."

"And you don't put on airs when you're with Gemma?" He paused. "And why aren't you with Gemma? How come you're all alone here, crying into your beer?"

"She's shut herself in the library. I can't understand what's taking her all this time. It's not like we're royalty. But she's going over every single journal and account book in there."

"What does that have to do with our family history?"

"Don't ask me," Callum said.

"She's pretty. Not as pretty as Payton, but pretty."

"I beg to differ," Callum said. "Gemma is much prettier."

"Payton told me she spoke with Teague today. He was talking like he'd started things up with Hayley Fraser again. And he took off in the middle of the night last night on horseback."

"Shit," Callum said. "When I heard she was back, I wondered if he was going to see her again. What do you think she's up to?"

"You never liked her, did you?"

Callum shrugged. "She put Teague through hell the first time they were together. He has a blind spot when it comes to her."

"Maybe that's our problem," Brody mused. "We've never had a blind spot when it comes to a woman. Maybe we're missing out on something."

Callum took a drink of his beer. "Maybe." He pulled his feet off the railing and stood. "I'm going to go check on Gemma. See if she might need some help." He stepped over Brody's outstretched legs and walked back inside the house.

Brody glanced over at the light shining from the window of the bunkhouse. If Gemma was in the library then that meant Payton was alone in the bunkhouse. He drank the last of his beer as he wandered off the porch toward the light.

When he rapped on the door, there was no answer from inside, but he heard the sound of running water and walked around the corner of the bunkhouse to the rough wooden shower. He pulled the door open and stepped inside, slipping his hands around Payton's waist.

She screamed, but he stopped the sound with his kiss, his tongue delving into her damp mouth until her surprise was subdued.

She brushed her soapy hair from her eyes and looked at him. "Your clothes are getting all wet," she said.

His fingers skimmed over her naked body, deliberately tempting her. "I just wanted to say good-night." He leaned forward, his lips barely touching hers.

"I thought you did that already," Payton said.

"I wanted to leave you with something a bit more memorable," he said. His hands slid around to cup her backside and he pulled her hips against his, making his desire completely evident.

Brody's mouth found Payton's again and he felt her melt against him. "If you want more, I'm in the first room at the top of the stairs." With that, Brody stepped out of the shower. "Good night, Payton. Sleep tight."

She didn't return the courtesy. He imagined that she was considering his offer. But Brody really didn't expect her to follow through. Not tonight. But maybe tomorrow night. A grin curved the corners of his mouth. He could be bloody persuasive when he wanted.

THOUGH SHE WAS EXHAUSTED, Payton couldn't sleep. Her head spun with thoughts of Brody. She wanted to go to him, to crawl into his bed and into his arms and just fall asleep with him beside her. The need was so acute it had become an ache.

Cursing softly, she tossed aside the bedcovers and swung her legs off the edge of the bunk. Gemma had come in an hour before and Payton had assumed she was asleep, but then she spoke.

"Can't sleep?" she called from across the room.

"No. You can't, either?"

"No."

A moment later, the light on Gemma's headboard came on. She sat up, crossing her legs in front of her, then ran her hand through her thick auburn hair. "Would you care to talk?" she asked. "I'm a good listener. All my friends tell me so."

"It's complicated," Payton replied.

"I can handle complicated. Is it Brody? You two seem to be…attracted."

"That's putting it mildly," Payton said. She crawled out of bed and crossed the room, then sat down on the edge of Gemma's bunk. "Can you keep a secret?"

"Of course."

"A month ago this last Saturday, I was putting on my wedding gown in Fiji and getting ready to walk across the beach and get married."

Gemma gasped. "Oh, goodness. What happened?"

"I got scared and ran away." She frowned, searching for the words to explain her actions. "I just wasn't sure he was the man I wanted to spend the rest of my life with. There was no…fire. Do you know what I mean?"

Gemma nodded. "Yes," she said. "I know precisely what you mean."

"So I grabbed a few things, stuffed them in my bag, exchanged my honeymoon ticket for a flight to Brisbane and…disappeared into the outback."

"And here you are," Gemma said.

"Yes."

"Have you called your family?"

Payton shook her head. "I left a message at the hotel

in Fiji after I landed in Australia. I said I'd call them soon, but they're going to be so angry with me that I don't even want to think about that now. The embarrassment and the expense of the wedding. The gossip will be awful."

"What of your fiancé?"

"I can't imagine what he's thinking. I'm sure he doesn't want anything more to do with me. Not that I want him to. I made my choice and I can live with it."

"Well, there it is, then," Gemma said cheerfully. "As Callum would say, no worries."

"Oh, I have plenty to worry about. Like this thing with Brody. I'm sure it's just a reaction to what I did. I was a little…repressed and now I'm testing my boundaries. And the attraction will probably fade soon. But then, I'm not sure I want it to." Payton paused. "He's like a rebound guy, but I think he might be more."

"A rebound guy?" Gemma said. "I understand. But wouldn't any man who came after your fiancé be a rebound guy? So, in theory, it would be better to go out with some git after you break up so you don't waste a good bloke as a rebound guy."

"I suppose that would be sensible. So you think I'm wasting Brody?"

"Or perhaps, you could consider the possibility that fate has put this man in your path and the reason you ran away from your wedding is that you were really meant to be with him all along."

"No," Payton said, the notion too absurd to consider. "You think so?"

"I think it's silly to try to figure out a relationship before it's really begun. Maybe you should just let it happen."

Payton considered Gemma's point, then slowly

stood. "Thank you," she said. She walked over to her bunk and grabbed her jacket from where it hung on the bedpost. "I'm just going to visit Brody for a few minutes. Don't wait up for me."

"I won't," Gemma said with a sly smile.

Payton slipped her shoes on and pulled the jacket over her T-shirt and flannel pajama bottoms. The night was chilly as she ran from the bunkhouse to the main house. Mary had left a light burning over the sink in the kitchen, but the house was silent. Tiptoeing through the kitchen, she headed toward the stairs. But when she reached the top, she was faced with two choices.

Brody had said his bedroom was the first door at the top of the stairs, but she couldn't remember if he'd said on the right or the left. She reached for the door on the right and opened it carefully. To her relief, she found a linen closet stacked with towels.

Drawing a deep breath, she opened the opposite door and slipped inside. The bedside lamp still burned and Brody's hand rested on a sports magazine that he had been reading before he fell asleep. He slept in a tangle of blankets, his chest bare and his hair tousled.

Payton slowly undressed, dropping her clothes on the floor. When she was naked, she stepped to the side of the bed and gently moved the magazine from beneath his hand. He looked so relaxed, almost boyish. His brow, usually furrowed into an intense expression, was now smooth, and his lips, so perfectly sculpted, were parted slightly.

Payton carefully pulled the covers back and slipped into bed beside him. He awoke with a start and stared at her for a long moment before he comprehended what was going on. Then, with a soft sigh, he rolled her beneath him and kissed her.

There was no need for words. They communicated with taste and touch, with soft moans and quickened breathing. Payton slid her hand down and wrapped her fingers around his rigid cock and at the same moment, he found the damp spot between her legs.

All the while, as they teased each other closer to the edge, he kissed her gently, murmuring her name and telling her how good it felt to touch her. At first, Payton was a bit inhibited talking about such things. But then, she let her insecurities go and began to take part in the highly charged conversation.

She could feel his body tense as she brought him closer, his breath coming in short gasps. Carefully, Payton drew him back from the edge, becoming more skillful with every caress. Brody took his cues from her and did the same until they were both almost frantic for release, writhing against each other, their limbs tangled in the sheets.

And when her need finally overwhelmed her, Payton knew that it was exactly what she was searching for. He surrendered a moment later, her hand becoming slick with his orgasm.

Brody's mouth found hers and he kissed her gently. Such a simple thing, Payton mused. And yet, every time they surrendered to each other, she felt the bond between them growing. It wasn't just sex. They were discovering each other and with each new experience, Payton found herself wanting more.

"Are you going to stay?" he asked, his lips brushing against hers as he spoke.

Payton nodded. It would be easy enough to sneak out before morning. But then, why even bother to deny what was happening between them? They were both free to enjoy each other. They were both consenting adults. Any shame she might have felt about sleeping with a man she barely knew was just residual guilt left over from leading a rather sheltered life.

She wasn't the same Payton who had flown to Fiji for her wedding. She wasn't even the same Payton who had run away in the middle of the ceremony. Every day she was on her own, she was learning more and more about the woman she really was inside.

She'd spent so much time in familiar surroundings, safe among family and friends, her every need met, her every worry soothed, that she hadn't really bothered to question who she was or what she wanted. But now, each day was a choice, a choice to go backward or to move forward.

"You're not a dream, are you?" Brody whispered, running his fingers through her hair.

"No," she said.

"You won't be gone the next time I open my eyes?"

"No."

Satisfied, Brody pulled her against his body, tucking her backside into his lap and wrapping his arms around her. His lips pressed to her nape and Payton closed her eyes, a warm feeling of contentment washing over her.

The world she'd once known seemed like another lifetime. She was happy here in Brody's arms. And whether it lasted a day or a year, she wouldn't question it again, for perhaps Gemma had been right. Perhaps fate had brought them together.

BRODY PARKED the Land Rover in front of Shelly's coffeeshop, waiting for the dust on Bilbarra's main street to
settle before stepping out of the truck. He had just
enough time for a late lunch before heading back to the
station.

Gemma and Payton had taken off with Teague at
sunrise for their girls' day out in Brisbane. To keep his
mind off Payton, Brody had driven into Bilbarra to pick
up a part for one of the windmills that had gone down
the previous week.

But the long ride in had left him plenty of time to
think about the past five days. It had only been five days
since he'd first set eyes on Payton. Hard to believe considering what had passed between them. It wasn't just
the desire, Brody thought. He'd felt that way about
other women, at least in the beginning. But he found
himself focused on different matters when it came to
Payton—like how long she'd stay and whether she had
any reason to go home.

They seemed to fit so perfectly, understanding each
other's needs without even having to speak, focusing on
the present instead of the future. He needed a woman like
that, a woman who wouldn't insist on plans and promises.

She'd spent the last three nights in his bed, though she hadn't been brave enough to face the group at the breakfast table. Instead, she'd slipped out in the hour before dawn, while the house still slept.

Oddly enough, his brothers wouldn't have even noticed her comings and goings. Teague hadn't bothered to come home the past two nights, only just turning up to grab a shower and change clothes. And Callum had his own preoccupations, disappearing with Gemma the night before last and returning the next morning.

It was strange that all three of them were suddenly involved when not one of them had bothered with dating for months. He headed toward the post office, but a shout stopped him in the middle of the street.

"Brody Quinn!"

Brody turned to see Angus Embley lumbering after him, his tie undone and his hair standing on end.

"I haven't done anything wrong," Brody said, holding up his hands in mock surrender.

"I've been wanting to speak with you," Angus said. He motioned Brody toward police headquarters and Brody jogged across the street, joining him on the porch. "Why have you been dodging my calls?"

"I'm sorry," Brody said. "I was just planning to go over to the Spotted Dog and pay Buddy for that mirror I broke last weekend."

"I'm not worried about Buddy's damn mirror. I'm on the organizing committee for Bachelors and Spinsters and we're going to hold an auction this year. You're the only celebrity we've got in Bilbarra besides Hayley Fraser and I don't think we can convince her to participate. You'd fetch a pretty penny. All the proceeds go to the library book fund. And you don't have to sleep with anyone, just have dinner together."

Though every unmarried person within a two-hundred-mile radius looked forward to the annual Bilbarra "ball," Brody and his brothers suddenly had three very good reasons not to attend—Payton, Gemma and Hayley. "I heard Hayley was back on Wallaroo Station," Brody mentioned, hoping for some additional news.

Angus looked surprised. "Really." He appeared to weigh his options for a moment, then shook his head. "Naw. She's a big telly star. She's probably got a whole building full of people telling her what she can and can't do."

"I think I'm going to have to pass," Brody said.

"Hey, there is something else." Angus braced his arm on the porch post. "There's a private detective hanging about."

"Looking for me?"

Angus chuckled. "One would think that might be a good bet. But he's looking for that lady you bailed out of my jail. Payton Harwell. What did you do with her after you bailed her out?"

Brody considered his answer for a long moment. He could trust Angus, but the man was an officer of the law. If Payton was a fugitive, Angus might not have a choice in taking sides. Brody shrugged. "I gave her some money and sent her on her way. She said she was headed back to Brisbane. That's the last I saw of her."

Angus frowned. "There's a reward for information. Ten thousand American."

"What did she do?"

"He wouldn't say. You could ask him yourself. He was looking to have a bit of lunch, so I pointed him toward the coffeeshop. He may still be there."

"Thanks," Brody said, starting off down the street.

Hell, this was all he needed. He was lucky he hadn't brought Payton to town with him. He'd been concerned about her flying to Brisbane with Teague, but she seemed almost anxious to get off the station and spend time shopping with Gemma. The testosterone-heavy atmosphere on the station did require time away occasionally.

If she was running from something—or someone—then who could say when she'd just up and disappear again? Maybe she planned to use the trip to Brisbane to make her escape. He shook his head. She'd promised to say goodbye before she left. He'd have to take her at her word.

The bell above the door of the coffeeshop jingled as he stepped inside. "Hey there, Shelly!" Brody slid onto one of the stools at the counter and picked up a menu.

Shelly Farris wiped her hands on a towel and strolled over to him. "Brody Quinn. What brings you into town on a weekday?"

Brody set the menu down and watched as she poured him a cup. "I'm picking up a few parts for Callum. I thought I'd check up on you. See if you made any of my favorite meat pies today."

"We have steak mince, steak and mushroom, and a few of our breakfast pies left."

"I'll have a steak mince," Brody said. "Make them takeaway." He closed the menu and glanced over his shoulder. There was only one other customer in the place. "Tourist?" he asked, nodding in the man's direction.

Shelly shook her head. "No. Private investigator. Looking for that girl who stiffed me on the bill last week. The bill you paid. I don't think you did society any favors there."

"Why? What did he tell you?"

"Nothing. Only that he's offering a reward for information. I couldn't give him more than what I just told you. Do you know where she is?"

Brody shook his head. "No, how would I? I was just doing a good deed."

Shelly disappeared into the kitchen to get his order while Brody sipped his coffee. If he wanted to know more about Payton Harwell, all he had to do was ask. But by asking, he might create undue suspicion. Still, idle curiosity wasn't out of the ordinary.

He slipped off the stool and wandered over to the booth where the middle-aged man sat, a half-eaten Lamington on his plate. "Don't like the dessert?" Brody asked.

The man glanced up from the study of his mobile phone. "What?" He looked at his plate and smiled. "No. It was great. Can I get my check?"

"I don't work here," Brody said.

"Oh, sorry."

When the man made a move to leave, Brody sat down on the opposite side of the booth. "I hear you're looking for someone."

"Yes. Yes, I am." He reached into a leather folder and pulled out a photo, then set it down in front of Brody. "Do you know her?"

Brody nodded. "I do. We were incarcerated to-gether."

His eyebrow shot up. "I knew she spent some time in the local jail, but I didn't know you were with her when she was arrested."

"I wasn't," Brody said. "We just happened to be confined at the same time. I paid her fine and settled her accounts. Why are you looking for her?"

"It's a private matter," he said. "Do you know where she is?"

"Did she break the law?"

"As I said, it's a private matter. But there is a reward for information leading to her location, if you know something."

"I bailed her out and then dropped her on the road out of town. I think she said she was going to make her way down to Sydney," Brody lied. "I told her she could probably catch a ride on one of the road trains that pass through."

"Road trains?"

"It's a semitruck that pulls a string of trailers. They pass through Bilbarra occasionally, hauling feed and building supplies." He leaned back and stretched his arms out to rest on the edge of the bench. "She could be anywhere by now."

"Yes, well, thank you," the man said. "That's the most I've found to go on. She didn't say anything about where she might be staying or whether she met up with any friends?"

Brody pretended to ponder the question for a moment, then shook his head. "Nope. She just wanted to get out of town."

The investigator threw a wad of cash onto the table, then held out his hand. "Your lunch is on me," he said. "Thanks for the information."

"No worries," Brody said. "I hope you find her." He watched as the man walked out the front door then went back to his spot at the counter. When Shelly returned with his meat pies, he pointed to the empty booth. "He's buying me lunch."

"Well, there's a clever boy. What did you tell him?"

Brody scooped up the pies wrapped in paper, and took a big bite out of one of them. "Not much," he said as he chewed. "But I got a free lunch out of it." He headed toward the door.

"Where are you going?" Shelly asked, disappointment tingeing her tone. "I just rang my husband to stop by. Arnie's got himself mixed up in some silly football scheme with the boys over at the Spotted Dog and he needs advice on his footy picks. He's been losing twenty dollars a week to those fools."

"I'm out of the game," Brody said, pointing to his knee. "I'm trying my best to forget footy."

"You were one of the best, Brody Quinn," Shelly called.

As Brody strode down the street, he inhaled the two meat pies. He was tempted to stop by the Spotted Dog for a beer to wash them down, then realized he'd been banished from the place until further notice. Instead, he decided to stop at the local library. A quick Internet search might turn up a few clues on Payton and her past…and maybe even outline her crimes.

The public library was attached to the small school in Bilbarra. Though nearly all of the children who lived on cattle and sheep stations took their classes by computer, those who lived within a short drive of Bilbarra attended a regular school. Some of the advanced classes were still taught online, but there were two teachers that guided the thirty or forty students through their studies, and the town librarian to see to their literary needs.

When he walked into the library, a trio of young boys gathered at a large table. One of the boys recognized him immediately and quickly informed his friends. The librarian, Mrs. Willey, looked up at the commotion, then smiled. "See there," she said. "Everyone uses the library, even football legends."

Brody grinned. "She's right, you know. The library is one of my favorite spots in all the world. Read more books!" He stopped at the counter. "There," he muttered. "I've done my duty as a role model, ma'am. Now, I was wondering if I could use a computer with Internet access."

"Certainly," Mrs. Willey said. "Use any one of those three along the wall. But I'll have you know, accessing adult material is prohibited and will result in the suspension of your privileges."

He caught her teasing smile and chuckled. "There'll be none of that," he said. "I'm here to look up some recipes."

He sat down and keyed in his favorite search engine then typed Payton's first and last name. Brody paused before he hit Enter, wondering what he'd find. Maybe it would be something he didn't like, something he'd rather not know. And shouldn't he wait for Payton to tell him about her past? Real relationships were supposed to be about trust.

He had to know all the facts before he could protect

her, Brody rationalized. If she was in trouble, he'd do everything in his power to help her. "So I have to know," he said as he hit the keys.

"Payton Harwell," he read. "Over one thousand hits?" Brody clicked on the first one and found her name mentioned as the winner of a horse show. But right below that was a startling headline: Payton Harwell to Wed Heir to Whitman Fortune.

He clicked on the article and an instant later, a photo of Payton and her fiancé appeared. He scanned through the text beneath it and stopped at the wedding date. "The couple will be married on the island of Fiji in late April with close friends and relatives in attendance. The bride will wear a gown by designer Sophia Carone."

Late April? If Payton had been married in late April and he'd met her the first of June, then her marriage hadn't lasted more than a month. "Oh, shit," Brody muttered. Had he been having a naughty on a nightly basis with a married woman?

There weren't many rules in Brody's book when it came to sex, but not bedding another man's wife was one of them. After witnessing the problems in his parents' marriage, he'd vowed never to be involved in breaking up a family. Besides, there had always been plenty of single women willing to jump into bed with him, he'd had no need to do it with the married sort.

He leaned back in his chair and studied the photo. They looked happy, their arms wrapped around each other, smiling for the photographer. Worse, they looked as if they belonged together, living in some fancy mansion in New York with servants to tend to their every need.

Well, at least she wasn't a criminal, Brody mused. She was simply a runaway wife. He paused. Or maybe a runaway bride. There was no proof that she'd ever gone through with the wedding. Maybe she'd arrived in Fiji and decided marriage just wasn't for her.

"Is there anything I can help you with?"

Brody quickly clicked back to the search engine, then glanced over his shoulder at Mrs. Willey. "No. Nothing. Just catching up on a few of my old friends." He stood, shoving his hands into the pockets of his jeans. "Thanks. I'm in a bit of a hurry right now, but I'll stop by soon and pick up some books."

"You do that," she said with a wide smile. "Be sure to come on a school day if you can. I'm sure the students would love to talk to you."

Brody strode out the front door of the library into the midday sun. He headed back to the Land Rover, parked near the coffeeshop. He'd have to decide just how to discuss his discovery with Payton. Though his rule regarding married women still stood, it seemed rather pointless to avoid sex now that that horse was already out of the barn.

Hell, the only way to avoid wanting her was to leave Queensland altogether. He could no more control his desire for Payton Harwell than he could stop breathing.

THE PLANE TOUCHED DOWN as the afternoon sun hovered near the western horizon. Payton peered out the window, catching sight of one of the station's utes, the name she'd learned to call the pick-up trucks that nearly everyone drove. She saw Callum leaning against the truck as the plane taxied to the near end of the runway, but Brody was nowhere to be seen.

When Teague had turned off the single engine, Callum approached and opened the door. He helped Payton out, grabbing shopping bags as she jumped lightly from the plane. He then turned back to wrap his hands around Gemma's waist. Payton watched as their gazes met and he gave her a quick kiss.

Though Gemma hadn't said anything about her relationship with the eldest Quinn, it was clear to everyone that something was going on. Callum didn't smile much, but he always seemed to be smiling when Gemma was present.

Callum helped Teague secure the plane before all four of them hopped into the truck and headed toward the house. Payton had hoped to find Brody standing on the porch or lounging on her bunk, but she was disappointed.

"He took off about a half hour ago," Callum said. "On horseback, toward the west. I'm sure he'll be back soon."

Payton forced a smile. She'd been looking forward to seeing Brody all day. She'd bought a sexy new swimsuit for the hot tub and some lacy underwear that she was certain he'd appreciate. Her nails and toes looked perfect and her hair smelled like fruit. In short, she was almost irresistible.

She set her bags inside the door of the bunkhouse then turned and jogged down the front steps. "I'm going to ride out and meet him," she said.

"It's getting dark," Callum warned.

"Don't worry, I won't go far. I can see the lights of the station from pretty far away."

She ran to the stables and found a gentle mount, then quickly saddled the horse. She tied a bedroll on the back in case she and Brody decided to make a stop at the swimming hole again. Then, after swinging her leg over the saddle, she steered the horse out of the stable and into the waning light.

Though she'd ridden to the pond with Brody the other night, this was the first time she'd been on a horse alone since her fall nine years before. "Like riding a bike," she said, settling into the rhythm.

She urged the horse into a relaxed gallop, letting the wind whip her hair into a riot of curls. It was still easy to see where she was going, the last rays of the sun shining on the red dirt of the outback.

As she rode, her thoughts wandered to Brody, to spending the evening alone with him. Brisbane had been so busy and exciting that she'd wished he'd been there to share it with her. Maybe next weekend they could go together, as he'd suggested. They could spend some time at the beach or find a comfy hotel room and revel in absolute privacy.

As the sun dropped lower, the air became chilly and Payton drew her horse to a stop. She scanned the landscape for Brody, but it was difficult to see. Tugging gently on the reins, she turned the horse around. Her breath caught in her throat. She couldn't see the station anymore.

Rubbing her eyes, she squinted into the distance, searching for the lights that would guide her back. Slowly, she realized she'd ridden too far, lost in her thoughts and unaware of the passing time. Everything looked the same. Starting off in the direction she'd come from, Payton kicked the horse into a gallop again.

But a moment later, the horse stumbled in an unseen gully and she found herself thrown forward.

Payton hit the ground with a hard thud, knocking the wind out of her. Groaning, she lay back in the dirt and took a quick inventory. Her limbs were still intact, no broken bones, just wounded pride. Levering to her feet, she brushed the dirt off her jeans and remounted, but as soon as she spurred the horse forward, she could feel the animal favor its right foreleg.

Sliding off again, she bent down and ran her hands over his leg. "What happened?" she cooed. There was no swelling and no broken bones. She's seen enough stumbles in her show-jumping career to suspect that it was probably just a bruise. Though riding was possible, there was no need to put the horse under any more stress. She mentally calculated the distance and figured she probably had at least an hour's walk.

Payton stared up at the stars, trying to remember what she'd seen in the night sky. The last traces of the day were visible on the horizon, so she grasped the reins and began to walk the opposite way, east, toward the station.

The outback looked deceptively flat, yet as she walked, she realized that a gentle rise could easily hide things in the distance. She tried to keep moving in a straight line, finding a cluster of stars to keep over her right shoulder. But it was difficult to maintain her bearings in the dark. In the end, she decided to give her horse its head. He knew how to get home better than she did.

But, to her surprise, the horse didn't lead her back to the station. Instead, she found herself standing at a low iron gate. She hadn't come through any fence on her way out, but the horse seemed to know what it was doing. "Do I trust the horse or do I trust myself?"

In the end, she opened the gate and led the horse through. A few seconds later, she noticed the outline of a small building, just barely visible in the growing moonlight. Obviously, the horse had been to the spot in the recent past. "What is this?"

The front door was unlocked, but she could see nothing in the black interior. Closing her eyes, she felt around with her hands, stumbling over what felt like beds along the walls. She wandered back to the porch, then noticed a lantern hanging beside the door and a tin box of matches nailed below it.

The match flared and she lit the lantern, then walked back into the small shack. It was obvious it was some kind of remote bunkhouse, though it seemed to be awfully close to Kerry Creek to be of much use. She found a couple more lanterns and, after lighting them, took the first one out onto the porch to serve as a sign that she was there.

Someone would come looking for her sooner or later. And if they didn't come tonight, she'd simply wait until the morning and then head toward the sunrise. Payton walked over to her horse and took off his saddle, dropping it onto the front steps of the shack.

She folded the saddle blanket and threw it on top. Then she carefully tethered the horse to a hitching rail in front of the cabin before stepping inside.

The interior of the cabin was cozy and almost as comfortable as the bunkhouse, though a bit dustier. From what she could tell, the place had been used recently. There was a stack of firewood next to the cast-iron stove and canned food in the small cupboard above the dry sink. She picked through the assortment and found a can of nuts.

A shelf of paperback novels, mostly mysteries, caught Payton's attention and she chose one and sat down at the small wooden table. Though it was hard to read in the flickering light, she managed to finish a few pages before her eyes grew tired. With a frustrated sigh, she laid her head down on the table and closed her eyes.

She wasn't sure whether she'd fallen asleep or not, but a loud crash brought her upright. She saw a shadow in the doorway and screamed. But a moment later, Brody stepped into the light.

He crossed the room in a few long strides, grabbed her arms and yanked her into his embrace. "What the hell were you thinking?" he muttered. "I got back to the station and they said you'd left on horseback."

"I was just going to ride out to meet you and then my horse came up lame. I thought he'd lead me back to the stable, but he came here."

"You're on Fraser land," Brody said. He pressed a kiss to the top of her head and then took a deep breath. "Do you know how dangerous it is out here? You can walk for a day and not see anything familiar."

"That's why I decided to stay here."

"The first smart move you made all day." He cupped her face in his hands and kissed her, his mouth harsh and demanding, as if he was exacting punishment for what she'd done.

But he didn't stop there. He tore off his jacket and tossed it aside, then began to work at the buttons of her shirt. When he wasn't removing her clothes, he was stripping out of his, and within a minute, they were both naked.

Payton wasn't sure what to say. She knew he was angry and maybe a bit shaken, but he seemed to need reassurance that she was safe. He buried his face in the curve of her neck, his hands skimming over her body as if to prove to himself she was unhurt.

Brody turned her around in his arms. Payton knew what was coming, but she wasn't prepared for the intensity of his need. "I don't have protection," he murmured.

"It's all right," Payton said, arching against him. She'd taken care of birth control a long time ago, choosing a method that was both constant and convenient. She wanted to experience him without any barriers, to feel just him inside her.

He buried himself deep in a single thrust, then held her, drawing a deep breath. She wriggled against him, silently pleading for him to move, but he held her still until he regained control.

He began slowly at first, with a delicious rhythm that she couldn't deny. Her mind whirled with a maelstrom of sensation and she felt herself losing touch with reality. Every stroke brought her closer to completion.

Payton moved with him, sending him even deeper. Every movement felt like perfection, as though their bodies were made to do just this. His fingers grasped her hips as she urged him on, so close to release that she was afraid they might both collapse onto the floor before they were through.

Brody moaned and she knew he was close. But then, suddenly he stopped. "Say it," he murmured. "Tell me you'll never leave me."

At first, she wasn't sure what he meant. Did he just want to hear the words, or was he demanding the promise behind them. In the end, Payton didn't really care. If he wanted her to stay, she would, for as long as this passion lasted. "I won't," she said. "I promise."

"Promise me," he said, his voice raw as he moved again.

"I promise."

Satisfied, he brought them both closer and closer. And then, in a blinding instant, Payton cried out and dissolved into powerful spasms of pleasure. He was there with her, his body shuddering with every stroke.

Brody sighed as he kissed her nape, his teeth grazing her skin. When he stumbled, Payton steadied them both, their bodies still joined. "I think we should sit down," she said.

"No," he murmured. "I want to stay just like this."

"All right," she said, reaching back to wrap her arm around his neck. She shifted and he groaned, slipping out of her.

Brody moved over to one of the bunks and gently lowered her onto the rough wool blanket. Then he stretched out beside her. Goose bumps prickled her skin and she pulled the edges of the blanket up around them both. "It's not as comfy as your bed," she said. "But it will do."

"We're trespassing. Considering the feud between the Frasers and the Quinns, we might end up shot, or in jail."

"It was worth it," she teased.

"No more adventures in the outback for you."

"I'll just take you with me." She closed her eyes and snuggled against him. At that moment, Payton couldn't imagine ever doing without this passion. Or without this man. What that meant, she wasn't sure. But it did mean something.

"TEAGUE?"

Brody awoke to the sound of a woman's voice. The door creaked and he pushed up on his elbow, squinting against the sunlight that shone through the door, Payton still sound asleep beside him. "Brody," he said.

He heard hurried footsteps on the front steps, then carefully rolled out of bed and tugged his jeans on. When he got outside, Brody found Hayley Fraser mounting her horse.

"Wait," he called, raking his hand through his tousled hair.

She paused, watching him warily from atop her horse. Brody hadn't seen Hayley in ages, not since she and Teague were teenagers. But he had seen photos of her in magazines and on television. Teague's ex-girlfriend had become one of Australia's most popular young actresses. She had a part on a television show that almost everyone in Oz watched every Thursday evening, and there were rumors that she was about to make a move to Hollywood.

"What are you doing here?" she asked, her wavy blond hair blowing in the morning breeze.

"We needed a place to sleep. This was close by. Was Teague supposed to meet you here?"

"No," she said, an edge of defensiveness in her voice. "Why would you think that?"

"It was almost as if you were expecting him," Brody said.

"I saw the Kerry Creek horses and I thought it

might be him. But I was mistaken. Sorry. I didn't mean to wake you."

She looked even more beautiful than she did on television. But instead of being dressed in some sexy outfit, with her hair fixed up, she wore jeans, a canvas jacket and a stockman's hat. "Should I tell Teague you were looking for him?"

"Why?" She shook her head. "No. You don't need to tell him anything."

Brody felt a hand on his arm and he turned to see Payton standing beside him, wrapped in the wool blanket. "Morning," she said, nodding to Hayley.

"Payton, this is Hayley Fraser," Brody said. "Her family owns this place. Hayley, Payton Harwell."

Payton smiled. "Thank you for letting us stay here. I got lost last night and wasn't really prepared to sleep outside."

Hayley nodded, her expression cool and guarded. She'd never really warmed to anyone else in the Quinn family or anyone connected with them. In truth, Brody's parents had discouraged a relationship to the point where they forbade Teague from seeing her. At the time, both Callum and Brody had sided with their parents. But Teague had never bothered to follow their advice. And he probably wouldn't now.

"I—I have to go," Hayley murmured. "Stay as long as you like. I won't say anything to my grandfather."

She wheeled her horse around and kicked it into a gallop, the dust creating a cloud behind her. Brody and Payton watched as she rode off. Brody glanced down at Payton, then slipped his arm around her shoulders. "That was odd," he said.

"She seemed nice."

Brody laughed. "What is it with you Americans?"

"Us Americans?" Payton looked around. "There's only one American here. Are you speaking of me?"

"Yes. Why do you always have such a positive attitude about everything? Everything is always…nice. Even if it isn't, you smile and pretend it is. Why don't you just say what you think? Hayley Fraser is a bitch."

"I don't even know her. Why would I think that?" Her brow creased into a frown and she shook her head. "And why are you such a grouch?"

"See, there you go. I *am* being a grouch." He turned and walked inside, grabbing his clothes scattered across the floor. "At least you said what you thought."

"My mother always told me if I couldn't say something nice, I shouldn't say anything at all. It's hard for me to forget those little lessons."

"People aren't always perfect," he said.

"I know that. I'm not naive. But I prefer to see the positive qualities rather than dwelling on the negative."

"Like the way you look at me?" Brody asked.

Payton sat down on the edge of the bunk and began to idly pick lint off the blanket, smoothing her hand over the rough wool every now and then. "You've been very nice—I mean, you've been generous and kind and understanding. You got me out of jail, you gave me a place to live and—"

"I sleep with you. I make you moan with pleasure, I touch your body like—"

"All right. You do have a nasty sarcastic streak that comes out when you haven't had enough sleep. You're not perfect. And neither am I. So can we leave it at that?"

Was that it? Brody's jaw twitched as he tried to control his temper. He'd been so happy to find her last night he hadn't even thought about what he'd learned from the Internet. She'd run away from her family and the man she was supposed to love and for some reason, she'd decided to hide out with him.

But sooner or later, she'd get sick of life on the station, just like his mother. She'd realize she'd made a mistake and she'd be gone, back to her comfortable life with her rich husband and his fancy job. So why hadn't she told him the truth about her past?

Maybe for the same reason he hadn't told her about his past—he wasn't proud of who he'd been, or of some of the things he'd done.

"Get dressed," he said. "We need to get back. Cal will be wondering where we are."

"If there's something you want to know, all you have to do is ask," she said.

"No." He shook his head.

"I'll tell you anything."

That was the problem. Did he really want to know all the details of her relationship with a man she loved enough to marry? Did he want her making comparisons between the two of them? He ought to be happy for the time they had together and just leave it at that. Brody certainly couldn't offer her the kind of life that Sam Whitman could.

"I'm fine," he said, forcing a smile. "You're right. I'm just cranky." He walked across the room and stood in front of her.

"Don't act like such a dickhead," she muttered, sending him a sulky look.

Brody laughed, taking a step back. "Well, there you go again. I see you're learning the lingo. You could tell me not to be such a drongo."

"That, too." She drew a deep breath. "What is that?"

"A dimwit," he said. "An idiot for not appreciating you. A fool for taking my bad mood out on you." He held out his hand and when she placed her fingers in his, he gently pulled her to her feet. "So, what are we going to do with our day today?"

"I have to work in the stables. I was gone all yesterday."

"I'll help you finish."

"I bought a swimsuit, so we could hang out in the hot tub. And I bought some new underwear. I might even model it for you."

"I'm feeling my mood getting much lighter," he said. "What color?"

"Is your mood?"

"No. What color is the underwear?"

"Black," she said.

He wrapped his hands around her waist drawing her body against his. "I like black underwear."

"Every man likes black underwear."

He bent down and brushed a kiss across her lips. "You know, we could stay here a little longer. At least we have some privacy."

A tiny smile curled the corners of her mouth. "For a little while," she suggested. "But only if we go back to bed."

With a low growl, he pushed her backward until they both tumbled onto the narrow bunk. "Maybe if I have a bit more sleep I won't be so cranky."

He felt her hand on the front of his jeans. "I know exactly how to make you feel better."

"Then I'll put myself in your capable hands—or hand."

6

THE MIDDAY SUN shone in a cloudless sky. Payton stood on the fence at the edge of the paddock and watched as Callum demonstrated the fine art of campdrafting. He'd declared a holiday from all work in honor of the queen's birthday—June 8. Brody had explained that it wasn't Queen Elizabeth's real birthday, but no one seemed to care about that small technicality. A holiday was a day off, something they all needed.

The stockmen had decided a barbecue was in order and had set up an afternoon of lighthearted competition between station employees followed by a sumptuous meal. They'd begun with a brief course on one of Australia's original sports, showing Gemma and Payton how campdrafting worked.

A calf was let out of a pen into the paddock and the rider carefully herded the calf around a series of obstacles, barrels and posts. Each rider was timed and the fastest to get the calf through the obstacle course would win a cherry pie that Mary had baked for the event.

Gemma and Payton watched from behind the fence, cheering on each stockman and wildly applauding their efforts against Brody and Callum. Though Payton had only known Gemma for a week, it was easy to like her.

She was witty and audacious, yet very levelheaded, someone Payton could turn to for advice. They'd taken to meeting up midafternoon for tea with Mary, the three of them enjoying freshly baked biscuits and a cuppa, as Gemma had called it.

To the surprise of everyone, Teague had turned up halfway through the competition with Hayley Fraser in tow. At first, she'd caused quite a stir among the men. Payton had informed Gemma that, according to Brody, Hayley was a popular television star in Australia and a huge celebrity. But the extra attention seemed to only make Hayley more uncomfortable and she chose to stand alone while she watched Teague compete with his brothers.

"She looks miserable," Payton said to Gemma. "I'm going to go talk to her."

"Callum certainly hasn't done much to make her feel welcome," Gemma commented. "Men can be so thickheaded."

Payton grabbed Gemma's arm. "Come on, let's go teach those boys a little bit about hospitality."

They walked over to Hayley and stood on either side of her, their arms braced on the top bar of the fence. "You know what I love about this," Gemma chirped in her charming Irish accent. "I love the chaps. A man wearing chaps just sets my imagination to working overtime."

"Why is that?" Payton asked, playing along.

"I just can't help but think about what those things would look like without the jeans underneath." She glanced over at Payton and pulled a silly face. Payton burst out laughing and Hayley couldn't help herself. A giggle erupted from her throat and she bit her bottom lip to stop herself.

"I was thinking exactly the same thing," Hayley said. "Why do I find those things so sexy?"

"It's the leather," Gemma said. "It's so…"

"Dangerous?" Payton asked.

"Smooth," Hayley said.

"Naughty," Gemma added. "I mean, I can understand how a man would enjoy lacy underwear on a woman. For me, a man in leather just gets me all tingly."

The trio stood and silently watched as Teague maneuvered a calf through the maze of posts and barrels, the rest of the stockmen shouting directions from across the paddock.

"Thanks," Hayley said.

Payton turned to face her. "For what?"

"For making it easier. I know how Brody and Callum feel about me and I don't think they were too chuffed to see me turn up here."

"Whatever is going on in their heads has nothing to do with us," Gemma assured her.

"Sistahs before mistahs," Payton said decisively. They both looked at her as if she'd suddenly begun speaking Armenian. "Sisters before misters. Girlfriends should come before boyfriends."

"Oh," Gemma said. "Yes. I completely agree."

"Do you ride?" Gemma asked Hayley.

"Like the wind," she said with a grin. "What about you?"

"No. If they did this on bicycles I might give it a go. But horses scare the bleedin' bloomers off me. And I don't care for the way they smell either." She sighed.

"Still, I wish I knew how to ride. Callum seems to be more comfortable on a horse than on his feet."

"I could teach you," Payton said.

"Me, too," Hayley offered.

Gemma smiled. "Callum offered, but I didn't want to look like a muppet in front of him, so I begged off. But as long as I'm here, I wouldn't mind trying."

"It's a date then," Hayley said. "Payton can bring you out to the shack. I'll organize a lunch and then we can ride back together."

The idea of making plans together seemed to solidify their new friendship and as they watched the boys, they chatted amiably.

"What do you think they're talking about?" Gemma asked, nodding in the direction of the three Quinn brothers. The men sat on their horses, staring across the paddock.

"Maybe they think we're plotting against them," Payton said.

Brody was the first to approach. He smiled as he drew his horse to a stop. "Ladies," he said, tipping his hat. "Are you having a lovely time?"

Payton smiled seductively. "Absolutely," she said.

"What are you doing over here all on your own?"

"Discussing our love of chaps," Gemma said. "With or without jeans. If I might be so bold, which do you prefer?"

Her question took him by surprise and he grinned. "That's between me and my horse." He turned to Payton. "Would you ladies like to give it a go? I'm sure the boys would love to see you jump into the competition. And there are prizes to be had for the winners."

"I'll try," Payton said.

"Me, too." Hayley crawled over the fence and started in Teague's direction.

"I'm afraid I'll have to sit this one out," Gemma said.

"Come on," Brody insisted. "Callum will ride with you. You can steer and he'll work the pedals."

Gemma grinned. "All right."

Payton helped her over the fence and they strode across the paddock, Brody riding beside them. When they got to the boys, Brody suggested that they all compete in pairs to make the game more equitable. The girls would hold the reins while the boys held the girls and used the stirrups.

As the eldest, Callum went first, settling Gemma on the saddle in front of him and wrapping his arm around her waist while his other hand gripped the saddle horn. Brody and Payton watched from a spot at the fence as Davey released a calf from the pen.

He stood behind her, his chin resting on her shoulder, his hand on her hip. "So what were you girls really talking about?" he asked, his voice soft against her ear.

"Sex," she said.

"Really?"

"That's all girls talk about when they're together. We were comparing the three of you."

"And how did I fare?" he asked.

"Oh, I spoke very highly of you," Payton teased.

His hand slowly moved forward on her hip until it was pressed flat on her lower abdomen, right above the waist-band of her jeans. "Did you tell them how good I am at making you moan?" His fingertips drifted a bit lower.

"Stop," Payton said. "Everyone is watching."

"No one is watching," Brody countered.

She closed her eyes and moaned softly. How was it possible that he could set her nerves on fire with a simple touch? They were both fully dressed, standing amidst a group of people, and all she could think about was his hand dipping into her pants.

"How far will you go, Payton? Can I make you come just by talking to you?"

"Don't even try," she said.

"I'll wager I can. Dare me."

"Brody, I—" He shoved his hand a bit farther beneath her waistband and she sucked in a sharp breath. "All right. You probably could. But that doesn't mean I want you to. Not here."

"Where?" he murmured.

"Your room."

"Hey!" Brody called. "We're going to grab some more coldies. Who wants one?" He took the time to count the takers then turned to Payton. "Come on, you can give me a hand."

They started off toward the house without attracting any attention. When they reached the porch, Brody pressed his finger to his lips, then poked his head inside the door. Though the smell of fresh-baked bread drifted out, Mary was elsewhere. He took Payton's hand and dragged her through the kitchen, then up the stairs, taking them two at a time.

When they were both inside his room, Brody slammed the door behind them and began to unbutton her jeans. Payton fumbled with the belt holding his chaps, but let go when he bent over to pull off her shoes. Her jeans and panties followed and by the time he stood, he was completely aroused, his erection pressing against the faded denim.

Getting him undressed was too much effort and in the end, she unbuckled his belt and pulled his jeans down around his hips. He picked her up and carried her to the bed.

In one exquisite movement, he slid inside her, her body ready for him, so wet with desire. From the moment he moved, Payton felt herself dancing near the edge. This wasn't a slow, easy seduction but a desperate attempt to possess each other.

She clutched at his shoulders, her mouth pressed against his throat. "Oh," she cried. "Oh, yes."

"Tell me you want it," he said, his voice raw with passion.

"I do," Payton said, her own desperation growing.

She felt her orgasm building, fueled by the almost violent nature of their bodies arching against each other. Every thrust became magnificent torture, pushing her closer to the edge and then drawing her back again. Payton let her mind drift, focusing on the spot where they were joined.

And then, she was there, her release shattering reality. Wave after wave of pleasure coursed through her and she felt him surrender to his own orgasm. He kept moving inside her until he couldn't move anymore. Then Brody rolled onto his back, carrying her with him.

The entire encounter had only lasted a few minutes, but Payton had never experienced anything quite so powerful. She'd wanted him so much that her desire had overwhelmed all rational thought. He owned her body and he was quickly taking possession of her soul.

"We're bad," he whispered.

"I know," Payton said. "I think it was the chaps."

Brody laughed out loud, wrapping his arm around her neck and rolling her onto her side. He faced her, his hand lazily trailing through her hair. "So all I have to do to get you into bed is wear leather?"

"I think you already know the answer to that question."

"Tell me anyway."

"You just have to touch me," Payton said softly. "That's all it takes."

He smiled boyishly, then stole another kiss. "I'll remember that." Pausing, he ran his finger along her jaw and met her gaze. "There is one thing. We haven't been using protection, and at the shack you said—"

"It's all right. There won't be any surprises."

"Good," he said. "I mean, not that surprises are always bad, but I'm not sure we're ready for that."

Sam had been obsessed about birth control, insisting that Payton find a method that would protect them both without fail. They'd been engaged and they'd always planned to have children, so Payton wondered why he'd been so adamant. Sam had acted as if an unplanned pregnancy would've been a disaster. Why hadn't she ever questioned him making such a decision about her body?

"Payton?"

She blinked, startled from her thoughts. What had brought Sam to mind? She hadn't thought of him in…days.

Brody was staring at her, a frown on his face. "What's wrong?"

Payton shook her head. "Nothing. We should probably get back outside. The boys will want their beers."

Brody levered to his feet, then held out his hand. He patiently helped her dress, patting her backside once she was completely clothed again. But as he turned for the door, Payton noticed a purple mark on his neck.

"Oh, no," she said, reaching up for his chin and tipping his head up. "Did I do that?"

"What?"

She laughed. "I think I gave you a hickey."

"What's that?" Brody asked.

She pulled him over to the mirror above his dresser and pointed to the spot on his neck.

"A love bite," he said, examining it closely. "I haven't had one of those since I was a teenager."

"Sorry."

He shrugged. "I like it. I like knowing I can make you do such things to me."

She stared at his reflection in the mirror and smiled. "I think we're both in trouble," she said.

He nodded. "I think you might be right."

"BRODY!"

They both turned to see a horse approaching at a fast gallop. Davey pulled the horse to a stop, nearly running into Brody. "What the hell are you about?" Brody shouted.

"Callum," he said, gasping for breath.

"What's wrong? Is he all right?"

"Yeah. Yeah, he's fine. He needs you back at the house. Right now. He said just you, not Payton. Just you. He made that very clear."

Brody frowned. "Well, I'm not going to leave Payton out here on her own," he said.

"No, I'm to help her out," Davey said. "Go ahead. I'll carry on."

Brody regarded the young kid suspiciously. Why was it so important for Payton to stay behind? What the hell was Callum up to? He maneuvered his horse next to Payton's, then reached out and placed his hand on her cheek. "I'll be back in a bit." Brody leaned over and dropped a kiss on her lips. "Don't let Davey boss you around."

She smiled. "I won't. I'll see you later."

Brody kicked his horse into a gallop and headed toward the house. This had damn well better be an emergency. The ride back to the homestead was almost fifteen minutes. As he rode, Brody's thoughts rewound over the past few days. He and Payton had settled into a life of sorts.

She'd managed to charm Davey into working the stables for the day while she worked the station with Brody. They enjoyed the long ride together and Payton had been fascinated with discovering new plants and animals in the outback. She'd nearly fallen off her horse when she'd spotted her first kangaroo.

He liked having her with him, and Callum hadn't seemed to mind that they'd paired up. After greasing two of the windmills, they'd eaten some lunch, then set off to ride the fence lines. Payton had quickly learned how to handle herself on a stock pony, eagerly taking tips from Brody when he offered.

Still, her fascination with station life worried him. Was she happy here or was she just avoiding her real life with Sam Whitman? He needed answers, yet he couldn't bring himself to ask the question. Was she married? And if she was, did it make a difference anymore? He wasn't sure that it did for him. Not now.

Brody had been considering his options, specifically another surgery on his knee. He was still covered under the team's insurance and he really didn't have anything to lose, except a month or two off his feet and at least a year spent in rehab. He cursed softly. The more time he spent with Payton, the more confused he became about his future.

He'd always trusted his gut instinct when it came to any decision, and his gut had never steered him wrong—until the accident. The rain had made the roads slick and he'd already been late for practice, caught up in an argument with Nessa. He hadn't been paying attention and had taken a turn far too fast. As he went down, his only thought had been that he ought to have trusted his gut and taken the Land Rover to work.

Right now, every instinct told him that Payton belonged in his life, that he should to do everything in his power to keep her there. So why couldn't he just say that to her? Why couldn't he tell her how he felt? Brody had never doubted himself until now. Maybe his feelings weren't as strong as they seemed. Or maybe, this was something more than just infatuation.

As he rode past the horse paddock and into the yard, he saw Callum standing on the back porch, pacing nervously. He waited for Brody to come to a stop before jogging down the steps. Brody hopped off, gathering the reins in his hand.

"Come on," Callum murmured.

"What's up?"

"Teague is in the house. There's a private investigator here looking for Payton."

"Shit," Brody muttered. "How did he find her?"

"You know about him?"

"Yeah, he was in Bilbarra trying to track her down. I talked to him. I thought I sent him off to Sydney to look for her."

"Well, he's a little bit smarter than you reckoned," Callum said. "Payton used her credit card at David Jones in Brisbane. And Teague bought something right after her with his card. The clerk mentioned that they were together, so that's why he's here. Teague is feeding him some story, but I'm not sure if he's swallowing it."

Brody frowned. Payton had spent time in jail for dining and dashing. Why had she suddenly chosen to use a credit card? Had she wanted to be found? Was she looking for an excuse to leave? Or was she unaware that a detective had been sent to find her? "We have to get her out of here," Brody muttered.

"What the hell has she done?" Callum asked.

"I don't know." Brody cursed softly. "She was supposed to get married in April. She ran out on her wedding. And I'd assume her fiancé or her husband wants her back, since he sent someone to fetch her. Bit of a problem there since I don't want to give her back."

"Brody, she's an adult. She should make these decisions for herself. If she wants to stay, she can just tell the guy to get lost."

"And what if she doesn't?" Brody asks. "What if she decides to leave with him?"

"Then that's her choice. You can't keep her here if she doesn't want to stay."

"She may want to stay," Brody countered. "Only she isn't ready to admit it yet. She might need more time."

"Did you ever think about asking her straight out?"

"I'm not going to ask her unless I'm sure she'll give me the right answer."

"Bloody hell, Brody, just talk to the girl."

"I will," Brody promised. "Soon. But right now, I have to get her off the station. I'll go back and get her and we'll ride to the airstrip. I need you to go to the bunkhouse and gather up her things and put them in your ute. Teague can meet us out there."

"Are you sure you want to do this?" Callum asked.

The backdoor squeaked and Teague stepped outside. The moment he saw Brody, he grabbed him by the arm and pulled him around the side of the house. "What the hell is going—"

"Don't ask," Brody said. "I'll explain it all later. Can you get away or is this guy going to follow you wherever you go?"

"I think I can lose him. Why?"

"I need you to fly Payton and me to Brisbane. I'm going to go and get her and we'll meet you at the airstrip. Callum is going to put her things in his ute. Whenever you can, get away and meet us there."

"All right," Teague said, nodding. "I better get back in there. He thinks I'm making coffee."

Brody jumped on his horse and turned it away from the house. "We'll be at the airstrip in a half hour," he said. "Don't let him follow you."

The ride in had taken twice as long as the ride back. He rode as hard and as fast as he'd ever ridden, as if his life depended upon it. In the end, his life did depend upon Payton. He'd grown attached to her and he couldn't imagine losing her, especially to another man.

He found them where he'd left them, working on a broken gate that led to the east horse pasture. Davey was holding the gate off the ground while Payton twisted the turnbuckle. They both stopped what they were doing and watched as he approached.

"Get on your horse," he told Payton. "Come on, we have to go."

"What's wrong?" she asked.

"I'll tell you after we get to the airstrip."

"Why are we going to the airstrip?"

"Payton, don't ask any questions. Just get on your horse and let's ride."

She studied him for a long moment, then handed Davey the spanner she was holding. Snagging her jacket from where she'd thrown it over the gate, she kept her gaze fixed on him. Then, in an easy motion, she put her foot in the stirrup and swung her leg over the saddle.

Brody didn't take the time to explain any further. He simply wheeled his mount around and took off, hoping she'd follow. A few seconds later, she caught up to him and they rode through the scrub, a cloud of dust forming behind them.

Their horses were winded by the time they reached the airstrip. Brody dismounted and then helped Payton do the same. He slapped both horses on the rump and sent them running, knowing they'd find their way back to the stables on their own.

"Are you going to explain what we're doing here?" Payton asked.

"First, you have to tell me something. And I want you to be completely honest, because I'll be able to tell if you're lying to me."

"All right," she said softly.

Brody grabbed her by the arms and pulled her toward him, his mouth coming down on hers. He softened the kiss immediately, hoping that it would serve as a last attempt to prove his feelings for her. Then he drew back and took a deep breath. "Are you married? Did you go through with your wedding or did you walk out before you said 'I do'?"

Her mouth dropped open and she stared at him in utter shock. "How do you know about—"

"Just answer the question. Are you married?"

"I…" She paused, as if she wasn't sure how to answer him. "No. Of course not. If I were married, I'd be with my husband. I certainly wouldn't be sleeping with you. How did you know about my wedding?"

"We have the Internet here, too."

She took a moment, then shook her head. "You Googled me?"

"Yes. And a private investigator tracked you here," he replied. "You used your credit card in Brisbane and he figured out where you were."

She groaned, closing her eyes and shaking her head. "I knew I shouldn't have used the card. I didn't use it earlier for food. But I thought since I was flying right back to the station, it wouldn't make a difference. They wouldn't be able to find me even if they were watching the card."

"Turns out Teague bought something at the same time and he used his card. They figured out you two were together." He rubbed her forearms. "I think you should tell me what's going on, Payton. Tell me about Sam Whitman."

She sucked in a sharp breath and looked at him, her eyes wide. "You know about— But, how—"

"It doesn't matter. Just tell me what happened."

She drew a deep breath. "I ran out on the wedding before we got to the vows." She took his hand. "I should have told you. But I wanted to leave that part of my life behind."

"Why did you run?"

She shrugged. "I'm not sure. I just had this feeling that I was making a huge mistake. I honestly can't say what it was. I'm not an impetuous person, but I had this—" She put her hand on her stomach.

"Gut feeling?"

"Yes," she said, as if his explanation suddenly made perfect sense of her actions.

"So what does your gut tell you to do now?" Brody asked. "We can ride back to the house and you can talk to this guy. Or we can leave. Teague will fly us to Brisbane and from there we'll catch a flight to Perth."

"Perth?"

"I have an apartment in Fremantle, just across the river. We can hang out until the investigator leaves."

She considered the offer for a long moment. "And then what?" she asked. "I can't avoid my family forever."

"Then we'll go back to the station right now and you can call them."

He waited as she weighed her options, hoping and praying that she'd choose to leave with him. He knew he'd have to let her go sooner or later, but he wasn't ready. He'd take another day, another week, as much time as he could get.

"I don't know what I want," she said.

He'd asked her if she was married and he'd gotten the right answer. But the second question had gone unasked. Was she still in love with her fiancé? The words were on the tip of his tongue, but he was afraid of what she might say. Right now, he'd rather not know.

He reached up and cupped her face in his hands. "Come with me to Fremantle," he said. Leaning forward, he kissed her again, softly, a silent plea.

"All right," she said. "For a little while. We'll go to Fremantle."

Brody released a tightly held breath and yanked her into his arms. He had a few more days, a week even. And this time, he wasn't going to waste it. He'd savor every second he spent with her. They'd walk on the beach and make love all night and sleep until noon and then do it all over again the next day. And, maybe, she'd decide she never wanted to leave at all.

BY THE TIME they landed at the airport in Perth, Payton had filled in the details of her story, from her parents' high expectations, to her belief that Sam was the man she was supposed to marry. And then she told him about her sudden decision to break free from the path that had been laid out for her. Until that moment, she'd simply deferred to her parents and her fiancé.

It felt good to pick apart her life, to examine her motives and try to make sense of them. And it almost gave her enough courage to call her parents and apologize for everything that she'd put them through. But after a half day's work on the station and two separate plane trips, she was exhausted. The thought of making that phone call twisted her stomach into knots.

"I know what you're thinking." She sighed, avoiding his gaze as they walked from the plane.

He held her hand, his fingers laced through hers. "No, you don't," Brody said.

"You think I'm…naive. Spineless. And maybe I am—or was. But I'm not that way anymore."

He pulled her to a stop, forcing her to face him. "Are you under the impression that this has changed the way I feel about you?" Brody asked.

"It hasn't?"

He shook his head. "No. Not at all."

They took a cab from the airport to Brody's apartment. Payton was curious about what she'd find on the other side of the front door. The building was luxurious, with its richly appointed lobby and thickly carpeted hallways. Brody hadn't told her much about his life off the station. What she knew had come from Teague—a career in football, the accident that had ruined his knee and a retreat back to the station.

He reached for the front door, then paused. "I don't remember what it looks like inside," he said, forcing a smile. "It's been a while since I've been home and I had to let my cleaning lady go." He shoved the key into the lock. "Maybe I should just check it out."

"It's all right," Payton said. "I've been working in a stable. Unless you have a dozen horses in there, nothing is going to freak me out."

Brody chuckled. "All right." The door swung open

and he stepped aside to let her enter first. She walked inside slowly, taking in the details of the interior.

It was a beautiful apartment, sleek and modern. A wall of windows overlooked the water and filled the apartment with light. It was furnished sparsely yet fashionably.

Payton wandered over to the windows and took in the view of a wide river and the city on the other side. "It's wonderful," she said. "So different from the station."

"One of the guys on the team gave me the name of his decorator. I didn't pick this stuff out myself. I would have been content with a couch and telly and a bed."

She stared up at a painting hanging on the wall above the sofa. "Very nice. So, is this what football buys?"

Brody smiled. "That's what football bought. Footy doesn't buy anything anymore."

"It's difficult to imagine you doing that. Dressed in all that gear."

"Aussie rules is not like American football," he said. "We don't wear anything but a shirt, shorts and shoes. It's more like rugby than what you think of as football." He paused. "So you know how I found out about your wedding. How did you find out about my busted career?"

"Your brother Teague. He said you were good, but that your motorcycle accident ended your career."

Brody nodded. "I was. I was the top scorer on our team. But that doesn't really matter anymore. Now some other bloke is the top scorer on the team. And I'm just a guy who spends his time working a cattle station in Queensland."

"There's nothing wrong with that," she said.

"It's not the same as being famous."

Payton ran her hands through her hair. "I'm still dirty from work. Can I take a shower?"

Brody took her bag off his shoulder. "The bathroom is through the bedroom," he said, pointing to a door in the far wall. "I'll show you."

She followed him into the bedroom and he set her bag on the bed, then turned and helped her out of her jacket. He smoothed his hands over her shoulders and nuzzled his nose in her hair. "It's nice to have you here," he said. "All to myself."

Payton leaned back against his chest and drew his arms around her. "It is funny how things work out. We've both lived such different lives, and then they touched for a moment in that jail cell. If you hadn't drunk so much beer or I'd paid for my meal, we would never have met. Gemma thinks it was fate."

"Maybe it was."

Payton turned in his arms and then pushed up on her toes and kissed him. She slipped her arms around his neck and drew him more deeply into the kiss, loving the way he tasted, the way his mouth fit so perfectly with hers. Just a simple kiss was all it took to ignite her desire.

She reached up and tugged his jacket down over his arms, then moved to work on the buttons of his shirt. They'd undressed each other so many times that it had become second nature to them. There was no longer any hesitation or embarrassment. They felt more comfortable out of their clothes than in them.

When they were both naked, he took her hand and led her into the bathroom. The shower was surrounded by glass block from floor to ceiling. He opened a door and stepped inside, turning the water on and then helping her inside when it was the proper temperature.

It was a shower made for a man who came home with bruises and sore muscles: a variety of shower-heads angled in all different directions. The door kept the steam inside and before long, the moisture created a fog around them both.

His hands smoothed over her body and she closed her eyes and enjoyed his caress. He turned her around and pulled her against him, his growing erection pressing against her backside. His palms slowly ran the length of her torso, from her breasts to her belly and then to the juncture of her thighs.

He delved between the soft folds of her sex and when he found the spot, began to touch her in a way he knew so well. Payton arched back, wrapping her arm around his neck and pulling him into another kiss.

But he wasn't content to just touch her. His mouth moved over her shoulder, his tongue tracing a path to the curve of her neck. Brody gently urged her to sit on the low bench at the center of the shower. And then he knelt in front of her, spreading her legs and continuing the seduction with his tongue.

Payton had always felt this was the most intimate ex-pression of desire and until now, they'd both been sat-isfied with other things. But Payton let go of the last shred of inhibition, surrendering to Brody, the shudders rocking her body. And as she surrendered to him, she realized that this was no longer just physical. She'd grown to need him in so many other ways.

She felt tears press at the corners of her eyes, but when he met her gaze she forced a smile. How could she ever consider living without him? He'd become part of her life, the new life that she'd found in Australia.

But was she really ready to walk away from her past, from her family and everything she'd known, to stay here with him? Payton reached up and brushed his wet hair from his eyes. She didn't need to tell him how she felt. It was understood between them, communicated by smiles and sighs and soft kisses in the dark.

Brody drew her slowly to her feet and then led her out of the shower. Her release only made her exhaustion more acute and when he wrapped her in a thick cotton towel, Payton closed her eyes and leaned against him for support.

They ended up on the bed, Brody stretched out beside her, his fingers gently stroking her cheek. "Tell me about him," he said softly. "Why did you love him?"

"That's a question," she said. "I'm not sure I have an answer."

"Try," he said. "Please?"

"I thought he was right for me. And I knew my parents would love him. I always tried to do what I thought they wanted me to. I was a very good girl."

"But there must have been something about this guy," Brody said.

"We were together so long, I guess I forgot what it was that attracted me in the first place. He was supposed to be perfect for me."

Brody was silent for a long moment, then drew a deep breath. "Do you still love him?"

"I'm not sure I ever did," Payton said. "At least not the way a woman should love the man she marries."

He seemed to take comfort in that answer. But did it make a difference? She was here, with him, running away from all her problems. She hadn't thought about how this might end between them. It was so simple to believe they would just continue, without any difficulties. They were living off the high of their infatuation. Real life hadn't intruded yet. But it would soon enough.

7

"PADDLE, PADDLE, PADDLE!" Brody shouted. He gave the surfboard a final shove, sending Payton off into the set of small waves on Cottesloe Beach. They'd practiced on the beach first and then he'd caught a few waves with her in front of him on his board. But she was determined to do it on her own.

"Pop up!" he called.

To Brody's surprise, she nimbly got to her feet. Steadying herself, she slowly straightened, her arms out to the side. Brody shouted as she rode the wave. There wasn't much that Payton couldn't do once she set her mind to something.

She stayed on her feet all the way to the shore, hopping off the board just before she hit the beach. She looked at him, waving and jumping up and down in excitement. Then she turned the board around and paddled back out to him.

The weather was perfect for a winter day in June. The sun was shining but the water was a bit chilly, so they both wore wet suits. Brody had made a gift of the surfboard and wet suit, hoping that they'd be staying in Fremantle long enough to enjoy them.

Life was certainly simpler here than it had been at

the station. Their days and nights belonged entirely to them. They strolled the streets, stopping to eat or browse through a shop when they wanted. They went to the movies and a concert in the park and rented bicycles to tour old Fremantle.

Brody had planned a trip to Rottnest Island for the next week, booking a room in the old hotel in case they wanted to spend a few hours alone together during the day. Though he knew she might decide to leave at any time, he wanted to believe she'd still be with him in a week.

They kept themselves busy during the day, but it was the nights that Brody found most satisfying. Blessed with absolute privacy, they had the time to explore the limits of their passion. Sex ranged from a silly romp, to a frantic drive for release, to a slow, methodical seduction—and all in one day.

"Did you see me?"

"I did," Brody said as she paddled up to him. "You were great."

"I was! It was so much fun. I want to try a bigger wave."

"All right, hang on. I'll just put in your order." He looked up at the sky. "Can we have some bigger waves, please?"

She splashed water in his face. "I meant, we should go to another beach with bigger waves."

He splashed her back, then reached out and grabbed her, both of them tumbling off their surfboards. Treading water, Brody pulled her into his arms and kissed her, his mouth searching for hers through the saltwater that dripped from her hair.

There was nothing more satisfying, he mused as he teased at her tongue. The fact that he could kiss and touch her whenever he chose to was something he had come to appreciate. In truth, he couldn't imagine doing without it.

He drew back and looked down into her eyes. Droplets of water clung to her lashes. "We'll find some bigger waves tomorrow," he said. He helped her back onto her board, then straddled his. "We need to get you in to shore and put some sunscreen on your face. You're starting to burn."

"Let me try one more wave. Then we can go."

"Only if you kiss me again," he said.

She leaned into him, her feet dangling off the sides of her board, and placed a quick kiss on his lips.

He frowned. "You can do better."

With a dramatic sigh, she leaned in again and this time, treated him to a full-on tongue kiss, her mouth warm against his. She knew exactly how he liked to be kissed and she used that knowledge to her advantage. When she drew back, she arched her eyebrow.

"All right," he agreed. "One more wave. I'm not going to give you a push this time. I'm just going to tell you when to go."

She lined her board up, watching over her shoulder as the next set rolled in. "Tell me when," she said.

"Go," he said. "Paddle hard. Paddle!"

This time, she got up right away. But she was so excited that she threw her arms over her head and disrupted her balance. She wobbled and then tumbled off the board into the water. Brody waited for her to come up and when she didn't, he paddled over to her board, cutting through the water in strong, even strokes.

By the time he reached her, she was up and

coughing water, clinging to the edge of the board. "Are you all right?"

She nodded. "Water up my nose." She coughed again. "That was bad."

"You shouldn't have put your hands up," he said. "You were doing so well." He held her board as she climbed back on. When they reached the shore, he helped her tuck her board under her arm before walking onto the beach.

"It's getting late," he said. "We should get some lunch." He jammed the surfboards into the sand, then peeled his wet suit down around his waist.

Payton took a deep breath and turned her face up to the sun. "I love it here. It's just like California. Only no earthquakes."

"I wish it was spring," he said. "We could go bush-walking and see the wildflowers. Western Australia is known for that. Miles and miles of flowers."

"Maybe we can," she said.

Brody knew it was just an offhand reply, that her words contained no promises. They hadn't made any plans or given any pledges to each other, beyond the promise of unbridled passion in the bedroom. He didn't want to think about that now. Instead, he was determined to show her exactly how much fun life was with him here in Oz.

"What do you want to do with the rest of the day?"

"I want to enjoy the good weather." She glanced over at him. "I noticed there's a football game this weekend. Could we go?"

"Why would you want to do that?"

"I'm just curious to see what you used to do for a living."

"I don't know," he said, shaking his head. "I haven't been to a game since I got dropped from the club."

"It's all right," she said. "If you don't want to, we don't have to."

He thought about her request for a few seconds. Denying her anything was impossible. And what did he have to lose? It might be fun to explain the game to her. There was nothing quite like Aussie football. "All right. I'm going to call and see if I can get us some decent seats."

She grinned. "Good."

"Any other requests?"

"I heard there was a nude beach around here."

"Yes," he said. "Swanbourne Beach."

"I've never been to a nude beach. I think I should try it at least once. I was really good at skinny-dipping, so I think I'd do well at the nude beach."

"You do realize you'd have to take off your clothes and go naked in front of strangers, don't you?"

"Yes. That's the point. I've never done that. I'm trying new things. Trusting my instincts. And it might feel good, liberating, don't you think?" She reached out and ran a finger down his chest. "It'll be fun."

"No," Brody said emphatically. "I'm not taking you to Swanbourne. You can go on your own if you like, but I'm not going."

"Prude," she teased. "You have a very nice body. And you're well endowed. There's nothing to be ashamed of."

"That's not it. You know exactly what happens to me when you get naked. And I'm not going to walk around the beach with a throb in my knob."

"I'd find that visual very entertaining," she said. She glanced down and fixed her gaze on his crotch.

"Stop," he said.

"What? I'm not doing anything."

"Stop it. You're going to get me all worked up."

"I'm not doing anything," she repeated in a voice filled with mock innocence.

"There's no extra room in this wet suit," he said. "So just knock it off."

She looked up at him and gave him a devilish smile. "I have such amazing powers," she said. "I surprise even myself."

He pulled her against him, wrapping his arm around her neck in a playful headlock. "Why don't we go home and you can give me a demonstration of your powers."

"I'd be happy to," she said. "I think it's important that I share my powers with as many people as I can."

"Now you've gone too far," he said, kissing the top of her head. "There will be no sharing."

They gathered their things and walked back to the car, Payton's hand tucked in his. It had been another perfect day, he mused as they strapped their boards on the BMW's roof rack. Brody couldn't imagine life getting any better than this.

PAYTON CLUTCHED the program in her hands as they walked through the crowds of fans to their seats. Brody's appearance seemed to cause quite a stir among those in attendance and he was stopped again and again with requests for autographs and photos. Payton waited patiently, watching as he handled each request with surprising grace and enthusiasm, giving special attention to the younger fans.

She hadn't realized how famous he was and she

found herself regretting her request to come. It couldn't be easy to answer all the questions about his injury, about the chances of him playing again, about the plays that everyone remembered him making.

When he finally pulled himself away from the fans, she held on to his arm and gave it a squeeze. "I'm sorry," she said.

"For what?"

"For asking you to come here. I didn't realize how difficult it might be for you. It was selfish of me."

"No," he said. "Actually, I'm doing all right. I thought it would be a bit dodgy, but it's not that bad."

They found their seats and settled in. Payton took a good look around, then turned to him. "All right, give me the scoop."

"You want ice cream?" he asked.

"No, the scoop. The skinny. The 4-1-1. Tell me what I need to know."

"Oh, all right. Well, this is the Subiaco Oval. And that's the team, my former team, out there warming up."

"The field is round," Payton said.

"Oval."

"I like the outfits," she added, observing the players on the field. "Not as hot as chaps, but pretty sexy. Nice short shorts. And sleeveless jerseys to show off the muscles." In truth, she could imagine Brody running around in that uniform. "Maybe you could take out your old outfit when we get home and we could play footballer and the surfer girl."

Brody laughed, glancing around to see if anyone had heard. "Better yet, I'll buy you a guernsey, you wear it and nothing else, and I'll show you some of my moves."

"A guernsey. Is that like a jumper or a cardie?"

"Jumper," he said. "Cardie has buttons down the front."

"And what is the team called?" she asked.

"Their official name is the Fremantle Football Club, but everyone calls them the Dockers. See, they have an anchor on their jumpers."

She nodded. "So, what's the deal? How do they get points?"

She listened as he explained the rules. Eighteen players on a side. The aim was to kick the ball through the poles on each end of the field. They could throw, kick and pass the ball to move it downfield, but they weren't supposed to hold on to it. When they kicked the ball through the center pair of four posts the team scored six points. But Payton became hopelessly confused when Brody tried to explain something called a "behind."

The game began and the crowd immediately grew noisy. She'd never been to an American football game, but she couldn't imagine more of a party atmosphere than she was experiencing now. There was music and cheering and dancing in the stands, along with a lot of beer. And incredibly dangerous activity on the field.

The players wore no padding or helmets, yet they seemed to slam into each other on a regular basis. Men were thrown to the ground and bloodied by flying elbows and knees. Payton was grateful that Brody was sitting safely next to her. She couldn't imagine watching him and not worrying herself sick.

Brody cheered the team, shouting out his displeasure at good plays by the opposition. As the game went on, he continued to explain the intricacies of the plays and by the time it ended, Payton actually could follow each play as it developed on the field.

The Dockers lost, but Brody didn't appear to be too upset by the result. In truth, he seemed to be quite happy that they'd come. Payton wrapped her arm around his waist as they walked out of the stadium.

"Brody Quinn!"

They stopped and Brody turned, then smiled as an older gentleman approached them dressed in a polo shirt with the Fremantle team logo stitched on the chest.

"Simon. How are you?"

"I'm well. You look grand. Healthy. Keeping fit, I see."

"Trying," Brody said, rubbing his abdomen. He turned to Payton. "Simon, this is Payton Harwell. Payton, this is the team doctor, Simon Purvis. He helped me through my rehab."

Simon held out his hand and Payton took it. "Pleasure," he said. "Did you enjoy the game?"

"I did," Payton said. "It's a little rougher than I expected, but it was fun to watch."

"We're a tough lot here in Oz." Simon grinned. "So, you're from America. I recognize the accent."

"I am," Payton said.

"Where do you call home?"

"Connecticut. Though I live in Manhattan. New York City?"

"Ah. New York Giants. New York Jets. Interesting. Almost bizarre, that."

"What?" Brody asked.

"I just met a scout for the Americans. For their NFL. He's come looking for kickers. I wasn't about to send any of our guys to see him. But you might want to give him a tingle, Brody."

"No," Brody said. "I'm in no condition to play."

"There's the thing," Simon said. "It's a different game. At least for kickers and punters. All you have to do is kick. They put the ball down and you kick it through the posts. Or you drop-kick it. They call that punting. Once or twice, they might knock you down, but if they touch you while you're kicking, it's a penalty. Brody, you've got a way with that foot of yours. It would be a shame to see it go to waste."

Payton turned to Brody, trying to read his expression. But she could see nothing that indicated how he felt. She expected him to be happy, or at least curious about the possibility. "I don't know. I was going to look into that surgery you told me about, but I'm not sure I—"

"You might not need the surgery," Simon said. "You don't have to carry the ball. There's no cutting or quick direction shifts. You might have to tackle, but that's really not your job." He paused. "I can ring him up, if you like. I'm sure he'd be interested in seeing you."

"I'll think about it," Brody said.

"Don't think too long," Simon warned. "He's only going to be here for a few weeks and then he's back to the States."

Brody shook Simon's hand, and as they walked back to the car, he was strangely silent. Payton wasn't sure whether he wanted her opinion on the matter, and decided to wait for him to speak first. But when he didn't, she decided to start the conversation. "That was interesting," she said. "But what is a tingle? And why do you have to give this guy one?"

"A phone call," he explained. "You know, there have been a couple of Aussies that have gone over to play in America. One was a kicker. He did pretty well."

"Do you want to play again?"

"Sure. But Aussie football is what I do."

"Have you ever seen an American game?"

"The Super Bowl once or twice. I never really paid much attention." He shook his head. "It's a crazy idea. They're not going to want anything to do with me once they see my knee."

"Maybe you could wear long pants. And show them how you can kick first, before you tell them about your injury."

Brody chuckled. "That might work. But the first thing they're going to ask is whether I've been seriously injured."

"It wouldn't hurt to talk to the guy," Payton said.

Brody opened the door of the car for her and helped her inside. "I'll think about it."

As they made their way out of the parking lot, Brody was lost in his thoughts. He held her hand, his fingers woven through hers, and every now and then, he brought her hand up to his lips and kissed it, as if to remind himself she was still there.

Payton drew a deep breath and then relaxed back into the seat. She wasn't quite sure how she felt about the possibility of him moving to the States. Here in Australia, she was the visitor. If things didn't work out, she could always leave. But having Brody in the U.S. seemed like such a serious shift in their relationship.

It was silly to worry over it now, though. When she

had to make a choice, she'd make a choice. And until then, she intended to enjoy her time with Brody.

BRODY STARED at the ceiling above the bed in the early-morning light. Sleep hadn't come easily for him, though he and Payton had exhausted themselves making love before she'd curled up in his arms and drifted off.

Instead, his head was filled with thoughts about the day's revelations. His life had taken so many sharp turns lately, he shouldn't be surprised at this one. Playing in America would give him a chance to get his life set up again. He'd be working, making a decent salary. He could save his money, instead of blowing it on expensive toys and exotic vacations. He'd have something to offer Payton then. But the chances of getting a job in the U.S. were slim, especially considering his injury.

Brody rolled over onto his side and stared at her. Her hand was curled next to her face, her hair tumbled over her shoulder. He still thought she was the most beautiful woman he'd ever met. There were moments when he believed he'd never be able to do without her, that waking up with her by his side and falling asleep with her in his arms was the only thing that mattered.

He reached out and smoothed his hand over her hip, her skin like silk beneath his fingertips. How was it that she suited him so perfectly? Whether they were living on the station or here in Fremantle, their lives seemed to mesh flawlessly.

He'd had his share of high-maintenance women—girls like Vanessa, who'd demanded far too much and offered far too little. They'd been extras in his life, like fast cars and expensive electronics, something to acquire and then grow bored with over time.

But he'd never felt as if he'd acquired Payton. She'd appeared in his life one day and decided to stay. He was well aware that she might choose to leave at any time. He wasn't in control of this relationship, she was. And maybe that's what kept the boredom at bay.

He was almost afraid to believe they might make it work. He'd always assumed he'd find the right woman, but he'd imagined it would happen at a distant point in the future, not now. She was the right woman. Brody was fairly certain of that.

So what was required to keep her? He needed a way to support them both, to give her a comfortable lifestyle. Without a job, he could give her four or five years. With a job, maybe a lifetime. And he needed to make sure her fiancé was out of her life for good. He ought to encourage her to contact her parents and smooth out the problems there. And then he needed to plead his case to her family.

Hell, they'd probably be suspicious of him from the start. He didn't come from some blueblood line with money coming out of his arse. He was a working-class bloke without a proper education. But he had one thing going for him—there wasn't another man in the world who loved Payton more than he did.

He drew a deep breath. He loved her. It was that simple. Brody gasped, stunned by the revelation. *Love* was the only way to describe how he felt.

But how did she feel? Payton had been silent on that issue. She seemed content to just go along as they were—lovers, friends, companions. She lived in the present, avoiding any discussion of what was to come.

Why was that? Brody wondered. Was it because she thought their relationship had no future? Or was it because she didn't want to face returning to her fiancé and family? If she truly loved him, she would have given him some hint by now. Every other woman he'd known was ready to profess love after the second date.

Maybe he just didn't measure up. Maybe she was biding her time until some other man caught her eye. Brody rolled over on his back and pressed his palm to his chest, aware of the ache in his heart. He'd never loved a woman before, so he'd never risked getting hurt. For the first time in his life, he was afraid. What if she didn't want him? Would he ever be able to forget her and move on?

He sat up and swung his legs over the edge of the bed, and pushed himself to his feet. Raking his hands through his hair, he wandered over to the windows and stared out at the river and the lights twinkling from the opposite side.

If he was going to make this work, he needed a plan. Hell, Callum was the planner in the family. Maybe he ought to go to his older brother for advice. Worst-case scenario, he could always work the station. They'd have a home and Payton seemed to enjoy living there. Best case, he'd find a job that allowed them to live wherever they wanted, on the station, in Fremantle, in Manhattan, if they chose.

Sighing softly, Brody walked out of the bedroom and into the kitchen. He grabbed a jug of orange juice and unscrewed the top, then took a long drink. Suddenly, he was wide awake, his mind spinning with the possibilities. If he couldn't play, maybe he could coach. Or he could be an analyst for one of the networks. Or a sports presenter on the local news.

Brody strode into the living room and picked up the remote, then flipped through the stations until he came to ESPN Australia. The network played mostly American sports, but there was a nightly program that focused on Aussie sports. He could talk football and rugby and make a paycheck doing it. And if ESPN didn't want him, perhaps he might convince someone to hire him at Seven Network.

He leaned back into the sofa and closed his eyes. His coaches and friends had all told him he could find a career outside football, but he'd been too stubborn to listen to them, too angry about his injury to even consider the alternatives. But now he had a reason to get serious about his future.

He switched the telly over to a DVD of his rookie season, listening to the analysts as they described the action. His attention shifted to the twenty-year-old kid in the green guernsey. It was hard to believe he'd ever been that young. Though it was only six years ago, it seemed like a lifetime.

"What are you doing out here?"

He turned to see Payton standing in the bedroom doorway. She'd pulled on the Dockers jumper he'd bought her at the game and she looked irresistible in it, her hair a riot of curls around her face.

"Just watching some telly," he said. He patted the sofa cushion next to him and she crossed the room and curled up beside him.

"Is this your team?" she asked.

"Yep. See, there I am. Number fifteen. Watch. I'll

score a goal." He waited, knowing every play by heart. This was the game when he'd broken the season scoring record for rookies. "There. There it is."

"Yay for you," Payton said, patting his belly. "Good onya."

He wrapped his arm around her neck and pulled her closer, pressing a kiss into her fragrant hair. "I want you to stay with me," he murmured.

"I'm not sleepy," she said, mistaking his request.

"No, I mean, I want you to stay with me. I want you to live with me, here, in Australia. I don't want you to go back to the States." He'd made the same request back at the shack that night she got lost in the bush. But then, he'd just wanted reassurance. Now, he wanted to focus on the future.

She pushed back and looked up into his eyes, her brow creased in an intense frown. "I'm not going anywhere."

"Promise me," he said. "I don't want to wake up some morning and find you gone. I want to make this work."

She sighed softly, then glanced away. "I'm here because I want to be, Brody. If I didn't want to be here, I'd tell you."

"Would you? You ran out on your wedding. You didn't tell your fiancé that you didn't want to be there."

"That was different," Payton said.

"How? Tell me how."

"I—I…" She paused for a moment, then shook her head. "I should have been brave enough to tell him the truth. I don't have any excuses for that. But I'm different now. I'm not afraid to speak up for myself, for what I want. I promise, I'll tell you if I want to leave."

It wasn't the promise he was looking for, but it was as good as he was going to get. Brody would have to be satisfied that it was enough. And yet he wasn't. Until Payton faced her family and her ex-fiancé, he'd always be looking over his shoulder, waiting for someone to turn up and lure her back to the States.

Did he really want to live with that kind of doubt? A sensible, secure guy would tell her to go back and clear up the mess she'd made and then return to him, free of any entanglements. But Brody had never cared for any woman the way he cared for Payton. And he didn't want to let her out of his sight for a moment, much less send her toddling back to Mr. Moneybags.

"Do you ever think about him?" Brody asked.

"Sam?"

Sam. There. She'd said his name. How many times had she said that name? How many times with love in her eyes and how many times with passion in her touch? She had a whole history with this man, a life that Brody knew nothing about.

"Never mind." He pushed to his feet. "I don't need to know. I really don't want to know." He raked his hands through his hair again, suddenly feeling a bit vulnerable, standing in front of her stark naked. This was exactly why he couldn't allow himself to believe in a future with Payton.

She might be able to handle it, but he'd surely find a way to fuck it up. "I'm going to go for a run," he said.

"But, it isn't even light out."

Brody shrugged. "It will be by the time I get back."

"I could come with you."

"No. I just need to clear my head." He walked back

to the bedroom and put on a pair of shorts and a T-shirt, then grabbed his trainers from the closet floor. When he returned to the living room, she was sitting where he'd left her, her knees pulled up beneath the oversize jumper.

"I'll be back in an hour," he said. "Why don't you get a little more sleep and then we'll go to breakfast."

Brody slipped out of the door before she could reply to his suggestion, then strode down the hall to the lift. He stepped inside, releasing a tightly held breath as the doors closed in front of him.

There was no sense trying to plan his future right now. Until he found work, it would be best to keep his feelings for Payton in check. He could enjoy their time together, enjoy the passion they shared, but anything beyond that would be a risk.

8

PAYTON STROLLED slowly through the Fremantle Market, searching for inspiration for the evening meal. She'd already purchased prawns at the fish market on the harbor and now she was studying the vegetables that filled the stalls.

Though they'd only been in Fremantle for a week and a half, she'd already settled into life with Brody. They'd spent their days touring the city and surfing and trying new restaurants. Yesterday, they'd sailed a friend's boat to Rottnest Island and ridden bicycles over the picturesque roads. Brody had even rented a room at the old hotel where they had their lunch and enjoyed a "nap" before continuing their tour.

Payton smiled to herself. Though they'd stripped off their clothes before crawling into bed, neither one of them had had any intention of sleeping. Instead, they'd spent a lazy hour kissing and touching before they made love.

It had been a wonderful day filled with long walks and quiet conversation. Brody was a complicated man, troubled by his own doubts and worries. He'd confessed that he was toying with the idea of calling the NFL scout and talking to him about a job.

Though she could sense his tension over scheduling

a tryout, Payton tried to reassure him that even if it didn't work out, it didn't represent a failure. In the end, Brody made the call.

The NFL scout had arranged to meet him at the Oval tomorrow. Brody had nearly canceled, but she'd convinced him she would be there when he came home, exactly as she was when he left, whether the tryout was a success or not.

The more she got to know Brody, the more she realized how vulnerable he was when it came to his emotions. He seemed so self-assured on the outside, but inside, he was a tangle of insecurities. There were moments when she caught him watching her, times when she woke up and he was clutching her hand so tightly it hurt. Was he really that afraid of losing her?

Though Payton had left a mess in Fiji, she didn't have any plans to return home. She would have to call at some point and had resolved to do that by the end of the week. The private investigator was probably still searching for her and it wouldn't do to waste more of her parents' money or cause them any more worry.

By now, they should be comfortable with the fact that she wouldn't be coming home anytime soon. They'd have accepted the notion that Sam would not be her husband and that she would not be living a comfortable life in Connecticut, raising their grandchildren and attending charity events.

She shook her head, a tiny shudder running through her at the thought. How close to that life had she come? If she'd pushed aside her fears and married Sam, it would have been her future—everything all planned out in front of her.

But her life with Brody was exciting. Every day was a new adventure. And though he worried about his career, Payton was truly convinced that she could live anywhere with him and be happy. She loved working at the station. And she loved Fremantle, too. But most of her affection for both places had come from being with Brody.

Payton strolled over to a vegetable stall and chose some colorful sweet peppers and fingerling potatoes. She waited for the vendor to put them in a bag for her. Then she moved on to the nearest fruit stall and picked out some red oranges, knowing they would make a wonderful tangy-sweet sauce for the prawns. At the last second, she picked up a kilo of strawberries for dessert.

It wasn't a long walk back to Brody's apartment and the weather was pleasant. She'd bought only enough for the evening meal and didn't mind carrying the bags.

As she approached Brody's building, she noticed a dark sedan parked across the street. A man was standing against the front fender, his arms crossed over his chest. He saw her almost immediately and Payton's breath caught as he removed his glasses.

"Sam," she whispered to herself. Her heart slammed against her rib cage as he slowly crossed the street to where she stood. She blinked, hoping that she was seeing things, but as he came closer, Payton knew he wasn't a figment of her imagination.

"Hello, Payton," he said. He reached out and grabbed her elbow, then brushed a kiss on her cheek.

"Hello, Sam. What are you doing here?"

He gave her a cool look, his icy blue eyes cutting through her. "What do you think, Payton?"

She opened her mouth, then snapped it shut. She didn't know what to say.

"Don't worry," he muttered. "I'll wait for your answer. I'm used to that."

His words dripped with sarcasm. She hadn't realized until now, but that was one of things she truly hated about Sam. When he was angry, he got nasty. She'd always just accepted it as part of his nature, but now she realized there were men who didn't feel it necessary to patronize the women they loved.

"I'd assume you're looking for me," she said, keeping her voice calm and detached. "How did you find me?"

"Your parents and I hired a private investigator. They thought you might have had a—a breakdown."

She bit back a laugh. "I'm mentally sound," she said. "I'm not crazy."

"The investigator tracked that Quinn fellow here after he figured out you'd left the station with him. He's spent the last few days following you. You've had quite a vacation. Or maybe we should call it a honeymoon?"

Payton glanced around. She and Brody had been so caught up in each other, they hadn't even noticed someone following them. "Why don't you just say what you came to say, Sam. I understand you're angry and I'm sorry for any embarrassment I caused. But you have to realize I saved us both a lot of heartache."

This seemed to soften his prickly facade. "Did you ever love me?"

"I think I did," she said, knowing it was probably a lie. "But I also think I was getting married to please my parents. They wanted me to be settled and happy and I never thought about what I really wanted."

"And this is it? Some guy you just met? I've read the report on him, Payton. Come on, you can't seriously be thinking of staying here with him. He's just some washed-up jock."

"I don't know what will happen tomorrow or the next day. But I'm happy right now, Sam. Happier than I've been in a long time."

"Payton, be practical. You don't belong here. You're thousands of miles from everything you know—your family and your friends. I forgive you. You made a mistake, but it's nothing that can't be fixed. We can begin again."

"I did make a mistake," she admitted. "I should have been honest about my feelings and my fears. I should have told you how I felt long before our wedding day."

"You got cold feet. Lots of women go through that. But give it a little more time and you'll realize who really loves you. And then you'll come home."

"Sam, I don't—"

He reached out and pressed his finger to her lips. "Don't. Just think about what I've said, Payton. I'm staying in Perth for the next three days. I think we should take some time to talk. To see if we can smooth out this wrinkle."

Wrinkle, Payton mused. She ran away from their wedding and took up with another man and Sam considered it a wrinkle. "I don't think we have anything to talk about."

"I'm at the Intercontinental. Room 1250. I'll be waiting for your call." With that, he turned and walked back to his car. Payton stared after him, wanting to shout out her anger. How dare he assume that she'd change her mind? She wasn't some feebleminded doormat who could be convinced by his mere appearance.

Sam could wait all he wanted, but she wasn't going to change her mind. She'd call her parents tonight and tell them exactly that. And then she'd tell them to talk some sense into her ex-fiancé. But first, she'd tell Brody about Sam's sudden appearance. Knowing Sam and his inability to accept losing at anything, she could expect another visit. She would not allow Brody to be caught off guard.

When she returned to Brody's apartment, she found him sitting on the sofa, examining his knee. He glanced up as she walked inside and she noticed the worried expression etched across his face.

"Is everything all right?" she asked. From the looks of things, now was not the time to bring up her ex-fiancé. That could wait until tomorrow, after the tryout.

"Sure," he said. He pushed to his feet and crossed to her, taking the bags from her hands. "Dinner?"

"Yes. I'm cooking something special. A good-luck meal. I figured it's about time to show you my true talents in the kitchen."

"You have talents in the kitchen too?" he teased, his mood shifting quickly. "I knew you were great in the bathroom, the bedroom and the living room. But the kitchen wasn't something I'd considered."

"I'm a very good cook," she explained.

He peered inside the bags, then pulled out the strawberries she'd purchased. Payton reached for them. "Those are for dessert," she said.

"Can't we have dessert first?" He took one from the bag and bit into it, then held it in front of her mouth.

Slowly, he drew the fruit across her lower lip. She ran her tongue over the sweet juice and smiled.

With a quick move, she bit down on the strawberry, then pulled him into a long, deep kiss. The taste of the berry exploded in her mouth, and Payton wasn't sure that she'd ever tasted something quite so wonderful.

The kiss went on forever, their hands moving over each other's body, so familiar yet still so exciting. He spanned her waist with his hands, then lifted her onto the granite countertop. The short shirt she wore bunched high on her thighs and he slipped his hand between her legs and began to caress her.

Payton knew his touch, yet every time he seduced her, he found a new way to take her to the heights of pleasure. He pushed her back until she was lying across the cool granite. Then he pulled her panties off and trailed kisses along the insides of her thighs.

She knew what was coming and waited, knowing the exquisite sensations his tongue could elicit. And then, he was there, sucking gently, making her writhe with the need for release.

She'd meant to tell him about Sam, but as her pleasure began to escalate, all thoughts of her former life dissolved. She was here with Brody now, and what they were doing was perfect. Nothing could possibly spoil it.

BRODY WINCED as he pushed up from a crouch and ran the width of the field. Though he was in pretty good shape, he hadn't really run full out since before his accident. When he reached the far side of the field, he gulped in a deep breath, then turned and ran back.

The scout scribbled something in his notebook, then nodded. "I understand your injury prevents lateral movement."

"Not prevents," Brody said. "Hampers. I'm just not as quick as I was. But it doesn't affect my kicking. You saw that. I put ten of them through the posts from fifty meters. I can do ten more. Hey, I can kick all day and I won't miss."

"But you'll have to run and tackle," he said. "And even though we have a rule against roughing the kicker, you will get knocked down. That knee isn't going to take much abuse."

"I know I can do this," Brody said. "Just give me a chance. I'll come to the States. I'll kick in your football stadium. I'll play for free."

The scout considered Brody's offer, then nodded his head. "You're a hell of a kicker. But I'm worried about the knee. The strength just isn't quite there. But you do some serious work and that might change. You should be running every day and doing some intense weight training. The NFL preseason starts the end of July. If a team is in need of a kicker, they'll be looking before the regular season begins in September." He held out his business card. "You call me after a month and we'll see where you're at."

Brody stared down at the card. "All right. I can do that. Thanks for taking the time."

"Good luck, son. I hope I hear from you."

Brody walked toward the exit, resigned to the fact that he'd given it his best try. Hell, he'd kicked well. No one could quarrel with that. But his knee wasn't what it should be. Even he knew it. He drew a deep breath, trying to push back the disappointment.

Though it wasn't good news, it wasn't really bad. He had a chance, if he put in a little work. He still had access to the team's training facilities and their physical therapists. Given a month, maybe he could gain more strength.

As he walked through the tunnel to the car park, he saw Payton standing in the entrance, her slender form outlined by the morning sun. She smiled and he felt his spirits rise. Even if the world was falling apart at his feet, she could still make him feel like a hero.

"How did it go?" she asked as he took her hand in his.

"I kicked well," he said. "But he didn't like the look of my knee."

"Well, you expected that," she said.

"He said I should work harder on rehab and then give him a call in a month."

"Are you going to do that?" she asked.

Brody shrugged. "I don't know. Maybe. It would give me more options." He smiled. "I can kick the damn ball. At least the next time one of their kickers goes down, he'll be thinking of me."

They drove back to his apartment, his mind distracted by the traffic. Every now and then, he caught Payton glancing over at him. He wanted to tell her how he was feeling—the frustration and the doubts—but his problems were his own. This afternoon, they'd find something to do that would take his mind off his troubles. And tomorrow, he'd figure out a plan.

As they drove up to the apartment, he reached out and took her hand. "Why don't we go surfing this afternoon." He looked over at her to see her gaze fixed on a car parked across the street from his building.

"What's wrong?"

"Keep driving," she said.

"Why? We need to get our gear if we're going surfing."

"Just keep going."

He did as he was told. After a few blocks, Brody drove in to an empty parking spot and pulled the truck out of gear. Then he turned to her. "Would you like to tell me what's going on?"

She gnawed at her lower lip, avoiding his eyes. "Yesterday, after I came back from the market, I saw Sam. My ex. He was parked in front of your apartment building waiting for me."

Brody felt as if he'd been hit in the gut. This didn't make sense. "You talked to Sam?"

She nodded, then risked a glance over at him. "I wanted to tell you yesterday, but you had the tryout today and I didn't want you to be upset. Besides, when I got home we got distracted and I guess I just forgot."

"You forgot?"

"Well, not exactly. It wasn't the right time."

"Which is it, Payton?"

She cursed softly. "What difference does it make? I'm telling you now. He asked if I'd come home. I told him no."

"Then what's he still doing here?"

"I guess he thinks I might change my mind."

Brody's fingers tightened on the steering wheel, his knuckles turning white. "And will you change your mind?"

"No," Payton insisted. "I don't want to marry him. I told him that. But he doesn't like to lose. And he certainly doesn't like to be embarrassed. He and my parents seem to think I've had some sort of mental breakdown and that if I just get a little help, I'll regain my senses."

"We're going back," Brody said. "I'll talk to the guy. I'll tell him to back off."

"No," Payton said. "This is my problem. I'll—"

"It's my problem now. He's screwing with *my* life."

"I know where he's staying. I'll call him tonight and tell him to go home. And I'll call my parents and let them know I'm going to stay in Australia for now."

Brody didn't like leaving it up to Payton. She'd obviously tried to convince Sam the first time they'd talked and it hadn't worked. Either Sam wasn't listening or she hadn't been forceful enough. But there would be no denying Brody's argument—either the guy would leave Fremantle immediately, or Brody would give him a thick ear.

"So what does this mean? We can't go back to the apartment?"

"Why don't we go get some lunch and maybe he'll be gone when we return." She reached out and pried his hand off the wheel, then laced her fingers through his. "As you've probably noticed, I'm not very good with confrontation."

"What are you talking about? You've told me off plenty of times."

"It's different with my family and with Sam. They make me feel—" Payton searched for the word "—small. They make me feel small."

He turned to look at her, noticing the uneasy expression on her face. Hell, he never wanted to do anything that made her feel that way. "You're one of the strongest, most determined people I know," he said. "Don't let them do that to you. Think of everything you've done over the past weeks."

Brody paused, carefully considering his next suggestion. He was tired of all the wondering—did she love him, would she stay, how did she really feel about Sam? There were too many unanswered questions that she had to settle once and for all. "I think you should go see him," Brody said.

"Really?"

"Why not? He was an important person in your life. Hell, you were going to marry him. Maybe he just needs some…what do they call that?"

"Closure?" she suggested.

"Right. Closure."

A long silence grew between them. "All right," she said softly. "If that's what you want, I'll go see him tomorrow."

It wasn't exactly what he wanted. But it was the quickest way to get to what he wanted. And for that, he was willing to take a risk. He'd give Sam Whitman one last chance to plead his case and if he didn't leave after that, Brody would personally escort him to the airport.

He wasn't about to let Payton go. At least, not without a good fight.

"WHAT DO YOU THINK?"

Brody frowned, staring down at the assortment of towels. He winced, then ran his hand through his hair. Payton could see the confusion in his eyes, but she suspected it had nothing to do with his choice of towels.

Payton had called Sam and agreed to meet him the

next morning. Since she'd made the decision, she and Brody hadn't spoken of it. In truth, she'd carefully avoided the subject. But she could see that it was killing Brody. He'd been hovering over her all day, obviously wanting to ask her what she would say, but afraid to bring up the subject.

"Ah…well, they're towels," he said. "I've never really had an opinion on towels. They're just sort of there when I need them." He nodded. "That's what I think."

"I mean the colors. Your bathroom is so neutral."

"Is it? What does that mean?"

He was going to make this difficult, Payton mused. She'd wondered if buying new towels for him was really a good idea. But she wanted to contribute something to the home they'd made together, even if it did mean spending a bit of his money. "Neutral means there's a lack of color."

"And color is good?"

"Yes. Now, do you like the ice blue or the burnt sienna? These are both masculine colors, but one is cool and the other is warm. I like the burnt sienna."

"Then I like that one, too. Don't I have towels?"

"Yes. But they're a little worn. And they're kind of mismatched. I just thought these would be pretty. And they're really soft. One hundred percent Egyptian cotton." He nodded mutely. Frustrated, Payton picked up the towels and shoved them back into the bag. "Never mind. I'll return them."

"No, no. Don't do that. I like them. I like the burnt sienna. And the blue, too. Maybe we could keep both. One color for summer and one for winter. Cool and warm, right?"

Payton gave him a grudging smile. "I just thought I could make your apartment look a little more homey."

"It doesn't look homey?"

She shook her head. "No. It looks like a bachelor's apartment. It's very nice, but very sterile. And if we're going to live here together, then I want it to be like a home."

A slow smile curled his lips. "A home. With me and you."

"Yes. I like it here."

"Is there anything else that needs fixing?" he asked.

"Well, the kitchen could use some nice towels. And a few accessories, maybe a bowl for the island, for fresh fruit. And some nice wineglasses to put in the china cabinet. Those refrigerator magnets have to go."

Brody chuckled softly. Then he dragged her into his arms, kissing her squarely on the mouth. "Do whatever you want," he said. "As long as you're staying, you can paint the place pink. And if you need more money, just ask."

She'd been thinking about exactly that subject. She wanted to contribute, to help pay for their living expenses. "I'm going to try to find a job," she said. "And to get a job, I suspect I'll need a work visa."

"We can think about that later. I have cash enough to last for a while."

"No, I want to contribute," she said.

"Then let's find out about a work visa." Brody reached out and removed the towels from the bag, stacking them up on the coffee table. "We'll go first thing tomorrow morning."

Payton forced a smile. "I'm going to see Sam

tomorrow morning. Remember?" She studied his expression. He didn't look happy. But then, he hadn't been very happy since Sam had appeared in Fremantle.

"We should go try out these towels," she said. "Let's take a shower."

Brody shook his head. "You think that if you seduce me, I'll stop worrying about him?"

"There's no need to worry," she assured him. "Brody, I'm decorating your apartment. I wouldn't do that unless I was planning to stay."

"He's leaving tomorrow?"

"That's what he said," Payton replied.

"Good. Then, day after, we can stop talking about him." He pushed her back on the sofa and crawled on top of her, rubbing his nose against hers. "Do you have a nice dress?"

"Not really."

"Then, go out and buy one. We're going out to a swank place tomorrow night for dinner. It's my birthday."

"It's your birthday? Why didn't you tell me?" Payton asked. "I'll make a cake. We'll have presents and a celebration."

"I just want to take my girl out," Brody said.

His girl. She liked the sound of that. It wasn't too serious. Yet, it did suggest a real relationship, one that was more than casual. "I'm not sure where to go to find something."

"There's a David Jones in the mall in Perth. It's the same store you went to in Brisbane."

"They have really pretty dresses there." She kissed him. "I'll go this afternoon. You can come and help me pick something out."

"Surprise me," he said. Brody brushed the hair out of her eyes. "When is your birthday?"

"August tenth," she said. "I was born twelve minutes before midnight."

Payton realized they didn't know the little details about each other's lives. Maybe it was time to find out. "What's your favorite color?" she asked.

"Neutral," he teased. "No, it was blue. But now, it's this really pretty shade of pink." Brody smiled. "Exactly the color of your lips."

Payton groaned inwardly. Her attempt to learn more about him was swiftly turning into a full-out seduction. But then, they had plenty of time to go over the silly little details. "What is your favorite sexual fantasy?" she asked.

He laughed sharply. "How did we go from colors to sexual fantasies?"

Payton shrugged. "Just curious."

He thought about his answer for a long time, then smiled. "There is this one. I'm asleep and I'm having this dream that there's a woman in bed with me. And she's doing all kinds of wonderful things with her lips and her tongue. And I open my eyes and it's not a dream."

"Has it ever happened before?" Payton asked.

"No," he said.

"Your birthday is coming up. That could be arranged, you know."

"Arranged? Only if you're the woman I'm waking up to. I'd reckon that would be a bonzer prezzy."

"Bonzer is good?"

"Very good. Great. Incredible. The best."

"Hmm. That's a lot to live up to. Maybe I should just buy you a bonzer watch. Or a bonzer shirt."

"Do not tease me," he said. "It's my birthday. And as my girl, it's your job to treat me special."

Payton giggled. "It's not your birthday yet." Now that she'd decided to stay, she had every intention of making all Brody's fantasies come true. Life—and sex—with Brody would be one long adventure.

9

THE BUZZER ON the security system startled Brody. Payton had left less than an hour ago to shop for a dress for tomorrow's birthday celebration. He hadn't expected her to return until just before dinner.

He pushed the button and leaned in. "Did you forget your key?"

There was a long pause on the other end. "I'm looking for Brody Quinn."

"And who might you be?" Brody asked.

"Sam. Sam Whitman."

Brody stepped back from the intercom, then cursed softly. What the hell was this? Payton had assured him that she'd called Sam and told him she would see him in the morning. Either he was a very impatient man or he wanted to talk to Brody directly.

Brody drew a deep breath. "She's not here," he said.

"I'm here to talk to you," Sam said. "Man to man."

Brody shook his head, then opened the front door and walked to the lift. If this guy wanted to talk, they'd talk. But Brody was going to have much more to say than "get the hell out of our lives." As he rode the lift down to the lobby, he carefully schooled his temper. The last thing he wanted to do was punch the guy. There was no need to get physical. But he was prepared to take it that far if the situation warranted.

He'd seen the photo of Sam on the Internet and knew what to expect. But when he walked into the lobby, Brody was surprised at how slight he was. In a bar brawl, Sam Whitman wouldn't last a minute.

To Brody's delight, Whitman seemed to be a bit intimidated by Brody's size. Brody had at least ten centimeters on him and a good fifteen kilos. "What do you want?" he demanded.

"I have some things to say about Payton."

"She plans to stay here with me. She was going to stop by your hotel tomorrow morning and let you know."

Sam paused, as if considering his next comment carefully. "You don't find it unusual that she'd abandon her family and friends? Without a second thought?"

"No," Brody lied. "Not after the way you treated her. She has a right to make her own decisions."

"I think we both have to be honest," Sam said. "Maybe I didn't give her the attention she needed. And I'll admit, I might have focused on work too much. But I can give her a very comfortable life. From what I know of you, you can't."

Brody quelled a surge of temper. He knew it was the only advantage that Sam Whitman had on him. And Whitman obviously wasn't afraid to use it.

"I have some opportunities," Brody said. "Besides, we can always live on the station with my family. Payton loves it there."

"For how long?" Sam asked. "How long until the novelty wears off and she grows tired of being isolated from everything she knows and loves?"

He was saying the same things Brody had said to himself. "Do you honestly think you can buy her back?"

"No. But I believe if you really love her, you'll consider what's best for her. I believe if you're selfish enough to keep her here, you'll pay the price later. And by isolating her from her family and friends, you're allowing her to avoid the consequences of her actions." Sam reached into his jacket pocket and pulled out a leather wallet, then withdrew an envelope from it. "This is an airline ticket and enough cash to get her home."

"What makes you think I'll give this to her?"

"Because you want to know as much as I do," Sam said. "You love her enough not to leave any stone unturned. Send her home. If she comes back to you, you'll know she's made her choice." He held out his hand. "May the best man win."

Brody bit back a curse. This guy was arrogant and condescending and in need of a good beat-down. But he was also right. If Brody did want to keep Payton in his life permanently, then she'd have to face up to her past mistakes. It was better to lose her now than later.

He reached out and shook Sam's hand, then nodded. "She loves me," he said.

"Then I guess you have nothing to worry about. Tell her good-bye. And I'll see her back home."

With that, Sam turned on his heel and walked out of the lobby. He watched as Sam jogged across the street and got into his car. Then Brody glanced down at the airline ticket. He ought to just toss it in the rubbish and forget it ever existed.

Why not? He could accept the risk that it would all explode in his face at some point. He'd have more time to convince Payton she'd made the best choice by staying. But Sam was right on one point. It was probably better to know how she really felt, before investing his heart in a relationship that was doomed from the start.

Brody walked back to the lift and pushed the button, then stepped inside after the doors opened. A single shot at an NFL career wasn't enough. If he wanted to compete with Sam Whitman's millions, he had to look at other options.

The moment he got back to his apartment, Brody found his phone and dialed the Dockers' office. When the receptionist answered, Brody asked to speak to John Cook. When the assistant coach got on the line, Brody drew a deep breath and said a silent prayer.

"John. Brody Quinn here. Say, I was wondering if you still had the name of that bloke at Seven Network. You know, the one you thought might be able to find a spot for me as an analyst?"

To Brody's surprise, Cook had the number at hand and encouraged Brody to make the call. They chatted for a few minutes about Brody's knee and the possibility of surgery, but Brody cut the conversation short and hung up. After a half hour, he had a list of seven contacts for a wide range of jobs, from school coach to equipment salesman.

He stared at the phone for a long time, trying to put his thoughts in order. Then he tossed the phone on the sofa and stood up. This was far too important to bungle. The NFL would pay the best, but television was more secure. He'd follow Callum's advice and write everything down first, the pros and cons of all his options.

Brody found a pad of paper, sat down at the table and carefully wrote out the skills that he possessed. He'd always been the club's best student of the game. He read the opposition like no other player and could talk at length about a player's strengths and weaknesses. He had a good mind for statistics and remembered almost everything he read. He didn't stammer or mumble and his teammates had often teased him about his pretty face. And he was considered quite charming.

"What more is there?" Brody asked himself, staring at the list. He owned a suit and tie and a decent pair of shoes. He wrote that down, though he assumed if he got a job in the business world, he'd need a better wardrobe. He started a list for the NFL job and even made one for getting back into Aussie football.

Brody heard the front door open and turned to see Payton walking in. Their eyes met and for a moment, Brody forgot to breathe. He still found himself amazed that she'd wandered into his life. How the hell had he gotten so lucky?

"You're home early," he said, glancing over at the plane ticket he'd left on the table.

She held up a sheaf of papers. "I stopped by the immigration office on my way back from shopping. I have to fill out all this paperwork and then call back for an appointment." Payton dropped her shopping bags on the floor, then sat down on his lap and slipped her arms around his neck. "What happens if they don't let me stay? What if they force me to go home?"

"Maybe you need to go home," he said. The moment the words slipped out of his mouth, he wanted to take them back. Why would he encourage her to leave? Was he compelled to test her feelings for him? Brody took the plane ticket from the table and held it out to her.

"What's that?"

"A ticket home," he said. "Sam dropped by. I guess he got tired of waiting for you and decided to talk to me."

Her expression turned angry. "I left a message that I was coming to see him tomorrow. He always has to control everything. God, I hate that about him. I'm not going home. And I'm not going to talk to him again. I'll just return the ticket. Or better yet, exchange it for tickets we can use together."

"I think you should go home. Payton, I don't want to constantly be looking over my shoulder, waiting for him to turn up again like he did today. You need to clean up the mess you left behind and then, if you still want to, come back. But this is always going to be hanging between us, Payton. I'm always going to wonder if I'll wake up someday and you'll be gone."

She bit on her lower lip, her eyes filling with tears. "So you want me to leave?"

"Of course not. But if you're going to stay, I want you to stay forever. And if you don't smooth things out with your family, you're always going to regret that. Do it now. Make amends. And then come home to me."

A long silence grew between them as she considered his suggestion. "You're right," she finally said. "This whole thing has been hanging over us like a dark cloud. I know what I want and I shouldn't be afraid to tell them." Payton cupped his face in her hands and stared into his eyes. "I'll go back day after tomorrow," she said. "After we've celebrated your birthday. And I'll call my parents and let them know I'm coming home." Payton leaned forward and gave him a fierce kiss. "I will come back. You can count on it."

Brody's pulse leaped. He cupped her face in his hands and molded her mouth to his. How would he live without this? After a day or two, he'd be ready to hop a flight to the States and drag her back.

But he'd have to be strong and hope that she would return and stay for good. Brody slipped his arm beneath her knees and stood, then slowly walked toward the bedroom, their mouths still caught in a deep kiss.

As he lowered her onto his bed, they broke apart for a moment. He stared down into her beautiful face and tried to memorize all the tiny details that he'd begun to take for granted. He didn't even have a photo of her. But then, perhaps that was for the best.

He could believe she'd existed in a dream, that what they'd shared hadn't been real. If she didn't return, he'd continue with the fantasy. And if she did, reality would be better than anything he could have ever imagined.

They undressed each other slowly, taking the time to touch each inch of exposed skin. There were so many spots on her body he'd lingered over, spots made just for his lips or his tongue or his touch. In his eyes, she was perfection and there would never be another woman like her.

And when they finally came together in a long, delicious possession, he was already regretting what he'd done. He should have burned the ticket, should have trusted his instincts and kept her with him.

He thrust deep and held her close, desperate to seal the bond they shared. Again and again, they moved together and when their release finally came, Brody knew just one thing was certain. He loved Payton and if giving her up meant assuring her happiness, he'd do it in a heartbeat.

JFK WAS CROWDED with summer tourists, the concourse a maze of luggage and late passengers. Her flight from Perth had been a marathon affair, though passed in the comfort of first class. She'd boarded a Qantas flight almost thirty-five hours ago and had changed planes in Melbourne and Los Angeles. At this point, she could barely summon the energy to lift her bag onto her shoulder, much less marshal the resolve to face her parents.

But her trip was far from over. Before she'd left Perth, she'd booked her return flight and a night at an airport hotel, putting the charges on her credit card. One last thing her father would pay for before she was completely on her own. She was due to get right back on the plane in another twenty-four hours. In all, she'd be apart from Brody for three and a half days—enough time to realize she could never stay away longer.

They'd had a wonderful birthday celebration, though it was laced with the bittersweet knowledge that they'd soon be miles apart. After returning from the restaurant, they'd stripped out of their fancy clothes and made love all night long.

When it was time for her to leave, he'd reluctantly let her go. He'd decided to call a cab, rather than drive her to the airport himself, and Payton was glad for it. Emotional goodbyes would have been too difficult to handle. She was determined to get her problems solved and then return. Neither one of them would have time to be sad.

Payton wondered why she'd even bothered to leave. She didn't need to see Sam again. As for her parents, she could have invited them to Fremantle for a visit and a chance to meet the man she loved.

Payton stopped short, causing a traffic problem on the concourse. She hadn't admitted it to herself until now, but she was in love with Brody. It had taken thirty-five hours in and out of the air for her to come to that realization, but at least she was dead certain of it. She loved Brody Quinn and deep down inside, she knew he loved her, as well.

"So what am I doing here?" she muttered, staring at her surroundings. Payton hoisted her bag back up on her shoulder and started off again. "Closure," she murmured.

How wonderful would it be to return to Brody without a single thing hanging over their heads? She smiled to herself as she walked, thinking about the last time she'd seen him. He'd stood in the doorway of his apartment building, watching her get into the cab. He'd looked so sad, almost as if he didn't believe he'd ever see her again. She'd prove him wrong.

Her parents had promised to meet her outside the security checkpoint and as she neared the spot, Payton said a silent prayer that they'd kept their promise. As she worked her way through the crowd, she caught sight of Sam. He waved at her and she started toward him. He met her halfway, then grabbed her bag.

"I thought my parents would meet me."

"They're waiting in the Red Carpet Club just down the concourse. I wanted to talk to you first."

"I don't have anything to say to you, Sam."

"I have something to say to you," he said. He took her elbow and steered her over to a row of chairs set against the wall. "Sit."

Payton gave him a withering look. She wouldn't be ordered around like some naughty pet.

"Please, sit down," Sam amended, motioning to the chair. "I have something I need to tell you before you talk to your parents."

She frowned, taking in the stricken expression on Sam's face. Payton had never seen him so worried. Her stomach lurched. "What is it? Are my parents all right? Has something happened? Did someone die?"

"No," Sam said. He sat down, then pulled her down beside him. "It's me."

"You're dying?" Payton asked.

A wry smile touched his lips. "Metaphorically, yes." Sam drew a deep breath, then met her gaze. "For the past three years, I've been carrying on an affair with my executive assistant. Your father found out about it and I'm sure your parents will bring it up. They think that's why you ran out on the wedding."

Payton stared at him, his words a jumble in her mind. "You were having an affair? You were cheating on me? And my father knew about it?"

"Yes. To all three questions. I know how you must feel and I can only beg for your forgiveness and spend the rest of my life making this up to you. It's over. It's been over for a month now and—"

"Wait," Payton said, holding up her hand. "A month? You mean, it was still going on while we were in—" She stopped, stunned by the realization. "She was there. In Fiji. Emily was there. We invited her to our wedding. Oh, my God. You were planning to carry on after we were married?"

"I know this must be a shock, but I can assure you that—"

Payton shook her head, a laugh bubbling up inside her. "I knew something was wrong. I trusted my instincts and I was right." She stood and picked up her bag from the floor, slinging it over her shoulder. "Do you want to know what I feel, Sam?" She shrugged. "Nothing. I feel nothing. I thought I loved you, but I know now that what we had wasn't love. It was obligation. And I'm fine with this."

He jumped up and reached for her arm, but Payton avoided his grasp. "Unfortunately, you won't be taking over Daddy's bank, but I'm sure you'll find comfort in the fact that you can keep sleeping with Emily." Payton held out her hand. "Goodbye, Sam. Have a nice life."

He took her hand and gave it a weak shake. Then, Payton turned on her heel and headed down the concourse. As she walked, she tried to make sense of what Sam had told her. Her parents had known about his affair and they'd still gone ahead with the wedding plans. How was that possible?

When she reached the first-class lounge, she stood in the doorway, her gaze falling on the handsome couple sitting at a nearby table. They spotted her at the same time and her mother rushed up to her, arms thrown open. She gathered Payton in a frantic embrace, hugging her tightly. "You're home," she cried. "Thank God. I was beginning to wonder if I'd ever see you again."

A moment later, her father appeared at her side and patted her on the shoulder. "There, there. Well, I'm happy to see you've come to your senses, Payton. Come on, let's get out of here. We have a car waiting."

"No," Payton said.

Her father arched his brow. "No? How do you propose we get home?"

Payton straightened her spine and took a deep breath. "I'm not going home, Daddy. Not tonight."

Her mother gave Payton's arm a gentle squeeze. "Oh, George. She's going to Sam's, of course. Darling, we couldn't be happier. You know how much we adore Sam. And he loves you. Just wait, this whole terrible embarrassment will be forgotten in no time."

"Mother, I'm not going to Sam's." She took her mother's hand and pulled her along with her toward their table. "I think we should order some wine, sit down and talk. I have something I need to tell you."

"She's pregnant." Her mother pressed a hand to her heart and closed her eyes. Her father held her elbow to keep her upright.

"I'm not pregnant!" Payton groaned. "Why would you think that?"

"Sam said you were—oh, how did he say it, George?"

"Shacked up, Margie," her father said. "He said Payton was shacked up with some unemployed soccer player."

"Football," Payton said. "Aussie rules football. Mother, Father, sit down," she ordered. It was time they started treating her like an adult and not some eager child always willing to please. This conversation would be between three reasonable adults—or one reasonable adult trying to calm two irrational-overbearing adults. She drew a steadying breath. "I'll be right back."

She strode up to the bar, ordered three glasses of Merlot and paid with one of the twenties that Sam had given her. Then she carried the wine to the table and sat down.

"Why are we staying here?" her mother asked. "Why don't we go home and have a drink? I'm sure the quality of this wine isn't up to the standards of what we have in our wine cellar." She took a sip and wrinkled her nose. "Just as I suspected."

"This is ridiculous." Her father pushed away from the table. "You're coming home with us right now, Payton. You are going to get a good night's sleep and then we are going to figure out how you can make this all up to Sam."

She shook her head. "I don't love him. And neither should you. He cheated on me. You knew and you were going to let me marry him all the same. You two spent a lifetime trying to protect me and then, when I really needed you the most, you were ready to walk away, to let me marry a man who didn't love me."

"Sam assured me the affair was over," her father said. "And that it wouldn't happen again."

"Well, he wasn't telling you the truth. Thank God, I figured it out."

"When did you find out?" her mother asked.

"A few minutes ago," Payton said. "But I knew something was wrong for a long time. I felt it in the weeks before the wedding. And in Fiji. That's why I ran." An image of Brody flashed in her mind and she smiled. "And I'm lucky I did. Because I've met a man I can really love and trust, a man who wants me and not the bank I'll inherit. I have to live my life now on my own. And I'm going to do that in Australia. With Brody."

"What is she saying, George?" her mother asked.

"She's just distraught. You need help," her father

said, turning to Payton. "We can get you help. A nice quiet place to get some perspective."

Payton giggled softly. "Daddy, I don't need help. I'm perfectly sane and I'm happier than I've ever been. And I hope someday you'll come to visit me. I'd love for you to meet Brody. He's a wonderful man. Or maybe, we'll come here for a visit. Brody might have a tryout with a football team later this summer." She gulped down the rest of her wine, then stood, satisfied that she'd said everything that needed saying.

Though she ought to have been angrier over her parents' deception, there wasn't really a point. Everything they'd done had led to Brody and that was all that mattered. She rounded the table and kissed them both on the cheek. "I have to go now. I think I might be able to catch the flight back tonight if I hurry."

"You only just got here," her father said.

"And now I have to go," Payton replied, picking up her bag. "I love you both. And don't worry, I know exactly what I'm doing."

She walked to the doorway of the bar, then turned and waved at her stunned parents. It was enough for them to see that she was healthy and happy. They'd get over her broken engagement and their disappointment that Sam wouldn't be a part of the family. And they'd find a way to explain the embarrassment of the wedding. And maybe someday they would meet Brody and understand why she loved him.

As much as she wanted to feel regret while walking away from them, Payton couldn't. She was returning to the man she loved, to a land she was learning to love and to a life that would be built on love. She

wasn't frightened or nervous or anything but bliss-
fully happy.

She checked the signs at the end of the concourse and
headed toward the Qantas desk. If she hurried, she could
hop the 7:10 flight to Australia, a full day before her
scheduled return. Then, in about thirty hours, she'd be
back in Brody's life—and in his arms—for good.

"DAVEY, GRAB ME that spanner." Brody crawled halfway
down the windmill and waited as the kid searched the
ground at his feet. "Next to my saddlebags."

He picked up a tool. "This one?"

"No, the big one."

Davey finally found the tool, then climbed up the
ladder and handed it to Brody. They'd been working
together all day, greasing and adjusting the six windmills
close to the station. Tomorrow they'd catch the ones on
the outlying pastures, traveling by ATV rather than horse.

Brody had decided to return to the station after just
one day alone in Fremantle. The apartment seemed so
empty without Payton there and he found himself
spending every waking minute thinking about her. He
could rehab his knee as easily on the station as he could
in Fremantle, and he'd have work to occupy his mind
the rest of the day. Station work was difficult and exhausting—and exactly what he needed.

He wasn't sure when Payton would return. She'd
promised to call once everything had been settled, but
he expected she'd spend at least a week or two in the
States before she left again. He'd decided to go on as if
she wasn't going to return. Then, everything after that—
if there was anything—would be like a gift.

Brody climbed back up to the top of the windmill, the spanner tucked into his jacket pocket and the grease gun still clutched in his hand. As he went through the maintenance routine, he heard the sound of a plane overhead and glanced up to see Teague coming in from the east.

He hadn't seen Teague at all since his return and Callum had ridden out an hour after Gemma had left a day ago, heading into the outback with his horse, his pack and his rifle. He'd left Skip in charge of preparations for the mustering, a sure sign that he was upset. Now that Teague was back, Brody would get some answers. He had tried not to dwell on his brothers' love lives. Thinking about their happiness only made his life seem emptier.

"What is he doing?" Davey asked.

Brody glanced over his shoulder to see Teague circling the plane. "I don't know." He watched as Teague made a wide sweep around the windmill, wiggling his wings before he headed toward the airstrip.

Brody finished his work, then carefully surveyed the landscape from his perch high above the ground. He used to love this view when he was a kid. He always thought if he just looked hard enough, he could see the real world in the distance. Now he took some comfort in the fact that he was isolated from that world.

If things didn't work out the way he'd planned, then he'd return to the station for good and make his life here in Queensland. He'd always have a place with his brothers and there was some comfort in that.

"Are we done?" Davey called.

"Yeah," Brody replied. "Pack it up. It's getting late. We should start back if we want to make it by dinner."

Davey gathered the tools, then strapped the pouch to his horse. By the time Brody joined him, Davey was mounted and ready to ride. There was no keeping him from a meal. Davey kicked his horse into a gallop, but Brody decided to take a slower pace.

"Come on," Davey shouted over his shoulder, pulling his horse up to wait.

"Go ahead," Brody called. "I want to enjoy the ride."

"Suit yourself. But Mary's got pork chops tonight. If you don't sit down on time, the rest of the boys will eat all the potatoes."

He waved Davey off and watched as the kid took off in a cloud of dust. Brody wasn't anxious to get back to the dinner table. Since he'd returned, he'd been grabbing a plate and eating by himself, too preoccupied to socialize. Mary and the jackaroos had given him a wide berth and he'd been grateful for it.

As he rode toward the house, he noticed the Fraser shack in the distance. His mind wandered back to the night he'd spent there with Payton. Everything had been so new with them then, so exciting. Only a few weeks had passed since, but it seemed like a lifetime.

He wondered what Payton was doing, trying to calculate the time difference between New York and Queensland. There was almost a twelve-hour difference, so it was the middle of the night there. Was she sleeping alone or had Sam convinced her to return to his bed?

Brody cursed beneath his breath, brushing the image from his mind. He wanted to believe that thoughts of him filled her mind, that she missed what they had together, that she ached for him the way he ached for her. Sleep hadn't come easily since she'd gone.

He fixed his gaze on the horizon and let the horse navigate. It felt good to think about her, to rewind every encounter and enjoy them all over again. They'd been wonderful together, both in and out of bed. He closed his eyes and tipped his face up, the sun warm on his back, exhaustion setting in.

Maybe he'd sleep tonight, he mused. Perhaps his bed wouldn't seem so cold and empty. It had to happen sooner or later. The loneliness would fade and he'd get his life back—pitiful as it was.

When he opened his eyes again, he noticed a rider approaching from the direction of the homestead. He squinted to see in the late-afternoon light, trying to make out who it was. Slowly, he realized it was a woman. Hayley?

Suddenly, the rider pulled to a stop and jumped off the horse. Brody's breath caught in his chest. He blinked hard, wondering if he was imagining her, like a mirage in the middle of the desert. He kicked his horse into a trot and covered the distance between them.

As he approached, she pulled off her stockman's hat and her curly hair fell down around her shoulders. Brody smiled. If this was a dream, then he planned to enjoy it.

He reined in his horse before he reached her, then slid down to stand beside it. For a long time, they stood facing each other, neither one of them moving. And then, at the very same moment, they covered the distance between them in just a few seconds.

Payton launched herself into his arms and he picked her up and spun her around. She felt real, warm and soft, the scent of her hair filling his head. "Is it really you?"

"I think so," Payton said. "I can't have changed that much in four days."

He set her down and stepped back to look into her eyes. "You're more beautiful, I think. Is that possible?" Brody took her face in his hands and kissed her, his tongue delving into her mouth and savoring her taste. "Did you even go home?"

Payton nodded. "I did. I saw Sam and my parents and I turned around and came back. When I got to New York, I realized it was the last place in the world I wanted to be. You shouldn't have made me leave, but I'm glad I put that part of my life to rest."

"I won't do that again," Brody said. "God, I missed you. How did you get here?"

"Teague picked me up. When I got to Fremantle and you weren't there, I figured you might have come back to the station. I flew to Brisbane and then called Teague and he came to get me. I thought it might be nice to surprise you."

"Nice," he said. "I like *nice* now. Coming back to me is definitely nice."

"I may have to leave again if they don't extend my visa. But maybe, we can go to New York for a visit."

"Or for that football tryout. I'm going to give that a go. And if it doesn't work out, I have some other interesting prospects."

She pushed up onto her toes and kissed him softly. "I don't care what you do or where we live. I don't ever want to be away from you again. I—I think I might love you."

Brody chuckled softly. For now, he was happy with a vague statement of love. He could wait for her feelings to grow stronger. "I think I might love you, too. A lot."

He grabbed her hand, then pulled it to his lips. "So, what are we going to do with ourselves?"

"Mary's making dinner. We could eat and then go for a swim."

"Aren't you tired? You've been on a plane for the better part of four days."

"About seventy hours," she said. "I've taken off and landed sixteen times."

"Then I definitely think you need to get to bed. Right now. For your own health. And mine." He glanced over his shoulder. "We could head over to the shack and spend the night there."

"But we're not lost. And that would be trespassing."

Brody smoothed his thumb over her lower lip. "This all started with a life of crime. I think we can live dangerously."

Payton threw her arms around his neck. "Forget about nice. I'm really starting to enjoy dangerous."

He wrapped his hands around her waist and set her back on her horse, then remounted. As they rode toward the sunset, Brody wondered at how his life had changed so much in such a short time. There were no answers to his questions, and maybe there never would be. But Payton was here, with him, from half a world away.

This hadn't been his dream, but it was now. And it was better than any dream he could have ever imagined for himself.

* * * * *

THE MIGHTY QUINNS: TEAGUE

BY
KATE HOFFMANN

To Dr Greg B., DVM, for his insights on
equine veterinary medicine.
And for taking such good care of
Chloe and Tally!

Prologue

Queensland, Australia—August 1996

TEAGUE QUINN STRETCHED his arms over his head and closed his eyes against the sun, the warm rays heating the big rock beneath him. The wind rustled in the dry brush. The sounds of the outback were so familiar they were almost like music to him.

He'd managed to escape the house before anyone noticed he was gone, saddling his horse and riding out in a cloud of dust, the shoe box tucked under his arm. When he wasn't working the stock with his father and brothers, he was tending to some other job his mother had conjured out of thin air. He wondered what it might be like to live a normal life, in a grand house in Brisbane, where daily chores didn't exist.

There'd be girls and parties and school and sports— all the things fourteen-year-old boys were supposed to enjoy. Teague sighed. Most boys his age didn't like school, but real classrooms with real teachers, chemistry and biology and physics and math, these were things he'd never experienced.

Instead, Teague was stuck on a cattle station in Queensland, with his parents, his two brothers and a rowdy bunch of jackaroos. Classes took place at the kitchen table, him and his brothers gathered around the radio listening to School of the Air. The closest town, Bilbarra, had a library and a small school, but that was a two-hour drive, much too far to make it practical day to day. Some of the kids on the more profitable stations were sent away to boarding school, but Kerry Creek wasn't exactly swimming in cash. Though the Quinn family wasn't poor, they weren't in the big bickies, either.

Teague heard the sound of hoofbeats and pushed up on his elbows, scanning the approach to the big rock and cursing to himself. Would he ever be able to get away from his brothers, or would they be following him around the rest of his life?

When he didn't see a rider coming from the direction of the homestead, he glanced over his shoulder and watched as a horse galloped full bore from the opposite direction, its rider hunched low in the saddle. Scrambling to his feet, Teague stood on the rock, ready to defend his territory against the interloper.

The boy drew his horse to a stop, the animal breathing heavily. From beneath the brim of a battered stockman's hat, he stared at Teague, a grim expression on his face. He wasn't very big, Teague mused, sizing up his chances if it came down to a fistfight.

But then suddenly, the boy smiled. "Did I scare you?" In one smooth motion, he brushed his hat from his head and a tumble of wavy blond hair revealed not a boy, but a girl. His breath caught in his throat as he stared into her pale blue eyes. Teague swallowed hard. She was the most beautiful girl he'd ever seen.

"I scared the piss out of you, didn't I? You should see your face. You're as pale as a ghost."

Teague scowled, embarrassed that she'd noticed his reaction. "Nick off. I wasn't scared. Why would I be scared of a mite like you? You couldn't knock the skin off a rice pudding."

She slid off her horse. "Oh, yeah. Well, you're so stupid, you couldn't tell your arse from a hole in the ground."

Teague opened his mouth, shocked to hear that kind of language from a girl. But then, he really had no experience talking to girls. With no sisters, he wasn't sure how girls were supposed to talk. On the telly, they always seemed to act so proper and prissy. This girl was acting more like his brothers.

She hitched her hands on her waist and stared up at him. "Well, are you going to give me a hand up or are you going to be mingy about the view?"

Teague studied her for a long moment. There wasn't much to fear from her. She was at least a head shorter than him and a few stone lighter. Though, in a verbal sparring match, she'd probably slice him into dinner for the dingoes. He reluctantly held out his hand and pulled her up beside him.

She scrambled to her feet and took a good look around. A frown wrinkled her brow, then she plopped down and sighed deeply.

"You don't like the view?"

She shook her head. "I thought I might be able to see the ocean."

Teague laughed, but when he saw the hurt in her eyes, he realized the depth of her disappointment. "Sorry," he mumbled as he sat down beside her. "You can't see the ocean from anywhere on this station. Even if you get up to the highest point. It's too far away."

She cursed beneath her breath before turning away from him. "I used to live near the ocean. I could see the water every day. I wish I could see it again."

A long silence grew between them. "That must have been nice," he finally ventured.

"It was better than living out here. Everything is so…dusty. And there are flies everywhere."

"Yeah, but you don't get to ride horses in the city," Teague offered, surprised to find himself defending the outback. "Or keep cattle. Or have a lot of dogs. And you don't see lizards and 'roos like you do here."

"You like animals?" she asked, her disappointment forgotten as suddenly as it had appeared.

Teague nodded. "Last month I found a bird with a broken wing. And I healed it." He pointed to the box beside him. "I'm going to let it go today."

"Can I see?" she asked, bending over the box.

Teague picked the box up, said a silent prayer, then lifted the lid. The sparrow immediately took flight and the girl clapped her hands as it flew into the distance. He felt his cheeks warm. "Maybe it healed itself. It's only a sparrow, but I kept it alive until it could fly again. I find hurt animals all the time and I know how to make them well again." He paused. "I like doing that."

A tiny smile tugged at her lips. "All right, there is one good thing about living on Wallaroo."

Teague swallowed hard, wondering if she'd just paid him a compliment. Then her words sank in. "You live on Wallaroo?" He hadn't even considered the possibility. But now that he thought about it, this was the girl his parents had had been talking about. "You're Hayley Fraser, then."

She seemed surprised he knew her name. "Maybe," she replied.

He'd heard the story by way of eavesdropping. Hayley's parents had been killed in an auto wreck when she was eight years old. She'd been moved from foster home to foster home, until her grandfather had finally agreed to take her. According to Teague's mum, old man Fraser hadn't been on speaking terms with his only child since Jake Fraser had run away from home at age eighteen. And now, his poor granddaughter was forced to live with a cold, unfeeling man who'd never wanted her on Wallaroo in the first place.

Teague's mum had insisted that Wallaroo was no place for a troubled young girl to grow up, without any women on the station at all, and with only rowdy men to serve as an example. Yet there was nothing anyone could do for her. Except him, Teague mused.

"You ride pretty good," he said. "Who taught you?"

"I taught myself. It doesn't take much skill. You hop on the horse and hang on."

"You know your granddad and my father are enemies. They hate each other."

Hayley blinked as she glanced over at him. "No surprise. Harry hates everyone, including me."

"You call him Harry?"

She shrugged. "That's his name."

Teague felt an odd lurch in his stomach as his eyes met hers. She had the longest eyelashes he'd ever seen. His gaze drifted down to her mouth and suddenly, he found himself wondering what it might be like to kiss such a bold and brave girl.

"It's because of that land right over there," Teague said, pointing toward the horizon. "It belongs to Kerry Creek, but Har—your grandfather thinks it belongs to him. Every few years old man Fraser goes to court and tries to take it back, but he always loses."

"Why does he keep trying?"

"He says that my great-grandfather gave it to his father. It's part of the Quinn homestead, so I don't know why any Quinn would ever give it away. I think your grandfather might be a bit batty."

Hayley turned and looked in the direction that he was pointing, apparently unfazed by his opinion of her grandfather. "Who'd care about that land? There's nothing on it."

"Water," he said, leaning closer and drawing a deep breath. She even smelled good, he mused. He reached up and touched her hair, curious to see if it was as soft as it looked, but Hayley jumped, turning to him with a suspicious expression.

"What are you doing?"

"Nothing!" Teague said. "You had a bug in your hair. I picked it out."

She sighed softly. "I better get home. He'll wonder where I am. I have to get supper ready."

Teague slid off the rock, dropping lightly to his feet. Then he held his hands up and Hayley nimbly jumped down. His hands rested on her waist as Teague took in the details of her face, trying to memorize them all before she disappeared.

Hayley quickly stepped away from him, as if shocked by his touch. "Maybe I'll see you again," she murmured, looking uneasy.

"Maybe. I'm here a lot. I guess if you came out tomorrow night after supper, you might see me."

"Maybe I would." She glanced up at him through thick lashes and smiled hesitantly. Then she gave him a little wave and ran to her horse. Teague held his breath as she hitched her foot in the stirrup and swung her leg over the saddle. "So what's your name?" she asked as she wove the reins through her fingers.

"Teague," he said. "Teague Quinn."

She set her hat on her head, pushing it down low over her eyes. "Nice to meet you, Teague Quinn." With that, Hayley wheeled the horse around and a moment later, she was riding back in the direction from which she'd come.

"Shit," he muttered. Now he knew exactly what his mother had been talking about when she'd insisted that someday he'd meet a girl who would knock him off his feet.

"Hayley Fraser." He liked saying her name. It sounded new and exciting. Someday, he was going to marry that girl.

1

THE DUST FROM the dirt road billowed out behind
Teague's Range Rover. He glanced at the speedometer,
then decided the suspension could take a bit more abuse.
Adding pressure to the accelerator, he fixed his gaze
down the rutted road.

He'd finished his rounds and had just landed on the
Kerry Creek airstrip when the phone call had come in.
Doc Daley was in the midst of a tricky C-section on Lanie
Pittman's bulldog at the Bilbarra surgery, and needed him
to cover the call. It was only after Teague asked for details
that he realized his services might not be welcomed. The
request had come from Wallaroo Station.

The Frasers and the Quinns had been at it for as long
as he could remember, their feud igniting over a piece
of disputed land—land that contained the best water
bore on either station.

In the outback, water was as good as gold and it was
worth fighting for. Cattle and horses couldn't survive
without it, and without cattle or horses the family station
wasn't worth a zack. Teague wasn't sure how or why the
land was in dispute after all these years, only that the fight

never seemed to end. His grandfather had fought the Frasers, as had his father, and now, his older brother, Callum.

But all that would have to be forgotten now that he was venturing into enemy territory. He had come to help an animal in distress. And if old man Fraser refused his help, well, he'd give it anyway.

As Teague navigated the rough road, his thoughts spun back nearly ten years, to the last time he'd visited Wallaroo. He felt a stab of regret at the memory, a vivid image of Hayley Fraser burned into his brain.

It had been the most difficult day of his life. He'd been heading off into a brand-new world—university in Perth, hundreds of miles from the girl he loved. She'd promised to join him the moment she turned eighteen. They'd both get part-time jobs and they'd attend school together. He hadn't known that it was the last time he'd ever see her.

For weeks afterward, his letters had gone unanswered. Every time he rang her, he ended up in an argument with her grandfather, who refused to call her to the phone. And when he finally returned during his term break, Hayley was gone.

Even now, his memories of her always spun back to the girl she'd been at seventeen and not the woman she'd become. That woman on the telly wasn't really Hayley, at least not the Hayley he knew.

The runaway teenager with the honey-blond hair and the pale blue eyes had ended up in Sydney. According to the press, she'd been "discovered" working at a

T-shirt shop near Bondi Beach. A month later, she'd debuted as a scheming teenage vixen on one of Australia's newest nighttime soap operas. And seven years later, she was the star of one of the most popular programs on Aussie television.

He'd thought about calling her plenty of times when he'd visited Sydney. He'd been curious, wondering if there would be any attraction left between them. Probably not, considering she'd dated some of Australia's most famous bachelors—two or three footballers, a pro tennis player, a couple of rock stars and more actors than he cared to count. No, she probably hadn't thought of Teague in years.

As he approached the homestead, Teague was stunned at the condition of the house. Harry Fraser used to take great pride in the station, but it was clear that his attitude had changed. Teague watched as a stooped figure rose from a chair on the ramshackle porch, dressed in a stained work shirt and dirty jeans. The old man's thick white hair stood on end. Teague's breath caught as he noticed the rifle in Harry's hand.

"Shit," he muttered, pulling the Range Rover to a stop. Drawing a deep breath, he opened the window. His reflexes were good and the SUV was fast, but Harry Fraser had been a crack shot in his day. "Put the gun down, Mr. Fraser."

Harry squinted. "Who is that? State your name or get off my property."

"I'm the vet you sent for," Teague said, slowly realizing that Harry couldn't make him out. His eyesight was clearly failing and they hadn't spoken in so many years there was no way Harry would recognize his voice. "Doc Daley sent me. He's in the middle of a surgery and couldn't get away. I'm…new."

Harry lowered the rifle, then shuffled back to his chair. "She's in the stable," he said, pointing feebly in the direction of one of the crumbling sheds. "It's colic. There isn't much to do, I reckon." He waved the gun at him. "I'm not payin' you if the horse dies. Got that?"

They'd discuss the fee later, after Harry had been disarmed and Teague had a chance to examine the patient. He steered the Range Rover toward the smallest of the old sheds, remembering that it used to serve as the stables on Wallaroo. Besides that old shack on the border between Wallaroo and Kerry Creek, the stables had been one of their favorite meeting places, a spot where he and Hayley had spent many clandestine hours exploring the wonders of each other's bodies.

Teague pulled the truck to a stop at the wide shed door, then grabbed his bag and hopped out. The shed was in worse condition than the house. "Hullo!" he shouted, wondering if there were any station hands about.

To his surprise, a female voice replied. "Back here. Last stall."

He strode through the empty stable, each stall filled with moldering straw. A rat scurried in front of him and he stopped and watched as it wriggled through a hole in the wall. While the rodent startled him, it was nothing compared to the shock he felt when he stepped inside the stall.

Hayley Fraser knelt beside a horse lying on a fresh bed of straw. She was dressed in a flannel shirt and jeans, the toes of her boots peaking out beneath the ragged hems of her pant legs. They stared at each other for a long time, neither one of them able to speak. It wasn't supposed to be like this, Teague thought, his mind racing. He'd always imagined they'd meet on a busy street or in a restaurant.

Suddenly, as if a switch had been flipped, she blinked and pointed to the horse. "It's Molly," she said, her voice wavering. "I'm pretty sure she has colic. I don't know what else to do. I can't get her up."

Teague stepped past Hayley and bent down next to the animal. The mare was covered with sweat and her nostrils were flared. He stepped aside as the horse rolled, a sign that Hayley's diagnosis was probably right. Teague stood and reached into the feed bin, grabbing a handful of grain and sniffing it. "Moldy," he said, turning to Hayley.

"I got here last night," she explained, peering into the grain bin. "When I came in this morning she was like this."

"She might have an impaction. How long has she been down?"

"I don't know," Hayley said. "I found her like this at ten this morning."

Teague drew a deep breath. Colic in horses was tricky to treat. It could either be cured in a matter of hours or it could kill the horse. "We need to get her up. I'll give her some pain medication, then we'll dose her with mineral oil and see if that helps."

"What if it doesn't?" Hayley asked. "What about surgery?"

Teague shook his head. "I can't do surgery here. And the nearest equine surgical facility is at the university in Brisbane."

"I don't care what it costs," she said, a desperate edge to her voice. "I don't care if I need to charter a jet to fly her there. I'll do whatever it takes."

He chuckled softly at the notion of putting the horse on a jet. "We'll cross that fence when we come to it," Teague murmured. "Help me get her up."

It took them a full ten minutes of tugging and prodding and slapping and shouting before Molly struggled to her feet, her eyes wild and her flanks trembling. The moment she got up, she made another move to go down and Teague shouted to distract her, slapping her on the chest and pushing her out of the stall.

He handed the lead to Hayley. "Keep her walking, don't let her go down again. I've got to fetch some supplies."

Teague ran toward the stable door, then glanced over his shoulder to see Hayley struggling with the mare. Thank God they had this to focus on, he mused. It was difficult enough seeing her again without demanding answers to his questions and explanations for her behavior.

He opened up the tailgate on the Range Rover and searched through the plastic bins until he found a bag of IV fluid, which he shoved in his jacket pocket. He took a vial of Banamine from the case of medication. Then he grabbed the rest of the supplies he needed—a hypodermic, IV tubing, a nasogastric tube and a jug of mineral oil—and put everything into a wooden crate.

When he got back to the stable, he saw Hayley kneeling on the dirty concrete floor with Molly lying beside her.

She looked up, tears streaming down her cheeks. "I couldn't stop her. She just went down."

Teague set the crate on a nearby bale of straw, then gently helped Hayley to her feet. In all the years he'd known her, he'd never seen Hayley cry. Not a single tear, not even when she'd fallen from her horse or scraped her knee. He'd never thought much about it until now, but it must have taken a great deal of strength to control her emotions for so long.

"Don't worry," he said, giving her hands a reassuring squeeze. "We'll get her up."

Then he brushed the pale hair from her eyes, his thumbs damp from her tears. It had been so long since he'd touched her, so many years since he'd looked into those eyes. But it seemed like only yesterday. All the old feelings were bubbling up inside him. His instinct to protect her had kicked in the moment he looked into her eyes and he found himself more worried about Hayley than the horse.

Teague didn't bother to think about the consequences before kissing her. It was the right thing to do, a way to soothe her fears and stop her tears. He bent closer and touched his lips to hers, gently exploring with his tongue until she opened beneath the assault.

Cupping her face in his hands, he molded her mouth to his, stunned by the flood of desire racing through him. They were teenagers again, the two of them caught up in a heady mix of hormones they couldn't control and emotions they didn't understand.

He drew back and smiled. "Better?" Hayley nodded mutely and Teague looked down at the horse. "Then let's get to work."

It was as if the kiss had focused their thoughts and strengthened their bond. Though he wanted to kiss her again, he had professional duties to dispatch first. And saving Molly was more important than indulging in desire. They managed to get the horse on her feet again and pushed her up against a wall to keep her still as Teague inserted the IV catheter into her neck. Drawing out a measure of the painkiller, he injected it into the IV bag.

"There. She should start feeling a little better. Once she does, we'll dose her with mineral oil. If it's an impaction, that should help."

They walked back and forth, the length of the stable, both of them holding on to Molly's halter. At each turn, he took the time to glance over at her, letting his gaze linger.

Without all the slinky clothes and the fancy makeup and hair, she didn't look anything like a television star. She looked exactly like the fresh-faced girl he used to kiss and touch, the first girl he'd ever had sex with and the last girl he'd ever loved. Teague clenched his free hand into a fist, fighting the urge to pull her into his arms and kiss her again.

"So you got home yesterday," he said.

Hayley nodded, continuing to stare straight ahead. He could read the wariness in her expression. If she was feeling half of what he was, then her heart was probably pounding and her mind spinning with the aftereffects of the kiss they'd shared.

"I've seen you on telly. You've become quite a good actress." This brought a smile, a step in the right direction, Teague thought. "I heard you won some award?"

"A Logie award. And I didn't win. I've been nominated three times. Haven't won yet."

"That's good, though, right? Nominated is good. Better than not being nominated."

"It's a soap opera," she said. "It's not like I'm doing Shakespeare with the Royal Queensland."

"But you could, if you wanted to, right?"

Hayley shook her head. "No, I don't have any formal training. They hired me on *Castle Cove* because I looked like the part. Not because I could act."

He wanted to ask why she had decided to run away from home. And why she hadn't come to him as they'd always planned. Teague drew a deep breath, then stopped. Molly had settled down, her respiration now almost normal. "See, she's feeling better," he said, smoothing his palm over the horse's muzzle. "That's the thing with colic. One minute the horse is close to death and the next she's on the mend. Have you ever twitched a horse?"

Hayley shook her head. "I don't want you to do that. It will hurt her."

"It looks painful, but it isn't if it's done properly. It's going to release endorphins and it will relax Molly so she won't fight the tube."

"All right," she said, nodding. "I trust you."

Three simple words. *I trust you*. But they meant the

world to him. After all that had happened between them, and all that hadn't, maybe things weren't so bad after all.

As they tended to Molly, they barely spoke, Teague calmly giving her instructions when needed. Hayley murmured softly to keep her calm, smoothing her hand along Molly's neck. Once the mineral oil was pumped into the horse's stomach, Teague removed the tube and the twitch and they began to walk her again.

"She is feeling better," Hayley said. "I can see it already." She looked over at him. "Thank you."

Teague saw the tears swimming in her eyes again and he fought the urge to gather her into his arms and hold her. The mere thought of touching her was enough to send a flood of heat pulsing through his veins.

He'd kiss Hayley again, only this time it wouldn't be to soothe her fears, but to make her remember how good it had been between them. And how good it could be again.

HAYLEY STARED OUT at the setting sun, her back resting against the side of the stable. A bale of straw served as a low bench. Teague sat beside her with his long legs crossed in front of him and his stockman's hat pulled low to protect his eyes from the glare.

They'd spent the last hour walking Molly around the stable yard, and to Hayley's great relief, the mare seemed to be recovering quite well. Hayley wanted to throw herself into Teague's arms and kiss him silly with gratitude. But she knew doing that would only unleash feelings that had been buried for a very long time—feelings that could sweep them both into dangerous waters.

She'd already turned into an emotional wreck over Molly. Since she'd returned to Wallaroo, she'd rediscovered her emotional side. It had disappeared after her parents died, when she'd stubbornly refused to surrender to sorrow or pain. But in these familiar surroundings, her past had slowly come back and she'd found herself grieving, for her parents' deaths, for her difficult adolescence and for her fractured relationship with Harry.

There was no telling what might happen if she and Teague revisited their past. With so many unresolved feelings, so many mistakes she'd made, she'd likely cry for days.

Now, it seemed so clear, his leaving. He'd been going off to university, starting his life away from home. But at the time she'd seen it as a betrayal, a desertion. Though she'd known he'd be back, Hayley's insecurities had overwhelmed her without Teague to help hold them in check.

From the moment she'd met Teague, she'd found a home, a family and someone she could trust. She'd come to depend on him. He had been the only person who loved her, the only person who cared that she existed and suddenly he was gone. She'd been angry. And though she'd tried to tell herself she'd be all right on her own, she'd been terrified.

So she'd run, away from the place that held so many memories, away from the boy who might not want to return.

She snuck a glance at him. He'd grown into a handsome man. Working in television, she'd met a lot of good-looking blokes, but none of them possessed Teague's raw masculinity. Teague Quinn was a flesh-and-blood man, seemingly unaware of the powerful effect he had on women.

"She looks almost frisky," Teague commented, nodding toward the horse.

"I don't know how I'll ever be able to thank you," Hayley said.

"Don't worry. I'm glad I could help. I know how much Molly means to you. I remember the day you got her."

"My sixteenth birthday," Hayley said. "My grandfather was never one for birthday celebrations. He'd shove money into my hand and tell me not to spend it on silly things. And then, he gave me Molly and I thought everything had changed."

"You rode her over to Kerry Creek to show me. You looked so happy, I thought you'd burst. You immediately challenged me to a race."

"Which I won, as I remember."

"Which I let you win, since it was your birthday. You were such a wild child. Looking back, I wonder how you managed to survive to adulthood. Remember when you were determined to jump the gate near the shack? You were sure Molly could do it. You even bet me my new saddle against your Christmas money."

"That wasn't my finest hour," Hayley admitted, wincing.

"She stopped dead and threw you right over the gate. It took a full minute for the dust to clear from your fall. And what about that time you decided to try bull riding?"

"Another embarrassing failure," she said with a giggle. "But at least I tried. You didn't."

"You were crazy. But I thought you were the most exciting girl I'd ever seen. You were absolutely fearless." He paused, then reached out and touched her face. "What's going on here, Hayley?"

She turned away, staring out at the horizon. "What do you… I don't know what you mean." Was he talking about the kiss? About the attraction that they still obviously felt for each other?

"Look at this place. It's a bloody mess. He's feeding your horse moldy grain. And she doesn't look like she's been exercised or groomed in weeks. Your grandfather used to take such pride in the place."

"I—I didn't know it was getting this bad," she said, grateful that she wouldn't have to analyze the kiss. "I haven't been home for three years. I thought Benny McKenzie was taking care of everything. I was sending money and they were cashing the checks. But then, I spoke to Daisy Willey last week and she told me Benny's mother had taken sick and Benny had left to tend to her. He's been gone a month. But this couldn't have all happened in a month."

"What about the other stockmen?"

"There are no others. My grandfather ran them all off. He thought they were lazy and not worth their pay. And when there was no one left to care for the stock, he sold it. Molly is the last animal on Wallaroo, besides the rabbits and kangaroos and dingoes." She forced a smile. "I'm going to try to convince him to sell the station. Or maybe lease out the land. His health is bad, he's still smoking and he hasn't been to a doctor since I came to live on the station thirteen years ago."

"You're not going to get him off this station," Teague said.

"I have to try," she said, her voice tinged with resignation. "And if I succeed, I want you to take Molly and find her a good home."

Teague nodded. "But until then, I'll bring some decent feed from Kerry Creek when I stop by tomorrow to check on her."

"You're coming back?" Hayley asked, unable to ignore the rush of excitement that made her heart flutter. She'd see him again. And maybe this time, she wouldn't be weeping uncontrollably.

"Follow-up visit," he said. "It's part of the service."

Joy welled up inside her and Hayley couldn't help but smile. Her arrival on Wallaroo had brought nothing but sorrow. And though she knew it would be best to get her grandfather off the station, she'd thought that selling the land would cut her last connection with the boy she'd once loved.

Now that connection was alive again. He was here with her, touching her and kissing her and making her feel as though they might be able to turn back the clock. "Thank you," she said again.

"You need to exercise her," Teague suggested. "Easy at first. A nice gentle walk. You could always ride out to the shack. That's not too far."

Surprised by the suggestion, Hayley couldn't help but wonder if it was an invitation. The shack had been their secret meeting place when they were teenagers. The place where they'd discovered the pleasures of sex.

"Maybe I'll do that."

"I mean, I don't know how long you're planning to stay, but—"

"I don't know, either," Hayley said. "My plans are… flexible. A week or two, at least."

This seemed to make him happy. He looked at his watch. "I really should go. Don't feed her tonight. Just water. I'll see you tomorrow."

She quickly stood up, wanting him to stay but unable to give him a good reason. "Tomorrow," she repeated. Hayley glanced down, wincing inwardly. There were so many things she needed to say, but now didn't seem like the right time. She looked up to find him staring at her. And then, acting purely on impulse, she pushed up onto her toes and kissed his cheek.

She slowly retreated, embarrassed that she'd shown him a hint of the emotions roiling inside her. But then, an instant later, Teague crushed her to his chest, his mouth coming down on hers in a desperate kiss.

In a heartbeat, her body came alive, her pulse quickening and her senses awash with desire. He was so familiar, and yet this was much more powerful than she'd remembered. Her knees wobbled but he was there to hold her.

They stumbled until she was pressed against the rough siding of the stable. His hands drifted lower, cupping her backside and pulling her hips against his. Hayley felt herself losing touch with reality. How many times had she dreamed of this moment? Over the years, she'd wondered what it might be like if they saw each other again. And now, the time had come and she wanted to remember every single second, every wild sensation.

Hayley clutched his shirt, fighting the urge to tear at the buttons. She wanted nothing more than to shed her clothes and allow him to have his way with her. She knew, just by the effects of his kiss, what he could do to her. It had been so long since she'd felt such unbridled passion. Was Teague the man she'd been waiting for all this time?

His palm slid beneath her shirt and up to her bare breast and she arched closer. Cupping her warm flesh, Teague ran his thumb over her nipple until it grew hard. God, it felt so good to have his hands on her body again. All the years between them seemed to drop away and the world was right again.

Hayley worked at the buttons of his shirt and when she pressed her hand against his chest, she could feel his heart pounding in a furious rhythm. "Make love to me," she pleaded.

Her plea seemed to take him by surprise and he stepped back and stared down into her eyes, as if searching for proof that she'd spoken at all. She saw confusion mixed with his desire. Had she made a mistake? Had she moved too fast?

"Hayley! Where are you, girl?"

The sound of her grandfather's voice shocked her

into reality. She quickly straightened her clothes and brushed her hair from her eyes. "Here," she called.

Teague reached for the buttons of his shirt as she turned to wait for her grandfather in the doorway of the stable. "We're watching Molly," she said with a bright smile. "She's better. See?"

He stepped out into the late-afternoon sun, shading his eyes as he searched the paddock. His eyesight had been failing for years, yet he refused to get glasses. Sometimes his stubbornness was downright silly, she mused. At this moment, though, it was convenient. "Where's that damn vet?"

"I'm here, sir."

Hayley steeled herself for what she knew would be a litany of harsh words between them. A Quinn setting foot on Wallaroo was unthinkable. "Grandfather, I don't think—"

"What's your name, boy?" he demanded.

Teague glanced at Hayley, sending her a questioning look and she frowned. Hayley quickly cleared her throat, stunned that her grandfather hadn't recognized Teague. "His name is Tom," she said. "Tom Barrett."

It was the name of one of the characters on *Castle Cove,* but her grandfather had never seen the program so there wasn't much chance of him recognizing the name.

"Dr. Tom Barrett," Teague said, holding out his hand.

"How much is this going to cost me, Dr. Tom Barrett?" her grandfather asked impatiently, ignoring Teague's hand.

"Don't worry, Harry," Hayley replied. "I'll pay for it. Molly is my horse. My responsibility."

"Suit yourself," the old man muttered. He squinted into the sun, then said something under his breath before turning and walking into the barn. Hayley released a tightly held breath. "He didn't recognize you."

"No," Teague said. "Good thing, since he was waiting on the porch with a rifle when I arrived."

She laughed softly, then shook her head. "I knew his eyesight was bad, but not that bad. For a second there, I thought I'd have to break up a fistfight."

"I think I could have taken him," Teague said. He slipped his arm around her waist, pulling her close. "Meet me tonight," he said. "I'll wait for you at the shack."

"I'm not sure I remember how to get there."

"There'll be a moon." He pointed toward the east paddock. "I'll meet you right there at the far gate. Just like we used to. Nine o'clock. We'll ride over together. Molly needs the exercise."

Never mind what Molly needed, she thought to herself. Hayley needed the touch of Teague's hands and the taste of his mouth, the feel of his body against hers. "What if I can't get away?"

"It's all right," he said. "I've been waiting for almost ten years. Another night isn't going to make much difference." With that, he kissed her again, only this time he lingered over her mouth, softly tempting her with his tongue.

A sigh slipped from her lips and Hayley lost herself in the sweet seduction. Every instinct she had cried out to surrender to him, to be completely and utterly uninhibited with her feelings. "Tonight," Hayley said.

He stole one last kiss, then walked backward into the stable, a wide grin on his face. "I sure am glad to see you again, Hayley Fraser."

At that moment, he looked like the boy she'd loved all those years ago. "Stop smiling at me," she shouted, a familiar demand from their younger years.

"Why shouldn't I smile? I like what I see." He picked up his bag and the crate of supplies and continued his halfhearted retreat.

She rubbed her upper arms, her gaze still fixed on his. When he finally disappeared through the door on the opposite end of the stable, Hayley sighed softly. She'd never expected to feel this way again, like a lovesick teenager existing only for the moments she spent with him.

She knew exactly what would happen between them that night and she had no qualms about giving herself to Teague. Of all the men she'd dated, he was the only one she'd ever really loved. And though time and distance had come between them, they were together now. And she was going to take advantage of every moment they had.

2

"WHAT DO YOU WANT to drink?"

Teague glanced up from the plate that Mary had placed in front of him. "Whatever you've got," he replied distractedly. "Beer is good."

She opened the refrigerator and pulled out a bottle, then twisted off the cap with the corner of her apron. Mary had been keeping house at the station for years, hired a few short weeks after Teague's mother had decided that station life was not for her.

He took a long drink of the cold beer, then picked up his fork and dug in to the meal. Dinnertime at the station was determined by the sun. When it set, everyone ate. But Teague had missed the usual stampede of hungry jackaroos tonight. The return trip from Wallaroo had taken longer than he'd planned after he stopped to fix a broken gate.

"Where is everyone?" he asked.

Mary shrugged. "Brody took some dinner out to Payton earlier. And Callum and Gemma disappeared after they helped me with the dishes. They said they were going for a walk." She sat down at the end of the table and picked up her magazine.

"Well?" Teague said. "Aren't you going to offer your opinion? I've met them both and they seem perfectly lovely."

She peered over the top of her magazine. "They add a bit of excitement to life on the station, I'll give them that. At least for Brody and Cal."

Teague chuckled. "Women will do that."

Women could do a lot of things to an unsuspecting man. Since he'd left Hayley at Wallaroo, his thoughts had been focused intently on what had happened between them. He'd replayed all the very best moments in his head, over and over again. The instant that he'd first touched her. The kiss they'd shared. And then the headlong leap into intimacy. His fingers twitched as he thought about the firm warmth of her breast in his palm. "There's nothing wrong with a little excitement every now and then, is there?"

"What about you?" Mary asked, slowly lowering the magazine. "Have you had any excitement in your life lately?"

Teague glanced up. "Excitement?" He chuckled softly. "Are you asking me if I've cleared the cobwebs in the recent past?" Though Mary had served as a mother figure to the three Quinn brothers, she was a bit of a stickybeak, insisting that she know all the relevant facts regarding their personal lives. "Not lately, but I'll let you know if my fortunes change."

She sighed. "I want to see you boys happy and settled."

"Why?" he teased. "So you can get off this godforsaken station and have a life of your own?" Teague watched her smile fade slightly. Mary had always been such a fixture in their lives that they'd hardly considered she might want something beyond her job at the station.

He took another bite of his beef and potatoes, then grabbed a slice of bread and sopped up some of the gravy. "You know, I think it's about time you had a little holiday. I'm going to talk to Callum about it. You could take a week or two and go visit your sister. Or go on a cruise. You could even rent a bungalow on the ocean. Get away from this lot of larrikins."

She shook her head. "There are too many things to be done on the station this time of year. Besides, we have guests. There's not a chance I'd leave those ladies to your care. Now, eat your dinner before it gets cold. My program is on in a few minutes." She stood up and wiped her hands on her apron, then slipped it over her head and hung it across the back of her chair. "Are you going to watch *Castle Cove* with me tonight?"

Teague shook his head. "No, I thought I'd take a ride. There's a full moon and I need to work off some excess energy." He pushed away from the table, then wiped his mouth on his serviette and tossed it beside his plate.

"You barely ate any of your dinner," Mary commented.

"I'm not hungry. Save it for me. I'll eat later." He pulled his saddlebags from the chair next to him, then crossed to the refrigerator. He'd already put the necessities—matches, bottled water, condoms—in the bags. He added a bottle of wine from the fridge and then tossed in a corkscrew from the drawer next to the sink.

He and Hayley had never shared a drink before, but they were old enough now. Maybe she liked wine.

Mary arched an eyebrow. "Do you plan on doing some entertaining tonight?"

"No."

She studied him for a time, then shook her head. "I heard Hayley's back on Wallaroo. But then, I expect you know that already, don't you?"

Teague shrugged, avoiding her glance. "I do. But how did you know?"

"I talked to Daisy Willey today. She called from the library to tell me my books had come in and she mentioned she'd heard Hayley was on her way home. Daisy's cousin, Benny McKenzie, helps take care of the place for old man Fraser, and Benny had to leave to see to his sick mum. So Daisy told Hayley she might want to check up on her grandfather while Benny is gone. Hayley makes a regular donation to the book fund at the library, so she and Daisy keep in touch."

"News travels fast," Teague said.

"Take care," she warned. "You know how your brothers feel about the Frasers. And with the lawsuit heating up again, you don't want to be stuck in the middle. Why Harry Fraser is starting this all over, I don't know."

Teague suspected he knew. If Harry planned to sell Wallaroo, it would be much more valuable with that land attached. "Hayley doesn't have anything to do with that mess," he said. "The land dispute is between Callum and Harry. Besides, I'm a big boy. I know what I'm doing."

"Like that time you did a backflip off the top rail of the stable fence and broke your wrist? As I remember, that was on a dare from Hayley Fraser."

"I'm older now." *But not much wiser,* Teague thought as he slung his saddlebags over his shoulder. He strode to the door and pushed it open, then stepped onto the porch.

He jogged down the steps and headed toward the stables. It was still early and the moon hadn't come up, but he could find his way to the shack blindfolded. When he stepped inside the stable, he flipped on the overhead lights. A noise caught his attention and he squinted to see Callum and Gemma untangling themselves from an embrace.

Gemma tugged at the gaping front of her shirt and Callum pushed her behind him to allow her some privacy. "What are you doing out here?" Callum asked.

"I'm going for a ride." Teague pulled his saddle and blanket from the rack and hauled it toward the paddock door. "Hey there, Gemma."

"Hello, Teague." She peeked around Callum's shoulder and waved. "Nice night for a ride."

He heard Callum mutter something beneath his breath and when he looked back, he saw his brother and Gemma making a quick exit from the stables.

Since the genealogist from Dublin had arrived, Callum had been besotted. Every free moment he could find away from running the station, he spent staring at Gemma. And Brody had brought home a girl of his own, Payton Harwell, a pretty American he'd met in a jail cell in Bilbarra.

Teague threw his saddle over the top of the gate, then whistled for his horse. A few seconds later, Tapper came trotting over, a sturdy chestnut gelding he'd been riding since he'd returned to the station a year ago. He held the horse's bridle as he led it through the gate and into the stable.

It only took a few minutes to saddle his horse and when he was finished, he strapped his bedroll on the back of his saddle, then slipped his saddlebags beneath the bedroll. Every month that he'd been home on Kerry Creek, he'd taken a ride out to the shack. Occasionally, he'd spend the night, sleeping in the same bed where they'd first made love, remembering their sexual curiosity and experimentation.

At least he and Hayley still had a place where they wouldn't be disturbed, a place that would conjure all the best memories. He pulled his horse around and gave it a gentle kick. It had been a long time since he'd felt this optimistic about a woman. And maybe it was silly to think they could return to the way things had been all those years ago. But he hoped they could start over.

As he rode into the darkness, Teague couldn't help but wonder what the night might bring. Would they discuss their past or would they simply live for the moment and be satisfied with that?

HAYLEY STOOD beside Molly, slowly stroking the horse's neck. She'd been waiting in the dark for ten minutes. And for every second of sheer, unadulterated excitement she felt, there was another of paralyzing doubt. Stay, go, wait, escape. She wanted to see Teague again, yet every shred of common sense told her she was setting herself up for heartbreak.

He'd called her fearless. But deep down, Hayley knew that wasn't true. Her childhood bravado had been a way to hide her fears, to divert attention from everything that terrified her. Though she still felt the urge to challenge him, to dare him to prove his devotion to her, she knew better than to risk bodily injury to get his attention, the way she had as a teenager. The only part of her body in peril this time around was her heart.

Over the years, the crazy memories had faded and she'd been left with just Teague, sweet and protective, loyal to a fault. She'd tried to convince herself that they had shared nothing more than a teenage infatuation. They'd discovered sex together and, naturally, there had been a bond between them. But they would have gone their separate ways sooner or later.

Teague had been there to help her through the difficult times. She'd been so confused and angry when she'd arrived on Wallaroo. Her life had been nothing but chaos since the death of her parents, most of the upheaval caused by her rebellious behavior.

Harry had been her only living relative, since her mother was orphaned at a young age, as well. But Harry had refused to take her, and she'd ended up in a series of foster homes. All of them had been fine places, but she'd wanted to be with her grandfather. She'd been constructing a perfect life for the two of them in her mind and was determined to make it happen.

But when he'd finally given in and allowed her to stay at Wallaroo, Harry had wanted nothing to do with her. He was cold and dismissive, barely able to carry on a conversation with her. It had been Teague who had given her a reason to go on with her life, a reason to accept her circumstances and make a place for herself on her grandfather's station—and in Teague's heart.

That's why his desertion had hurt so badly. For months before he'd left for university, she'd tried to tell herself their feelings were strong enough to survive their time apart. And then, after only a few weeks, he'd forgotten her. No letters, no calls. Every letter she'd written had gone unanswered.

Isolated as she was on Wallaroo, she'd assumed the worst of Teague. In the years that had passed after she'd left the station, she'd often wondered what had really happened. Maybe now she would find out the truth.

Hayley had wanted to go to him back then, to demand answers. She'd packed her meager belongings, said goodbye to Molly and hitchhiked as far as Sydney before she ran out of money. After a month there, she'd decided she didn't need anyone to depend upon—or love. She could fend for herself. And in the end, that's where she'd stayed, starting a new life, a life that didn't include anyone who could possibly hurt her.

The sound of an approaching horse caught her attention and she stepped out from behind Molly and peered into the darkness. She held her breath as he came closer, wondering how long it would be before he kissed her again.

Teague maneuvered his horse up next to her, then held out his hand. It had been forever since they'd ridden together. It had been this way when they'd spent nights at the shack. They'd ride out on the same horse, Hayley's body nestled against his so they could talk and touch on the ride home. A few hours before sunrise, Teague would return her to the gate.

He wove Molly's reins through the leather strap on his bedroll, then settled Hayley in front of him. Wrapping his arm around her waist, he gave his horse a gentle kick and they started off at a slow walk.

For a long time, they didn't speak. Hayley felt her heart slamming in her chest and she found it difficult to breathe with Teague so close. She focused her attention on the spot where his arm rested against her belly, shifting back and forth and creating a delicious friction as the horse swayed.

Even after all the time that had passed, this felt safe and comfortable and right. Hayley sighed softly and leaned against him. He nuzzled her neck and she tipped her head to the side to allow him more freedom. His mouth found a bare spot of skin.

Arching against him, Hayley wrapped her arm around his neck, drawing him closer. She was almost afraid to speak for fear she might break the spell that had fallen over her. There was no need to revisit past mistakes and dredge up old resentments. They were here, together, and that was enough.

Teague pressed his palm to her stomach, his fingers splaying across the soft fabric of her T-shirt. But as they continued their silent ride, he slipped his hand beneath her shirt to caress her breast. Hayley inwardly cursed her decision to put on her sexiest underwear. She wanted to feel the warm imprint of his hand on her flesh like she had that afternoon.

The night was chilly and the moon shone golden as it rose over the outback. She had lived so long in Sydney she'd forgotten how desolate it was on Wallaroo—and how incredibly beautiful.

By the time they reached the shack, the silence between them had become part of their growing desire. She didn't need to speak. There'd be time for words later. Teague slid off the horse, then held out his hands for her. Grasping her waist, he held tight as she dropped to the ground. Her breath caught in her throat as he looked down into her eyes. She couldn't read his expression in the dark, but the moonlight outlined his mouth and she fixed her gaze on it, waiting for him to make the first move.

He drew a slow breath, then reached down and ran his fingers through her hair. His lips met hers in a kiss so soft and sweet that it caused a lump in her throat. He took his time, drawing his tongue along the crease of her mouth, teasing until she allowed him to taste more deeply.

Her body pulsed with desire, a current racing through her bloodstream. She shuddered, anticipation nearly overwhelming her.

"Cold?"

Hayley shook her head.

"Scared?"

"Never," she replied, her voice breathless. It was true. She had nothing to fear from Teague. Whatever happened between them, she could handle it.

He took her hand and tucked it inside his jacket, pressing her palm to his chest. "Nervous," he whispered, a smile curling the corners of his mouth.

"It's been a while," she admitted. "For you, too?"

He nodded. Teague took his horse's reins in his other hand and led Hayley toward the shack. He untied Molly's reins and secured both horses to the hitching rail before grabbing his saddlebags. Then he took her hand and they walked up the steps. Hayley paused on the porch. If this shack looked anything like Wallaroo did, she wasn't sure she wanted to go inside.

"It's all right," he said, opening the door.

Hayley waited as he lit an oil lamp. A wavering light filled the shack and she walked inside. Nothing had changed. It was exactly as it had been ten years before. She'd expected cobwebs and dust, but the interior was surprisingly tidy.

"I come out here every now and then and do a bit of housekeeping," Teague said. He set his saddlebags on the small table in the center of the room. "I guess maybe I was hoping I'd find you here one day." He pulled her into his arms. "And here you are."

Teague pushed the door and it swung shut. He slowly drew her jacket down over her arms then tossed it aside. He shrugged out of his own jacket, letting it drop to the rough plank floor behind him.

When he paused, Hayley reached out and began to

unbutton his shirt. She wouldn't be satisfied until they both were naked and lying next to each other in the narrow bed against the wall. As soon as he saw what she wanted, Teague grabbed the hem of his shirt and yanked it over his head.

Hayley's breath froze as she looked at his body in the soft light from the oil lamp. This was no boy. He was Teague, but a different Teague—tall, broad shouldered and finely muscled. Where he'd once had a dusting of hair on his chest, there was now a soft trail from his collarbone to the waistband of his jeans.

Her hand trembled as she smoothed her fingers over his torso. He reached for her T-shirt and pulled it over her head. His gaze immediately dropped to her breasts and he smiled, running his finger beneath the lacy edge of her bra. "Pretty," he said. "I now have hair on my chest and you have expensive underwear."

"I guess we really have grown up," Hayley teased.

Slowly, they continued to undress each other, tossing aside items of clothing one by one. When he was left in his boxers and she in her panties and bra, they stopped. Years ago, she'd always been a bit apprehensive about getting completely naked. It was the only thing that made her feel vulnerable.

But Hayley wasn't a girl anymore. And she wanted to show Teague she was ready to make love to him as a woman, completely free and uninhibited. She reached back and unhooked her bra, then let it slide down her arms. Catching her thumbs in the lacy waistband of her panties, she pulled them down over her hips. Then, without hesitating, she reached over and skimmed his boxers down, his erection springing upright as the waistband passed over his groin.

Hayley straightened and let her eyes drift over his body, taking in all the details. Teague had been a lanky young man, but now he was a fully formed male, with a body that would make any woman weak in the knees.

"God, you are beautiful," he murmured, reaching out to run his hand over her shoulder. "But then, you always were."

"We've both changed," she said.

"One thing hasn't changed," Teague countered. "I still want you as much as I did the first time we made love."

"And I want you," she said.

Teague pulled her against him, soft flesh meeting hard muscle. He was so much taller now, and stronger, and she was surprised by how fiercely he took control. But this was still Teague, still sweet and gentle as he laid her on the bed, then stretched out beside her.

How many times had she fantasized about this? And it had always been the same, the two of them, here in this place, lying naked in each other's arms. Now that her fantasy had come true, she didn't want it to end. Was it possible for the scene to play out again and again, not in her head, but in a brand-new reality?

THE SENSATION OF Hayley's skin meeting his set Teague's desire ablaze. Though he'd often thought back to their times together, he hadn't remembered feeling this incredible. Her skin was silk, her scent like an exotic aphrodisiac. And her body was made to be slowly explored.

Making love with her now would be different from when they were teenagers. They'd both had other partners, and experience was always the best teacher. He stretched out above her, bracing his weight on his hands as he kissed her. But he was like a man parched with thirst. There had been no other women for him, not like Hayley. Desire had been fleeting, something easily satisfied by a one-night stand. But this was much more. As their mouths met again and again, teasing, tasting, he challenged her to surrender.

Her hands smoothed over his face, and every time he drew back, her eyes met his. There was no doubt about what she wanted. Desire suffused her expression, from her damp mouth to her half-closed eyes.

Teague slowly moved his hips and the friction of his cock against her belly sent currents of pleasure shooting through his body. He was hard and ready and longing for the moment when he'd bury himself inside her. But there was no telling how he might react. It felt like the first time, as if every sensation were multiplied a thousand times over. And if he responded as he had that night so long ago, it would be over before it really began.

Her hands drifted down his chest, then grasped his hips, pulling him into each stroke. She moved beneath him, twisting and arching, deliberately taunting him with what she offered. He wanted to take it, right then and there. But Teague fought the impulse and slowly slid down over her body.

The bed was narrow, not made for full-scale seduction. In the end, he knelt beside it, his lips trailing kisses from her belly to her thighs. Everything about her was perfect. This was his Hayley, the girl who had owned his heart for all those years. And yet, she was something more now. She was a woman who had the capacity to break that heart all over again.

Teague didn't care. He didn't care if she disappeared from his life tomorrow. Tonight was all he needed. It was a perfect ending, a way to close the book on all the questions. He would be satisfied and he'd sure as hell make certain she was, too.

Hayley's fingers tangled in his hair as he continued to explore her body with his lips and his tongue. He waited, wanting her to guide him. And when she did, when she drew him to the spot between her legs, Teague didn't hesitate.

He knew exactly how to make a woman writhe with pleasure, how to bring her close to release and then draw her away from the edge. She moaned and whimpered as he took her there, controlling her pleasure with each flick of his tongue.

But Hayley was impatient with the teasing, and every time he slowed his pace, she tightened her grip on his hair. The pain only added to his need to possess her. Teague brought her close one more time, then slid up along her body.

He was breathless now, his need driving him to seek her warmth. She reached down between them to stroke his cock and Teague held his breath, determined to maintain control. He knew he'd have to retrieve a condom, but her touch felt so good that he didn't want her to stop.

She rolled on top of him, her fingers still firmly wrapped around his shaft, then straddled his thighs. Teague watched her as she bent over and placed a kiss on his belly. As she moved up his chest, his fingers tangled in her hair and he relaxed, grateful for the respite.

Yet Hayley wasn't about to stop. She was damp from his tongue and when she shifted above him, he found himself suddenly buried inside her. A tiny gasp slipped from her lips and Teague clutched at her hips, determined to stop her.

He should have known better. When Hayley wanted something, anything, there was nothing that could stand in her way, safety be damned. And it was obvious what she wanted. "Should we stop?" he whispered. "I brought condoms."

"It's all right," she said. "I'm on the pill. And you're the only person I've ever had unprotected sex with."

He smiled. "So are you. We're safe, then."

She didn't answer. Instead, she began to move above him. Hayley braced her hands on his chest, her hair tumbling around her face as she focused on her need. Her eyes were closed and a tiny smile curled the corners of her mouth. Teague watched her, taking in the sheer beauty of her face and body. It was as if she'd been made purely for his eyes. Everything about her was perfect.

Hayley slowed her rhythm, then rose on her knees, until the connection between them was nearly broken.

Then she opened her eyes and moaned as she slowly, exquisitely impaled herself once again. The sensation was more than he could handle and Teague felt himself nearing the edge.

She bent down and kissed him as she repeated the motion. He tried to stop her, holding tight to her hips, but she brushed his hands away, grabbing his wrists and pinning them above his head.

It was no use, Teague mused. She was in control and he had no choice but to enjoy it completely. Her breasts brushed against his chest and he found himself lost in the feeling. He refused to close his eyes, to shut himself off from her beauty.

As Hayley began to increase her rhythm, he knew she was close. He knew her body, her reactions, probably better than she knew herself. He'd taught her how to surrender, how to let go of her inhibitions and fears and experience her first orgasm. The signs were still there— her brow knitted and her bottom lip caught between her teeth.

Teague concentrated on her face, allowing himself to move as she did, closer and closer to the edge. He wanted to share in her release and when the first spasm hit her, he was ready.

She came down on him hard, arching her back as the shudders rocked her body and crying out in pleasure. It came just as quickly to Teague and he grasped her hips as he exploded inside her. He tried to maintain a grip on reality, but the sensation was too overwhelming.

He'd made love to a lot of women since Hayley, but

there was something about being with her that seemed
to go beyond mere physical gratification. When he was
inside her, he felt a connection deeper than shared pleasure and mutual passion. It was like a silent promise
between them, that this intensity, this release, bound
them together forever.

It had been nearly ten years since they'd made love,
with almost as many lovers in between, but here with
her again, time seemed to drop away. He pulled her
down beside him and ran his fingers through her hair.
Hayley kissed him, still breathless, her face flushed and
her lips pliant.

"I guess it's true what they say," she whispered. "It's
just like riding a bike. You never forget how to do it."

3

HAYLEY SNUGGLED into the warmth, floating between sleep and consciousness. She opened her eyes, waiting for her vision to clear before completely comprehending where she was.

It all returned to her in a rush, his body, his touch, the feel of Teague moving inside her. And then the overwhelming pleasure of her release. She had wondered what it might be like between them, now that they were both more experienced. But she'd never anticipated the earth-shattering encounter that they'd shared tonight.

How had she ever believed it would just be sex between them? She'd known her desire for Teague was undeniable, something so powerful it had to be satisfied. But she'd been so sure that, once sated, she'd be able to walk away. After all, they no longer loved each other. And without an emotional attachment, sex should be sex and nothing more. That's how she'd approached all the men in her life since Teague—they were useful for physical gratification, but she wasn't interested in emotional attachments.

Yet now that she was here, all she wanted to do was

stay safe in Teague's arms and in his bed. Hayley drew a shaky breath. This was not the smart choice, she reminded herself. It had taken her years to forget him, or at least put him out of her day-to-day thoughts. And now she'd be forced to fight that battle all over again.

It would be so easy to depend upon Teague, to believe that he'd always be there for her. But they lived completely separate lives now, with miles between them, both physically and emotionally. And the only person she could truly depend upon was herself.

Hayley pushed up on her elbow and stared down into his face in the dim light from the lantern. If she concentrated hard enough, she could push aside her memories of the boy she'd loved and see the man capable of breaking her heart. She was stronger now, independent and in charge of her own life. She had a career and plenty of money to assure her security. Everyone told her she had a future in films. There would be no time for a man in her life.

But all the money and fame in the world could never feel like this, Hayley thought—the pure exhilaration and freedom of being herself, the Hayley she'd been before her role on *Castle Cove* had made her a celebrity. She picked up the edge of the blanket and, holding her breath, slipped out of bed.

The early-morning air was chilly against her naked skin as she tiptoed around the shack retrieving her clothes. The sun was already brightening the eastern horizon and if she wasn't back at the house by the time her grandfather got up, he'd come looking for her.

Hayley dressed quietly, watching Teague as she pulled on her clothes and stepped into her boots. She fought the urge to wake him and kiss him goodbye before she left. But she wasn't sure what to say to him. Perhaps it was better to let this settle in before trying to explain it all.

Shrugging into her jacket, she turned for the door. Molly was tied to the rail next to Teague's horse. She unwrapped the reins, then swung up into the saddle, gently wheeling Molly around and pointing her toward Wallaroo.

Hayley drew a deep breath. Though she enjoyed living in Sydney, there were times when she missed the solitude of the outback. The air smelled sweeter and the sun shone brighter on Wallaroo. Though she'd run away from this place, she still considered the station home.

Hayley glanced over her shoulder, taking one last look at the shack, then prodded Molly into a slow gallop. The horse's step was quick and energetic and Hayley was amazed at how Molly's circumstances had changed from the day before. Once again, Teague had been there to save her from certain disaster, to set things right and to make her happy.

Hayley laughed softly. She'd dreaded her visit to Wallaroo. Since she'd first left, she'd only been back twice. But this trip was different. The last two times she'd returned, she had still been so confused and conflicted. This time, she was ready to accept her life as it was. She tipped her face up and whooped as loud as she could, startling Molly.

Teague had promised to return to the station to check

up on Molly and to bring over some fresh feed. She'd see him again in a few hours and maybe they'd make plans to spend the night at the shack again. "I can handle this," she assured herself.

She could, if she managed to maintain a bit of perspective. She wasn't in love with Teague anymore. They were old friends. Lovers who'd rediscovered each other. There would be no strings, no serious attachments. And when it was time to go their separate ways, they would part without anger or hurt feelings. They weren't teenagers. They were rational, sensible adults.

When she reached the stable, Hayley slid out of the saddle and held the reins, leading Molly inside. To her surprise, her grandfather was waiting, sitting on a bale of hay, smoking a cigarette.

"Where were you?" he demanded.

"I took Molly out for some exercise," Hayley said. "You shouldn't smoke in here, Harry."

How easy it was for her to lie to her grandfather. And to divert his attention by changing the subject. She'd done it throughout her teenage years. But now it bothered her. There was no reason to lie anymore. It was her right to spend the night with a man if she wanted, even if that man was Teague Quinn.

"I can smoke any damn place I want to," he said. "Answer my question."

"I couldn't sleep. I've been worried about Molly all night. I came out here to check on her and I thought I'd take her out for some exercise."

He squinted at her, his expression suspicious. "If

you want breakfast, you're going to have to make it," he muttered.

"I'll be in as soon as I get Molly settled. And you don't have to worry about taking care of her. I'll do that from now on."

"I would think so," he said, pushing up to his feet. "She's your damn horse." He walked off toward the far end of the stable with a stoop-shouldered gait.

"Harry, wait a second. I want to talk to you."

"We can talk at breakfast," he called, continuing his retreat.

"No!" Hayley shouted.

Her grandfather froze in his tracks and slowly turned to face her. She prepared herself for his anger, something that she'd become accustomed to in the past. But she wasn't afraid anymore. This man held no power over her. After all this time, she'd resigned herself to the fact that he'd never love her. So what did she have to lose?

"We need to talk," she said in a measured tone as she straightened her spine. "I've noticed your vision isn't what it used to be. I think it's time you go to the eye doctor and get a prescription for glasses. We're not going to argue about this. There's an optometrist that comes out to Bilbarra once a month. I'm going to take you to see him on Thursday."

"There's nothing wrong with my eyes."

"You've been feeding Molly moldy hay. If you couldn't smell it, you should have been able to see it. The station looks bloody awful, the house is a wreck, the yard is all overgrown and you don't see it. I know you wouldn't want Wallaroo to look like this, Harry. But you can't fix what you can't see."

He scowled. "You don't know what you're talking about, girl."

"I have eyes and, unlike you, I *can* see. So, go into the house and get yourself cleaned up and shaved and I'll make breakfast. From now on, I want you to take more care with your appearance. If I have to look at you over the breakfast table then you're at least going to make an effort to look decent. After breakfast, we're going to talk about getting this station back to rights."

Harry thought about her suggestion for a good ten seconds, then, to Hayley's surprise, gave her a curt nod. He turned and shuffled out of the stable, muttering to himself. Hayley smiled. Things had certainly changed. And maybe it wasn't such a long shot trying to convince her grandfather to move off the station. Her powers of persuasion had obviously improved over time.

"The first battle won. Now for the war," she said. She had to be in Sydney by the end of the month, when she'd film her character's return from a short stay in a mental institution, so she didn't have much time. As long as the station wasn't making money, Harry would continue to fall further and further into debt. No doubt her contributions were covering most of his expenses, but she had no idea how he was paying the taxes—if he was paying the taxes.

Though Wallaroo was a small station, just half the size of Kerry Creek, it was worth millions. At least four million, perhaps more. But Harry couldn't spend a dime of it unless he sold the station. He might be able to lease the grazing land, but he'd still be all alone on Wallaroo, without anyone to watch over him. By selling, he'd have enough money to buy a mansion in Sydney and live out the rest of his life in comfort.

And if he lived close by, she could keep on eye on him, make sure he was taking care of himself. After all, for better or for worse, Harry was the only family she had left.

As she tended to Molly, Hayley's mind wandered to thoughts of the man who'd shared her bed the previous night. There had been a time when she'd considered Teague family. When she'd first met him, he'd been like a brother. And then he'd become her best friend. But gradually, her feelings had changed, shifting from affection to sexual attraction.

Hayley smiled, remembering the confusion those emotions had caused. She could recall the exact moment Teague had gone from best mate to object of lust. She'd been fourteen, Teague fifteen, and it had been only days after his mother had left the station with Brody in tow.

She'd found Teague at the rock and he hadn't seemed to be happy to see her. He'd haltingly explained what had happened and Hayley had been surprised to see tears swimming in his eyes. For the first time since her parents had died, she felt the urge to reach out and touch another human being. She'd put her arm around his shoulders to comfort him and then wrapped him in her embrace.

They'd sat that way for a long time and then, when he'd finally gathered the courage to look at her, she'd done something incredibly stupid—or so it had seemed at the time. She leaned forward and kissed him, square on the lips. In the moments after the kiss, her mind had raced for some way to excuse her behavior. But she hadn't needed one. Teague had stared at her as if she'd suddenly sprouted horns and a tail. His face had gone beet red before he'd scrambled off the rock, jumped on his horse and ridden as fast as he could away from her.

Hayley's lips twitched into a smile at the memory. It was at that moment she'd realized her power over him. How something as simple as a touch or a kiss could render a boy speechless. That night, as she'd lain in bed, Hayley had replayed the day's events in her mind. But she'd come away with only one certainty—things had changed between her and Teague Quinn.

From then on, every time she saw Teague, she experienced a physical reaction. Her heart skipped or her stomach fluttered or her cheeks got all warm. That first kiss had led to many more and, eventually, to a slow experimentation in adolescent desire. The relationship had become their little secret, a secret that, if revealed, could bring an end to their time together.

All those silly feelings had come rushing back the moment she'd seen Teague standing outside Molly's stall. But Hayley wouldn't let herself be swept away by emotions this time. Losing her heart to Teague again was not an option. Sexual attraction did not have to include emotional attachment. She'd managed to prove that with the men who'd recently populated her social life. And she'd prove it with Teague.

Hayley took the porch steps two at a time, then

turned and surveyed the yard of Wallaroo station. She had plenty of work to keep her occupied for the next few weeks and plenty to keep her mind off the man who had made her ache with desire the night before. And when she found denial too difficult to bear, they'd meet at the cabin again for another night of unbridled lust.

She smiled as she pulled the screen door open, a delicious shiver racing through her. How long would it be before she saw him again? And what would happen when she did? The answers to those questions were far too intriguing to consider. For now, she'd focus on breakfast.

"WHERE ARE YOU GOING with that feed? And my ute?"

Teague heaved the bale of hay into the tray of Callum's pickup, then slammed the tailgate shut. "I don't have enough room in the back of my Range Rover. And I'll only be gone a few hours."

"What the hell is going on with you?" Callum asked. "I catch you sneaking in this morning before sunrise and—"

"I wasn't sneaking," Teague said.

"And now you're loading feed into my ute. You could at least tell me where it's going."

"To someone who needs it," Teague muttered. "Charity begins at home." He reached into his back pocket and pulled out his wallet. "All right, how much do I owe you? I'll pay for the bloody feed. I've got three bales of hay, a bag of oats and a bag of the premix."

"You don't have to pay me," Callum said, pushing the

money aside. "Hell, take what you need. I don't care where it's going."

"Thanks, brother," Teague said, patting Callum on the shoulder. "If Doc Daley calls, tell him to ring my satellite phone."

Callum shook his head as Teague hopped into the pickup. If his older brother suspected anything, he wasn't saying, Teague mused. Maybe he didn't really want to know. Callum had inherited their father's distaste for the Frasers and was even crankier now that Hayley's grandfather was making another play for the disputed land.

Of all the Quinns, Teague probably knew Harry Fraser the best, and the old man didn't like to lose, not his money, not his reputation and not his land. Oddly, he didn't seem to care a whole lot about his granddaughter.

Teague turned the ute onto the long, rutted road that led from Kerry Creek to Wallaroo. Though he and Hayley were only a half hour apart over land by horseback, it took a full ten minutes longer than that by road.

As he drove, he picked through his brother's selection of music. Callum had always been a country-music kind of guy, preferring Keith Urban and Alan Jackson. Brody went for hard rock, anything loud and obnoxious. Teague's taste in music leaned toward alternative, little-known bands and singers with interesting lyrics. He managed to find a Springsteen CD in the mix and decided it was the best he'd do. He popped it into the player then sang softly along with the tune.

Just yesterday, he'd taken the same route, his thoughts

filled with memories of Hayley and the time they'd spent together as kids. But now, those thoughts were a pale prelude to what had actually happened between them last night.

He still couldn't believe she was here, within his reach and eager for his touch. She was different, yet she was the same girl he'd fallen in love with all those years ago. The same pale blue eyes, the same honey-colored hair, the same lush mouth and tempting smile.

They hadn't spent much time talking, but there would be time enough for answering all his questions. As he drove, Teague thought about the circumstances that had torn them apart. For months afterward, he'd tried to figure out what he'd done wrong, why it had ended as it had.

But after beating himself up for mistakes he wasn't sure he'd made, Teague realized there had been other forces at work. Maybe her grandfather had driven them apart. Or maybe she'd decided that she didn't love him anymore. Whatever the reason was, he needed to know the real story and Hayley was the only one with the answers.

By the time he reached Wallaroo, Teague had made a mental list of all his questions. He was prepared to take the blame for whatever he'd done wrong and hope that she'd forgive him. As he drove up to the house, he caught sight of her standing on the porch, her hair blowing in the breeze.

The ute skidded to a stop and Teague jumped out, his eyes on Hayley. She hadn't changed in the few hours since he'd seen her last. If anything, she looked more beautiful. Suddenly, all his questions were replaced with an overwhelming need to kiss her. "Hi." The word slipped from his lips like a sigh.

"Hello," she said, a smile playing at her mouth.

Teague took a deep breath and found his voice. "I brought some fresh feed. And I phoned in an order to the feed store in Bilbarra, but they said they wouldn't be able to deliver until later this week. I'll bring more over if you run out."

They stood at a distance, staring at each other, as if afraid to approach. Teague knew that the moment he got within arm's length he'd want to pull her into a long, deep kiss. He glanced around. "Where's Harry?"

"He's inside. I've got him tidying up the house. He's not happy about it, but at least he's not sulking around."

"I'm going to go check on Molly," Teague said, pointing toward the stables. "Do you want to—"

"I'll come with." Hayley bounded down the steps.

He helped her into the ute, then jogged around to the driver's side. As he backed the truck away from the house, Teague glanced over at her, his gaze fixed on her mouth. Kissing her again had become an obsession, something that he couldn't get beyond.

As soon as the truck was far enough from the house, he slammed on the brakes and turned to her. Reaching out, Teague tangled his fingers in the hair at her nape and pulled her toward him. "I missed you," he murmured before bringing his mouth down on hers.

A tiny moan slipped from her lips as he deepened the kiss, his tongue teasing hers. Though the sensation of kissing her was familiar, the passion they'd shared as teenagers was only a fraction of what he felt now. He knew what he could do to her body and what she could do to his.

There was nothing standing in their way now, no silly insecurities or fears of pregnancy. He looked down into her eyes, a frown wrinkling his brow as he thought back to that time. They'd taken a lot of chances when they were younger. Chances that could have changed the courses of both their lives.

"What?" she asked, staring up at him.

Teague shook his head. "Nothing."

She drew a deep breath and forced a smile. "We should check on Molly."

Teague nodded. If they went much further, he'd have to make love to her in the front seat of the ute. Though it might be fun, they certainly could afford to find a more comfortable spot. "How is she doing?" he asked, throwing the pickup into gear and steering toward the stable.

"Good, I think. We had a nice ride back this morning. She doesn't seem to be suffering from any aftereffects of the colic."

"With proper feed, she'll be fine," he said. "And I brought some supplements you can add to her food."

"Thank you. You're a good vet. I knew you would be."

"You always had a lot of faith in me," Teague said, pausing as he stopped the ute at the wide stable doors. "Why didn't you wait?" The question came out before he could stop it. He was afraid to look at her, afraid he'd see anger in her expression.

"I had to get home before Harry woke up," she explained. "And you were sleeping, so—"

"I'm not talking about this morning," Teague said, keeping his eyes fixed straight ahead.

"I—I don't know what you—"

"You know exactly what I mean." He turned to face her, stretching his arm across the back of the seat. "I expected you to be here when I came home. And you were gone. You didn't even bother to let me know where you were."

Hayley stared down at her lap, twisting her fingers together. "I was supposed to wait, I know. And I tried. I was so angry when you left."

"I thought you wanted me to go. You said—"

"What was I supposed to say? I was confused. I thought I could survive alone but as soon as you left, I was…lost. I felt like part of me had been cut away. Once you were gone, there was nothing left for me at Wallaroo, nobody who cared whether I stayed or left."

"But we'd talked about it over and over. I wasn't going to be gone forever. And once you turned eighteen, you could leave on your own and come to Perth."

"My parents were supposed to come home, too, and they never did. I guess I was sure once you left, you'd find someone else, someone smarter, someone prettier. And I didn't want to wait around for that to happen."

"But we made plans, Hayley."

"I know. But the longer you were away, the angrier I got. I wasn't exactly thinking straight. I was confused and scared and a little self-destructive. It's taken three years of therapy to deal with all my rubbish and, believe me, it goes real deep."

"I tried to phone, but Harry wouldn't let me speak to you. And I wrote. Almost every day."

"Harry never told me you'd called, and I never got your letters," she said, frustration filling her voice.

"Would that have made a difference?"

"I don't know. I was in love with you and you left me behind and that's really all I could think about. It was like my parents all over again." She sighed softly. "We can't fix the past, Teague. There's no use talking about it now."

Hayley opened her door and hopped out of the truck. He followed her to where she stood at the tailgate. She picked up a bag of feed and carried it into the stable, and Teague hauled a bale of hay in, as well. An uneasy silence grew between them as he watched her feed Molly.

He sat down on the hay bale, bracing his elbows on his knees, refusing to let the subject die. "Tell me what happened. I mean, I've read the stories in the magazines, about how you were discovered. But tell me."

She stood next to Molly, smoothing her hand along the horse's neck as if it brought her comfort. "I got to Bilbarra hidden in the back of a feed truck. And from there I hitched to Brisbane and then to Sydney. I didn't have any money, so I did odd jobs where I could, mostly washing dishes at restaurants along the way. And then, when I got to Sydney, I found a job at a T-shirt shop on the beach. I lived on the streets and in the parks, in the bus station and the train station. And then one day, this guy walked into the shop and next thing I knew, I was standing in front of a camera, reading lines from a script."

"I came home for semester break and I rode out to

the shack and waited for you. Three days I hung out there. I didn't eat, I didn't sleep. And then Callum told me he'd heard you left Wallaroo two months before. I was...I was scared. Scared I'd never see you again."

"But here I am," she said, glancing over at him.

"That's not what I meant," Teague snapped. She seemed to be so unaffected by what had happened. Surely she must have felt something. She'd walked away from a relationship that had meant the world to him. It wasn't just a teenage crush. He'd loved her. He'd planned his whole life around her. Irritated, Teague stood and strode to the truck, then grabbed another bale of hay.

When he returned to the stall, she was vigorously grooming Molly, wielding the currycomb with careful efficiency. She was angry, too. He knew the signs—the stony silence, the refusal to meet his gaze, the haughty expression.

"I think I have a right to be angry," Teague said.

"I don't know what you want to me to say. I was a kid. I was seventeen. I didn't understand what I was feeling."

"And now?"

Hayley turned to face him, her arms crossed beneath her breasts. "We're both older and wiser. And just because we slept together last night doesn't mean— It doesn't mean anything."

Teague crossed the distance between them. He slipped his hands around her waist and spun her around, pinning her against Molly. His eyes searched her face, then focused on her lips. "I know you, Hayley. Don't forget that. You can't hide from me."

He leaned forward, his mouth hovering over hers, her breath mingling with his. He wanted to kiss her. But he thought better of it. Instead, he let go of her and stepped back. If she was so determined to push him away, then he'd be happy to oblige. "I have to go. I've got calls this afternoon."

"Thanks for the feed," she said.

"No worries."

Teague returned to the ute and dumped the last bale of hay in front of the stable door, then got inside and started the engine. He glanced in the rearview mirror to see Hayley watching him, her chin tilted up in a defensive manner so familiar to him.

She was like one of his wounded birds, so fragile, yet so frantic to escape. He'd been too stupid and naive to see the true depth of her pain when they were younger. But now, he could read it on her face, in the grim set of her mouth and the indecision in her eyes. She was terrified and he knew exactly what was frightening her.

It scared the hell out of him, too—the possibility that what they'd shared all those years ago was real. That the connection between them was still there, as strong as ever. And that she was the only woman he could ever love.

He had his answers now. And yet, Teague found himself plagued with a whole new list of questions.

HAYLEY STARED at the ceiling above her bed, watching a fly crawl across the painted surface. She picked up the script she'd been reading and attempted to finish the page she'd started an hour ago.

The house was silent. Her grandfather usually went to bed immediately after watching the evening news, still keeping stockman's hours even though Wallaroo no longer kept stock. Once the sun went down, there really wasn't much to do…except…

Tossing the script aside, Hayley sat up and brushed her hair out of her eyes. She walked to the bedroom window and looked out into the darkness. It was past ten and the moon hung low in the night sky, softly illuminating the landscape.

Though she and Teague hadn't planned to meet that night, Hayley knew he'd be there waiting. She'd spent the evening devising a litany of excuses not to go to him. Reasons why giving in to her desire was dangerous. But as the night wore on, the reasons became less and less important.

Turning from the window, Hayley retrieved her jeans from a nearby chair. She tugged them on, then stepped into her boots. Her jacket hung on a hook behind the bedroom door. She shrugged into it, buttoning it over her naked breasts, then tiptoed into the hallway.

The stairs squeaked as she made her way down to the kitchen. She slipped out the back door, then ran across the yard toward the stable. Molly's stall was near the door and there was just enough light to see the bridle hanging from the hook on the wall. Hayley grabbed it, went inside and slipped it over the horse's head. But as she reached for the buckle, she felt an arm snake around her waist and lift her off her feet.

She screamed and a hand came down over her mouth.

A moment later, she was outside the stall, twisting against the grasp that held her tight. His grip loosened and she spun around, ready to defend herself. But when his mouth came down on hers, the instinct to fight dissolved, leaving her heart slamming in her chest and her breath coming in shallow gasps.

He didn't say a word and every time she tried to speak, he covered her mouth in another demanding kiss. His palms smoothed over her body, finding bare skin beneath her jacket. Teague turned her around, tucking her against him as kissed her neck.

His touch seemed to be everywhere at once, teasing each nipple to a peak, sliding over her belly, then dipping beneath the waistband of her jeans. He wasn't in any hurry to undress her and in truth, Hayley found the seduction incredibly erotic.

His fingers fumbled with the button at her waist and when it was undone, Teague lowered the zipper. He found the damp spot between her legs and slipped his finger between the soft folds of her sex.

Hayley's breath caught in her throat as desire snaked through her body. Slowly, he caressed her, drawing her closer to the edge while he moved her backside against his hard shaft. They were like teenagers again, too impatient to undress, too desperate to bring each other to release. It was safe, but it was still seduction.

His breath was hot on her neck and she shifted against him, the contact causing a moan to slip from his throat. Hayley wanted to stop, to strip off all their clothes and begin again. But this headlong rush toward completion was impossible to resist.

Her knees grew weak as she lost herself in the pleasure he was providing. Rational thought was replaced by single-minded focus. A burst of sensation spread through her body and then she was there, quivering, waiting, then tumbling over the edge, the spasms too delicious to deny.

She arched back, and his lips found hers, possessing her mouth in the same way he'd taken her body. The orgasm seemed to last forever and Teague wasn't satisfied until she was completely spent and limp in his embrace.

When she could stand on her own again, she turned to face him, ready to return the pleasure that he'd given her. He was still hard, his erection pressing against the faded denim of his jeans. She ran her hand along the length of him and he sucked in a sharp breath.

There were so many ways she could please him, but in the end, she brought him to completion with her fingertips, teasing him, edging him closer and closer, until he came in her hand.

Teague chuckled softly as she continued to stroke him. "The things you do to me," he murmured, nuzzling her neck.

"How long have you been waiting for me?"

"Not long." He brushed her hair away from her temples. "I went out to the shack first and got tired of waiting there. So, I decided to come here and kidnap you out of your bed."

"That would have been exciting," she said. "Although, you may have ended up on the business end of Harry's rifle again."

"It would have been worth it." He looked into her eyes, his features barely visible in the moonlight. "I'm sorry about this afternoon. I shouldn't have gotten angry."

"And I shouldn't have been so irrational. Sometimes, I get a little scared."

"Hayley, you never have to be frightened of me. I would never hurt you."

"You already did," she said. "Once."

"But not deliberately. I was a teenager. I didn't know how you felt. Hell, I couldn't even figure out how I felt. But I think I understand now and I'm sorry I hurt you."

Hayley pushed up on her toes and kissed him softly. "I'm not sure I understand," she said. "But I know we need to be careful. It would be so easy to depend on you again, to feel safe. But I have a life in Sydney and maybe a life in Los Angeles. It wouldn't be a good idea to get all wrapped up in each other."

"Los Angeles?"

Hayley nodded. "My contract with *Castle Cove* is up in September. My agent thinks I could have a career in films, maybe even in Hollywood. He says Australian actresses are hot now. I'm supposed to go there and meet with some casting directors before the end of the month. And he's trying to set up some auditions, as well."

"Los Angeles," Teague repeated. "That's a long way to go for a job. Especially when you have one right here in Australia."

"And the work is good here, don't get me wrong. But if I got a movie, a good movie, then things would change. I'd make more money. My future would be more secure. I wouldn't have to worry. And maybe people would start to see me as a serious actress."

"Is that what you want?"

"I guess. I'm not really qualified to do much else. I didn't go to university. I don't have any other talents or skills. Acting is what I do."

Teague forced a smile. "Then I hope everything works out for you. I mean it, Hayley. I want you to be happy."

"This doesn't mean we can't see each other," she said, reaching up to rest her palm on his cheek. "I just think we should try not to…"

"Fall in love?"

She giggled. Teague didn't mince words. "Yes. Fall in love. I think we should avoid any infatuations. We have to be practical. You have your life and I have mine, and when I leave in a few weeks, everything will return to the way it was."

"But until then, we'll be friends. Friends who might happen to have sex occasionally?"

"Friends with benefits," she said. "I think that's the proper term."

"Ah. So this is a familiar concept to you?"

Hayley shook her head. In truth, she didn't have many friends and certainly no male friends. And the lovers that she'd had were temporary diversions at best. "I've heard it works."

"I'm willing to give it a try."

She held out her hand. "Come with me. I'm sleepy and I want you in my bed."

"Don't you think that's a little risky? With your grandfather in the house?"

"You've slept in my bed before, don't you remember? Two or three times as I recall. The first time was on a dare. You crawled up on the porch roof, then shinnied over to my bedroom window. I'll need to sneak you out before the sun comes up, but we should be safe if you don't act like a yobbo once your clothes come off."

"I can be very quiet," Teague said. "But we're too old to be doing this, Hayley. I don't want to have to watch what I say in bed or sneak out before the sun comes up. If we want to sleep with each other, then we shouldn't need permission."

"We can go back to the shack, then," she suggested.

"That's not exactly five-star accommodations, either," he said. "Hell, I have a plane. We can go anywhere we want."

"No, we can't," she said.

"Why not?"

"Because people recognize me everywhere. Anyone who has a telly knows who I am. My personal life is all over the tabloids. And yours will be, too, if you're seen with me."

"So what do we do?" Teague asked.

"We take what we can get. We ride out to the shack and spend the night together. And in the morning, we go our separate ways."

"Then let's go," he said. "We'll ride out there right now. I want you in my bed tonight."

She wanted to test her resolve, to prove that she could resist if she had to. But in the end, Hayley saddled Molly and they rode out into the moonlight. There'd come a time when she would have to refuse. It wouldn't be tonight. Tonight, she'd give him what he wanted—her body. But she'd take care to keep her heart safe.

4

"DAVEY SAID the colt in the next stall has been sold. He's
beautiful."

Teague watched as Payton Harwell tended to his horse,
cleaning the gelding's hooves with a pick. Since Payton
had arrived on the station a few days before with Teague's
younger brother, Brody, the stable had undergone a make-
over. The tack room was tidy, the stalls clean, the feed
arranged in stacks against the wall. Though Callum
hadn't been enthusiastic about hiring the American,
Teague could vouch that she knew her way around horses.

She moved with an easy efficiency, feeding and
grooming and mucking out the stalls, all in a very
orderly fashion. She wasn't afraid to work hard and
seemed to enjoy what she was doing, curious about the
breeding operation that he oversaw.

"He's going to be trained as a show horse," Teague
said. "Some of our horses are used for polocrosse. And
some for campdrafting."

At any other point in time, he might have been attracted to Payton. She was smart and beautiful and she
seemed to be very well educated. The kind of woman

he ought to want. But there was only one woman who captured his imagination these days.

Funny how a few days with Hayley could change his outlook so completely. He found himself anticipating the end of the day, searching for an excuse to see Hayley again. He'd spent the morning and early afternoon making calls, but he didn't intend to spend the evening alone.

Payton set the horse's hoof onto the concrete floor and straightened, brushing her dark hair out of her eyes. "What's that?"

"Besides Aussie rules football, polocrosse and campdrafting are the only native Aussie sports. Polocrosse is a mix of polo and lacrosse and netball. And I reckon campdrafting is kind of like your rodeo riding. The horse and rider cut a calf from the herd, then they have to maneuver it around a series of posts."

"I'd like to see that," she said.

"I'll take you sometime," Teague promised. "There's a campdrafting event in Muttaburra in August if you're still around."

"I'd like to try it."

"Then I'll teach you."

"Teach her what?"

Teague turned to find Brody standing at his side. Though his brother was smiling, Teague sensed an undercurrent of aggravation. Brody was sweet on the new arrival and wasn't doing much to hide his feelings. "Hey, little brother. Where have you been?"

"I went out with Davey to fix the windmill in the high pasture," Brody replied.

"Good to see you putting in an honest day's work," Teague teased, clapping his brother on the shoulder. He smiled at Payton, then tipped his hat. "I've got a call. I'll see you later, Payton. Maybe you can give me a hand tomorrow morning. I've got vaccinations to do on the yearlings."

"Sure," Payton replied. "I'd be happy to help."

He nodded again. "I think I'll like having you here," he said. Teague turned to Brody. "Have you had all your shots?"

Brody's jaw grew tense and Teague decided to make his exit before his little brother decided to reply with an elbow to the nose. Brody had spent five years playing Aussie rules football on a pro team. Aussie rules was a mix of rugby, soccer and professionally sanctioned assault. There was no question who the toughest of the three Quinn brothers was.

"Don't mind Teague," Brody called as Teague strolled out of the stables. "He has a bad habit of yabbering to anyone who'll listen."

Teague pulled off his gloves and shoved them into his jacket pocket, heading toward the house. He had the evening to himself, with only one call on his agenda, a stop at Wallaroo to see Hayley.

Mary was preparing supper in the kitchen when he walked inside. He tossed his hat on the table and washed his hands in the sink.

"Where have you been?" she asked. "Or maybe I needn't bother asking."

Teague put his finger to his lips. "Let's make this our

secret, eh, Mary? I don't need to listen to any whinging from my brothers about my choice of companions."

"I don't think they're in a place to be complaining," Mary said. "They're a bit preoccupied with their own romances."

"I'm heading out," Teague said. "I'm taking my satellite phone, so if Doc Daley calls, tell him to ring me at that number. And I don't plan to be home for a while."

"You haven't slept in your own bed for the past two nights," she said.

Teague grinned. "Yeah. Well, I'm saving you the trouble of making my bed. You should be happy."

Mary shook her head and laughed. "You take care," she said. "I remember what happened the last time that girl broke your heart. You were impossible to live with."

"No one is going to break anyone's heart," Teague reassured her. He pulled open the refrigerator and searched through the contents. "I thought there was another bottle of wine in here."

"Brody took it last night," she said. "Wine consumption has gone up on the station since the ladies arrived." She opened the cabinet above the sink and pulled out a bottle. "Red. It should be served at room temperature."

Teague leaned over and kissed her cheek. "You're a sweetheart, Miss Mary." He strode out of the kitchen onto the back porch, then crossed the yard to his Range Rover. Callum approached from the opposite direction, wiping his hands on a rag as he walked. Teague slipped the wine into his jacket pocket, pushing the neck of the bottle up his sleeve.

"You leaving?" Callum asked.

"Yeah, I've got to drive into Bilbarra to pick up some medicine from Doc Daley."

Callum frowned. "Why don't you take the plane. You should be able to make it home before dark."

Teague shrugged. "I don't mind the drive. I thought I might spend the night. Do a bit of socializing. Since you and Brody have corralled the only two decent-looking women in this part of Queensland, I'm going to have to look elsewhere."

Callum stared at him for a long moment. "You are so full of shit," he muttered. "Who do you think you're fooling? I know Hayley Fraser is on Wallaroo and I suspect you've been seeing her."

"And what if I am?" Teague asked.

Callum shook his head. "Did you ever think that maybe Harry Fraser is using his granddaughter against us?"

Teague laughed. "I think you've got a few kangaroos loose in the top paddock there, Cal. The land is ours. He'll lose, whether I'm seeing Hayley or not. Unless you think he has a valid claim to the land."

"Doesn't matter what I think," Cal said. "Harry's the one raising a stink. He's gone completely round the bend thinking he'll win. This is costing money to defend ourselves once again. I'm ready to sue him right back for the fortune I've spent on solicitors."

Callum had no idea how close he was to the truth

about Harry. He *had* gone a bit berko. And maybe the lawsuit was part of that. "If you must know, Hayley is trying to convince Harry to sell the station."

Callum gasped. "What?"

"He's out there all by himself. He's got no stock, the place is falling down around him and he's probably spending his last cent trying to get that land back. I don't know what good the land will do him, unless he thinks it will raise his asking price for the station."

Callum frowned, shaking his head. "If you really think Harry will sell Wallaroo, you're the crazy one. The only way Fraser is leaving that station is in a casket."

"Hey, I'm just telling you what I know," Teague said as he pulled open the door on the Range Rover. "Hayley is not involved with what her grandfather is doing. She doesn't give a stuff about that land."

As Teague drove the road to Wallaroo, he thought about Cal's attitude toward Harry Fraser. Callum was a reasonable bloke and he always made decisions after careful thought. But his dislike for Hayley's grandfather seemed completely irrational. Yes, the land was valuable. But if the situation were reversed and Callum thought he'd been cheated out of the land, he would do everything he could to get it back.

What difference did it make? Teague mused. He and Hayley were friends. What Callum and Brody thought about their relationship was irrelevant. And if they became more than friends, then he'd have to deal with that when the time came.

When he got to the house on Wallaroo, he found

Harry sitting on the porch, his feet resting on the railing, his hands folded over his stomach. He sat up straight as Teague leaned out of the window of the Range Rover. "Hello, Mr. Fraser."

"She's in the stables. If you're here to collect on your bill, she's going to pay it. It's her horse."

"No worries," Teague said. "I'm sure she's good for it."

"If you're not back for money, what are you doing here?"

"Just another follow-up call," Teague said.

"Get on with it, then," he said, calling an end to their conversation.

By the time Teague reached the stables, Hayley was headed toward the house. He pulled up beside her and reached out, smoothing his hand along her bare arm. "Get in," he said.

"Where are we going?"

"Out," Teague replied.

"There is no out in the outback. We're already out."

"Well, I have a destination in mind. We'll have a little wine, maybe a bite to eat. After that, maybe we'll see a show." He reached over and opened the passenger-side door. "Come on. We're going to be late."

She gave him a dubious look, but hurried around the SUV and jumped inside. Instead of driving toward the road, Teague drove through the yard and past the stables. The Range Rover bumped along toward the sunset, dust billowing behind them. Teague had seen the landing strip from the air the last time he'd passed over Wallaroo and he wanted to see it up close. When he reached the long, flat stretch, he turned the SUV around, its tailgate facing west.

"What are we doing out here?" Hayley asked.

"The best show in all of Queensland," Teague said as he helped her out. He pointed to the brilliant pinks and purples on the horizon. "We're just in time." Teague opened the tailgate of the Range Rover, then lifted Hayley up to sit on it. Then he retrieved the bottle of wine from behind the driver's seat. "And I brought refreshments."

Hayley smiled. "Is this a date? Are you trying to impress me?"

"Is it working?" Teague asked.

"Yes."

"Then this is a date," he said. He took a corkscrew out of his pocket and opened the wine. "I didn't bring glasses. We'll have to drink out of the bottle."

"It's so much more sophisticated that way," Hayley teased. "That's the way they do it at all the best restaurants in Sydney." She crossed her legs in front of her. "You know, this is our first date. In all the time we knew each other as kids, we never went on a real date. No school dances, no parties. I wish we would have had something like that to remember."

"We'll have this," Teague said.

"Maybe we shouldn't." Hayley sent him a sideways glance. "Maybe we're getting ahead of ourselves. We're so anxious to rekindle a teenage romance that we aren't thinking about the effect it will have on our lives."

"Are you saying you don't want to be with me?" Teague asked.

"No. I'm saying, when this is over, I might not be able to cope with losing you again. I feel happy when I'm with you, Teague. The world seems right."

"You'll always have me," he said. "You don't have to worry over that."

She took a sip of wine, then smiled ruefully. "We'll be eighty years old and I'll show up on your doorstep wondering if our 'friends with benefits' deal is still good."

"And I'll invite you in for a cup of tea and a Vegemite sandwich and we'll watch a nice game show on the telly." He bumped her shoulder with his. "And you'll be wearing some of those sexy stockings that end at the knees and comfortable shoes and a nice hairnet and I won't be able to keep my hands to myself."

"Now you're making me really depressed," she said.

Teague took the wine and set it down beside her. Then he leaned forward and dropped a kiss on her damp lips. "I can make you feel better," he offered. "It's the perfect remedy. Have you ever had sex on the roof of a Range Rover at sunset?"

"I can't say that I have," Hayley answered.

Teague reached into the rear of the SUV and pulled out a blanket, then tossed it over his head. He stood up on the tailgate and pulled her up to her feet. Spanning her waist with his hands, Teague lifted her up to sit on the roof, then handed her the bottle of wine.

"I knew there was a reason I didn't get the optional roof rack," he said as he crawled up beside her. "Sweetheart, you are never going to forget our first date."

A MANTLE OF STARS filled the inky sky. Away from the lights of the city, Hayley was amazed at the sight, like a million diamonds scattered above her. Only in the outback, she mused. Snuggling against Teague, she sought the warmth of his body to ward off the chill of the night air. They lay facing each other, the blanket wrapped around them both, their noses touching.

"This was the nicest first date I've ever been on," she teased, her lips brushing against his as she spoke.

"I know what a woman likes," he said. "I'm pretty smooth that way. Wine directly out of the bottle, a beautiful sunset and really incredible sex on the roof of my car."

"So, how many other women have you had since me?"

"I don't remember," he said.

Hayley drew back. "You're lying."

"I'm saying that none of them were memorable. You were the one who stuck in my mind. I think I can recall every single time we made love." His hand ran up along her hip, then down again. "Would you like me to recall them all for you?"

Hayley shivered, nuzzling against his neck. "I guess it's true what they say. You never really forget your first love."

"Very true," he agreed.

"We should probably go. Harry is going to wonder where I am."

"It's not that late. We can stay a bit longer." He kissed her again, this time lingering over her lips. "I want to say something to you and I want you to listen carefully."

"What is it?" Hayley asked, wondering at his serious tone.

"I plan to spend as much time as possible with you, Hayley. I don't know how long you'll be here, but I'm determined to make every minute count. So when we're together, there'll be no talk of getting home or worrying about Harry or maybe we shouldn't be doing this or that. If you're not prepared to spend every free minute with me, you need to tell me now."

"You have to work," she said.

"I do. But I figure you can come along. That's why I wanted to check out the landing strip. I'll buzz the house and you can meet me out here and off we'll go. What are you doing tomorrow? I have to fly into Bilbarra to cover a couple surgeries for Doc Daley. After we're done we can fly to Brisbane for lunch."

"I have to take Harry into Bilbarra. The eye doctor stops there tomorrow and he has an appointment to get his vision checked. We're leaving first thing in the morning. Two hours in the car on the way to Bilbarra and two hours back. I'm not sure how that's going to go."

"Why don't you let me fly you both. It's about a half hour by air. Once I'm finished at the surgery, we'll have lunch."

"Harry would never get on a plane," she said. "I'm going to have the devil of a time getting him in my car. He's very suspicious of everything I suggest to him. He'll probably think I'm planning to dump him off at some retirement home."

"He must leave the station occasionally. Doesn't he?"

"From what I can tell, not recently. He'd been living off tinned food for a month before I arrived. This station was his whole life. It's kind of sad to see what's happened to it. Makes the feud seem a bit silly, doesn't it?"

"Why is he bringing this up again? He's lost the last two times in court. And the time before that, he only won because he found some old document that the judge thought was real."

"I don't know," Hayley replied. "He has no money to pay for this lawsuit. He's not using the land he has. He's so fixated on winning." She drew a deep breath. "Couldn't you let him win?"

Teague frowned. "You mean turn over the land to Harry? Cal would never go for that."

She nodded. "Why not? I'm beginning to think the feud is the only thing keeping my grandfather on this land. He simply refuses to leave until he wins."

"He's not going to win this time," Teague said.

"What if I bought the land from Cal? How much would your brother want for it?"

"He won't sell," Teague said. "Why do you care? Harry never did anything for you except drive you away from the only home you had left. You don't owe him anything, Hayley."

"You don't understand," she countered.

"Explain," he said. "Make me understand."

Teague waited, watching as she tried to put her thoughts in order. "You're right, I don't owe Harry anything. But he's the only family I have. And I can't continue to push him away. There's going to come a day when he isn't around anymore and I don't want to have any regrets about what I did or didn't do."

Teague caught her hand and drew it to his lips. "You can't make him love you. Even if you handed him that land on a silver platter, it wouldn't change who he is."

"I know." She drew a ragged breath. "He seems so old. And sad. And when he's gone, I won't have anyone left."

"You'll have me," he said in a fierce tone. "How many times do I have to say that for you to believe it?"

"Kiss me again," she said. "Then maybe I'll believe it."

Teague cupped her face in his hands and kissed her softly. Tears pushed at the corners of her eyes and she fought against them. She never cried. She hadn't cried since her parents' funeral. And now, twice in one week. Teague was the dearest friend she'd ever had, the only person in the world she could trust. Yet, she couldn't allow herself to surrender to those feelings.

He pulled away and Hayley swallowed the lump in her throat. Before he had the chance to see her tears, she rolled over on top of him, pushing the blankets aside. Goose bumps prickled her skin as the chilly night air stole the warmth from her body. She ran her fingers down his chest from his collarbone to his belly.

The cold magnified every sensation, the simplest touch warming her blood and making her heart race. Teague smoothed his thumb over her nipple and Hayley sighed softly, bracing her hands on his chest.

She moved above him, teasing at him until he began to grow hard with desire. And when he was ready, Hayley shifted and he was suddenly inside her. She moaned as he thrust deep, his hands clutching her hips.

She could lose herself in this passion. When he was

inside her, all her doubts and insecurities vanished. The connection became strong and the trust unshakable. But they couldn't spend the rest of their lives making love. They both had to live in the outside world, where other forces would pull them apart.

If only she knew what to do, how to commit to a man. Without an example to follow, without loving parents to watch, she'd been left to find guidance from romantic movies. But that wasn't real life.

Her parents had loved each other, against all odds. They'd met and fallen in love in the course of a day, then married young, just a year after her father had left Wallaroo. They'd started with nothing and built a life together. But how did it happen? She'd been too young to see the truth in their relationship. To her, they'd seemed perfect. Yet they must have had their problems just like any other couple.

Had it begun like this? Hayley wondered. With desire and passion and need? Or was there some other secret to making love last a lifetime? She looked down at Teague, his face cast in silver light from the moon, then bent closer and kissed him.

He twisted his fingers through her hair, holding her close, whispering his need against her mouth. Then he reached between them and touched her. She drew in a quick breath, then moaned, an unspoken plea for him to continue.

Hayley gave herself over to him, light-headed with desire and unable to think rationally. It felt so good to let go, to know that he would be there to catch her when she fell. She could allow herself to be vulnerable without the usual fears.

The seduction was slow and deliberate, a gentle climb toward release. And when it finally came, she and Teague found it together, their bodies joined in perfect pleasure. Hayley didn't know much about love, but she knew what they shared sexually was as good as it got.

He pulled her into his embrace again, tucking her against his warm body and wrapping the blanket around them. "We can't go on like this," he murmured.

"We can't?"

"I don't want to leave you. I want you with me."

"That's not very practical," she said.

"I'll find a way to make it happen. Twenty-four hours together with no one to get between us. Two days would be even better."

"I'm cold," Hayley said, anxious to change the subject.

"I think I'm going to have to find our clothes." Teague wrapped her up in the blanket, then slid off the top of the Range Rover.

She sat up and watched him, appreciating his body naked in the moonlight. He gathered his clothes first, pulling his shirt over his head before he tugged on his jeans. Then he searched for his boots and socks. When he was finished dressing, he returned with her clothes.

"So, tomorrow you have to take Harry into Bilbarra. I'll drive you. I'll be here at seven sharp. You can take care of your business in town while I stop at the surgery. We'll drive home in the afternoon and then spend the night at the shack."

"I don't think this is a good idea. A Quinn and a Fraser in the car together for four hours."

"Dr. Tom Barrett will be taking you to Bilbarra. Your grandfather loves me. I'm the one who saved your horse, remember? And I gave you a discount on the bill."

"You didn't charge me anything," Hayley said as Teague pulled her T-shirt down over her head.

He helped her find the sleeves, then gave her a quick kiss. "I prefer to get compensated in other ways."

"Where are my panties?" she asked, searching through the pile of clothes.

"I think a dingo ran off with them."

"This is awful. I lose my panties on our first date."

"I can hardly wait for the second date." Teague winked at her.

"Don't be so certain. Harry will be coming along tomorrow."

"Maybe I can find *him* a date," Teague joked.

TEAGUE FIXED HIS GAZE on the road in front of him. He fought the temptation to glance at the clock on the dashboard. No matter how much he wanted this day to be over, counting down the minutes wouldn't make it go any faster.

"Have you seen the horses they breed?" Harry asked. "Scrawny creatures. A wonder they manage to sell even one. But then, the Quinns have always been cheats— every last one of them."

Teague gritted his teeth. His jaw was beginning to ache with the effort to remain silent. He'd listened to

Harry blathering all the way to Bilbarra. The old man seemed determined to offload every imagined insult and slight that the Quinn family had ever perpetrated against him. Teague was beginning to wonder if Harry knew who he really was and was provoking him deliberately. Likening Teague and his brothers to con men was over the top.

Hayley sent him an apologetic smile. "How are your new glasses working, Harry?"

"I don't need glasses."

"Put them on. You won't get used to them if you don't wear them."

"They make me look like a fool," he muttered.

"They make you look very clever," Hayley countered.

"What would you know, girl?"

"Don't speak to her like that," Teague said, staring at Harry in the rearview mirror. "She doesn't deserve that."

"What do you know about what she deserves?" Harry snapped.

With a low curse, Teague slammed on the brakes. The Range Rover skidded to a stop and Teague twisted around to face Harry. But Hayley put her hand over his. "Nature break!" she said, sending him a warning look.

She jumped out of the SUV and ran around to Teague's door. "Come on," she said, yanking the door open and grabbing his hand. "I want you to watch for snakes."

They walked into the brush, Hayley clutching his hand and tugging him along behind her. "What are you doing?"

"What am I doing? What is *he* doing?"

"He's being Harry. That's the way he is."

"He's rude. And he treats you like crap. I'm not going to listen to him speak to you like that. I won't have it, Hayley."

"It's just the way he is," she said. "It doesn't bother me. I've learned to tune it out."

"Well, you shouldn't have to." He braced his hands on his hips and shook his head. "You're not staying on Wallaroo any longer. You're coming to Kerry Creek with me."

"What?"

"I won't allow you to be subjected to his tantrums. And you wonder why you're carrying around so much baggage? Well, there's one big windbag you can get rid of right now."

"He's family," she said. "You don't have any idea what it's like to have no one. You have two parents and two brothers. I have him. And yes, he can be a pain in the arse at times, but he's still my grandfather."

"He's also the guy you ran away from ten years ago. And the guy who refused to take you in right after your parents died."

"Well, I've had time to realize my mistakes," she said. "And now, I'm waiting for him to realize his."

"Why is it so important? He'll never be what you want, Hayley."

"I'm not going to argue about this," she said, turning to walk away from him. "Not here."

Teague followed her, grabbing her arm and spinning her around to face him. "We're not getting in that car until you agree to come to Kerry Creek and stay with me."

"Then we're going to be out here all day and night, because I'm not going to Kerry Creek. Do you think I'll be any more welcome under your brother's roof than I am under my own?"

"You won't even give *us* a chance, will you?"

"What is that supposed to mean? What do *we* have to do with me coming to Kerry Creek?"

"No matter what I do, you're never going to need me. You're too scared to need anyone, Hayley. That's why you ran all those years ago. And that's why you're still running right now."

"Don't try to analyze me. You're no good at it."

"I know you better than anyone in this world."

"You used to know me," she said. Hayley turned and walked toward the road. She got inside the Range Rover and slammed the door behind her.

Teague cursed, then kicked the dusty ground in front of him. Hayley was the most beautiful woman in the world, but there were times when he wondered what the hell he was doing with her. She stubbornly refused to acknowledge she might deserve a bit of happiness in her life. The closer he tried to get, the more she pushed him away.

Last night, under the stars, he'd felt as if they'd finally gotten past her insecurities. But then, hours later, she'd found a way to sabotage what they'd shared. They were running around in circles and he was getting dizzy.

Teague walked back to the SUV and got inside. He threw the car into gear and pulled out onto the road. The problem was he and Hayley would never get things right between them if there was always someone standing in the way. His brother, her grandfather and Hayley herself.

He glanced over at her and found her staring out the passenger-side window. Maybe trying to reestablish a relationship with Hayley wasn't worth the trouble, Teague mused. They'd be going their separate ways in a few weeks. The more time they spent together, the more they seemed to be at odds with each other.

The rest of the ride passed in silence. When Harry made a move to speak again, Hayley quickly shut him down. To Teague's surprise, the old man followed her order, slumping in the rear seat with his arms crossed over his chest. He'd seen that posture from Hayley too many times. Maybe they were closer than he'd thought.

When they reached Wallaroo, Teague pulled up in front of the house. Harry shoved his new glasses onto his nose and peered out the window. "Jaysus," he muttered. "That house needs to be painted." He got out of the SUV and walked up to the porch, examining the peeling paint, then disappeared around the corner of the house.

"Come home with me," Teague said.

"I can't. Thanks for the ride. I know he can be a horror sometimes. But I can handle him now. He doesn't bother me."

"You deserve better."

She forced a smile, then nodded silently. A moment later, Hayley jumped out of the truck and closed the door. She gave him a little wave, before turning and running into the house.

As the Range Rover bumped down the road, Teague tried to put the day in perspective. Life couldn't always be perfect. They weren't kids anymore and there would be differences between them. But he knew more now than he had ten years ago. It wasn't easy to fall in love or to stay in love. Sometimes the differences between two people were too large to overcome.

There was an upside to staying away from Hayley. He wouldn't have to think about her 24/7. He could get his work done without having to hurry home so he might spend the night with her. And he and Callum would be on better terms.

So that was it. He'd given seeing Hayley a go and it hadn't worked. "Nothing ventured, nothing gained," he muttered to himself. Would she be that easy to give up? Though it would be a challenge to stay away from her, he was determined to try. He had calls to make tomorrow and the next day, he'd promised to fly Gemma and Payton to Brisbane so they could do some shopping.

He wouldn't have time to even think about Hayley until Sunday. By then, maybe he'd be ready to forget her and go on as if nothing had happened between them. "Right," he said, knowing that was all but impossible. His attempts to stop thinking about Hayley would only lead to more thoughts about her.

All the way home to Kerry Creek, Teague tried to figure out a way around the walls Hayley had constructed. If anyone could breach them, he could. But as he was furiously taking them apart, brick by brick, she was frantically building them thicker on the other side.

It was her move, Teague decided. He would wait for her to come to him. She couldn't run away if he refused to chase her.

When Teague got to the station, he didn't bother stopping at the house. Instead, he drove directly to the landing strip. He had a few hours left until sunset. If he stayed on the station, he'd only be tempted to ride out to the shack. He'd have to put some space between himself and Hayley.

He'd fly back to Bilbarra. Once the sun went down, he couldn't land on the station. He'd be stuck where he was. He'd spend the evening getting pissed at the Spotted Dog, sleep it off on Doc Daley's office sofa and then make his calls tomorrow.

It was a decent scheme, with no room to make a fool of himself. And that's all he really wanted from here on out—to keep from playing the fool.

5

HAYLEY WOVE Molly's reins through her gloved fingers, then turned the horse away from the stables. With a gentle kick, she urged her into a slow gallop. The early-morning air was chilly, the breeze whipping at her hair. But a ride was exactly what she needed.

She'd spent the last two nights wide-awake, fighting the temptation to ride out to the shack and see if Teague was waiting for her. Her therapist would probably say she was reverting to the self-destructive patterns of her childhood, making a bad decision simply to punish herself. But Hayley knew it was something more than that.

Was she trying to test him? To see how deep his affection ran? Or was she trying to drive him away before he had a chance to leave on his own?

Her stomach fluttered as she thought about what she'd say if he was waiting for her. She managed to stay away from the shack partly because of the fear that he might not be there. If he wasn't there then he didn't care and it was all over. She'd half expected him to stop by the station with the excuse of checking up on Molly, even though the horse had recovered completely. And he hadn't come. In two days, no word from the only person in the world who claimed to care for her.

She urged Molly to gallop faster and faster. Hayley's legs ached and her breath came in shallow gasps, but she didn't want to stop. As she came over a small rise, she saw the shack in the distance. Two horses were tethered out front.

Drawing a deep breath, she headed toward the shack. Had he been there all night waiting? When she reached the porch, Hayley slid out of the saddle and dropped softly to the ground. She walked up the steps, then rested her hand on the doorknob. As she opened it, the hinges creaked. "Teague?"

Hayley froze as she saw the two naked bodies intertwined on the small bed. She felt her world shift, the ground moving under her feet. Teague had brought another woman to their special place. How could he have done this? Was he trying to punish her?

With a soft sob, Hayley turned and ran down the steps. She heard a voice call out behind her, but her heart was beating so hard and fast that it obliterated every sound around her.

She fumbled to put her foot in the stirrup, frantic to escape before he discovered her here. She swung her leg up and over the saddle, then reached for the reins.

"Wait!"

Hayley glanced up, tears swimming in her eyes. Slowly, she realized the man who stood on the porch wasn't Teague at all. Though the family resemblance was obvious, she found herself looking at a man who could only be Teague's younger brother, Brody. She'd only seen him once, when he was much younger, but she knew it was him.

"What are you doing here?" she demanded, her voice shaky and her hands trembling.

"We needed a place to sleep," Brody explained. "This was close by. Was Teague supposed to meet you here?"

"No," she snapped, keeping a tenuous hold on her emotions. "Why would you think that?"

He shrugged, then shoved his hands in his jeans pockets. "It was almost as if you were expecting him," Brody said, his eyebrow arched.

Hayley swallowed hard and tried to steady her voice. "I saw the Kerry Creek horses and I thought it might be him. But I was mistaken. Sorry. I didn't mean to wake you."

"Should I tell Teague you were looking for him?" Brody asked.

"Why?" Hayley shook her head, unwilling to reveal her true feelings to Teague's brother. "No. You don't need to tell him anything."

A moment later, a woman joined Brody on the porch, her eyes sleepy and her long mahogany hair loose around her shoulders. He turned to her and smiled, slipping his arm around her shoulders. "Morning," she said, nodding to Hayley.

"Payton, this is Hayley Fraser," Brody said. "Her family owns this place. Hayley, Payton Harwell."

Payton smiled warmly. "Thank you for letting us

stay here. I got lost last night and wasn't really prepared to sleep outside."

Hayley nodded, still suspicious of Brody's friendly attitude. She knew what Teague's brothers thought of her, what his whole family thought. She was trouble, a girl who didn't deserve a brilliant boy like Teague. His parents had tried to put an end to their friendship early on and when Teague had been forbidden to see her, they'd simply snuck around, taking whatever time they could find together.

"I—I have to go," Hayley said. "Stay as long as you like. I won't say anything to my grandfather."

Hayley couldn't contain her humiliation as she rode back to the house. Once again, tears flooded her eyes and she brushed them away with her fingers. What was wrong with her? She'd never been this emotional before. This was what romance did to her—it caused her heartache and pain.

But mixed with the humiliation was a large dose of frustration. She'd been the one to mess everything up. Teague had done nothing but offer her his friendship and affection and she'd thrown it in his face. He was right. She didn't owe anything to Harry. If it came down to a choice between Teague and her grandfather, she should have chosen Teague.

Harry may be family, but Teague was something more. Teague was a true friend. Hayley sighed. No, he was more than a friend. A lover. "A lover that I don't love." She groaned. A soul mate? Was that it? The notion seemed so sentimental, but it came the closest to describing how she felt.

There was no one in the world she trusted more. Considering she usually trusted no one but herself, that was saying a lot. And there wasn't one other man with whom she'd rather spend an evening. He knew what she was thinking before she said it, as if he could see right into her mind. And Hayley was certain that no matter how much time had passed, she could depend on him if she needed help.

As she approached the stable, Hayley noticed Teague's truck parked nearby. Her heart leaped and she kicked Molly into a quicker pace. When she got inside the stable, she saw him sitting on a bale of straw at the far end. He glanced up at the sound of Molly's hooves on the concrete and then got to his feet.

Hayley jumped to the ground and took a step toward him. For a long moment, they stared at each other, and then a tiny sob racked her body and Hayley ran toward him. Teague gathered her in his arms, lifting her off her feet as he kissed her.

"I'm sorry. I'm sorry," he whispered between kisses.

"No, I'm sorry," Hayley said. "I was such a bitch to you. And you didn't deserve that."

"I need to be more patient," he said, setting her on the ground. He held her face in his hands and kissed her again. "I've been miserable these last few days. All I could think about was you. I was in Brisbane yesterday and I was walking through David Jones and everything I saw reminded me of you. I wanted you there with me."

"You went shopping to get your mind off me?"

Hayley asked. "Don't men usually go to a pub and get themselves drunk?"

"I did that on Thursday night. Saturday I took Gemma and Payton shopping in Brisbane."

"I met Payton," she said softly. "I rode out to the shack this morning and she was there with Brody."

"So that's where they ended up," Teague said with a soft chuckle. "I guess that's not our private place anymore."

"She seemed nice," Hayley said. "Very pretty."

"I've never known Brody to be this far gone for a girl before and he's had lots of girls. And Cal, he's got a sweetheart, too. Though I'm not sure he knows what the hell to do with her. Her name is Gemma and she's a genealogist from Ireland. Things have changed at Kerry Creek in the past week."

"Is that why you asked me to come and live with you? So you'd have someone there, too?"

"No. And I shouldn't have asked. I know how you feel, and Cal and Brody haven't ever done anything to get to know you better. But that's going to change."

"How? Are you going to beat them up if they say anything nasty about me?"

"Yes," Teague said, nodding his head. "I will thoroughly thrash them to defend your honor. But before I do, I'm going to give them a chance to get to know you. I want you to come to Kerry Creek tomorrow. We're having a little celebration for the queen's birthday, a barbecue. And I'm inviting you to be my guest."

"I don't know, Teague. If I come, Callum and Brody will be upset and I'll ruin everyone's good time."

"But if you don't come, you'll ruin my good time," he said. Teague slowly rubbed her arms, searching her gaze until she couldn't help but smile at him. "It will be fun. We're going to have games and a campdrafting competition. It will give you a chance to show off your skills on a horse. And you can see Payton and meet Gemma and talk about…girl stuff."

In truth, Hayley would have been happy to avoid Callum and Brody for as long as she could. But Brody had been rather nice to her at the shack. Maybe their feelings had softened a bit now that they were older. "All right. I'll come, but if your brothers don't want me there, then I'm going home."

"I'll pick you up at—"

"No, I'll ride over," Hayley said. "In case I decide to leave early."

"You won't want to leave." He kissed her again. "I promise. You'll have a good time. Now, I have the day off. What are we going to do with ourselves?"

"We could go riding," Hayley said.

"We could fly to Brisbane to see a movie," Teague suggested.

"We could drive to Bilbarra and have lunch at Shelly's."

Teague bent close, his forehead pressed to hers. "Or we could ride out to the shack, kick Brody and Payton out and spend the rest of the day in bed."

"I vote for the shack," she said.

"Me, too."

He walked over to Molly, who had been munching on some loose hay in her stall, and led her to the door.

He swung up into the saddle, then shifted to make room for Hayley. He held out his hand and pulled her up to sit in front of him, then clucked his tongue.

Hayley settled against him, holding tight to the arm he'd wrapped around her waist. Everything was all right now. She hadn't made a mess of things. Teague still cared and she had another chance to show him how much he meant to her.

"I'LL GIVE YOU THIS," Brody said. "She's not hard to look at. I've watched her program a few times with Mary. They make her look like a real tart on the telly. She looks much better in person."

"They say the camera adds ten pounds," Callum said soberly.

"Who says that?" Teague asked, laughing at his brother's comment.

Callum shrugged. "I don't know. They. People who know that kind of shit. I'm not saying she's fat, because she isn't. And I think she's pretty enough, but Gemma is much prettier."

"Payton has them both beat. Dark-haired girls are always more attractive," Brody said. He nodded in the girls' direction. "What do you suppose they're talking about?"

The three women were standing along the far fence, their arms braced on the top railing as they chatted. The conversation must be going well, Teague mused, because Hayley was smiling.

Callum folded his hands over his saddle horn. "I

don't know. Maybe recipes. That's probably it. They're exchanging recipes."

This time both Brody and Teague laughed. "You don't know anything about women, Cal," Brody said. "They're probably talking about shoes or clothes."

"Or they could be talking about us," Teague offered. "The same way we're talking about them."

"What? Like they're discussing how pretty we are?" Brody asked. "There's not much to discuss. I'm a better-looking bloke than the two of you. End of story."

"Brody has always been the pretty one in the family," Callum said. "We've always thought of him as our little sister, haven't we, Teague?"

"And since you're the one with all the experience around women, little sis, you go over there and find out what they're talking about," Teague suggested.

"I'd guess they're probably talking about what a pair of dills you two are," Brody muttered as he rode away.

"You're not upset that I brought her here, are you?" Teague asked.

"No," Callum said. "My fight is with Harry Fraser, not his granddaughter. Besides, you could always marry her and then Wallaroo would be yours someday."

"What the devil are you talking about?"

Callum gave him a dubious look. "Don't tell me you haven't thought about it. She'll inherit. Harry doesn't have any other heirs. Though Wallaroo is smaller than Kerry Creek, it has some prime grazing land. And it would be the perfect place to raise horses. You've always wanted to do that. Isn't that why you went to vet school?"

"I told you, Hayley isn't interested in the station. She's going to try to convince Harry to sell it."

"You should talk her out of that," he said. "That land is worth a whole lot more than what anyone will pay for it now, especially since it borders Kerry Creek."

"You could always buy it," Teague said.

"Yeah. If three or four million dollars falls out of the sky tomorrow, I could. But I'm not holding my breath on that one."

They watched as the ladies climbed over the fence and walked across the yard toward them. Brody had talked them into taking part in the campdrafting competition. They'd compete as pairs against each other.

Though Callum was the best at driving cattle, it was obvious Gemma wasn't comfortable around horses. Payton, however, was an experienced horsewoman, but she'd never attempted campdrafting, so Brody's chances were about the same as Callum's—fifty-fifty. But Teague knew Hayley would throw herself headlong into any competition, especially if it involved riding.

"Two on a horse," Brody explained. "The girls steer, the guys work the stirrups. This should be fun."

Teague reached down and grabbed Hayley's arm, then swung her up in front of him. "We've got this won," he whispered in her ear.

"I don't know," Hayley said. "I think Payton might be a decent rider."

"And you could probably beat half the stockmen," he said. "With your hands tied behind your back."

"Oh, adding a little bondage to the competition might be fun," Hayley teased.

"Be careful," he warned, holding her close. "I won't be able to concentrate on winning."

Callum decided to go first and called out to Davey to release a calf from the pen. Payton and Brody watched from the other side of the fence, Brody's arms wrapped around Payton's waist and his chin resting on her shoulder.

Gemma screamed as she tried to maneuver Callum's horse. When Callum tried to grab the reins, the stockmen began to jeer at him for cheating. He finally told Gemma to drop the reins and he steered his horse using only his knees and feet.

Though the effort wasn't Callum's best, he did manage to get the calf through the obstacle course and back into the pen in under five minutes. Gemma looked as if she could hardly wait to get off the horse.

"Hey!" Brody called from the fence. "We're going to grab some more coldies. Who wants one?"

Both Hayley and Teague raised their hands, as did half the stockmen. Brody took Payton's hand and pulled her along toward the house.

"I sure hope you boys aren't too thirsty," Callum shouted. "They may be a while."

Teague gave Tapper a gentle kick and Hayley maneuvered the horse over to the gate. "Ready?" Teague asked.

"I'm ready."

Teague shouted to Davey and a moment later, the gate swung open and a calf ran out. Teague jabbed his heels into Tapper's sides and Hayley pulled the horse to the right, cutting off the calf's escape.

Over the next ninety seconds, they worked as a perfect team, anticipating each other's movements without speaking. Hayley was firm but aggressive with the reins, and Teague couldn't help but admire her determination. When they returned the calf to the pen and Davey slammed the gate shut, the stockmen erupted in wild cheers.

Teague glanced over at Callum to find his brother looking at the two of them in disbelief. "What?" Teague said. "You didn't think we could do it?"

"You beat Skip's time and he's the best on Kerry Creek," Callum said. "Ninety seconds."

"No," Teague replied, shaking his head. "You must have the time wrong. Skip Thompson's the best stockman we have. No one can beat him." He reached around Hayley and took the reins, then trotted Tapper over to the gate.

"It was only ninety seconds," Hayley said beneath her breath. "I think we won."

"I know. But we can't humiliate the boys. Skip will get the prize and everyone will be happy."

"What about my prize?" she said, turning around and sending him a sexy pout.

"I'll think of something I can do to make it up to you."

"You could rub my backside," Hayley suggested. "I've been spending too much time riding and I'm a bit sore."

When they reached the stable, Teague helped Hayley off his horse, then removed Tapper's saddle. He led him into the stable yard, then carried the saddle to the tack room. When he emerged, Hayley was waiting for him, a devilish smile on her pretty face.

"I'm not going to rub your bum," he said.

"Please," Hayley teased. She turned away from him, then looked over her shoulder, pursing her lips in another pretty pout.

Hayley was growing less wary of him, he mused. Allowing herself to tease and act playful. Maybe they were making progress. Teague was still unsure, but as long as their relationship kept changing for the better, he wasn't going to complain. "What if someone walks in?" he asked.

She pulled him into an empty stall. Then, taking his wrists, she placed both of his palms on her backside. Wriggling, she pressed up against him, her arms draped around his neck. "You do it so well when I'm naked. What's a little denim between friends?"

"Friends with benefits," he reminded her. "You really are determined to make me squirm, aren't you? Is this payback for my dragging you here in the first place?"

"No. Actually, I'm having a lovely time. Gemma and Payton are very nice and your brothers have been quite cordial."

"I told you you'd have fun."

"I'd have more fun if you rubbed my bum."

With a low growl, Teague grabbed her legs and picked her up, wrapping her thighs around his waist. Hayley yelped with surprise, then laughed as he stumbled. Pressing her against the wooden wall, Teague kissed her, his hands smoothing over the sweet curves of her backside.

"Oh, yes," Hayley moaned, her voice deep and dramatic. "Oh, that feels so good."

"I thought you were a good actress," Teague teased.

She pushed her hands against his shoulders and looked at him, a shocked expression on her pretty features. "And I thought you were a good lover."

"I am," Teague said.

"Prove it."

It was like one of those challenges she used to issue when they were kids—I can ride faster than you can, I can jump higher than you can, I can hold my breath longer than you can. He'd never refused one of her challenges in the past and he wasn't about to now.

"Here?"

"Are you afraid? Oh, don't be such a big girl's blouse."

"And you're going to get a reputation as the town bike if you don't watch out." He chuckled as he set her back on her feet. "I'm not going to start something here that might be interrupted, especially by one of my brothers."

"Then you'll have to work quickly," she said, reaching down and unbuttoning his jeans. "Ingenious design, these chaps. Good for riding and better for sex."

He moaned softly as she began to tease him erect. Strange how the prospect of getting caught made the desire even more intense. It was silly, this desperate need to hide their sexual relationship. Their romance was in the open now and there didn't seem to be any objections from the Quinn side of the equation. And sex was all part of that.

Still, Teague wasn't anxious for his brothers to know how obsessed he was with Hayley Fraser. She'd become the single point around which his universe revolved. And he was beginning to believe that he wouldn't want to live his life any other way.

"So what are you looking for in the way of a massage?" Teague whispered, his lips trailing along the curve of her neck.

She drew in a slow breath, then tipped her head to the side, inviting him to move lower. "I'll leave that up to you."

Over the next minute, they tore at each other's clothes, pulling aside just enough to allow the basics of sex. And when he slipped inside her, Teague was already on the edge. This was all he needed in life. That thought whirled round and round in his head as her warmth enveloped him.

And when he finally lost control and buried himself one last time, he made a silent promise. He would do whatever it took to make her happy, whatever it took to keep her with him. She was his—she always had been, from the moment they'd met out on the big rock until forever.

HAYLEY HEARD THE PLANE before she saw it. Shading her eyes from the sun, she stared up into the sky and caught sight of it coming in from the west. He flew low over the house and she ran out into the yard and waved. Teague wiggled the wings in response.

With a laugh, she hurried to her car and hopped inside, then made a wide turn toward the old airstrip. It had been a week since the queen's birthday celebration and she and Teague had seen each other only a few times. His work had called him off the station several times on overnight visits, and when he returned, he was off again within the next few hours. On top of that, he'd had to make a quick flight with Payton and Brody to Brisbane when they'd decided to visit Fremantle for a few days.

Though Hayley knew this was what a real relationship between them would be like, she'd found herself feeling more lonely than she'd ever imagined she could. No matter how hard she tried to convince herself they were involved in a purely physical relationship, it was becoming more delusion now than determination.

She and Teague weren't just sexual partners. They'd rediscovered their friendship and rekindled an affection that had never really disappeared. And though it might have been easy to say they were falling in love again, Hayley wasn't ready to take that step—not yet. Perhaps if they could meet the challenge of spending so much time apart, she might consider love.

The odds had been against them when they were kids and now that they were adults, not much had changed. She had her career in Sydney and the possibility of much more. And he had his new practice in Bilbarra. Perhaps if Teague had been free to practice in Sydney, it might work between them.

But he'd made a commitment to buy Doc Daley's practice. It was his chance to run his own business. And it could take years to establish himself in Sydney, especially as an equine vet. He'd probably be forced to join an existing practice and work for someone else. This had been his dream, to live in Queensland, to expand the horse-breeding operation on Kerry Creek.

He was standing beside the plane when she arrived at the airstrip, his arm braced on one of the wing struts. Hayley hopped out of the car and walked up to him. "Are you trying to impress me?" she asked in a teasing voice.

"Come on," he said. "Let's go."

"Where are we going?"

"We're getting away. You and me, alone, for a few days. I've made all the regular visits on my schedule and now I've got some time."

"I can't just leave," she said. "I don't have anything packed and I—"

"You won't need anything," Teague said.

"But—"

"But what? Where's your sense of adventure, Hayley Fraser? As I recall, you called me a big girl's blouse just last week. You used to do anything on a dare. I dare you to get in this plane."

"I can't leave without telling Harry I'm going to be gone. He'll notice I'm not there to make him supper."

"All right. Go," Teague said. "I'll give you fifteen minutes. If you're not back, I'm going to leave without you. I'll have to find another girl who's more adventurous."

Hayley frowned. Then she stepped up to him, threw her arms around his neck and kissed him. The kiss was long and deep and meant to show him that leaving her behind would be a big mistake. When she finally drew away, she looked up into his eyes to see desire burning there.

"Yeah, I thought so. You're not going to leave," she assured him. "And there are no other girls more adventurous than I am."

A smile curled the corners of his mouth and he sighed. "No. But I still want you to hurry."

"Are you going to tell me where we're going?"

He grinned and shook his head. "Do you have something against surprises?"

Hayley usually preferred to be in control, but she knew Teague would never plan a surprise she wouldn't like. "I'll be right back."

By the time Hayley returned to the house, Harry was already pacing a path along the length of the porch. When he saw the car, he stopped and stormed into the yard. "Where did you go?" he demanded as she jumped out of the car. "Was that a plane I heard?"

"Yes. I'm going to be leaving for a few days. I have…business. It's important, so they sent a plane." It was an outright lie, but Hayley didn't want to take the time to make up a more plausible excuse. She paused. Maybe she ought to tell Harry the truth. There was no use hiding it anymore. "That's not right," she said, facing him. "Teague Quinn has invited me on a holiday and I'm going. I don't care if you don't like it. I'm an adult and I make my own decisions."

Harry cursed and wagged his finger. "I'll not have you taking up with that Quinn boy again!" he shouted.

"I can do what I want, Harry. There'll be no letters for you to intercept and no phone calls for you to ignore. I've cooked and cleaned for you for the past two

weeks and I deserve a bit of a break. I'll be home…
when I get home."

She moved to the door, ready to return to her room
and pack a few belongings. But then, Hayley realized
she'd only have to put up with Harry's badgering the
whole time. Teague said she wouldn't need anything, so
she would trust him on that, as well.

"Goodbye, Harry." Hayley jogged down the steps
and got into her car. She saw Harry in the rearview
mirror, glaring at her from his spot on the porch. She'd
never really stood up to him when it came to Teague and
now that she had, Hayley realized Harry wasn't nearly
as powerful as she'd thought he was. What was the
worst he could do, kick her out of the house? She had
a place of her own in Sydney. And a place with Teague,
if she needed it.

Harry would have the next few days to cool off before
she had to face him again. But there was no longer a
reason for her to be ashamed of seeing Teague. He made
her happy and she hadn't felt truly happy since the last
time they'd been together. Nearly ten years of searching for the one thing she needed, and she found it in the
place where it had all begun.

When she drove up to the plane, Teague was waiting.
He helped her inside, showing her how to strap in, then
circled around and climbed into the pilot's seat. A few
seconds later, the engine roared to life.

"When did you learn how to fly?" she shouted.

"Four years ago," he said. "Figured I'd need a plane
if I was going to be an outback vet. I bought it last year.

Lived like a pauper when I was working in Brisbane, saving everything I made. This baby comes in handy."

Hayley had never been in a small plane before. She drew a deep breath as they headed down the bumpy runway, the plane gathering speed. She was afraid it might fall apart with all the bouncing and bumping, but then they lifted off and the ride was suddenly smooth.

Teague reached over and captured her hand, then brought it to his lips to kiss it. She felt a familiar thrill, the same feeling she'd had when they were kids and they'd found an adventure to experience together. There was a certain satisfaction in sharing something new with Teague. As if it was something no one could ever take from them.

"Will you tell me where we're going now?"

He shook his head. "Look in the bags behind your seat."

She twisted around and found two huge shopping bags from David Jones, a department-store chain. "What's this?"

"I picked up a few things while I was shopping with the girls."

"How long have you been planning this?"

He shrugged. "Awhile. Well, ever since we spent that first night in the shack. I wasn't sure I'd be able to get away, but Doc Daley told me I could take a few days if I cleared my schedule."

She pulled out a tiny pink-flowered bikini and held it up. "We're going to the beach?"

"Yes." He nodded.

She found a matching sarong and a pretty pair of sandals in the same bag. In the other bag, she found two sundresses along with a pale yellow cotton cardie. In a smaller bag, a selection of underwear, bras and panties in pastel colors. "You bought these yourself?"

He nodded again. "I think they'll fit. I had to guess on the sizes." He glanced over at her. "I don't think you'll need more than that."

"I suspect I'll be spending a fair number of hours without any clothes at all."

"Yes," he agreed with a boyish grin. "I didn't pack much, either."

As they flew northeast, Teague pointed out all the major landmarks. They flew over Carnarvon National Park and then over the Blackdown Tablelands before turning directly north. Soon, the coast was visible, the turquoise-blue water shimmering in the afternoon sun. Hayley sat back in her seat, watching the landscape float by below them. When they got over the water, Teague brought the plane lower and pointed out the window at a pod of whales breaking the smooth surface. They circled once so she could get a better look, then he navigated north again.

"It's so beautiful," she said. "I love the ocean."

"I know." He turned and smiled at her. "You told me the day we met. You stood on the top of the rock and tried to see the ocean. And when you couldn't, I was afraid you might cry."

"You remember that?"

"I remember everything about that day," he said.

Islands dotted the coastline and Teague headed farther east until they could see waves breaking over the Great Barrier Reef. She'd never really appreciated the true beauty of her homeland, but here, with Teague, everything looked different somehow. The coast was greener, the sky bluer, the water sparkling with the light of a million diamonds.

How was it possible that life seemed so much more exciting when he was near? He was just a man, nothing more. Yet, when she was with him, she felt…complete. As if all the pieces that had been missing over the years had found their place again in her heart.

Her body buzzed with a strange anticipation. While they were on Wallaroo and Kerry Creek, it was simple to think of their time together in finite terms. But now that they were in the real world, the possibilities seemed endless. Could they continue after they both returned to their regular lives? Would there be shared holidays and weekends away? The more she thought about how it might work, the more Hayley realized that it could work.

Lots of people carried on long-distance relationships. And she and Teague had spent nearly ten years apart, yet it hadn't changed anything between them, except the intensity of their feelings for each other. What was a week or a month compared to ten years?

"Which beach are we going to?" she asked.

"Why don't you let me surprise you," he insisted. "I know it's not in your nature, but give it a try, just this once."

"I have to warn you again that wherever we go,

people will recognize me. They'll either ask for my autograph or tell me what a horrible person I am. They sometimes get me mixed up with my character."

"You *are* a very bad girl on the program. How many marriages have you destroyed?"

"Three, I think," Hayley said ruefully. "And two engagements. I seem to like sex far too much for my own good."

"How does that work?" Teague asked. "When you have to do those scenes?"

"Sometimes it's uncomfortable. Especially when you don't know the other person very well. But it's part of the job." She paused. "And sometimes, it creates a false sense of intimacy."

"And how did the men in your life handle you doing love scenes with other guys?"

"You mean my boyfriends?"

Teague nodded. "I know you've had boyfriends. I've read all the magazines. Whenever there was a story about you and some fella, I'd have to read it. You've had some very famous boyfriends."

"I suppose they didn't care. They never really knew me, anyway. I never let them get close enough."

"I know what you mean," Teague said. "It's never felt right with other women."

"So you were abstinent for ten years," she joked.

"No. And I don't expect you were, either. But I never found anyone that felt as…right as you did. As right as you *do*. With me."

"What are we going to do about that?" she asked.

"I don't know. I'm still figuring it out."

A long silence grew between them as Hayley considered what he'd told her. Everything he'd said had been the truth and she'd felt it as strongly as he had. They belonged together. But admitting that fact made everything so much more complicated.

She could figure it all out later, she decided. For the next few days, she was going to enjoy her time with Teague and not worry about the future.

6

TEAGUE SAT on the edge of the bed and stared out the open doors onto the bungalow's wide veranda. Hayley stood facing the ocean, her body outlined by the setting sun. The breeze caught a strand of her hair and he watched as she distractedly tucked it behind her ear.

She was the most beautiful thing he'd ever seen. And it was obvious to him that he couldn't consider a life without her. How was that possible? Had they really fallen in love as teenagers? Was this merely a continuation of those feelings? If he couldn't figure that out here, alone with her, then maybe he'd never know for sure.

They'd landed at the only commercial airport in the Whitsundays, on Hamilton Island, and then had hopped onto a helicopter for the ten-minute flight to the resort. Teague had heard of the resort when he was living in Brisbane and when he'd called to make a reservation, he'd been assured that it was very private. There were only sixteen bungalows, set near the water's edge, the lush rain forest spreading out behind them. This being the off-season, he and Hayley were the only guests midweek.

The bungalows were furnished in plantation style with high ceilings and polished wood floors. A fan whirred above his head, the sound mixing with the rush of waves on the shore. If they were going to fall in love all over again, this would be the place to do it, Teague mused. They had three days and nights together to figure out their relationship.

She turned to face him, her expression soft and her smile satisfied. "It's beautiful," Hayley said as she walked toward him.

"The helicopter pilot told me we're the only guests right now. We have the whole island to ourselves. Besides the staff, the wallabies, the goannas and—"

She put her finger to his lips, then sat down on his lap. "No people to bother me with autographs," she said.

"Nope."

"A real bed with a down comforter," she said, leaning back to smooth her hand over the bed linens.

Teague nodded.

"You know how to spoil a girl, don't you."

"I do my best," he said.

She gave his chest a gentle shove and they tumbled onto the bed together. "Now that we're here, what are we going to do with ourselves?"

"I have some ideas," Teague teased. "But they all involve taking off your clothes."

Hayley scrambled to her feet and, without hesitation, pulled the cotton dress up and over her head. Then she kicked off her shoes and jumped onto the bed. "Now what?"

"Use your imagination," Teague said.

She stretched out at his side, then ran her hand from his chest to his groin. She rubbed the front of his khakis, waiting for the customary reaction to her touch. As he grew hard, she smiled. "You're far too easy," she said.

Teague caught her wrists and rolled her beneath him, pinning her hands above her head. "What about you? It doesn't take much to make you all warm and wet."

"I can last longer than you can," she said.

Another challenge. Funny how he enjoyed these challenges so much more than the silly challenges of their younger years. He loosened his grip on her wrists and slowly slid down along her body, his lips pressing against her silken skin. He stopped long enough to dispense with her bra, then let his mouth linger over each tempting breast.

Hayley arched beneath him as he brought each nipple to a stiff peak, then blew on it softly. Teague's fingers twisted in the waistband of her panties as he pulled them over her hips and thighs. When she was finally naked, he lay beside her and gently caressed the damp spot between her legs.

Her eyes were closed and her lips slightly parted. When he looked at her, every detail of her face suddenly became important to him. Her bow-shaped upper lip, the long lashes that fluttered against her cheeks, the tiny mole on her chin. He'd known them all by heart so many years ago, but now he didn't want to forget.

Teague bent over and kissed her gently as he slipped

his finger inside her. Hayley's breath caught in her throat and she moaned. He knew she was close, but he wanted to prolong her pleasure. They had a comfortable bed and a long night ahead of them. There was no need to rush.

But Hayley wasn't ready to surrender. She gently pushed his hand away, then rolled over and straddled his body. Her hair fell in waves around her face and she smiled down at him as she tugged at his T-shirt.

Carefully, she undressed him, Teague touching her at every turn, his hands searching out the sweet curves of her body. He'd been so long without a woman before Hayley had come into his life again. And now that he'd grown used to having her near, Teague wondered if he'd ever be able to do without. There was something so comforting in knowing that, for at least this moment in time, she belonged entirely to him.

Her lips were warm against his bare skin. A shiver skittered over him as she teased his nipple. Then, her lips drifted lower until her hair tickled his belly. He knew her game but he also knew how close he was to losing control. Teague groaned as her mouth brushed along the length of his shaft.

There were certain aspects of passion that they hadn't enjoyed as teenagers and this had been one of them. But it was obvious that new skills had been acquired in ten years. Her mouth closed around him and Teague felt a current race through his body, making him flinch in response.

He slid his fingers through her hair, holding her back when he felt too close, then loosening his grip when he wanted more. Teague lost himself in the wild sensations her mouth and hands were bringing him.

"All right," he groaned. "You win."

"Not yet," Hayley said. "Not until you give up." She went to work and Teague knew she wouldn't be satisfied until he was. Did he want to surrender? Or would he rather find his release inside her?

In the end, Teague didn't have a choice. The feel of her tongue on his cock was more than he could handle. He held his breath and felt his body grow tense with anticipation. And then, a spasm shook his core. His fingers tangled in her hair, gently pulling her away as the warmth of his orgasm pooled on his belly.

When it was finally over and his body had relaxed, Teague opened his eyes to find her looking up at him, her chin resting on his chest. "I win," she said, a satisfied smile on her face.

"No. I'm pretty sure I won that round." He reached down and drew her up alongside him, tucking her into the curve of his arm. "If this is any indication of the rest of our holiday, I think I'm going to need a holiday from our holiday."

"I like this," she said, staring up at the ceiling. "It feels so grown-up."

"We are grown-up," Teague said.

"Sometimes I don't feel like an adult. I keep waiting for my life to start, as if there's supposed to be a big sign that tells me when I need to begin paying attention. Your Life Starts Now," she said, emphasizing each word with her hands.

"Your life has started."

"But it doesn't seem like it's mine," Hayley said. "It feels like it belongs to someone else."

"What did you think it was supposed to be?"

She considered his question for a long moment. "I thought that you and I would live on a station and we'd raise horses and spend all day riding them. And at night, we'd live in a little shack, like the one on Wallaroo. And we'd sleep in the same bed and wake up together every morning. And that would be our life."

"It sounds pretty nice to me," Teague said.

"Not very practical, though. Where would we have found the money to buy a station and horses? How would we have supported ourselves? It was a silly dream."

Not so silly, Teague thought to himself. He'd had the same dream himself when he was younger. Only, he'd have a job as a vet to help support them both. They'd work the station together and breed the best horses in all of Australia.

But as he looked at Hayley now, he wondered whether she'd be happy with station life. He'd seen what it had done to his own mother, driving her away after eighteen years of marriage. And raising a family in the outback wasn't a piece of cake, either.

Hayley had a glamorous life in Sydney, enough money to live quite comfortably. She was a celebrity, people recognized her. That wasn't the kind of life someone walked away from.

But he could walk away and join her. His deal with Doc Daley wasn't finalized yet. Though they'd reached a verbal agreement, they were due to sign the papers at the end of the month. If he backed out, there would certainly be other vets who'd jump at the chance to take over the practice. Teague could return to clinic work, like he'd done after he graduated from vet school. City life hadn't been that bad. He could get used to caring for dogs and cats again and forget about horses.

Teague closed his eyes. He'd promised himself that he wouldn't think about the future while they were at the resort. There was time enough for that later.

"There's a very large shower in the bathroom. I think we should try it out," he said.

"We've never had a shower together," she said. "Or a bath."

"Well, if you don't count the time you snuck over to the pond on Kerry Creek and talked me into skinny-dipping."

A smile spread slowly across her pretty face. "I remember that."

"Yes. You spent half the night laughing at the effect the cold water had on my bits and pieces. I was humiliated."

"Yes, but you forget that a few days later, we found something much more interesting to do with your bits and pieces." She dropped a kiss on his lips. "We had sex for the first time."

"That's right," he said. "And look where we are now. Still naked, still having sex. And you're still issuing challenges."

"We have come a long way," Hayley said. She rolled off the bed and held out her hand. "Shower. I think it's time we ticked that off the list. I'll wager you dinner that I can wash your back better than you can wash mine."

Teague followed her into the bathroom, his gaze fixed on the sweet curve of her backside. If this was the way their holiday was starting, three days and nights would never be enough.

HAYLEY SAT on the wooden lounge chair, her feet tucked under her. The sun was beginning to brighten the morning sky. The mist rising from the dense rain forest on the island would soon burn off, leaving them with another beautiful day.

She'd learned to love mornings on the island. Right before the sun came up, birds would awaken and begin chattering in the trees that surrounded their bungalow. Teague slept so deeply he never noticed. But for Hayley, they were like an alarm clock, reminding her that she had another whole day to spend with Teague.

They'd walk on the beach or take a trek on the paths through the forest. They'd sip fresh juice for breakfast and enjoy a gourmet meal for dinner.

Sadly, this was their last day on the island. At noon, they'd take the helicopter back to Hamilton Island and then Teague's plane home to Wallaroo. She didn't want their holiday to end. It had all been too perfect.

Was she wrong to believe that real life would never match the fantasy of their time on the island? It was easy to fall in love in this place. They had no responsibilities, no worries, no careers tugging them in different directions.

Was their relationship strong enough to survive time

and distance apart? If they didn't make any promises to each other, there wouldn't be any failures or regrets. Why couldn't she accept this for what it was—temporary?

If she knew what was good for her, she'd return to Sydney before she lost her heart completely. She had scripts to memorize and she hadn't been to the gym in ages. Plus, she'd promised her agent she'd make the trip to L.A. before she was due back on the set.

She pushed to her feet and walked inside the room, the dew from the veranda creating tracks across the wooden floor. Slipping out of the expensive robe that the resort provided, she crawled beneath the down comforter.

Teague was warm, his naked body stretched out beneath the cotton sheets. This was the third morning she'd awoken beside him without having to think about the repercussions of spending the night together. This was how it should be.

Hayley slid her arm around his waist and pressed her body against his, throwing her leg over his thigh. He stirred and then slowly opened his eyes, turning his sleepy gaze on her.

"Your feet are freezing," he complained.

"I was sitting out on the veranda. Listening to the birds."

"What time is it?"

"Early, she said. "The sun is just coming up."

"I like waking up with you," Teague said, drawing her closer.

"How would it have been," Hayley asked, "if I had come to Perth to be with you?"

Teague frowned. "What brought this on?"

"I'm curious. How would it have worked?"

He drew a deep breath then raked his hand through his tousled hair. "Well. We would have had to find a place to live. I don't think they would have allowed you to stay in my room at Murdoch. We would have found a flat in the city, something we could afford. I worked while I was in school, so we would have had some money, although my parents might have cut me off if they'd known we were together. You would have had to find a job. I'm not sure we could have both afforded to go to school, but I could have—"

Hayley reached up and pressed her finger to his lips, stopping his words. "Do you realize how complicated it would have been? Teague, it would never have worked. As much as we dreamed it could."

"You don't know that," he said.

"I found a job when I first got to Sydney and I could barely afford to eat, never mind rent a place to live. We were so young and so stupid. We thought love would solve all our problems. Love doesn't pay the bills. It was best that things turned out the way they did, don't you think?"

"We spent ten years apart," Teague reminded her.

"But we both made something of ourselves in that time. We're happy with our lives, aren't we?" she asked.

"Are you? You don't seem anxious to get back to yours."

"Don't try to analyze me," she warned. "Best leave that to professionals."

He sighed softly. "I wish I could find a bandage to

fix all the bad things that happened to you in your life, Hayley. I wish there was medicine or some kind of cure for all the pain that you've had to endure."

"I know I'm pretty much a wreck," she said with a weak smile. "It's a wonder you can tolerate me. But don't stop trying."

"You're not a wreck. You're a little banged up. A few dents here and there, but nothing that will stop me from wanting you."

"So do you think you can fix me, Dr. Feelgood?"

"I'm Dr. Feelamazinglygood." He pulled his hand out from under the comforter. "These fingers are magic. They can cure anything that ails you."

"What about what ails you?" Hayley slipped her hand beneath the comforter and smoothed it along his belly until she found his shaft, which was already growing hard with desire. "I think you have a problem. Something very strange is happening here. There's an unusual swelling. Oh dear, I've never seen anything like it."

"Very strange," he said, kissing her softly.

Hayley giggled, then felt a warm blush creep up her cheeks. "I remember the first time I touched you down there. I had absolutely no idea. I mean, I'd seen horses and cattle, but I never imagined that boys would function the same way."

"Are you saying I resemble a stallion? Or a bull?"

"Oh, definitely a stallion," she said. "Long legs, a nice mane, beautiful eyes."

"So, you want to go for a ride or what?"

Hayley gasped at his request, then gave him a playful slap. "You're terrible. All you think about is sex."

"No, all I think about is sex with you. There's a big difference."

"You don't ever think about other women?"

"Not since you came back into my life. You're it. All my fantasies, you're right there. Dressed in sexy lingerie, doing all kinds of nasty things to me, whispering in my ear, telling me how much you want me."

"We need to take another holiday together," she said. "This has been perfect."

"It would be this way all the time if we lived together," he said.

Hayley shook her head. "You'd toss me out in less than a week. I'd make a horrible roommate." She knew what he was offering, but if she made a joke of it, she wouldn't have to answer him.

She sighed inwardly. She'd like nothing more than to accept. It would be wonderful to share a place and to share their lives. But marriage was difficult enough, even without long periods apart. If she was going to commit to Teague, then she'd have to be prepared to give up her life in Sydney and start a new life with him.

"You haven't been a bad roommate these last few days. I wish we could stay longer," he said.

"Me, too. I'm not looking forward to my homecoming at Wallaroo. In fact, I've been thinking maybe you ought to fly me straight to Sydney."

"You want to go home to Sydney?" he asked, a trace of hurt in his voice.

"No. It's just that...I told Harry about us. Right before I left. That I was going away with you. I'm not sure if he's going to want me staying with him anymore."

"Why did you do that?"

"I was tired of pretending. It was silly. And you and I have nothing to do with the fight between him and Callum. So what difference does it make?"

"He won't see it that way," Teague said.

Hayley shrugged. "I expect all my things will be tossed in a big pile in the yard. Or maybe he'll have burned them. When he's given enough time, he can work up a pretty bad temper."

"The longer that feud goes on, the more ridiculous it seems."

"It's a matter of honor," Hayley said.

"What are you talking about?"

She pressed her face into his naked chest. "That's what Harry says. It's a matter of honor. Promises were made and promises were broken."

"What promises?"

"You don't know?"

"No. I assumed it was some mistake made on the deed years ago."

"According to Harry, his father traded a mail-order bride for that piece of land. Your great-grandmother fell in love with your great-grandfather and didn't want to marry my great-grandfather. So they made a trade. Only, your great-grandfather kept the land and the girl."

"Why did I never know that story?"

"Probably because it proves that Harry is right about

the land. It belongs to Wallaroo. Unfortunately, the paperwork was never filed. It was a gentleman's agreement, which doesn't count for much these days." She glanced over at him. "So, I guess that if it weren't for my great-grandfather and that little piece of land, you and your brothers wouldn't exist."

Teague frowned. "I'm not sure I believe anything Harry says. He'd do anything to have his way."

"It is a good story, though. Especially if it proves to be true."

"Maybe I should trade Harry the land for you," Teague teased, nuzzling her neck. "That would end the feud and we'd both get what we wanted."

"What about what I want?" Hayley said. "Doesn't that count?"

Teague pulled back, his gaze searching her face. "What do you want, Hayley?"

It was a simple question and Hayley ought to give him an answer. She could tell he was getting weary of always asking where he stood. And truly, if she knew, she'd give him an answer. But fabulous sex and long, romantic meals with Teague had only made her more confused. It wasn't just about a relationship now, it was about a lifetime together.

"Breakfast might be nice," she said.

"Don't do that," Teague warned. "Don't brush me off like that. Whenever I talk about the future, you seem to find a way to make a joke out of it. We've spent three incredible days together, just the two of us and no one else. Has that made any difference?"

She tried to twist out of his arms, but Teague wouldn't let her go. "Hayley, I'm falling in love with you all over again. But you've got to let me know if I'm making a fool of myself. Or if there's a chance for us."

"Don't do this," she said. "I can't— I don't know how—"

"What?"

"I can't go through that all again. Watching you walk out of my life. I can't do it."

"But you won't have to. That's the point. If we decide to be together, then that's it. Neither one of us will be walking out."

"I will be. All the time. My work doesn't exactly allow me to stay in one place for very long. Not if I want to be successful."

"Is acting what you want to do for the rest of your life?"

"I'm not sure. But my career is the only thing in this world that truly belongs to me. I made it happen. And I don't think I can give that up."

He exhaled slowly and drew her closer. "All right. At least I know where we stand on that. And I'm all right with a long-distance thing. You'll come home when you can. We can make it work, Hayley."

"Are you going to come to Sydney? Are you going to follow me around the world when I have work outside Australia? Would you give up everything to be with me?"

"I'm not sure I'd have to give up everything," Teague said. "We don't need to be together every minute of every day in order to be happy."

Hayley felt tears of frustration pushing at the corners

of her eyes. "Oh, brilliant," she muttered. "Now I'm crying again. I seem to do that a lot lately."

Teague ran his hands through her hair, then dropped a soft kiss on her lips. "Don't cry. There's no need for tears."

"I just...can't."

"I know," he murmured, pressing a kiss to her temple and then another to each of her eyelids. "I know."

Hayley drew in a ragged breath, then let the tears come. She had fought so long against her emotions. But now that they'd finally broken free, she realized how much good came of crying. It felt as if all the pain was draining out in her tears.

Teague held her close as she wept. After a time, she wasn't sure why she was still crying. Was it for her parents? For the perfect childhood she'd never had? For the love and loyalty that Teague was so determined to give her?

It didn't matter. All that mattered was that she was finally capable of crying. And whether Teague understood her tears or not, the ability to let loose her emotions meant more to their future than anything she might say.

"I CAN'T BELIEVE we have to leave in a few hours," Hayley said. She glanced up at Teague and then reached across the breakfast table to take his hand. "This was the best holiday I've ever had. Thank you."

"Next time it will be your turn to plan," he said. "I'll provide the plane."

"All right," Hayley agreed. "It's a date. No matter what happens, we'll have another holiday together."

"And then another and another," Teague said. "We

could survive on a string of holidays." He paused. "I would be satisfied with that if that's what you're offering."

Teague felt like a fool willing to settle for scraps when he might have the entire meal. But if it was what Hayley wanted, he didn't have much choice.

She nodded. "We'll choose a date and I'll make the plans. And this time, it will be my treat."

"Christmas," he said. "I'd like to spend Christmas with you."

"Christmas it is."

They finished their breakfast in silence. Teague was happy they'd managed to agree on future plans at last. But it hadn't escaped him that the plans didn't address the things standing between them and a real relationship.

In a few weeks, he would sign the papers that would give him ownership of Doc Daley's practice. When he'd first returned to Kerry Creek, Teague had been certain that taking over an established practice would be the perfect opportunity. Doc Daley had been ready to retire, and Teague figured he could make enough to buy Doc out in five years. He already had the plane, so he could handle much more business than Doc had ever managed, which would increase his income substantially. His future had looked brilliant.

But now Teague had to wonder if tying himself down in Queensland was really the answer. He could establish a practice on the outskirts of any large city—Brisbane, Sydney, Melbourne. Or he could work for another vet and not worry about keeping a business afloat.

Funny how he'd spent the last ten years of his life

happily cruising along, never worrying about his future. It was easy when he was on his own, with no responsibilities for another person. But he'd begun to see how complicated things could become once he'd decided on a life with Hayley.

Hell, there was no point thinking about it now. He had a few weeks. Things might be completely different between them by then. They'd just planned a holiday together. Who knew what could be waiting around the next corner?

"Mr. Quinn?"

Teague looked up at the waiter. "We're fine. The breakfast was great." He glanced over at Hayley. "Would you like more juice?"

She shook her head. "No. Thank you."

"Mr. Quinn, there's a phone call for you in the office. It's a Dr. Daley. He says it's urgent."

Teague frowned. He'd nearly forgotten they'd been without phones for the past three days. Messages were delivered in person. No telephones, no television, nothing to distract from the solitude.

He pushed away from the table. "This will only take a minute," he said to Hayley. "He's probably wondering if I can make a call on my way home to the station."

He followed the waiter to the small office where the manager was waiting with the phone. "Thanks," Teague said. "Doc?"

"Sorry to interrupt your holiday, Teague."

"No worries. Is something wrong?"

"I got a call from Cal early this morning. He's been

looking for you and thought I might know where you were."

He'd told his brother that he'd be gone until Friday afternoon. He hadn't given him all the details, but had assumed he wouldn't be bothered with station business. "I'll call him. I'm sorry that he—"

"No, he wanted me to pass along a message. This is for Hayley Fraser. She is with you, isn't she?"

"Yes," Teague said.

"Hayley's grandfather took a bad fall. He rode over to Kerry Creek and wanted to stir things up with Cal. He fell getting off his horse and broke his hip. He's in the hospital in Brisbane. Things aren't looking too good. He's refusing care and insisting that they let him go home. They want Hayley there as soon as possible to try to talk some sense into him."

"Which hospital?" Teague asked.

"St. Andrew's."

"Call Cal and tell him we'll get there as soon as we can."

"Take a few more days to be with your girl," Doc said. "I can handle things here."

"Thanks," Teague said. He returned the cordless phone to the manager. "Can we get an earlier flight to Hamilton? We've got a bit of an emergency."

"I'll call the pilot right now," the manager said. "Why don't you get packed and I'll send someone to let you know when the helicopter will arrive."

Teague hurried back to the dining room. This was going to be difficult. Hayley had finally asserted herself with her grandfather and now she'd get drawn in again by guilt. Teague wasn't sure how she'd react to the news.

She saw his expression before he had a chance to sit down. "What's wrong?"

He took a deep breath. "It's your grandfather. He must have rode Molly over to Kerry Creek. He was looking to mix it up with Cal, probably over the land dispute. He somehow fell off Molly and broke his hip."

Hayley gasped. "Oh, no. That's serious, isn't it?"

Teague nodded. "They've taken him to the hospital in Brisbane. But he's refusing treatment. They want you to come and convince him."

"He has a broken hip. He can't walk with a broken hip. What does he expect to do?"

"I don't know, Hayley. But we need to go there. The resort manager is calling for the helicopter. We can fly directly to Brisbane from Hamilton. We'll be there in a few hours."

"Could he die from a broken hip?" Hayley asked.

"No," Teague said. It was the truth. But Teague knew the complications that came with an injury like that. For a man Harry's age there was pneumonia and blood clots to consider. And if he refused treatment, he'd be stuck in a wheelchair for the rest of his life, probably living in a great deal of pain.

Teague stood and held out his hand and Hayley laced her fingers through his. "Everything will be all right," he said.

Hayley nodded, her face pale and her eyes wide. He walked to the room with her, then packed for both of them while Hayley stood on the veranda, looking out at the ocean. Without her grandfather on Wallaroo, there was little to keep her in Queensland.

Teague said a silent prayer that the old man would see reason and accept treatment for his injury. Maybe, with rehab, he could live on his own. But it was unlikely he'd be fit to run Wallaroo again. Chances were far better that Hayley would have to find him a place where she could watch over him.

A soft knock sounded at the door and Teague pulled it open. The resort manager stood there, a solemn expression on his face. "The helicopter will be here in ten minutes. Would you like me to take your bags?"

Teague nodded, then stepped aside to let him pass. The manager gathered up their meager belongings. "I'm sorry your holiday had to end so abruptly," he said.

"I am, too," Teague said. "But it's been wonderful. Truly, the best holiday I've ever had."

"We hope you'll come again soon."

Teague closed the door behind the manager and walked across the room to the veranda door. "Ten minutes," he said.

Hayley turned around. Her face was wet with tears. In three long strides, he crossed the veranda and gathered her into his arms. "Don't worry," he whispered. "Everything will be fine."

"Promise?"

"I promise. Harry is being stubborn. It always takes him a while before he gives in."

"He's not going to want to see me. He thinks I deserted him. For you."

"Well, now you're coming back. And if he doesn't forgive you, well…I'll have to set him straight."

Teague gave her a fierce hug, picking her up off her feet and shaking her. A tiny giggle slipped from her lips and he kissed the top of her head. "Come on. Let's go."

As they walked to the helicopter pad, Hayley held tight to his arm. This wasn't the way he wanted their holiday to end, but he couldn't help but wonder if it might finally breach the last wall between them. Hayley needed him right now, needed his strength and his counsel. He'd help her through this hard time and perhaps they'd come out better for it on the other side.

7

TEAGUE GLANCED UP from the newspaper he was reading as Hayley approached. She'd left him in the hospital waiting room nearly an hour ago. With a soft sigh, she sat down beside him, glad for a break from the endless conversations with doctors and nurses.

They'd arrived at the hospital and she'd gone directly into a meeting with Harry's doctors. Teague had asked if she wanted him there for support, but Hayley had prepared herself to deal with the crisis on her own during the flight to Brisbane.

In truth, Hayley knew Teague had his own opinions about her grandfather, none of them very good. He thought Harry was a cranky old bastard who seemed to take delight in making Hayley miserable. Teague would always stand up for her first, especially against Harry. And now was the time to avoid conflict at all costs.

"He's refusing an IV," Hayley finally said. "And he won't even consider surgery."

Teague took her hand. "He'll change his mind once he gets tired of lying in that bed."

She tried to control the tremble in her voice, but then

realized it didn't matter. She was talking to Teague. He could handle her emotions. He'd seen plenty of them over the past few weeks. "But if he doesn't get enough fluids, then they can't do surgery. And if he doesn't have surgery, he won't walk again. I don't know what to do. He won't listen to me."

"Would you like me to talk to him?"

"No! He'd probably break the other hip trying to chase you out of the room. They're bringing in a counselor to talk to him later today. They asked that I get some of his things from home. They think if he has some reminders of his life at Wallaroo, he'll be more apt to want to get well so he can return home." She turned to him. "I don't want to leave. I—I made a list and I was hoping you could go to Wallaroo and pick up a few things." She handed him the piece of paper.

"I'll do that," Teague said, taking the list from her. "But first, why don't we get you settled in a hotel, somewhere close by."

Hayley shook her head. "No, I'm going to stay here. They have a small room for family members. There's a bed if I need to sleep. I think I should try to talk to Harry again later tonight after the counselor leaves."

"Why is he doing this?"

"He told the doctor that he's finished living. He's done. If he can't ride a horse without falling off, then he's pretty useless on a cattle station."

"He's feeling sorry for himself."

"Well, he has good reason. Wallaroo isn't what it used to be. I think all of the troubles at the station might come from this anger of his. He's mad at his body, that it doesn't work the way it should, that he can't spend twelve hours in the saddle, seven days a week. He's seventy-five years old. What does he expect?"

"I suppose I can sympathize. I know I'd be pissed off with the world if I were stuck in that hospital bed. He's always been so independent and now he needs help. Harry Fraser has never needed another human being in his life."

Hayley leaned over and rested her head on Teague's shoulder. "I often wonder whether he would have been different had my grandmother lived. I never knew her, but he has a picture of her next to his bed."

"How did your grandmother die?"

"Complications after childbirth," Hayley replied. "Three days after my father was born. She gave birth on Wallaroo and I guess everything was fine until a couple days later. She got sick and by the time they got her to the hospital, it was too late." Hayley paused. "I can see why Harry hates hospitals. Can you blame him?"

"How come you never told me that story?"

"I didn't know it until just a few years ago. I asked Daisy Willey and she told me." She sighed. "Maybe Harry would have had a happy life and they'd have moved off the station in their retirement and lived in a cottage on the ocean. Or maybe they would have gone to the city, like your parents did."

She glanced at the clock on the wall. It was already three in the afternoon. Teague needed to leave for the airport soon or he'd be spending the night. "You should go. You're not going to make it to Kerry Creek before sunset if you don't leave now."

"I'm going to stay. I'll fly to Wallaroo tomorrow morning. We'll get some dinner and I'll get a room. That way, you could rest for a while before coming back here."

"No, you should go," Hayley insisted. "You've been away from work for three days. And you'll be back tomorrow with Harry's things, remember?"

Though it was generous of Teague to offer to stay, Hayley felt it was her duty to deal with Harry. He was her family, her responsibility. Besides, it felt good to do something. She'd been all but useless to Harry for most of her life. Now she could help him get through this, help him get well.

Teague pulled her hand up to his lips and kissed her fingertips. "Walk me down to the door?"

"I should—"

"Harry isn't going anywhere. He'll be fine." Teague stood, then drew Hayley up beside him. They headed toward the lift and once inside, Teague gathered her into his arms and kissed her softly. She held on as tightly as she could, hoping to draw some strength from him.

He always knew exactly the thing to make her feel better, to lift her spirits. She closed her eyes as he gently smoothed his hand over her hair, her face nuzzled into his chest. A memory of her childhood flickered in her mind. Her mother had often done that when Hayley had awoken from a bad dream, soothing her fears until she'd fallen back asleep.

But this wasn't a bad dream. It was bad reality. She

had no one to blame but herself for this disaster. She'd been the one to take off with Teague, leaving her grandfather to fend for himself. If she'd been watching over him at Wallaroo, he would never have gotten on a horse and ridden to Kerry Creek.

Hayley couldn't believe they'd run out of time. She wanted some of those years back, years that she could have used to get to know her grandfather better. She barely remembered her parents, had never known her grandmother and she couldn't face losing the last member of her family. Without Harry, she'd be utterly alone in the world.

The doors opened and they stepped out into the lobby of the hospital. She sat down while Teague walked to the reception desk to call a taxi.

If Harry agreed to the surgery, she was willing to deal with all the consequences. There would be a long rehabilitation, but the promise of going home might tempt him to work harder. And he would go back to Wallaroo, to live out his days on the station he loved.

Harry wouldn't sell. He had never looked at his land as a financial asset. It was part of his family heritage, something that didn't have a monetary value. In truth, the station was part of who she was, too. Whether she wanted to admit it or not, the land she'd played on as an adolescent was more a parent to her than Harry had been.

He'd always lived his life by his own rules and he had a right to make his own choices. Hayley closed her eyes. Maybe she ought to respect Harry's wishes now and let him do as he wanted—no IV, no surgery. Who was she to stop him? If he wanted this to be the end, then maybe it should be, on his own terms.

But she didn't want to lose him—not yet. Hayley had always held out hope that she'd find a way to make him love her. When she'd run away, she'd wanted him to come looking for her, praying he'd show that he really did care. But Harry had never once tried to find her. And when Teague had tried, Harry had stood in his way.

Grandparents were supposed to love their grandchildren. Yet she'd managed to get the world's worst set of grandparents. Three were long gone, her mother's parents unknown to her and her grandmother just a photo beside Harry's bed. And then Harry, who'd never come close to the kindly, indulgent old folks she'd seen on the telly.

"Hayley?"

Startled out of her thoughts, she turned to find Teague standing in front of her. "Yes?"

"The taxi's outside," he said. "I have to go."

She quickly rose, then pushed up onto her toes and kissed his cheek. "Thank you," she said. "For bringing me here. And for the holiday. With the rush to leave the resort, I never told you how much fun I had."

He grinned. "We're going to do it again. Remember? You're making the plans."

"And thank you for going to get Harry's things from Wallaroo. I feel like you give so much to me and—"

"Don't," he warned. "Don't even say it. If I didn't want to be here, I wouldn't be here. It's as simple as that."

"You're a good friend, Teague," she said. "My only

true friend." She suddenly wanted to drag him off to a dark corner and lose herself in a frantic seduction, anything to take her mind off her troubles. But the distraction wouldn't last. Harry would still be lying in a hospital bed once they were through.

They walked outside and stopped next to the waiting cab. "I've been thinking," Hayley said. "I wonder if Harry is the way he is because he's been alone for so long. Because he lost the one person he loved in the whole world."

"I think Harry was born mean."

"But what would you do if you lost the person you loved?" Hayley asked. "I mean, not if she went away. But if she suddenly died? Wouldn't you turn bitter like Harry did?"

He considered her question for a long time, lazily playing with her fingers as he did. "I can't believe I'm going to say this, but, yeah, maybe I would. I guess it does explain his behavior a little better. He had his reasons."

"He did," Hayley agreed.

Teague reached for the door of the taxi. "I'll see you tomorrow morning," he said. "Ring my satellite phone if you need anything. In fact, call me later and let me know how things are going."

"I will."

Teague pulled her toward him, his mouth coming down on hers in a deep and stirring kiss. Hayley felt her legs go weak and she clutched at his shirt to maintain her balance. When he finally drew back, she remained limp in his arms, her eyes closed. Just hours ago, she would have tumbled him into their comfortable bed at the resort. Now, he was leaving.

When she looked up, he smiled softly at her. "Love you," he murmured.

"I love you," she replied, the words coming without a trace of hesitation.

With that, he let go of her, the impact of his revelation slowly sinking in and stealing her breath away. He jumped into the taxi and then gave her a wave as it drove off.

Hayley fought the urge to run after him, to demand an explanation. What did he mean? How could he say such a thing and then leave? He loved her like a best friend loves a best friend, right? And what about her? What did she mean?

She sat down on a nearby bench, numbly staring down the driveway, a frown wrinkling her brow. Maybe he'd said it to make her feel better, to boost her spirits. Hayley swallowed hard. Or—or maybe Teague really loved her.

A shiver raced through her body and she rubbed her arms to smooth away the goose bumps. *Love*. Such a simple word, a word they'd used so many times as teenagers. But back then, they hadn't known what it meant, how deep the feelings could run, how strong the bond could be. Did they know now? Or was it still only a word with vague emotions behind it?

"Are you all right, miss?"

She looked up to see an orderly standing beside the bench, a wheelchair in front of him.

"Yes. I'm fine. Just getting a little air." Hayley drew in a deep breath, then let it go. From the moment she'd first seen Teague again in the stables at Wallaroo, she'd felt as though she were clinging to the neck of a runaway horse. She wanted to jump off, to take some time and reestablish her bearings, to clear her head and think. But if she got off, could she climb back on or would the ride suddenly be over?

She pushed to her feet, the weight of emotional exhaustion making it hard to move. Perhaps the hospital had a nice quiet psychiatric ward where she could spend the next few days sorting through her feelings.

"I'VE NEVER ASKED YOU for anything, but I need this."

"No," Callum said, shaking his head. He shoved away from his desk and began to pace the width of the room. "I can't believe you'd even ask."

Teague schooled his temper, knowing only a calm discussion would get him what he wanted. Callum could be so stubborn at times, but he was also a reasonable man. And though Teague was asking an awful lot, he hoped his brother would relent. "I'll give you whatever you want for it. You know I'm good for it. I have the practice. I'll pay you back with interest."

"That's Quinn land," Callum said.

"Harry Fraser would dispute that."

"Now you're taking Harry's side?" Callum cursed beneath his breath. "I should have known this would happen."

"She doesn't have anything to do with this," Teague said. "It's me. I'm making this request."

The door to the office swung open and Gemma

stepped inside before she noticed the two of them. "I'm sorry," she said, turning to leave.

Callum's expression softened. "No, come on in. We're done here."

Teague stood and walked to the door. "We're not done here. Could you excuse us?"

Gemma glanced at them both, then nodded and quickly made her retreat. Callum made a move for the door, but Teague blocked his way. "We're going to finish this," Teague said.

"We are finished."

"You forget that all three of us have a share in this station. You may have a larger share because you run it. But I've been providing free vet service for over a year now and that's worth something."

Callum sat down at his desk and pulled out his check register. "How much do I owe you?"

"I don't want to be paid. I want you to sell me the land at a fair price."

"I'm not selling that land," Callum insisted.

"If you don't agree, then I'm going to have to call Brody and we'll bring it to a vote. If he votes with me, then you lose."

Since his father had moved off the station and turned the operation over to Callum, he'd given his sons an equal vote in any major decisions that had to be made regarding their birthright. Though Brody might side with Callum, the threat of bringing any subject to a vote underscored the serious nature of Teague's request.

"If there was one thing you could do to make Gemma's life happier, you'd do it, right?"

"Yes," Callum said.

"And I'd do the same for Hayley. That's why I need to give her grandfather that land. I wouldn't ask if it wasn't really important. You'll need to trust me on this, Cal. It will all work out in the end."

Callum gave Teague a shrewd look. "You're not a stupid bloke. But I honestly think you're being suckered into this."

"You know when it comes to the land, we each own a third. That piece doesn't even come close to a third. I'll take it and you can have the rest of my share."

"You're mad. You're willing to give up everything for a few hundred acres and a water bore?"

"I am," Teague replied.

Callum shook his head. "No. I'm not going to let you do that." He slowly closed the check register. "I'll sell you the land. But for the next five years, anything comes to a vote, you vote with me."

Teague smiled. "Thank you. This will all turn out in the end. I promise."

"I'm going to hold you to that promise," Callum warned. "Now, get the hell out of my office. And tell Gemma she can come in."

Teague had one more request and knew it wouldn't go over very well. "If it's possible, I'd like the agreement today. Before I head to Brisbane."

"Today? Why today?"

"Because I need it today." He glanced at his watch.

"In the next hour or two would be good." Teague walked to the door, then turned and sent Callum a grateful smile. "Thanks, Cal. I owe you. Free vet services for the next fifty years."

"That would about cover it," Callum said. "As long as you throw in ownership of the plane, too."

Teague left the office and climbed the stairs to his bedroom. He'd have to pack for at least a week if he expected to run his part of the practice out of Brisbane and spend his nights with Hayley. Though he'd use extra fuel flying back and forth, he could extend his workday by at least three or four hours by landing in Brisbane at the end of the day, taking advantage of the illuminated runways there.

He wasn't the kind of guy who folded when times got tough. And he knew how fragile Hayley could be when she felt as if she'd been deserted. The deal he'd made to give Harry the land would make her smile. And it might change Harry's mind about checking out early. Teague gathered some clean clothes from the pile Mary had put on the end of his bed and tossed them into a duffel bag.

He'd gotten up at sunrise and driven over to Wallaroo. He'd felt a bit strange going through Harry's belongings, but he'd found everything on Hayley's list—a flannel robe, a battered stockman's hat, a framed photo of Harry with Wallaroo's prize bull and a key chain with a lucky rabbit's foot.

He'd thought about taking the photo of Hayley's grandmother, then realized why Hayley hadn't put it on the list. Maybe Harry was ready to be with her again and the photo would only remind him of that. Teague couldn't imagine how any of the other things would be important to Harry, but then, he didn't know Hayley's grandfather.

He'd also ventured into Hayley's room and packed some of her clothes into one of her designer bags. Teague had actually enjoyed picking through *her* things, remembering when she'd worn each item of clothing, inhaling the scent of her perfume and her shampoo, flipping through some of the scripts she'd brought along.

He hadn't spoken to Hayley last night and was left to assume she was all right. Sleep had been impossible, his thoughts rewinding to their time at the resort. It seemed as if their holiday was weeks ago, even though they'd just left the island the day before.

A knock sounded on his door and he turned to find Gemma standing in the hallway. "Hi," she said. "I heard about Hayley's grandfather." She held up a paper bag. "Mary and I baked some biscuits. Shortbread. I know she probably won't have time to eat, so… It's not much, I know."

Teague crossed the room and took the bag. "Thanks. I'm sure she'll appreciate it."

"Tell her I hope everything turns out well. And if she needs anything, she should call."

"I will."

"My grandfather passed on last year. I used to spend summers with him. He was such a kind man, always looking out for me. I was devastated. I cried for days."

"Hayley and her grandfather aren't really close," Teague said.

"But I thought she grew up on the station."

"She did. But—"

"No need to explain," Gemma said, holding up her hand. "And tell her I hope we have a chance to see each other again before I go home."

"You're going home?" Teague asked.

"I'm almost done with my work. I'm needed in Dublin."

"You wouldn't have to leave," Teague said. "I know Cal enjoys having you here. And you haven't learned to ride yet."

Gemma giggled. "I've tried. But I'm fairly certain that, even if I stayed for a year, I'd never be much good at it."

"A year? That would be about enough time," he said. Teague studied her for a long moment, wondering how much he ought to say, then realized that Callum could probably use as much help as he could get. "My brother has spent his whole life working this station. There's no one who works harder than he does to make sure this place turns a profit. He's not the most romantic guy in the world, or the smoothest, but he has a lot of good qualities."

"You don't have to—"

"I do, because I know Cal never would. He's a pretty humble guy. But he's steady and loyal and—" Teague chuckled. "And I'm making him sound like the family dog."

"I understand what you're saying. And I do appreciate all his fine qualities. It's just that…well, it would be a huge thing for me to leave my life in Ireland behind. And there's no question that I'd have to do that if we were to be together." She paused. "And he hasn't asked me to stay."

Teague nodded. He wasn't going to try to sell Gemma on life at the station. It wasn't easy and she and Cal would have to love each other deeply in order to make it work. His mother hadn't been able to take it, Hayley had left and even Brody and Payton had escaped to the city.

"Well, I'll leave you to your packing," Gemma said. "Enjoy the biscuits."

Teague nodded. How odd was it that all three of the Quinn brothers now had women in their lives? And that all three of them risked losing those women. Payton and Gemma were foreigners and would probably be returning home soon. And Hayley? He figured he still had a shot with her.

They, at least, lived on the same continent.

TEAGUE SAT ACROSS the table from Hayley, watching as she picked at the pasta salad he'd brought her for dinner. Shadows smudged the skin below her eyes, betraying her lack of sleep the previous night.

"You're not staying at the hospital tonight," Teague said. "I've got a room. After you're finished eating, I'm taking you with me and you're going to get some rest."

Hayley nodded and sighed. "All right." She glanced around the hospital cafeteria. "Do you think anyone would be bothered if I crawled over the table and curled up in your lap?"

Teague grinned. "That lady behind the cash register looks strong enough to toss us both out."

"I want to kiss you for an hour or two," she said, stifling a yawn. "And then I want to pull the covers over my head and sleep for a year."

"How is Harry?"

She shrugged. "Still stubborn. But I think the things you brought him made an impact. He was wearing his hat when I left his room. And I heard him joking with one of the nurses and Harry never jokes. I think they're flirting with him. The counselor was in again today and has made some progress. If Harry agrees, they'll do his surgery tomorrow morning."

"I have something else for you," Teague said. "Actually, for Harry. But you can give it to him." He reached into his jacket pocket and withdrew an envelope, holding it out to her.

"What is it?"

"An agreement to deed the land over to me. And another to transfer it from me to Harry. It's his."

Hayley gasped, her eyes suddenly wide. "You did this for Harry?"

"I did it for you," Teague said. "And Harry. Maybe it will help."

"Oh, it will," she said, excitement filling her voice. "The court fight was weighing on his mind and this makes it all so simple. Thank you." Hayley glanced down at her uneaten dinner and pushed it aside. "I want to go tell him. Now."

"Let's go," Teague said.

They rode the lift up to Harry's floor, but before they got to the room, Hayley took Teague's hand and pulled him into through a doorway in the middle of the hall. Three cots lined the walls of the darkened room. This was obviously where Hayley had slept the night before.

She pressed him back against the closed door, his body blocking the window and their only source of light. Then she wrapped her arms around his neck and kissed him, deeply and desperately. Her need to touch him seemed frantic and she pulled at the buttons of his shirt until she'd undone them all.

He tipped his head back as she smoothed her hands over his chest. Her touch set his body on fire, every nerve tingling with anticipation. His cock grew hard almost immediately.

Hayley nuzzled his chest. "I missed you," she murmured.

Teague chuckled as she trailed kisses along his collarbone. "It's been less than twenty-four hours."

"It seemed like days," she said. "Weeks."

"Maybe because we'd spent the previous three days in bed."

"We weren't in bed the whole time. We did walk on the beach and eat."

"But it was pretty much a sexfest."

She looked up at him, grinning. "I like that. A sexfest. I think we should have another one of those."

"I know exactly where to find one. My hotel room. Fifteen minutes."

She quickly buttoned his shirt. "Let me go give Harry

the news and then we can leave." She reached down and ran her fingers along the front of his jeans. "You can stay here if you'd like. Until you…calm down. I'll only be a few minutes." She pulled the envelope out of her pocket. "Harry is going to be so surprised."

Hayley slipped out of the room and Teague sat down on the edge of the cot. He drew a deep breath, trying to douse the fire that raged inside him. Would his desire for her ever fade? Perhaps a long-distance relationship would be the perfect thing for them. All that time apart for their need to increase and then coming together again for an explosion of lust.

Yet, there was something to be said for the everyday events, the tiny things in life they could share if they lived together. He could touch her and kiss her whenever he chose. He could read her moods and soothe her worries. They could build a real life, together, maybe have a family.

Teague wanted to believe it would happen that way. Maybe not tomorrow or even next year, but someday he and Hayley would be together for good. He pushed to his feet and opened the door, stepping out into the brightly lit hallway.

He stood outside Harry's room, trying to hear the conversation inside. There was no shouting, which was a positive sign. Maybe this scheme of his would work.

A few minutes later, Hayley emerged, a smile on her face. Teague breathed a silent sigh of relief. She was happy. That was all he cared about.

"How did it go?"

"Good," she said. "We had a really nice talk." Hayley shook her head in disbelief. "He said he wanted me to be happy. And he said he'd go ahead with the surgery." She reached up and pressed her palm to Teague's chest, right over his heart, her eyes fixed on the spot. They stood that way for a long time, silent, the heat of her fingers warming his blood. "And he'd like to see you."

"Me?"

She nodded then glanced up at him. "Try to be nice."

Teague gave her hand a squeeze, then reached for the door. He wasn't quite sure what to expect. Was Harry going to throw the agreement back in his face? Or was he going to accept the land graciously?

The room was dimly lit, the blinds on the window turned down. Teague was shocked by Harry's appearance. He was immobilized by traction, ropes and slings and pulleys keeping his right leg at an angle. The man had always seemed so powerful. But he looked so small in the big bed, his skin pale, his beard grizzled.

"Hello, Mr. Fraser."

"Quinn," he said. He pointed to the chair beside the bed, but Teague shook his head. "I'm good."

"Hayley showed me this." He waved the paper. "Is it real?"

Teague nodded. "Yeah. My brother gave me the land and I'm giving it to you."

"Does your brother know about this?"

"Yes. As soon as you're out of here, we'll get all the papers signed and make it official. But it's yours."

"Why are you doing this?"

"For Hayley."

"You expect me to turn her over to you because you gave me the land?"

Teague laughed. "Jaysus, Harry, she's not a horse. You can't trade her like a piece of property. I did this because I thought it might keep your arse alive. That's what Hayley wants and I want what she wants."

Harry scowled. "Are you in love with her?"

"Yes," Teague said. "I have been since I was a kid."

"So, I guess you figure once I leave this world, she'll get everything and you'll waltz right in and share in the wealth?"

Teague cursed beneath his breath. "Go to hell, Harry. I don't give a shit about Wallaroo. But after all you've put Hayley through, the mess you made of her childhood, I think she deserves the place after you depart this life. Although, I don't expect you'll be dying anytime soon since it's your goal to make her as miserable as possible."

"I don't want that," Harry said. He went silent for a long time, turning his head away from Teague to look out the window. "I know I didn't do well by her. But I didn't know how to take care of her any more than I knew how to care for my own son."

"It's not that hard to love her," Teague said. "I fell in love with her the very first time I saw her."

"I guess it's my fault, then. I never knew what to say to her. Hell, I drove her father off Wallaroo and I figured she wouldn't have any interest in sticking around, either. She proved my point when she ran away."

"I don't know why, but she does care about you."

Harry shifted, wincing as he tried to sit up a little straighter. "They have me so shot full of pain medicine, I'm not sure what I'm saying, but I'm going to say it anyway. If I don't make it through the surgery, I want you to watch over her. I may have had my troubles with your father and your brother, but you seem like a decent sort, Quinn. And Hayley likes you."

"I think she does," Teague said. "But you are going to make it through this operation. And then you'll go somewhere where they'll get you walking again. And then you'll go home to Wallaroo. And I'm going to see that you're a lot nicer to Hayley from now on."

"You seem pretty damn sure of yourself," Harry said.

"I am. And if you don't try to make that happen, then you and I are going to have a problem."

"Good enough," he said. "Then I guess we have an understanding?"

"We do," Teague said.

"Now get the hell out of my room and let me sleep," Harry ordered.

Teague turned and walked to the door, smiling to himself as he stepped into the hallway. Hayley was waiting for him outside the door. He wrapped his arm around her shoulders and walked with her toward the lift. "It went well. We had a nice talk. Now let's get out of here."

They found Teague's rental in the car park. Teague pulled the door open for Hayley, then circled around to the driver's side. The hotel was less than a mile away, but Hayley wasn't in the mood to wait. She ran her hand along his thigh as he turned onto the street, then slid it in between his legs.

He grabbed her wrist to stop her from going farther, but she just smiled and ignored him. By the time they reached the hotel, he was completely aroused, his erection straining at the fabric of his jeans.

When they pulled in to the hotel car park, Teague retrieved his jacket from the rear seat and held it over his groin as he and Hayley strolled into the lobby. He glanced over to see a satisfied grin on her face. "Thank you," Teague said. "I always appreciate walking around like this. It makes me look like a pervert."

They rode the lift in silence. When he opened the room door and stepped aside, Hayley trailed her fingers across the front of his jeans as she walked past him.

The moment the door closed, she began undressing him. He reached for her shirt, but she brushed his hands away. Teague decided to let her have her way with him, curious how far she would go to pleasure him.

By the time she had him stripped naked, he really didn't care what she did. The feel of her fingers wrapped around his shaft was enough to bring him to the edge. But Hayley had other plans. She kissed a trail from his mouth to his chest and then lower.

He felt oddly vulnerable. She was still dressed and he was naked. But the moment her mouth closed over him, he realized that this situation was fantasy material. She was in control, seducing him, and he could simply relax and enjoy the ride.

It hadn't taken Hayley long to learn what he liked,

exactly what stoked his desire. They'd had plenty of practice during their holiday. Teague drew in a deep breath and held it, her tongue sending him closer to release. But she read the signs and slowed her pace, smoothing her hands over his belly as she pulled back.

He was so hard, he wasn't sure he could be any more aroused. But then, Hayley stood. Her gaze fixed on his, she slowly stripped out of her clothes, as if performing for him. The striptease was even more intriguing than physical contact.

He reached for her, but she evaded his grasp. And when she was completely undressed, she didn't return to touching him. Instead, she ran her hands over her own body. Teague groaned, aching to touch her but still caught up in the game she was playing. But when she slipped her fingers between her legs, he growled softly and grasped her waist with his hands.

Picking her up off her feet, Teague wrapped her legs around him, holding tight to her hips. Her lips found his and she twisted her fingers through his hair as she kissed him. Slowly, Teague entered her, a surge of desire washing over him. And when he was buried deep, Hayley sighed softly, a satisfied smile curling her lips. "Oh, don't move. That feels so good," she said breathlessly.

"I have to move," he said.

"No, you don't."

"Let me move," he said.

She shifted above him and he gasped. Maybe he didn't need to move. But the pleasure was too strong to deny. Teague held her tight as he slowly withdrew, then drove forward again. She whispered his name, her lips soft against his ear.

This was all he needed, Teague thought. The only thing in his life he couldn't do without. Her body was the perfect match for his, her heart and her soul the prize he wanted to possess. And though he hoped to spend a lifetime with her, Teague knew he'd be happy with one more day and the night that followed.

8

THE SKY WAS GRAY and overcast as the plane flew low over the outback landscape. Hayley had thought about canceling the trip, leaving it for a sunnier day, but then decided that the weather matched her mood. It had been nearly a week since she'd last smiled, the evening after Harry's surgery, when she'd sat by her grandfather's bed and told him that she loved him.

Hayley looked down at the urn on her lap, running her hands over the cool ceramic surface. The numbness had begun to wear off and reality had set in. Harry was gone.

He'd written detailed plans before going into surgery, scribbling everything he wanted her to know on a small scrap of paper. She'd found it a day later, after the hospital had returned his belongings. No funeral, no mourning, scatter his ashes over Wallaroo.

His death had been unexpected. He'd survived the surgery and had been making plans to enter a rehabilitation center. She'd said good-night to him that evening, happy that things had gone so well, and the next morning, when she'd arrived at the hospital, the staff had told her Harry had passed away during the night.

It had been a quiet death, in his sleep, and though the doctors wanted to give her all the details and the cause, Hayley really didn't want to listen. She knew why Harry had died. He'd done as she had asked, and then chosen his own time, on his own terms. In the end, Hayley was grateful that he never had to know a long, debilitating illness.

She had wanted to grieve for him, but she knew Harry wouldn't approve. There had been tears, but after the tears had come comfort in knowing that Harry's spirit would always live on at Wallaroo, in the beautiful sunsets and wide, sweeping vistas, in the shimmer of light off the slow-moving creeks and in the soft breeze that brought the rain.

"This looks like a nice spot," Teague said. "With the creek and that outcropping right there. It's very peaceful."

"It is," Hayley said. "What should I do?"

"Open the window and take the top off once you're holding the urn outside. Then tip it toward the tail of the plane."

Hayley slid the window open. "Goodbye, Harry." She followed Teague's instructions and watched as the cloud of ashes flew past the plane and drifted down to the ground. It was difficult to believe Harry wouldn't be there when they got to the house, sitting on the porch, watching over his property. She'd never have to cook him supper or pick up after him again. She'd never have to listen to him complain.

Hayley had been so young when her parents had died that she barely remembered feeling anything then. One day, they were there and the next day they weren't. The minister had told her to be brave. The people at the funeral home had patted her on the head and whispered behind her back. And though she felt the loss, she hadn't been old enough to understand the true impact it would have on her life.

"He was all I had left," Hayley said.

"You have me." Teague reached for her hand and gave it a squeeze. "Cal asked if I'd bring you over for dinner tonight. Gemma is going to be leaving soon and she wanted to say goodbye."

Hayley smiled weakly. "I can't. I'd really rather go home. I've got a lot to do."

"Nothing that can't wait," he said.

"I have to make some decisions. I have to get back to Sydney. I'm supposed to fly to Los Angeles next week. And I'm due at the studio right after that to finish taping *Castle Cove.*"

"So you're going to leave?"

"I don't have much choice," Hayley said.

"The station is yours now. You've watched Harry run it. You could do the same. You could raise horses, give the Quinns some competition. And you've got free vet services. There are plenty of station owners who'd kill for that."

"I can't live out here alone," she said.

"You wouldn't be alone," Teague replied. "I'd be here. I could move my things over and come and go from Wallaroo."

Hayley felt her cheeks warm. Was this a marriage

proposal or a business proposal? "And what would we be?"

"Whatever you wanted us to be," he said. "Friends? Lovers? Partners? Roommates?"

She turned away, her pulse racing at the thought of accepting his offer. She could have Teague with her for as long as she wanted. Or as long as he wanted, whichever came first. Though the thought of losing him terrified her, it wasn't half as bad as the thought of never having him in the first place.

"I know what you're thinking," Teague said. "Where's the parachute? I gotta get out of this plane."

Hayley couldn't help but laugh. "You planned this so I couldn't escape?"

"It looks that way. You don't have to give me an answer now, Hayley. But at least consider the option."

"Good. Because I don't have an answer now," she replied.

"But you'll think about it?"

Hayley nodded. It was the least she could do. Besides, it was a plan worth examining. She could imagine a life on Wallaroo with Teague. It would be simple, but satisfying. She could also picture her life in Sydney, her career, making movies and traveling the world.

If she decided not to stay, the sale of the station would provide her with the kind of lifelong security she'd always wanted. She could take the time to choose good projects, to build a film career slowly and carefully. And she'd never have to depend on another person for her day-to-day existence.

But Teague wouldn't understand that reason, her need to be able to survive without help from anyone. He seemed happy to have her dependent on him, to provide for her and make sure her life was easy.

They landed on the airstrip on Wallaroo, then rode to the house in Hayley's car. They bumped along the rough dirt track, Teague bracing his hand on the dash. "If you're going to live on Wallaroo, you're going to need a better way to get around. The suspension on this thing will last about a week."

"Right," she said softly. As she focused on the road ahead, she thought about the other changes she'd have to make. She'd have to sell her place in Sydney, give up acting and walk away from the life she'd built for herself. To live in the middle of nowhere.

But here, on the station, she would have love. And no matter how she turned it over in her head, there was no possible way she could have both.

When they reached the house, Hayley stopped the car and got out. But she couldn't bring herself to go inside. She'd spent the past week wandering around the station, cleaning the stables and the yard, taking long rides in the outback with Molly, sitting on the porch and memorizing her lines for the next three episodes of *Castle Cove*. She'd avoided the house as much as possible, knowing she'd have to face sorting through Harry's things.

Teague had been occupied with work and had only spent a few nights with her, sleeping by her side while she passed the night wide-awake and restless, her mind a jumble of disparate thoughts.

"I can't," she said, staring at the house. "I can't go inside. Not now. It's too sad."

He pulled her along, holding tight to her hand. "We don't have to go inside," he said. "Let's ride out to the shack. We haven't been there for a while. It'll be fun."

Hayley nodded and they walked toward the stables. She sat on a bale of straw as Teague saddled Molly. When he was finished, he gave her a knee up and then settled himself behind her. He gave Molly a gentle kick and they started out into the gray daylight.

"When I go home to Sydney, I want you to take Molly to Kerry Creek. Find someone to ride her every day."

"I can do that," Teague said.

She sank against him and closed her eyes. Exhaustion seemed to descend on her all at once, the gentle gait of the horse lulling her toward sleep. Everything seemed so right when Teague was with her. He was strong when she couldn't be and he made her laugh when she felt gloomy. He talked to her when she needed an opinion and listened when she didn't.

From the moment she'd seen him standing outside Molly's stall, Hayley had known what she was risking. And now, she was left to deal with the consequences of falling in love with Teague all over again. Only this time, she'd be the one to walk away and leave him behind.

Somehow, that didn't make her decision easier. It made the prospect of leaving almost impossible to bear.

"I'M NOT QUITE SURE why I'm here," Teague said, looking around the interior of the solicitor's office. Both he and Hayley had been summoned to Brisbane for the reading of Harry's will. Teague had assumed that it had to do with the land he'd given Harry.

The solicitor cleared his throat as he rearranged the stacks of files on his desk. "Since both you and Miss Fraser are mentioned in the will, it's customary."

Teague frowned. "I'm in the will? How can that be?"

"Harry made some last-minute changes. He called me over to the hospital the morning of his surgery so he could sign the new addendum."

"Let me guess. He left me the Quinn land that I gave to him."

"No," the solicitor said. "He left you half of Wallaroo."

Both Teague and Hayley gasped at the same time, then looked at each other. "Say that again," Teague murmured.

"You two are to share ownership in the station. Fifty-fifty. Harry decided if his granddaughter did not want to keep the station, then it should go to the Quinns. You are both required to live on the station for at least six months out of the year or you will forfeit your right to ownership. After ten years, if you both agree to sell, then you will split the profits from the sale fifty-fifty. If there is no agreement to sell, then this arrangement remains in force."

"But I can't live on the station," Hayley said. "I have a career in Sydney."

"Then I'm afraid the station will go to the Quinns, as long as Mr. Quinn is following the residency clause. Are you willing to live on Wallaroo?"

"Yes," Teague said.

"Of course he is," Hayley said. "It's perfect. The Quinns have always wanted Wallaroo. And now they have it." She turned to Teague. "What kind of deal did you make with him? Did you talk him into this?"

"No!" Teague said. "I'm as surprised as you are."

"You're sure you didn't figure out some way to force the issue, to make me stay on Wallaroo? Because this seems awfully suspicious to me."

"Well, it seems downright crazy to me. Harry asked me to take care of you, but I never thought—"

"And what did you say?" she demanded. "Did you tell him you would?"

"Of course."

"See. That's what it was. He assumed you'd marry me and we'd live happily ever after on Wallaroo."

"Well, it's not such a bad idea," Teague said. "Didn't you say you'd always dreamed we'd have a station together, with horses?"

"I was a kid," Hayley said. "And it was just a stupid dream. I have a life of my own now. I don't need you making decisions for me."

"Would you two like a moment alone?" the solicitor asked.

"No!" Hayley said.

"Yes," Teague answered.

The solicitor got up and Hayley shook her head. "Why do you listen to him and not to me?"

When the solicitor shut the office door behind him, Hayley turned to Teague. "You can't force me to live on Wallaroo."

"I'm not forcing you to do anything, Hayley. This was Harry's deal, not mine. But I can understand his thinking. Wallaroo has been in your family for years. He didn't want to see it sold. And you shouldn't, either. It's part of your heritage."

"I make my own decisions about my life. Not you, not Harry, me."

"So you don't want to be with me?"

"Not because of some scheme you and Harry cooked up," she said.

"I see." Teague shrugged. Hell, there were times when Hayley's ability to reason flew right out the window. Instead of thinking things through, she reacted. They could make this arrangement work. Teague could run the station and she could come and go as she pleased. He wouldn't hold her to the residency clause— at least not down to the letter.

But if he did decide to enforce the rules, he'd have her for six months out of the year. If he couldn't convince her they belonged together given that amount of time, then maybe they didn't belong together at all.

"If you don't like the terms, then don't follow them."

"I'd lose my share of Wallaroo," she said.

"You hate Wallaroo."

"I don't hate it. I just never appreciated it until I came back this last time."

"What do you want me to do?"

"Give me your half," she demanded. "That's the only fair thing to do."

"No," Teague said. "You aren't prepared to run it

alone. And it's the perfect place to raise horses. What land we don't use for that, we can lease to Callum for cattle."

"You have it all planned out, don't you? This plays right into your hand. Why don't we both agree to break the rules and sell it. You can come to Sydney with me and start a practice there." She raised her brow. "How about that scheme? Now you have to turn *your* life upside down for me."

"Would that make you happy?" Teague asked. "Would that mean we could spend the rest of our lives together?" He waited for her answer, knowing it wouldn't come. The question actually seemed to make her even angrier.

Had he really expected the fairy tale to last forever? Everything had been going so well for them, beyond Harry's passing. Hayley had been quiet and thoughtful, though a bit confused. But here was the Hayley he'd always known. Scrappy and opinionated, a girl who didn't let anyone push her around. Until she was backed into a corner. Then she clawed like a tiger to escape.

"I'm going to fight this in the courts," Hayley said, snatching up her bag and getting to her feet.

"Great!" Teague replied. "Now that one feud is finally over, we'll start another one."

"Tell your solicitor that he will be hearing from mine," she said as she strode to the door.

"How are you going to get home?" he shouted. "It's a long walk."

Hayley slowly turned. "I am perfectly capable of getting to Wallaroo on my own. I see you share Harry's rather low opinion of my intelligence. You two should have made friends long ago. You're so much alike."

She yanked on the door. At first, it didn't open, and when it did, it hit her on the head. Teague winced, jumping to his feet to help her. But Hayley warned him off, waving her finger at him.

Teague sat down in the chair, cursing softly as she slammed the door behind her. A few moments later, the solicitor returned, a file folder clutched in his hands. "I suspected she might be upset," he murmured as he took his place behind his desk. "These last-minute changes are always a problem. But the doctors assured me that Harry was of sound mind and all the necessary signatures were made. If there is a lawsuit, I'd be happy to testify."

"I don't think that will be necessary," Teague said. He stood and held out his hand. "Thank you. I'll be in touch."

Teague half expected Hayley to be waiting in the reception area, but when he got there, she was gone. Her behavior wasn't surprising. He'd been expecting it for some time. It was Hayley's way of coping when she felt herself growing too close to someone, depending too much on another human being.

She'd done it when they were teenagers, refusing to speak to him for days after some silly fight. He'd always figured that must be the way all girls behaved. But now he saw it for what it was—a defense mechanism. It probably would have come earlier had her grandfather's death not delayed her.

It was the "love you" he'd mumbled to her outside the hospital that probably set it off. Too much, too soon.

It'd seemed like the proper thing to say, considering the situation. He'd wanted to reassure her, not box her into a corner. But his declaration and then the will were enough to convince her that he expected to be a part of her future—and she had no say in the matter.

"What the hell were you thinking, Harry?" Teague muttered as he walked to the car park. Though he suspected Harry had noble motives for changing his will, it only proved that he'd never really known his granddaughter. If he had, he'd have realized she'd see the move as another attempt to control her life.

Harry had suspected Hayley wouldn't want to run the station, so he'd given half of it to a Quinn. He'd thought Hayley might sell the station, so he'd made it impossible for her to do so without a Quinn's permission. If Hayley did want to run the station, then she would have help…from a Quinn.

Harry's attempt to keep the two of them together, in at least a legal and working arrangement, may have driven them apart emotionally. But Hayley would have to see the sense in it. She had a career away from the outback. And Teague was in the perfect position to make something out of Wallaroo. If he succeeded, she would profit from it, too.

Teague walked up the stairs to the second level of the car park and searched the rows of cars for his rental. He spotted it parked at the far end, right where he'd left it. As he approached he noticed Hayley leaning against the passenger-side door, her arms crossed over her chest, an annoyed expression suffusing her pretty face.

Teague ignored her, unlocked the driver's side and got in. Two could play this game. If she wanted a ride home, she'd have to ask. He wasn't going to offer.

God, she could be so exasperating. There were times when he almost believed they'd be better off giving up on their romance and beginning a chaste friendship. She wouldn't be half so skittish and any disagreements between them could be worked out in a rational fashion.

"Are you going to get in or will I have to drive over you?"

She turned and pulled on the door handle, but the passenger side was still locked. Hayley sent him a withering glare and he pushed the button to unlock it. She got inside, looking straight ahead and refusing to speak.

"You're really beautiful when you act childish," he said.

"You don't think I have a right to be angry?"

"No. Because you've assumed things that aren't true. I didn't ask Harry to do this. I was as surprised as you were. And I understand why you're angry, but don't take it out on me."

"Why not? I'm sure you think this is a perfect solution. With the station between us, you'll have exactly what you want."

"And what is that?"

"Me," she snapped.

Teague shoved the key in the ignition and started the car. "And what's so bloody wrong with me wanting you? I happen to like spending time with you. I think you're the most beautiful woman in the entire world.

And I think we'd make a good team. We could make a success of Wallaroo, turn it into something really grand. But you've got your knickers in a twist because of the way it happened."

"I can't be tied to that station."

"It's not only the station. It's everything. You're like a mare that can't be broken." As soon as the words were out of his mouth, he realized his mistake.

"Oh, that's lovely," she retorted. "As if I should want to be tamed, so I can live with a bit in my mouth and haul your arse around all day long."

"All right, maybe that wasn't the best comparison. But there are some benefits to settling down and making a commitment."

"I don't want to talk about this right now," she said. "I would rather we pass the ride to the airport in complete silence. Can you manage that?"

He felt her pulling away and there was nothing he could do to stop it. She'd been under so much stress, the weight of Harry's injury and death bending her to the breaking point. But now, with the will, she'd cracked. The wall was back up and they'd returned to where they began.

Maybe Hayley wasn't capable of a long-term relationship. He'd always wanted to believe she was perfect, but the more time he spent with her, the more he understood the ghosts that haunted her. No matter how hard he pushed, she simply pushed back.

It would be up to her to decide if they had a future. And nothing he could say or do would change that. He just hoped he wouldn't have to spend the rest of his life waiting for her to realize she loved him…and wondering what might have been if she had.

"HAYLEY!"

Teague's voice echoed through the empty house. Hayley folded the T-shirt and tucked it into her bag. Then she bent down and picked up the sandals Teague had bought her and placed them in the plastic bag with her other shoes.

"Hayley!"

She found the letter she'd written to him and tucked it into the back pocket of her jeans. His footsteps sounded on the stairs as she closed the zipper on the tote and set it beside the bed. Then she sat down and folded her hands in her lap, knowing that the next few minutes might be more difficult than she'd ever imagined.

"Hayley?" He stepped inside her bedroom. "Didn't you hear me calling?" His gaze dropped to the bag at her feet. "What's going on?"

"I have to go," she said.

"You don't have to be back in Sydney until next week."

"My agent got me an audition for a television series. They want me in Los Angeles right away. I have to go now."

He frowned, shaking his head. "A television series? In Los Angeles?"

She nodded.

"But you're not going to do it, right? You have a job like that right here in Australia."

"This would be different. This would be a lot more money."

"Hayley, you own half this station. You don't have to worry about money anymore."

"But I can't sell my half unless you agree to sell yours. So I really don't have anything except a lot of land and no money."

"If you need help, you know I'll be there to help you. Do you need money?"

"See, there's the problem." She stood up and returned to her packing, grabbing her tote and stuffing a pair of jeans inside. "Any actress would kill for an opportunity like this."

In truth, she still hadn't decided whether it was a good idea. She was *supposed* to want a better career. Her agent had said so and she usually listened to her agent. This might open the door to American movies or at least a big role in an Australian movie.

But since she'd returned to Wallaroo after the reading of the will, she hadn't thought much about her acting career. There had been long stretches of time when it hadn't even entered her mind. If acting was her passion, wasn't she supposed be obsessed with it?

Instead, she'd spent her time wandering around the house, making a mental list of the changes that needed to be made, imagining life at Wallaroo with Teague. With so much time alone, she'd found herself fantasizing an entire existence—and she'd liked what she'd seen in her head.

"I need to find out what it's all about before I get too excited," Hayley said in an indifferent tone.

"You were going to leave without saying goodbye?"

"I wrote you a letter." She risked a glance up at him. "I want you to make sure you look after Molly. And if you need any money, call me. We should share the expenses of fixing this place up. If you don't want to do that, then just keep a tally. If we ever sell the place, you can take it out of my share."

Teague cursed softly. "You're not coming back."

"That's not true. I have to come back. I'm under contract with *Castle Cove* through September."

"I meant to Wallaroo. You're not coming back here."

"I'll visit when I can." She sat down on the edge of the bed. "When are you moving in?"

"I brought some of my stuff over today. Callum is coming later to pick me up and then I'll fly the plane over here. I can't very well get this place in shape if I don't live here."

"No. There is a lot to do."

"I figure we ought to upgrade the homestead a bit while we're looking for stock. I spoke to Cal and he's interested in leasing some of the grazing land for Kerry Creek cattle. So we should have some money to invest."

He made it sound as if she was going to be part of it all. Was that wishful thinking or did he believe he could change her mind about leaving? "That's brilliant," she muttered. "You have it all figured out."

"Not all," he said. "There are still a few pieces missing, but I'm working on those."

"I don't know when I'll be able to come to Wallaroo

again," she said. "Our production schedule is always really busy. Maybe sometime in September."

"No worries. You'll be surprised when you come the next time. I'll have this place in top shape."

Hayley drew a deep breath and flopped back on the bed, staring up at the ceiling. What did he want from her? Was she supposed to feel guilty for leaving all the work to him while she ran off and became a movie star?

Teague lay down beside her, turning to face her. He reached out and toyed with a lock of her hair. "We can make this work," he said.

"Can we?"

"Only if you want to, Hayley. Do you? If you don't, then you should get up and leave right now. Because I'm not sure I'm going to be able to say goodbye without making myself look like a damn drongo."

Hayley rolled onto her side. "Kiss me," she said, saying a silent prayer that one kiss would make everything clear in her head.

"Why? Do you expect that to change anything? I could tear all your clothes off and make love to you and you'd still leave. You decided to leave the day you got here and nothing that's happened since has made a bit of difference, has it?"

"That's not true. You don't have to be cruel."

"I'm being honest," Teague said. "We've always been honest with each other, haven't we?"

Hayley heard the anger in his voice, the bitter edge that sent daggers through her soul. Teague understood her too well. He knew exactly what was running through her mind right now, the desperate need to run away and the overwhelming temptation to stay.

He rolled over and threw his arm over his eyes. "Get the hell out of here, Hayley. You don't belong here. You never have. The same way I don't belong anywhere *but* here."

"I'm—"

"Don't. I don't need any explanations. Just go."

Hayley sat up. Bracing her hand beside his body, she leaned over and brushed a kiss across his lips. "Goodbye, Teague." When he didn't reply, she slowly stood and picked up her bags. He was still lying on the bed, his arm over his face, when she turned to take one last look.

As she walked down the stairs, she slowed her pace, waiting for him to come after her, to drag her back to the bedroom and make love to her for the rest of the afternoon. By the time she reached her car, Hayley realized he wasn't going to come. He was going to let her walk away.

Drawing a ragged breath, she tossed her bags in the rear seat and got behind the wheel. She glanced up at her bedroom window, where the breeze ruffled the plain cotton curtains. He wasn't there watching.

Hayley reached for the car door, then let her hand drop. She shoved her keys into her pocket, turned and walked toward the stable.

Molly was in her stall, munching on fresh hay. She watched Hayley with huge dark eyes, blinking as Hayley smoothed her hand over the mare's nose. "You be a good girl," she said. "Teague will take care of you now. He'll make sure you have plenty to eat and get exercise. He's good with horses and you'll like him."

Hayley's eyes swam with tears. How was it she could walk away from Teague, yet the thought of leaving Molly made her cry? She kissed Molly's muzzle, then turned and ran out of the stable.

As she approached the house, she saw Teague standing on the porch, his arm braced against one of the posts, his expression unreadable. Hayley stood next to the car, watching him. Their eyes locked for a long moment. Then she smiled and gave him a small wave.

He didn't respond. Gathering her resolve, she got into the car and started the engine, then slowly drove out of the yard. She couldn't bring herself to look in the rearview mirror. No, from now on, she couldn't focus on the past. She had to look forward. Without regrets and without doubts.

This was her life and she'd make her own decisions. And whether they were right or wrong, she was willing to live with the consequences.

9

HAYLEY HAD NEVER SEEN anything like it. Miles and miles of traffic stretched out in front of the taxi, the landscape of cars wavering in the heat from the freeway pavement. Though traffic could be slow in Sydney, the government had quickly moved to fix the problem. Here in Los Angeles, people seemed to accept it as part of the lifestyle.

The airport had been worse than the freeway. Her flight had been delayed twice. She'd been scheduled to arrive twelve hours before her audition, giving her time to settle into a hotel and get some rest. Instead, she'd arrived with just two hours to spare and had to go from the airport to the studio directly.

"How long will it take to get there?" she asked the cabdriver.

He shrugged. "Maybe hour, two, could be," he replied in a heavy accent. She glanced at his name card. Vladimir Petrosky. She'd heard that all the cabdrivers and waiters and store clerks in L.A. were aspiring actors. If that was true, she'd probably have plenty of competition.

"You call," he said. "Tell them you be late."

"I don't have a phone," Hayley replied.

He passed a mobile through the window between them. "Use mine," he said. "No problem."

Hayley pulled out the copy of her itinerary and searched for the number of the studio. When she found it, she punched the digits into the phone. A receptionist answered and put her through to the assistant producer's assistant. Who put her through to the assistant producer. Who politely informed her that the producer had another appointment in an hour and if she didn't make it, they would have to reschedule for next week.

"I'll be there," she said. Hayley handed the phone to the driver. "Is there another way? Perhaps we could get off this highway and find another route?"

"Other could be bad," Vladimir said. "You have audition, yes?"

"Yes?"

He twisted around in his seat and looked at her. "You give me producer's name and phone number, I get you there on time."

Wasn't this extortion? Not a very serious case, but an actor had to do what an actor had to do. "All right," she said. "But I'm going to write it down and leave it here on the seat. If anyone asks, you don't mention my name. Deal?"

"I not know your name," Vladimir said.

"Good, that works out well for the both of us."

True to Vladimir's word, he managed to get her to the studio in under a half hour, taking the first exit off the freeway and then winding through busy city streets.

She paid him with the cash her agent had given her, then hurried through the doors of a plain two-story building on the studio lot, dragging her bags along with her.

The receptionist pointed to a long sofa and Hayley sat down. The office was decorated with photos from the programs they produced. Like her show in Australia, this was an hour-long weekly drama. Set in an American hospital, the show had launched movie careers for three of its lead actors, so a place in the cast was considered a stepping stone to bigger things.

Bigger things, she mused. Was that really what she wanted? Her mind flashed back to the room she'd shared with Teague on the island, to the perfect solitude of their waterfront bungalow. All that seemed like a dream to her now, stuck in the middle of this noisy city with a haze of smog all around it.

She closed her eyes and pictured Teague in bed, his naked limbs twisted in the sheets, his hair rumpled. That's what she wanted. Teague, naked and aroused, his lips on hers, his hands exploring her body, making her ache with desire. She wanted to go to bed at night knowing he'd be there in the morning. She wanted to talk to him about little things she'd discovered in the course of her day. And she wanted to be assured that he would always love her, no matter what.

But wasn't that exactly what she'd walked away from? Hadn't he offered that life to her? Why was it so easy to see, now that she was miles and miles away from him? Hayley pressed her palm to her chest, trying to ease the emptiness that had settled in her heart. Though she'd tried her best to convince herself otherwise, something had changed inside her.

The thought of loving him and then losing him no longer frightened her. Anything truly important always came with risks. Her real fear was that she'd go her entire life and never find another human being who would understand her the way Teague did. Had she deliberately ignored her true feelings simply because they'd begun when she was a child?

It was so easy to consider their connection a teenage infatuation, something never meant to survive to adulthood. But it had survived. And they did still love each other. And she'd been a... "Fool," Hayley whispered.

She glanced up to see the receptionist watching her with an odd expression. "Is everything all right?"

"No," Hayley said with a groan.

"Are you going to be ill?"

Hayley shook her head. "I don't think so." She stood up. "I have to leave. Can you call me a taxi?"

"But, Miss Fraser, Mr. Wells hasn't seen you yet."

"I know. But I don't want to be seen. Tell him I'm grateful for the opportunity, but I'm not interested in doing American television. I don't want to live in America. It's too far away."

"Are you sure?"

Hayley smiled. "I am. I've never been more sure of anything in my life. Isn't that crazy? I walk away from him a few days ago and now all I can think of is getting home to be with him."

The receptionist smiled. "Oh, I understand. Love?"

"Yes!" Hayley cried. "I think it might be. And I don't want to be living here while he's there. I'm not even sure I want to be in Sydney. I mean, that's at least fifteen hours by car. Although he has a plane, so he could probably come for visits. But I don't like the idea of not seeing him every day. I think if you're in love, you should be together. Don't you?"

"Yes?"

"Exactly," Hayley said. "I need to get to the airport right away. How long will it take for a taxi?"

"I'll call right now," she offered. "It will only be a few minutes."

"That would be brilliant," Hayley replied, picking up her bags. "I think it would be best if I waited outside."

She didn't want to have to make her excuses to Mr. Wells. After all, what would she say? *I'm sorry, I can't audition today because I just realized I'm still in love with my childhood sweetheart.* "I'm such an idiot!" Hayley cried as she shoved open the main door and stumbled out.

She stood beneath a wide awning for five minutes before she saw a taxi approach. The car stopped in front of her and she got inside, only to find Vladimir behind the wheel. He got out and tossed her bags in the boot. "It went well? You smiling."

"No," she said as she crawled inside. "It didn't go at all. But that's all right. I've got something really good waiting for me at home."

Vladimir got behind the wheel. "Where can I take you?"

"To the airport," she said.

"Quick trip," Vladimir said. He started the meter and Hayley sat back and sighed softly. Her agent was going to be furious, but she didn't care. He'd get over it. As for her acting career in Australia, she still had obligations, but once she'd fulfilled her contract, she was free to take projects she found interesting and exciting, and not just projects that would pay the bills.

Teague had been right. She owned half the station and though it wasn't money in the bank, it was financial security. She'd always have a place to live, work that she found satisfying and the chance for a comfortable future. That was all she'd ever wanted from her acting career.

What would it feel like to leave celebrity behind? She'd never really enjoyed the notoriety that her career had brought and it wasn't something she'd miss. And perhaps, someday, someone would ask what had happened to that girl who used to play the vixen on *Castle Cove.*

They'd find her living on Wallaroo with her childhood sweetheart, raising horses—and maybe a few children, as well. Although Hayley wasn't sure about the children. How could she be a good parent when she'd never had a good example to follow? But, though she barely remembered her own parents, she did remember being loved. There had been smiles and hugs and giggles.

She let her thoughts drift, images flowing through her head, all of them comforting, happy, the pieces of her life she wanted to remember. There was no reason to always expect the worst, to be waiting for some disaster to befall her. Teague had tried to tell her that, but she hadn't listened.

The next thing Hayley knew the driver was calling out to her. She opened her eyes and realized that she'd fallen asleep. Rubbing her face, she sat up and looked around. They were at the airport again, in the same spot from which Vladimir had picked her up. "Qantas?" he asked.

"Yes," she said. She fumbled with her wallet, then withdrew the rest of the American money she'd brought along. "Here, keep the change."

He frowned. "But this is too much."

"Don't worry. I don't need it. I'm going home. And I'm not going to be leaving again anytime soon."

"IT'S GOOD GRAZING LAND," Callum said, staring out across the landscape toward the horizon. "If we have more land, we can increase the size of the mob. How many hectares do you want to lease?"

"As much as you want. I plan to start small," he said. "Maybe twenty-five mares. Good stock. We won't need a lot of grazing land. I'm hoping you'll sell me five or six Kerry Creek mares."

"I don't know if I should be helping you. You're going to be competing with us."

Teague drew a deep breath, ready to lay out his plan. "You never wanted the horse-breeding operation in the first place. I'm the one who talked you into it. Why don't you let me move the whole thing over here. You'll get your pick of stock ponies at a good price and you can concentrate on cattle."

Callum thought about the offer for a moment. "He won't go for that," Brody said, his hands folded over his saddle horn, his hat pulled low over his eyes. "Cal would never pay for anything that he could get for free."

"There's where you're wrong, little brother." Callum turned to Teague. "All right. It's a deal. I'll trade you the Kerry Creek horses for lease rights on Wallaroo grazing land."

Teague glanced over at Brody. "What's wrong with Cal?"

"Lovesick," Brody said. "Right now he'd say yes to just about anything. Gemma has turned him into a shadow of his former self."

"Not only me," Cal countered. "Look at poor Teague. We're both alone again. You're the only lucky guy in this bunch. How does that figure?" He paused. "And what the hell are you doing here with us when you have Payton waiting back at the homestead?"

"She has a serious case of jet lag. I think she's going to be sleeping for the next week," Brody said.

The three brothers turned and silently surveyed the land in front of them. Teague found it odd that three women had swept into their lives in a single week, turning their lives upside down before sweeping back out. What were the chances of that happening to one of the Quinn brothers, much less all three? Well, at least Brody's girl had come back.

"Yep, we're a pretty pathetic pair," Teague said, patting Callum on the shoulder. "Do you think it's something in the genes?"

"Must be," Brody muttered. "I have plenty in my jeans to satisfy a woman."

"Genes," Teague said. "G-E-N-E-S. You know, DNA? Not your trousers, you big boof."

"Right," Brody said. "Leave it to you to get all scientific on us, Dr. Einstein."

"So, Casanova, what do you propose we do about this mess?" Teague asked.

Brody shrugged. "Why do you think you should do anything? Gemma and Hayley went home. Obviously they weren't interested in living out here in the middle of nowhere. Do you blame them? Our own mother couldn't handle it. Why would they even try?"

"It's not that bad," Callum said, leaning forward in his saddle to look at Brody. "Payton likes it here."

"She does," Brody agreed. "With Teague over at Wallaroo all the time, you're going to need some help running the place. We thought we'd stick around and give you a hand."

"But you're going to take the tryout, right?" Cal's expression turned serious. "You can't give up that chance."

Brody nodded. "Once the knee is stronger."

"Hell, if I could pick this station up and move it to Ireland, I'd do it straightaway," Callum said. "Without a second thought." He turned to Teague. "And you. Why should you even be worried? Hayley has a job in Sydney. At least for a few more months. If that's not enough time to convince her to move in with you, then you're not as smooth as I thought you were."

Callum was right. At least he and Brody had more

options. Cal was pretty much stuck. He'd never walk away from the station. He'd dreamed about running Kerry Creek since he was a kid. But then, he'd never been in love before.

"Maybe you ought to try and convince Gemma to come back," Teague said. "Go to Ireland. Explain to her how you feel and ask her to come home with you."

Callum shook his head. "She wouldn't want to live here."

"Why not? If she loves you, she probably won't care where you live. And Brody and I can watch over the station while you're gone."

"No, I'm fine."

"What did she say when you asked her to stay?" Brody inquired.

Callum frowned. "I didn't ask. She had to go home. She didn't have a choice. Besides, I didn't want to deal with the rejection."

"Jaysus, Cal," Brody and Teague said in unison.

"You don't get anything unless you ask." Teague chuckled. "This is the problem. You've been trapped on this station for so long, you've never learned to deal with women. You are completely clueless."

"If you know all the right moves, then why are you alone?" Cal countered.

"Point taken," Teague muttered.

"I have an idea," Callum said. He pushed his hat down on his head. "Follow me." With a raucous whoop, Callum kicked his horse, and the gelding took off at a gallop. Teague and Brody looked at each other, then did the same, following after him in a cloud of dust and pounding hooves.

Teague assumed they were going to Kerry Creek for a few coldies and some brotherly commiserating. But instead, Callum veered north. As they came over a low rise, he saw the big rock and instantly knew what his brother had planned.

Brody looked over at him and laughed, then urged his horse ahead, overtaking Callum to reach the rock first. He threw himself out of the saddle and scrambled to the top, waiting as Teague and Callum approached.

Brody gave them both a hand up and when they were all standing on top of the rock, he nodded. "Doesn't seem as big as it used to, does it?"

Teague couldn't believe it, either. The rock had once seemed like a mountain, but now he could understand how it might have been rolled here from another spot. "So what do we do? I'm not sure I remember."

"We have to say it out loud," Callum replied. "One wish. The thing you want most in the world."

"How do we know it will work?" Teague asked.

"It worked for me. Remember? I wished I could be a pro footballer. And it happened."

"And I wished I could run a station like Kerry Creek," Callum said. "And I'm running Kerry Creek. I remember what you wished for. You wanted a plane."

"Or a helicopter," Brody said. "I guess you got your wish, too."

"So what makes you think it will work again?" Teague asked.

"We won't know unless we try." Callum drew a deep breath. "I wish Gemma would come back to Kerry Creek for good."

"I wish Hayley would realize I'm the only guy she will ever love."

"I wish Payton would say yes when I ask her to marry me," Brody said.

Teague and Callum looked over at him in astonishment and Brody grinned. "You don't get anything in life unless you ask."

"Well, I guess that's it," Callum said in his usual down-to-business manner. "We'll see if it works. Are you riding back to Kerry Creek with us?"

"I've got work to do on Wallaroo," he said. "But I'll come by tomorrow to talk about our deal."

They jumped off the rock and remounted their horses. Then Brody and Callum headed toward Kerry Creek and Teague toward Wallaroo. The ride to the homestead was filled with thoughts of Hayley. She'd left for L.A. four days ago and he hadn't heard from her since. He'd tracked down her phone number and tried calling, but had gotten her voice mail and hung up.

He thought if she answered, he would know what to say. Something would come to him. But he couldn't leave a message. So he called occasionally, hoping that she'd answer. And when she did, he'd be able to put into words how he felt about her.

But didn't she already know how he felt? Hadn't he made it clear? Or, like Cal, had he forgotten to ask her to stay? He rewound every one of their conversations. No, he'd asked, over and over. And she'd refused.

"Guess I'll have to find a better way to convince her," he murmured.

When he reached the stable, he groomed and fed Tapper then sent him out into the yard with Molly and two other horses he'd brought over from Kerry Creek. As he got the operation running, he'd bring over more and more stock until all the breeding mares were stabled at Wallaroo.

There were still repairs to make on the paddock fences and supplies to buy. Between working on the house and the stables, he spent his time making calls, flying out of Wallaroo and returning each evening before sunset. The airstrip on Wallaroo was much closer to the house than the one on Kerry Creek had been, and he'd considered running electricity out for some crude landing lights. Then he wouldn't have to worry about the length of his workday.

But that was a project for a later date. There were too many things to be done. He strode to the house, slowing his pace when he reached the porch. He'd managed to paint the facade a bright white and the trim a deep green. When he'd chosen the colors, he'd thought about what Hayley might have picked and wished she'd been there with him. But without her input, he'd depended on an old color photo of the place.

It looked good. In fact, he couldn't remember ever seeing the house looking quite that nice. He planned to get flowers and bushes for around the porch in spring. And he'd put a porch swing up and buy some comfortable chairs so they could—

"They," he repeated out loud. He was still thinking in terms of "they." He and Hayley, together on Wallaroo. It was always good to be optimistic, but when did optimism turn into delusion? "Give her three months," Teague said. "No, six." After that, he'd be forced to come to terms with the possibility that she wouldn't come back.

He pulled open the front door and walked inside. The interior smelled like fresh paint. He'd finished the front parlor and rearranged the furniture, bringing over his favorite chair from his room at Kerry Creek.

He walked across the parlor to the small desk that Harry had used to keep the accounts for the station. He'd been meaning to go though the papers and see if there was anything he should keep.

Grabbing a chair, he sat down and started with the top drawer. He pulled it out, then dumped it at his feet. A packet of letters caught his attention and he picked them up and examined the envelope on the top.

His breath caught as he recognized his name and his old address at Murdoch University, all written in Hayley's careless scrawl. He slipped the string off the packet and flipped through each envelope. There were letters to him and from him, all of them unopened.

Teague rose and walked out the front door to the porch. He sat down on the step and opened a letter in his handwriting.

As he read the text, memories flooded his mind, memories of a nervous teenager, alone in a strange city, wishing he was home with the girl he loved. Teague chuckled at the clumsy declarations of love, the silly questions, the assurances that they'd be together again soon.

Harry had obviously intercepted his letters, probably meeting the mail plane himself each week. And he'd obviously searched through the outgoing mail for Hayley's letters, as well. Teague had never imagined her grandfather might interfere with the mail. Would things have been different if the letters had been delivered? There was no way of knowing.

He opened a letter from Hayley, written on stationery he'd given her right before he left, stationery decorated with an ink drawing of a horse. It was nearly the same as his letter, declarations of affection and news of her days on Wallaroo.

He stared out across the yard. It was a bit ironic. Now he was the one left waiting and wondering when he'd see her again, hoping for any type of communication. "Come home, Hayley," he said softly. "Come home soon."

HAYLEY'S EYES drifted closed. She shook herself awake and squinted at the deserted road in front of her. She'd landed in Sydney about fifteen hours earlier. She'd lost an entire day on the trip back, but she'd managed to sleep most of the way home. After landing, she'd packed the car and headed north on the Pacific Highway.

A breakfast stop outside of Brisbane provided the opportunity for a short nap before heading west toward

Bilbarra and Wallaroo. The drive had been pleasant when she'd made it a month ago. She'd taken her time, traveling over two days, rather than driving straight through.

But she was anxious to get home, to see Teague again and to try to repair the damage she'd done by leaving. They hadn't spoken for a week and Hayley hadn't bothered to call and warn him of her arrival. She didn't want to explain her actions. She just wanted to walk up to him, throw herself into his arms and kiss him until she was certain he understood how she felt.

She felt like a fool for leaving him in the first place. Teague had put up with a lot of foolish behavior from her, but she hoped he would forgive this one last mistake. She wasn't about to walk away again, at least not until they'd come to an understanding.

They needed to discuss whether they would live together at Wallaroo as friends, as lovers or as two people who were planning to spend the rest of their lives together. Hayley preferred the latter, but she was willing to settle for the other two choices.

As she passed the road to Kerry Creek, she slowed her car, wondering if she ought to stop there first. Over the past week, she'd wondered if Teague had changed his mind about living on Wallaroo. The house was a wreck and it would be a lonely place to live compared to the hustle and bustle of his family's station.

If he wasn't at Wallaroo, she'd take the time to clean up, maybe catch a few hours of sleep and then drive over to see him later in the day. She glanced in the rearview mirror then groaned at the sight she saw.

Dark shadows smudged the skin beneath her eyes and her hair was a mess of tangles. The makeup she'd worn for her audition was long since gone. She hoped he'd be so happy to have her home he wouldn't notice the details of her appearance.

As she drove down the road to Wallaroo, her energy began to surge and she felt a jolt of adrenaline kick in. She was about to change the course of her life for the second time. Only this time, she was steering directly toward what she'd left behind.

She stopped the car at the end of the long driveway into Wallaroo, then got out and retrieved her bag from the rear seat. She tugged off her T-shirt and jeans and slipped on a soft cotton dress. Then she found her brush and tamed her unruly hair, tying it back with a scarf.

When she bent down to look at her reflection in the side mirror, she thought about lipstick and a bit of mascara, but then decided against it. Teague had always preferred her without makeup. She didn't want to look like Hayley, the television star. She wanted to look like Hayley, the girl he'd fallen in love with years before.

Gathering her resolve, she hopped back into the car and started off down the driveway. As she got closer to the house, she noticed something odd. It seemed to gleam in the morning sun. It was only when she entered the yard that Hayley realized the house had been painted.

A tiny gasp slipped from her lips. The two-story clapboard structure looked so shiny and new she barely recognized it. Teague had painted the trim around the windows and the porch floor a deep green. And she noticed a row of new green shutters drying in the sun.

She stopped the car and slowly got out, taking in the other changes that had been made in the course of a week. The yard was clean and raked, the various bits of junk that had collected over the years hauled away. Teague had dug up the ground along the front side of the porch as if to make a garden. And the weather vane that had once perched on the roof at a precarious angle was now fixed and functional.

The front door was open and she peered through the screen, wondering if Teague was inside. She hesitantly opened the screen door, calling out his name, but the house was silent. Hayley looked around in astonishment. He'd worked miracles on the interior, as well. The walls had been painted and the woodwork had been oiled. The plank floors now gleamed with a fresh coat of wax and all the furniture had been rearranged.

It was Wallaroo as it had been, back in its early days, when everything was bright and new, back in the days when her grandmother had been alive and this had been a real home. She walked into the parlor and sat down in a soft leather chair, a chair she recognized from Teague's bedroom at Kerry Creek.

Hayley noticed a pile of mail on the table nearby and reached for it. A tiny sigh slipped from her lips as she realized what she was holding. Her letters to Teague! They were all here, all neatly addressed with the stamps unmarked. She pulled one out of the envelope and read it, each word ringing in her mind as if it had been yesterday.

"I found them in Harry's desk drawer."

She glanced up to see Teague watching her from behind the screen door. He was dressed in work clothes, his stockman's hat pulled low over his eyes. She couldn't read his expression and didn't know if he was pleased or displeased that she'd returned.

Hayley slowly stood and dropped the letters onto the chair. "Hi," she said.

"Hi, yourself," he replied.

"I'm back." She swallowed hard. It wasn't sparkling conversation, but it was the best she could manage between her pounding heart and her dizzy head.

"I can see that."

"I thought I should come home."

"To check up on me?"

She frowned. "No. I mean, yes. To see you. I wanted to see you."

"Why are you here, Hayley?"

She sighed impatiently. "Can we at least be standing in the same room when we have this conversation?"

"What conversation is that?"

"The one where I tell you that I was stupid to leave and that I'm in love with you and I hope you're in love with me." The words came out in a rush and after she said them all, she felt a warm blush creep up her cheeks. So what if it hadn't been scriptworthy romantic dialogue. This wasn't a scene from a television program, this was real life. And real life wasn't perfect.

"Say that again," he murmured.

"No," she said. "Not until you come inside."

He reached for the door, then thought better of it. "I'm going to stay out here."

"Why?"

"Because if I come inside, I'm going to have to kiss you. And once I start, I'm not sure I'm going to be able to stop."

"That sounds nice," Hayley said, smiling at him. "Please come inside." She walked to the door and pushed open the screen door. "Come on." She stepped aside to let him pass. But as he did, his arm slipped around her waist and he pulled her against him.

In a heartbeat, his mouth came down on hers in a deep and soul-searching kiss. He left no doubt about his feelings. In a single instant, Hayley knew he was glad she'd returned. She ran her hands over his shoulders and arms, enjoying the feel of his body. She hadn't realized how much she'd missed touching him.

Teague scooped her up in his arms and walked into the parlor. She grabbed his hat and tossed it aside, taking in the details of his handsome face as they continued kissing. He sat down in the leather chair, settling her on his lap, molding her mouth to his until she felt as if she might pass out.

Hayley smiled as she teased him with tiny kisses, first on his mouth, then his jaw and finally on his neck. "So you're happy to have me home."

"That depends on how long you're planning to stay."

"I was thinking maybe the rest of my life." She looked up at him.

He drew back, then held her face between his hands. "What does that mean?"

"Exactly what I said. This is my home now. I'm going to come and go from Wallaroo. I'll have to return to Sydney to finish up my contract on *Castle Cove*. Then I'll sell my place and move everything up here."

A grin broke over his face. "You're going to live here with me," he said, as if to reassure himself that he'd heard her right.

"Yes. It's my house, too."

"What about your career?"

"Well, if something interesting comes along, then we'll discuss it. We may need money for buying stock. Or for fixing up the station. I'm not going to make any plans right now, except to spend the next week with you. Then I have to go back."

"We have a week? What will we do with ourselves?" He cupped her breast.

"You'll have to work and I'm sure I'll find something to do around here." She chuckled.

"About that. Work, I mean. I spoke with Doc Daley and we've made a few changes in our plans. I'm not going to take over his practice, at least not all of it. I'm going to do the equine cases only, so I can spend more time on the station. And he's going to find someone else to take over the rest of the work. I figured, if we wanted to make a go of Wallaroo, I needed to be here as much as possible."

"So, I guess it's all settled then. You and I are business partners."

"And friends," he said.

"Lovers, too," Hayley added.

"Roommates."

She smiled. "Soul mates."

"And the rest will come," he assured her. He ran his fingers through her hair and pulled her into another kiss, lingering over her mouth. "I love you, Hayley. I always have and I always will."

"And I love you, Teague."

He smoothed his fingers through her hair. "You must be very tired from your trip. I can tell you'd like to lie down."

"Oh, you can tell?" she teased. "I think you want to get me into the bedroom."

"Actually, I want to show you the bed." He stood and pulled her along to the upstairs, past the door to Harry's old room, past the door to her room, to the largest of the bedrooms. Harry had used it for storage, like an attic, filling it full of old furniture and things he couldn't bear to throw away. She'd always suspected it was the room he'd shared with her grandmother. The beautiful bedroom set was too fancy for a single man to use.

But Teague had cleaned the room out. The old bed was there, but dressed with brand-new linens. He tossed her onto it, then flopped down beside her. "Do you like it?"

"Yes." She turned and ran her hands over the down

comforter. It was exactly like the— "These are the bed linens from the resort."

"I liked them so much that I bought some. They sell the bed linens and the soap and the shampoo right from the hotel. I bought the sheets and the down comforter. Oh, and the down pillows. And I got one of those nice showerheads, too."

Hayley rolled over and threw her arms out. "It's perfect. I could spend all day in this bed."

"Is that a request or a demand? Because I'd be quite happy to keep you in this bed all day."

She rolled over and wrapped her arms around his neck, remembering that first day at the big rock. He'd saved her life that day. Without Teague, Hayley probably wouldn't have survived her teenage years. But he'd made every day an adventure, every moment something wonderful to be shared.

"Promise me you'll love me forever," she said.

"I will love you forever and beyond," Teague said, his declaration simple and direct and honest.

"My life starts today," Hayley said. "No more fears, no more running away. And if I ever get a little crazy again, I want you to drag me back into this bedroom and prove to me why we belong together."

"Can I do that now?" Teague asked.

Hayley laughed, then kissed his mouth. "Yes," she said. "And don't stop doing it until I tell you."

As Teague began to seduce her, Hayley closed her eyes and gave herself over to the man she loved. How something so complicated had suddenly turned so simple, she would never understand. It was like a switch had been thrown and a light turned on, illuminating all the things she knew deep in her heart yet had never acknowledged.

She was exactly where she belonged now—in Teague's arms. And after so many years of searching, she was finally home.

*   *   *   *   *

THE MIGHTY QUINNS: CALLUM

BY
KATE HOFFMANN

To my readers
in that wonderful land down under.

Prologue

"YOU KISSED HER?" CAL QUINN stared at his younger brother Teague in disbelief. It was one thing to kiss just any girl, but quite another to kiss a Fraser. Harry Fraser and Cal's dad were in the midst of a land feud, a fight that had gone on for years.

"I'm not spilling my guts to you boofheads," Teague said. "You'll tell Dad and then he'll lock me in my room until it's time for me to go to university."

Cal turned his gaze to the horizon. He and his brothers had spent the day riding the fence line along the west boundary of Kerry Creek Station, looking for breaks. On their way back to the homestead, they'd decided to make a stop at the big rock, a landmark on the station and a favorite spot for him and his brothers. They'd discarded their shirts in the heat, their bodies already brown from the summer sun, and crawled up on top of the rock.

"Dad would be mad as a cut snake if he knew what you were doing," Cal warned. "He hates Harry Fraser. All the Frasers."

"There are only two. Hayley and her grandfather. And Hayley doesn't care about the land."

Cal scowled. "Still, you shouldn't be talking to her. It's—it's disloyal."

"Oh, nick off," Teague muttered, growing impatient with the conversation. "You can't tell me what I'm allowed to do. You're not the boss cocky on this station."

Cal's temper flared. The hell he couldn't. He was the oldest of the three Quinn brothers and if Teague or Brody were doing something that might hurt the family, then it was Cal's duty to step in. "I will be someday. And when I am, you won't be kissing Hayley Fraser."

"If you tell Dad about—"

"I kissed a girl," Brody confessed. "Twice."

Cal leaned forward to glare at his youngest brother. Brody had always done his best to keep up, but he usually didn't resort to lies. "Twice?"

"Yeah," Brody said. "Once with tongue. It was kind of nasty, but she said we should try it. I thought I'd give it a fair go."

Brody had been living in Sydney with their mum, attending a regular school filled with real girls. He'd been to a proper dance and played footy with his school team and went to the flicks almost every weekend. Maybe he was telling the truth. If he was, then at fourteen, Brody had already passed Cal in worldly experience.

"Tongue?" Teague asked. "What does that mean?"

"When you kiss her, you open your mouth and touch tongues," Brody explained. "It's called French kissing. I guess the French do it all the time."

Teague considered the notion, his eyebrow raised in suspicion. "So who opens their mouth first, the guy or the girl?"

"Whoever wants to French kiss," Brody said. "If you don't want to do it, you just don't open your mouth. It's probably not so good to do if you're sick. Or if you have food in your mouth. Or if you haven't brushed your teeth."

Cal listened as his brothers discussed their experiences with girls, unable to add anything to the conversation. Cal was seventeen, yet he'd never kissed a girl, or touched a girl, or even carried on a conversation with one his own age. He'd lived on the station his entire life, miles from any female worth talking about.

Sure, he'd been to Brisbane a bunch of times with his family and he'd seen lots of pretty girls there. And his cousins had visited Kerry Creek when he was younger, and some of them were girls. But he'd never gotten close enough to…

He knew what went on between men and women. He listened to the jackaroos after they'd come back from a weekend in town. And he'd discovered self-gratification and teenage fantasies years ago. But he wanted to know about the real thing. Sex. Something that Teague and Brody might end up experiencing long before he did.

Cal had considered going into Bilbarra the next time the jackaroos took a weekend off and find himself a willing girl. He was old enough. His mother might disapprove, but she was living in Sydney and would have no idea what he was up to.

As for his father, Jack Quinn had left his two eldest sons to their own devices since the separation. Brody was out of his control in Sydney, but Teague and Cal had only Mary, the housekeeper, to watch over them. Though she was strict about schoolwork, and their father firm about station chores, Cal and Teague were allowed to spend their free time in whatever way they chose.

"Mac and Smithy said they'd take me into town the next time they went," Cal said, trying to maintain an air of cool. "They know a lot of women in Bilbarra."

"Yeah, only they all live at the knock shop," Teague said.

"Not all of them," Cal said. Though the boys did frequent the local brothel, they also spent time at the pubs. From what the jackaroos had told him, the brothel in Bilbarra was still a well-kept secret, one almost everyone in the territory knew. But there were other places in Oz where that type of thing was perfectly legal.

Maybe that's what he needed to do. Go find a place like that, pay his money and have done with it. He'd ask for a pretty girl, one with long hair and a nice body. And he wouldn't need to be embarrassed by his lack of experience. He'd be paying for a tutor.

Something would have to change. Cal had always dreamed about running Kerry Creek someday. But if he never left the station, there wasn't much chance of meeting females. Maybe he ought to do like Teague and make plans to attend university for a few years. He could study business, learn things that would make him a better station manager and at the same time, find a wife.

But the idea didn't appeal to him at all. He felt comfortable where he was. He'd learned how to run the station from watching his father. And he loved the work, loved the animals and the people who populated Kerry Creek. There was nothing more beautiful to him than a sunrise over the outback and nothing more peaceful than the sounds of life all around him at day's end.

Cal lay back on the rock and stared up at the sky, linking his hands behind his head. Though he wanted to believe the opposite sex might find him interesting, Cal knew life on an outback cattle station wasn't all sunshine and roses. His mother had left Kerry Creek just six months ago, unable to stand the isolation any longer.

Still, there had to be girls who liked riding horses and mustering cattle and fixing fences. Girls like Hayley Fraser. It might take a while to find someone like that, but when he did, maybe he could convince her to visit him on Kerry Creek. If she liked it, he would ask her to stay.

"I've seen lots of knockers, too," Brody said.

"Yeah, right," Teague said. "In your dreams, maybe."

"No, I'm not lying," Brody said. "Me and my mates go down to Bondi Beach on the weekends and there are girls sunbaking without their tops all over the place. You just walk down the beach and look all you want. You don't even have to pay."

Cal cursed softly, then sat up. "Is that all you droobs can talk about? Girls? Who needs them? They're all just a big pain in the arse anyway. If you two want to sit around sipping tea and knitting socks with the ladies for the rest of your life, then keep it up. I've got better things to do with my time."

He slid off the rock, dropping to the ground with a soft thud. Cal grabbed his gloves from his back pocket and put them on, then swung up into the saddle, shoving his hat down on his head. "Well, are you two coming? Or do you need help getting down?"

Teague and Brody glanced at each other, then slid to the ground, their boots causing a small cloud of dust to rise. "Come on, I'll race you back," Cal challenged.

"I'm in," Teague said, hopping on his horse and weaving the reins through his fingers.

"Not fair," Brody complained. "I haven't ridden in four months."

"Then you better hang on," Cal said. He gave his horse a sharp kick and the gelding bolted forward. The sudden start surprised his brothers. They were just getting settled in the saddle while he was already fifty meters in front.

This was what he loved, the feeling of freedom he had, the wind whistling by his ears, the horse's hooves pounding on the hard earth. He was part of this land and it was part of him. And if staying on Kerry Creek meant giving up on women altogether, then he'd made the choice already. This was home and he'd spend his life here.

1

May 31, 2009

THE SUN WAS BARELY ABOVE the horizon as Cal got
dressed. He raked his hands through his damp hair, the
thick strands still dripping with water. He usually
showered at the end of a long workday rather than first
thing in the morning, but he'd come in so late last night
that he'd flopped onto the bed and fallen asleep with his
dusty clothes on.

Strange how a year had flown by so quickly. It
seemed like just last month that they'd finished the
mustering and now they were about to start all over
again. He should have been accustomed to the rhythms
of the station by now, but the older he got, the more Cal
was reminded that time was slipping through his
fingers.

He sat down on the edge of the bed and pulled his
boots on, then rolled up the sleeves of his work shirt.
As he reached for his watch on the nightstand, Cal
noticed the letter he'd received from the matchmaking
service sitting out. He grabbed it and shoved it into the
drawer. Better not to let anyone know what he was con-

templating, especially Mary, the station housekeeper. He'd be facing the Aussie inquisition over the dinner table if she found out.

He'd discovered the Web site a few months back— OutbackMates—an organization devoted to finding spouses for country men and women. He'd filled out the application last week and sent it in with an old photograph of himself. According to the letter, his profile would appear on the site next week. It was a bold move, but he was nearing thirty and he hadn't had a long-term relationship with a woman for...ever.

The station kept him so busy that he rarely took more than a day or two away. Cal knew all the single women in Bilbarra and not one of them would make a suitable wife. The past few years he'd been forced to go as far as Brisbane for feminine companionship. Unfortunately, the single women he'd met there weren't interested in romance with a rancher who lived five hours away, either—except when he happened to be in town. Then he was good for a quick romp between the sheets.

He stood and stared at himself in the mirror on his closet door. Reaching up, Cal smoothed his hands over his tousled hair. He wasn't a bad-looking bloke. Though he didn't possess the charm and sophistication his two younger brothers did, he could show a girl a good time. And he could be romantic if required. That had to count for something, right?

As he jogged down the stairs, Cal turned his thoughts to the workday ahead. The month of June would be spent preparing for mustering, herding the cattle back into the station yards for inoculations, branding, tagging and sorting. From the first of July through the end of that month, every jackaroo on Kerry Creek Station would exist on caffeine, fifteen-minute meals and barely enough sleep to get them through a day's work.

The six station hands were already gathered around the table, devouring heaping platters of scrambled eggs, bacon, baked beans and toast. Mary hovered nearby, filling requests for coffee, juice and tea in her calm, efficient manner.

As he entered the room, the stockmen shouted their greetings. Cal took his place at the head of the table, observing the scene before him. Was it any wonder a woman would find station life unappealing? Table manners were all but nonexistent. Not a one of the stockmen had bothered to comb their hair that morning and he'd wager that most hadn't shaved in the past three days. What was the point when they all looked the same?

"I don't see why Miss Moynihan can't take her meals with us," Davey said, glancing around at his fellow jackaroos. "We can act polite." He snatched his serviette from his collar and laid it on his lap. "See?"

Cal reached for a piece of toast, then slathered it with strawberry jam. "Who is Miss Moynihan?"

"We have a guest," Mary said, setting a mug of coffee in front of him. She smoothed a strand of gray hair back into the tidy knot at the nape of her neck.

"We do?"

"Since you weren't here, I took it upon myself to offer her a place to stay. She's a genealogist come all the way from Dublin, Ireland, to do research on the Quinn family. She's been driving back and forth between here and Bilbarra for the past two days, waiting for you to get back."

"You invited a genealogist to stay at Kerry Creek?" Cal frowned. "What does she expect to find here?"

"She'd like to talk to you about Crevan Quinn, in particular. She's documented the Quinn line going all the way back to the ancient kings of Ireland. You ought to take a look at her work. It's all very interesting."

"Where did you put her?" Cal asked.

"She stayed in the south bunkhouse last night. She'll be driving back to Bilbarra to fetch her things this morning, if you approve. I don't think her research will take long."

"I'm not going to have time for her," Cal said, grabbing the platter of eggs and scooping a spoonful onto his plate. He sent Mary a shrewd look. "If you ask my opinion, I think you're happy to have another woman on Kerry Creek who will sip tea and eat biscuits with you all afternoon."

Mary gave his head a playful slap. "I'm the only one on Kerry Creek who has managed to maintain a bit of civility. Look at the lot of you, gobbling down your food like hogs at a trough. I'd wager you'd all act differently if we had a lady at the table."

"Oh, so you invited her to stay so we'd improve our manners?" Cal picked up his serviette and placed it daintily in his lap, holding out his little fingers as he did so. "Hear that, boys? Our Mary thinks we're all a bunch of uncouth cane toads."

"Can I tell her you'll meet with her after dinner tonight?"

"Let Brody or Teague take this one," Cal said wearily. "I've got far too much on my list."

"Brody took off for Bilbarra on Friday and hasn't been seen since and Teague has responsibilities with Doc Daley. He spent last night at Dunbar Station and isn't supposed to be back until later this morning."

The phone on the wall rang and Mary wiped her hands on her apron before picking it up. When she finished with the call, she sighed and shook her head.

"What is it?" Cal asked.

"That was Angus Embley. Your brother raised quite the stink in town last night. It appears Brody's lost his keys down the dunny at the Spotted Dog. Angus asked if someone could bring him a spare set and bail him out of jail."

"I'm not going," Cal said. "This is the third time in as many months."

"You will go," Mary said, her voice firm. Though she wasn't related to the Quinns, she had served as a surrogate mother ever since their own mother had left the station twelve years before. Cal recognized the tone of voice and knew not to argue.

Since Brody had arrived on Kerry Creek a few months ago, he'd been nothing but trouble. A motorcycle accident had ended his career as a pro footballer and Brody had found himself at loose ends, unable to deal with the loss of everything he'd worked for. Though he wasn't a pauper, the money he'd made wouldn't last forever. Sooner or later, Brody would have to make a decision about a new career. But for now, he'd been living off his notoriety and the patience and generosity of his oldest brother. But this had gone far enough.

"Teague probably has to fly into Bilbarra today. He can just—"

"You'll not leave your brother sitting in the nick," Mary scolded. "Besides, it will do you good to get off this station for a few hours. You can pick up supplies and the mail, and maybe even get yourself a decent haircut."

"All right, all right," Cal said. He pushed away from the table and stood, then snatched another piece of toast from a passing platter. "If I leave now, I'll be back before lunch."

Mary fetched her list and handed it to him. "Stop by the library, too, will you? Daisy called to tell me my books were in."

"Any other requests?" he asked, looking around the table.

"The windmill up in the northwest paddock is rattling," Skip said. "We should probably take it apart before mustering and replace the bearings."

"I'll order the parts," Cal said. He grabbed his stockman's hat from the peg near the door, then nodded to the men gathered around the table. "Comb your hair for once, will ya, boys? I'm sick to death of looking at you."

Cal jogged down the porch steps to his ute. He tucked Mary's list into his shirt pocket, then hopped behind the wheel. A cloud of dust billowed out behind him as he drove down the long dirt road.

Though the drive into Bilbarra took two hours, Cal had made it so many times in his life that he barely noticed the time passing. The closer he got to town, the smoother the roads became, though none of them were paved. He slipped a CD into the player and let his mind wander, thinking about his chances of finding a wife.

He'd always known his place was at Kerry Creek. From the time he was a boy, he'd carefully watched each element of the operation, taking on more and more responsibility with every year that passed. He'd never expected to be boss cocky before he turned thirty. But when his parents had decided to reconcile, his father had reluctantly handed the reins over to Cal and left for Sydney.

Cal imagined that Jack Quinn's decision had been made easier knowing the station was in good hands. And after his parents' last visit, he could see the choice had been right for them both. His mother taught school in Sydney and his father had started a small landscaping business. They'd bought a house near the ocean and were happy being together again.

As he turned east on the main road into Bilbarra, Cal squinted as the early-morning sun emerged at the top of a rise. He grabbed his sunglasses from the dashboard, but they fell to the floor of the ute. Bending down, he searched for them with his fingers. But when he glanced out the windshield again, Cal was startled to find himself heading directly toward a figure standing in the middle of the road.

GEMMA SAW THE TRUCK COMING toward her and frantically waved her arms above her head. She'd been stuck here, at the edge of nowhere, for nearly thirty minutes. Not a single living creature had happened by beyond a few hundred flies and a small, evil-looking lizard. But now, as the vehicle was coming closer, she realized the driver hadn't seen her—or he didn't intend to stop.

She shouted, jumping up and down to gain the driver's attention. For an instant, she thought he might run her down and she scurried to safety, but then suddenly, the truck veered sharply and drove off the edge of the road. It came to a dead stop when the front wheels hit the bottom of a shallow gully. Gemma held her breath, afraid to move, adrenaline coursing through her. She'd been the cause of this accident and now she wasn't sure what to do. Her mobile wasn't working and she was at least fifteen kilometers from Bilbarra and help.

"Oh, please, oh, please," she chanted as she raced over to the truck, climbing down into where it had come to rest. The driver's-side window was open and she could see a man inside. He was conscious and staring out the windscreen. "Are you all right?" she asked, coughing from the dust that hung in the air.

He turned and looked at her, then blinked vacantly. "Yes," he murmured. He closed his eyes, then opened them again, shaking his head. "Are you real? Or am I dead?"

His question caught her by surprise and she reached inside and grabbed his arm, then pinched it hard. "Do you feel that?"

"Ow!" He rubbed his skin, glaring at her.

"I'm very real. And you're fine. You haven't hit your head, have you? Are you bleeding anywhere?"

He reached up and pushed his hat off. The moment he did, Gemma got a good look at his face. She took a step back, a shiver skittering through her body. Suddenly breathless, she tried to inhale. But her lungs had ceased to function properly. She felt a bit dizzy and wondered if all that adrenaline was wearing off too quickly. Her fingers gripped the edge of the window as she tried to remain upright.

The driver pushed against the door with his shoulder and it swung open, sending her stumbling backward. "I'm so sorry," she said. Good Lord, he was absolutely the most gorgeous thing she'd ever seen in her life. Although Australia was teeming with beautiful men, Gemma felt quite certain that she'd hit the jackpot with this bloke.

He was fine, handsome without being pretty. His features, taken individually, were quite ordinary, but together they combined to make up a man of unquestionable masculinity, rugged and powerful and perhaps a tiny bit dangerous.

Gemma took another step back as he approached and her heel caught on a rock. An instant later, she landed on her bum, the impact causing her to cry out. Gemma felt something move beneath her hand and she looked down to see a lizard squirming between her fingers.

This time, it was a shriek that erupted from her lips as she scrambled to her feet to escape. But she lost her balance again and pitched forward into his arms. He held on to her until she was back on her feet, looking down at her in utter bewilderment.

"Is it poisonous?" she asked, frantically wiping her

hand on the front of his shirt. "Jaysus, I hate those things. They're slimy little buggers. Look, did he bite me?"

Her question seemed to shake him out of his stupor. "It's a gecko." He smiled crookedly. "I—I reckon you are real. I don't expect angels screech like that." He gradually loosened his grip on her arms. "I almost hit you, miss. What the hell were you doing in the middle of the road?"

"I was trying to wave you down," Gemma said. "I have a punctured tire. I've tried to change it myself, but I can't get the bloody things off. The…screws. The bolts. Didn't you see me?"

"Nuts," he said. "They're called nuts." He took her elbow and gently led her back to the road. "The sun was in my eyes." Drawing a deep breath, he surveyed the scene, his attention moving between his truck and her car. "Come on, I'll help you change it."

She looked back over her shoulder. "Shouldn't we get your truck back on the road first?"

"No worries," he said with a shrug. "It's not stuck." He walked up to the Subaru wagon she'd rented in Sydney and squatted down beside the flat.

Her attention was caught by the way his jeans hugged his backside. They fit him like a glove, not so tight that it looked like he was trying too hard to be sexy, but just tight enough to attract her notice.

Her eyes moved to his shoulders, and the muscles shifting and bunching beneath the faded work shirt. Then he stood and faced her. Gemma liked the way he moved, so easy, almost graceful.

"These roads around here are shite," he said, wiping

his hands on his jeans. "If you hit enough holes, a tire will go flat without a puncture."

Gemma pointed to the jack, lying in the dust. "I tried to change it myself, but I have no earthly clue what I'm doing. I was starting to get worried when no one came by."

"This road doesn't go many places," he said.

She stood over him as he put the jack together and hooked it beneath the front of the car. Watching him, Gemma realized she never would have figured out how to change the tire on her own. She bent down beside him. From this vantage point, she could get a better look at his face. He was deeply tanned and his eyes were an odd shade of hazel, more gold than green. "Thank you so very much for stopping."

"I didn't have much choice," he said. "It was that or run you down." He straightened and began to pump the handle. Slowly, the front end of the car rose. Then he started on the nuts that held the tire to the car.

As he worked, she studied him more closely. He wasn't much of a conversationalist. She'd always thought the strong, silent type was just a myth, but here was a man who proved it. He was tall, over six feet. His clothes were well-worn and she suspected he worked on one of the stations in the area. She made several more attempts to engage him, but he seemed intent on his task.

Since the weather and the flies hadn't sparked a discussion, she decided to try asking about places to eat in Bilbarra. He'd been headed in that direction and once he was through with her tire, she'd offer to buy him lunch.

Though Gemma had been anxious to get back to

Kerry Creek with her things, the Quinn brothers had
been scarce. According to the housekeeper, Cal had
been camping in the outback for a few days and Brody
had stayed overnight in Bilbarra. She'd met Teague
briefly on the morning she'd first arrived at the station,
but he hadn't had time to talk. Since she wasn't getting
anywhere with the Quinns, why not spend a little time
with this stranger?

Her plan had seemed so simple back in Dublin. But
now that she was here in Queensland, ready to play the
part of a curious genealogist, Gemma was getting nervous.
What if they didn't believe her? What if she tripped herself
up and revealed her real reason for coming?

For a long time, she'd thought the Emerald of Eire
had been nothing but an overblown legend, based more
in fantasy than truth. Her mother had told her about it
when she'd been little and it had piqued Gemma's imagination—not because of the jewel, but because it had
something to do with Gemma's father, David Parnell.

Before the age of twelve, her father had been nothing
more than a faded photo. But suddenly, Gemma
realized she was part of something bigger, a family
history.

According to her mother, the jewel had been stolen
from Gemma's fourth great-grandfather, Lord Stanton
Parnell, more than one hundred and fifty years ago.
Some of the Parnells believed that with the loss of the
emerald, the fortunes of the family had been cursed.

The fortunes of Orla Moynihan had definitely fallen
the moment she set eyes on David Parnell. According
to her mother, they'd fallen in love instantly. David had

promised to find the emerald so they might run away together and get married. Gemma suspected this was only a ploy to lure her mother into his bed. A pregnancy followed and David disappeared, behind the protective walls of the Parnell family estate. The baby was named Gemma, after an emerald and a dream.

It was no surprise that David had abandoned her mother. The Parnells were part of the old English aristocracy that had made their fortunes in the Belfast textile industry. And Parnell sons didn't marry poor Irish girls, no matter what the circumstances.

Gemma had met her father twice, once when she'd barged into his office on her twelfth birthday and the other on the day she'd turned eighteen, when she'd demanded he pay for her university tuition at University College in Dublin. He had his own family, including a wife not ten years older than Gemma, so he had sent her away with a promise. He would pay if she'd never approach him again.

But throughout her childhood, Gemma had dreamed of someday being part of that family, of living in a posh house, of having servants to wait on her, of never having to worry about whether they could afford to pay the rent that month. And the emerald had come to represent that dream, something precious and beautiful.

Finding the Emerald of Eire was her chance to claim her birthright. Whether it fixed things with the Parnells or she just threw it in her father's face, it would prove that she had Parnell blood running through her veins, even though it had been tainted by the Irish of the Moynihans.

So she'd gone to university, thanks to the Parnell scholarship. Gemma had focused her studies on medieval Irish history and after receiving her doctorate, she'd been offered a teaching position. One day, last year, while researching an article on medieval prisons, she'd decided to see if there was any truth to the family legend. To her astonishment, everything her mother had told her was there—the emerald, the theft, the trial of the pickpocket, Crevan Quinn.

Yes, there had been an Emerald of Eire, a 72-carat jewel that Stanton Parnell had bought in Europe to give to his young bride. He'd been carrying it in his coat pocket on the streets of Dublin in February of 1848 when a local pickpocket had stolen it. Though Crevan Quinn had been tried and later shipped off to Australia for his crime, the jewel had never been recovered.

Even now, she imagined the headlines in the papers, the proof in black and white that Gemma Moynihan, illegitimate daughter of David Parnell, was an heir to the Parnell millions. Though her mother refused to ask for a DNA test, the emerald would be Gemma's bargaining chip. If they wanted it back, then David would have to acknowledge her as his daughter.

She'd completed her research in six months and was armed with a list of leads, all of which led her to Australia and the descendants of Crevan Quinn. One didn't possess a jewel like that without either selling it or passing it down as an heirloom. And since an emerald that size would have caused some notice had it been sold, it was probably still in the Quinn's possession.

"Can you hold these?"

Gemma brushed a strand of hair out of her eyes, startled back to reality by the stranger's voice. He handed her the nuts. "That was quick. I don't think I'd ever have been able to get those off on my own. I—I hope I'm not keeping you from anything," she said.

"Nothing important." He stood and wiped his hands on his jeans, then walked to the tailgate to retrieve the spare. "You should get the tire repaired straight away. You don't want to get stranded out here again without a spare." He shoved the spare onto the bolts and she handed him the nuts, one by one.

"Good advice," she murmured.

"You're from Ireland." He looked at her again, this time with a rather odd expression. "Are you here for a visit?"

It was the closest they'd come to a two-sided conversation and Gemma jumped at the chance. She was known to be quite charming, with a ready wit. But she hadn't had a chance to prove herself with this man. "I am. I'm staying out at Kerry Creek Station. Do you know it?"

She saw his shoulders stiffen. "Is that where you're headed now?"

She nodded. "And you? Do you live out here or in town?"

He pointed off toward the west. "Right out there, beyond the black stump. In the back of nowhere."

Well, if she wanted to find him, it wasn't going to be easy with those directions. Was the black stump a local landmark, or just another Aussie saying? For such a gorgeous man, he was impossible to flirt with.

Gemma stared down at his back as he let the car down with the jack, fascinated by the way his dark hair curled around his collar and his muscles flexed beneath the fabric of his shirt. Her fingers twitched as she fought the urge to touch him again. She held her breath in an effort to focus her mind.

When he'd finished, he bolted the flat to the rack on the tailgate and tossed the jack inside. "There you go," he said, wiping his hands on his jeans. "Good as new. Or almost."

"You must let me pay you," Gemma insisted. "Or let me treat you to lunch. There's a lovely coffee shop in town. They make the best meat pies."

"No, thank you," he said. "I'm happy to oblige, miss." He hesitated and she was certain he was about to change his mind, but then he moved toward his truck. "G'day, miss. Drive safe." He gave her a quick tip of his hat and walked away. She watched as he hopped inside, then slowly backed the truck out of the gully and onto the road. As he drove off toward town, Gemma stared after him.

She pressed her hand to her chest, her heart beating furiously beneath her fingertips. "Idiot," she muttered. She'd made a botch of that. All the other men she'd met here in Australia had seemed to like her. He was probably involved, or married. Or not attracted to her in the least. Maybe Australian men didn't fancy pale Irish girls with red hair and small breasts.

Besides, not all white knights were supposed to fall in love with their damsels in distress. It was a historical fact. Once she got back to Dublin, she'd research it thoroughly and write a paper. Gemma smiled to herself.

Whenever she found herself faced with a dilemma, it always helped to put it in historical context.

"I SAID I WAS SORRY."

Cal stared at the toes of his boots as his brother apologized. Though he knew he ought to kick Brody's arse for his behavior, he was tired of being his brother's keeper. If Brody wanted to stuff up his life, then that was his choice. Cal was much more interested in thinking about the woman he'd met on the road.

Gemma Moynihan. When Mary had mentioned her, he'd assumed the genealogist would be older, a granny sort with gray hair and glasses. Instead, she was stunningly beautiful, with flawless skin and a riot of auburn hair that fell in waves around her face. Though she looked quite young, Cal guessed she was probably about his age, give or take a few years on either side.

From the moment he heard her speak, in that lilting Irish accent, Cal had wondered if she was the one. And when he learned her name, he thought of introducing himself right then and there. But she'd already left him tongue-tied and he didn't want to make a fool of himself right off. He needed time to gather his wits about him.

It had taken him the entire ride into town to calm his racing pulse and consider what their encounter had meant. Though he'd maintained his calm while speaking to her, it had taken a tremendous effort not to stare at her, to analyze her every word and to fantasize about what she'd look like naked.

He rubbed his hands together, remembering the feel of her silken skin beneath his fingertips. Would he have another chance with her? Or would things change when she found out who he really was? Suddenly, he wanted to get out of Bilbarra and return to the station to find out.

"You're turning into a fair wanker, you are," Cal muttered. "You could find something better to do with yourself. Like lending a hand on the station. We could use your help mustering now that Teague's practice is starting to take off. He's been taking calls almost every day. And when he's home, he spends his time doing paperwork."

"I haven't decided what I'm going to do," Brody replied. "But it bloody well doesn't include stockman's work. Now, can I have my keys? I've got some place to go."

Cal reached in his jacket pocket for the spare key to his brother's Land Rover. "Buddy doesn't want you back at the Spotted Dog. You're going to have to find yourself another place to get pissed. Or you could give up the coldies. It would save you some money." Cal patted his brother on the shoulder. "I'm sorry things didn't turn out the way you wanted them to. Sometimes life is just crap. But you pick yourself up and you get on with it. And you stop being such a dickhead."

Brody gave his brother a shove, then stood up. "Give it a rest. If I needed a mother, I'd move back to Sydney and live with the one I already have."

Brody snatched his keys from Cal's hand, then jogged down the front steps and out into the dusty street. "I'll catch you later."

Cal watched him stride toward the Spotted Dog. He

heard the screen door of the police station creak and
Angus Embley, the town police chief, stepped outside.

"How much trouble did he make?" Cal asked.

"Nothing too serious. Just a broken mirror."

"Well, if he can't drink at the Spotted Dog, he's going
to have to drive halfway to Brisbane to find another
pub."

"Give the boy a break, Cal," Angus said. "It's got to be
an adjustment coming back here after all that time away."

Cal slowly stood and adjusted the brim of his hat.
"Thanks for taking him in, Angus. I don't like the
thought of him driving back to the station when he's
pissed. It's good to know he has a place to sleep it off."

"No worries," Angus said with a nod.

Cal walked back to his ute and jumped inside.
Though he had Mary's grocery list in his pocket and
orders to stop for the mail and her library books, he was
tempted to head right back to Kerry Creek.

It felt odd to be preoccupied with thoughts of a
woman. Running a successful cattle station usually
consumed all his attention. But there were times when
Cal worried needlessly over business because there was
nothing else in his life to think about. The genealogist
was worth additional consideration.

He steered the ute towards the post office. Many of the
outback stations got their mail by plane, but Teague and
Brody spent enough time in town that they usually picked
it up and brought it home, saving the mail plane a trip.

He grabbed a stack of letters from Mel Callahan, the
seventy-five-year-old clerk, then returned to his ute.
But one of the envelopes caught his eye and he stopped

to open it. "You have been matched with three lovely mates," he murmured, reading the note inside. He flipped through the three photos, then continued reading. "To learn more, visit their profiles on the Outback-Mates Web site."

He looked at the three candidates again, studying them carefully. There wasn't one who came close to Gemma Moynihan's beauty, though they were all quite pretty by anyone's standards. But there was something about the Irish girl he found compelling, something that made him want to get to know her a lot better...and more intimately.

"Sorry, ladies." Cal jumped back into the pickup, then opened the glove box and shoved the envelope inside. For now, he was taking himself off the menu. As long as Gemma was staying at Kerry Creek, he'd focus his modest charms on her. After all, what did he have to lose? She was beautiful, intriguing and close at hand, three qualities that he found irresistible.

Cal reached for the key, then stopped. What if he fell in love with her? Still, that wasn't likely. He'd never been in love before, so he probably wouldn't know it if it dropped out of the sky and hit him on the noggin. But he did know about lust. And his feelings for Gemma were definitely of the lustful variety.

After she left Kerry Creek, he'd get back to his search for a wife. Cal pulled out onto the street and headed out of Bilbarra toward the station, the groceries forgotten. Unfortunately, the ride dragged on forever. He'd covered the distance between the station and town so many times it had become second nature. He knew all the landmarks and could probably find his way home blindfolded. But now that he had something important to do, every kilometer passed at a grindingly slow pace.

By the time he pulled into the yard, Cal figured he was about an hour behind Gemma. It was nearly time for lunch and if he was lucky, he'd find her sitting at the kitchen table with Mary. He took the steps two at a time and pulled the screen door open. But the kitchen was empty.

A huge pot of mutton stew bubbled on the stove and Mary had freshly baked bread to go with it. Cal decided to use the extra time to clean up. He hung his hat on the peg, then strode through the house to the stairs. He met Mary coming down.

"Oh, wonderful. You're back. I'm almost out of coffee and I need yeast to—"

"I didn't get supplies," Cal said. "Sorry. We'll call Teague. He can pick them up when he's in town today. Where is Gemma Moynihan?"

Mary gave him an odd look. "She's in the bunkhouse unpacking her things. She drove into town at dawn to get them. She said she had a flat tire on her way back to the station but some bloke stopped and changed it for her."

"Yes. That was me," he said.

"So you met her?" Mary asked.

"Not properly. Why didn't you tell me she was… you know."

"Young?"

"Pretty," he said.

"I thought you'd find out soon enough."

"Did you invite her to lunch?" Cal asked.

"I told her I'd take her out something to eat after the boys were fed."

"Leave that to me," he said. "I'm just going to change and I'll be right down."

He ran up the stairs and into his room, stripping off his shirt along the way. Though he'd taken a shower before breakfast, he figured another wouldn't hurt. The road had been dusty and his hair was sticking up all willy-nilly. He only had one chance to make a first impression—or a second impression.

He managed a shower in less than five minutes, then grabbed a towel for his wet hair. Luckily, he'd taken the time to shave off three days of stubble that morning. A splash of cologne was probably overkill, so he set the bottle back on the shelf.

Cal stepped into the hallway, rubbing his head with the towel until his hair was barely damp. But when he pulled the towel away, he found Gemma standing next to the linen closet, a blanket clutched to her chest, her eyes wide. A tiny cry of surprise slipped from her lips as the blanket dropped to the floor.

They both bent to pick it up, Cal getting to it first. He held it out to her as he rose. Gemma straightened, her gaze drifting along his naked body. He struggled to wrap the towel around his waist, but with only one hand, it was impossible to do. It seemed like an eternity before she took the blanket from him.

A long embarrassed silence followed as he tried to come up with a clever line. Of all the scenarios he'd gone over in his mind, this was not the way he'd intended their first meeting to go—him starkers and her all fascinated with his bits and pieces. Cal swallowed hard, realizing there was only one thing to say. "Hello," he said.

Her gaze quickly returned to his face and a pretty blush stained her cheeks. "Wha-what are you doing here?"

"I live here," he said. Though this wasn't exactly the way he wanted it to go, he'd have to make the best of it. "I'm Callum Quinn. Cal."

Stunned, she slowly took his outstretched hand, her fingers soft against his palm. "I'm—"

"Gemma Moynihan," he said. "I know. The genealogist. Mary told me."

She frowned, shaking her head in confusion. "But why didn't you introduce yourself on the road?"

"I didn't realize who you were at first. I thought you'd be older—I mean, I just assumed. Mary didn't say that you—weren't. Older."

She looked around, as if searching for the quickest means of escape. "I—I should let you get dressed. Mary just sent me up to fetch another blanket for the bunkhouse."

"I'm sure she did," he muttered, wondering at the housekeeper's motives. "I'll see you later?"

Gemma nodded. "Right. Later, then. All right." She turned and hurried back to the stairs, looking over her shoulder once before descending. Cal listened as her footfalls echoed from the lower hallway, then leaned back against the wall.

He'd always been the one who'd struggled to speak

around women. It was obvious his lack of clothing had something to do with her unease. Maybe that was the key with this woman? To shed his clothes as quickly as possible whenever the conversation slowed so neither one of them would have to talk?

Fate had dropped Gemma Moynihan into the middle of the outback and he was going to make the best of the opportunity. In reality, she was trapped here, waiting for him to enlighten her about his family history. He'd dole out a few interesting tidbits here and there, just enough to keep her around long enough for him to explore this attraction between them.

But the first thing he'd do was make it clear to every man on Kerry Creek Station, including his two brothers, that Gemma was off-limits. Though he knew she wouldn't be staying long, he could use the practice. When the right woman did present herself, he wanted to be ready.

"Lunch," he murmured. He'd get Mary to make up something for them both and then he'd take her on a tour of the station. The more time they spent alone, the better his chances of charming her. And if that didn't work, he'd just strip down and tempt her with his other attributes.

2

GEMMA RACED DOWN THE STAIRS, her face hot, her pulse pounding. She stopped at the bottom, grasping the newel post and drawing a deep breath. Had she just imagined that entire encounter? She'd spent the drive to Kerry Creek mentally undressing the man she'd met on the road, trying to conjure an image of him without his clothes. Was it any wonder that all came back when she met him again?

"No," she murmured. He had definitely been naked. She had imagined a good body beneath those clothes, but nothing quite as perfect as what she'd seen upstairs. She took a ragged breath, then continued on to the kitchen, desperate to return to the bunkhouse where she could enjoy her embarrassment in solitude.

"Did you find it?" Mary asked as Gemma hurried through the kitchen.

"Yes, thank you," Gemma called, shoving the screen door open with her free hand.

Some of the ranch hands were coming in for lunch and they watched her with unabashed interest as she passed. She wondered if her face was as red as it felt. It wasn't like she'd never seen a naked man before. She had—many times. But what had ever possessed her to stare in such a blatant way?

Gemma walked inside the bunkhouse, then slammed the door behind her. Crossing to the bed, she flopped onto it, facedown into the pillow. An image of Cal flashed in her mind again. Oh, God. He had an incredible body, from top to toe, and the all the interesting parts in between. She groaned again. Yes, there, too.

"Be careful what you wish for," Gemma said as she rolled onto her back. From the moment he'd driven off, she'd regretted not being more aggressive. She had always been the one in control of a relationship. She'd decided when it began and when it ended.

Similarly, she'd decided she wanted the post as senior instructor at University College, and had convinced the entire department that, even at her young age, she was the perfect person for the job. Her article on Irish religious icons made the cover of the university's history journal, because she'd decided that was where it belonged. And when they'd demanded that she teach during the summer, she'd convinced them that her time would be much better spent doing research for a new book.

But here, she'd seen something she wanted—a man— and she was suddenly afraid to go after him. A summer romance was exactly what she needed, even though it was technically a winter romance here in Australia. It had been months since she'd been with a man. Yet, it didn't seem quite ethical.

She was here to extract information from Cal. If

they had a physical relationship at the same time, wouldn't she be using her body to further her agenda? Gemma pinched her eyes shut. Wasn't that what sex was about? Most women had an agenda—first sex, then marriage, a comfortable life, a good future. Her plan was just a wee bit different.

But if he knew what she was here for, then she wouldn't be deceiving anyone. An emerald worth a half million English pounds wasn't something he'd just turn over, simply because she said it belonged to her family. And if she found proof of the sale of the stone, then she could demand he return the ill-gotten profits.

The more Gemma became involved in her scheme, the more she realized how complicated things could become. But a few nights of brilliant sex was nothing compared to assuring her identity as a Parnell. She'd wanted Cal Quinn's body for about three hours. She'd wanted to be a Parnell for years.

Gemma had always been so practical about sex. The physical release was enjoyable but she'd carefully avoided emotional attachments. Though there had been a number of lovers in her life, she'd never been in love. Watching her mother gradually destroy herself over a man she couldn't have was enough to make Gemma cautious.

A knock sounded on the bunkhouse door and she sat up, tossing her hair over her shoulder. Gemma weighed the chances that Cal was on the other side. How could she face him without thinking about his naked—? She groaned as the knock grew more insistent.

"Come in," she called.

The door swung open and Mary walked in with a

tray. "Hello, there. I've brought you some lunch. Just a sandwich and some crisps. And a lovely slice of apple pie." She set it down on the table near the door. "The boys are having stew, but I thought you'd prefer this. What would you care to drink? We have beer, lemonade and wine. There's even milk, if you prefer that."

"Lemonade is fine, thanks. But you don't have to wait on me. I'll come in."

"No, no, I'll send Cal out with it. You two can meet—again."

Gemma covered her face with her hands. "Oh, Jaysus, he told you about that?" She shook her head and peeked between her fingers at the housekeeper. "He startled me and I didn't know what to do or where to look. One isn't often confronted with a naked man."

Mary gasped. "Naked? What was he doing driving around in the nuddy?"

"Driving?" She paused, then smiled. "Oh, no. I'm not talking about the first time we met. I'm talking about the second time. Upstairs. He was coming out of the bath and I was—"

"Oh dear," Mary said, a look of horror on her face. "Oh, I am so sorry. He said he was going up to change his clothes. I just assumed he'd come down and gone outside." Flustered, the housekeeper began to rearrange the lunch on the table.

"Don't worry," Gemma said, crossing the room to stand beside her. "It's not like I didn't enjoy the view. He is quite fetching in the nip."

Mary glanced over at her, then laughed. "I see you'll fit in just fine around here. Living with all these men takes a certain amount of tolerance. That's why I think it best you work your way up to meals in the kitchen. Their behavior can be bawdy and their language a little raw."

"I'm Irish. We invented bawdy," she said.

"Well, then, we'll see you at dinner. And I'll just go get that lemonade."

Gemma pulled on her cardie and grabbed her sandwich and crisps, following Mary out onto the porch. The winter weather in Queensland was much warmer than winter in Dublin, pleasant enough to eat lunch alfresco. She plopped down on the top step and set her plate beside her. The sandwich was huge—a thick slab of warm ham between two slices of home-made bread. Mary had added mustard, remembering that Gemma had liked it from their lunch the day before.

Gemma had left so early for Bilbarra that she hadn't bothered with breakfast. Famished, she took a huge bite of the sandwich and sighed. Food tasted so much better here. Maybe it was because someone more competent than herself was doing the cooking.

She heard the screen door slam and Gemma looked up to see Cal striding across the yard, a glass of lemonade in his hand. She chewed furiously and managed to swallow right before he stopped in front of her. "Hi," she croaked, pasting a bright smile on her face.

"Mary sent this out."

Gemma took it from his outstretched hand, avoiding his gaze. "Thanks."

He rocked back on his heels and nodded, his hands shoved in his jean pockets. "Well, enjoy your lunch."

"Would you care to join me?" Gemma asked. "This sandwich is big enough for the both of us."

Cal thought about her offer for a long moment, then shrugged. "Sure. But first, I want to apologize for—"

"Oh, no," Gemma interrupted. "You don't have to— It was my— I didn't mind." She laughed nervously. "I mean, it didn't bother me. I have seen a man naked before. Several times. More than several. Many." She winced. "Not that many. Enough."

"And you'd rather not see any more?"

"No," she said. "Yes. I'd rather not be surprised by one. But I don't mind…looking." Gemma took another bite of her sandwich. She wasn't having much luck using her mouth to speak. Perhaps she ought to stick to chewing.

"Mary said you wanted to talk to me about our family history."

"I do."

"Why?"

She'd expected the question and had a story all worked out. "Because I'm interested in what happened after your ancestors left Ireland. I'm working on a book. On the Quinn family."

"Why the Quinns?" he asked.

"Because a Quinn is paying me to do the research," she lied. "Edwin Quinn. He's a very important man. And he wants to know more about his family." She held her breath, waiting for him to either question her further or accept the story as it was.

"Why would someone pay to know all that? All those people are dead. That's the past. Aren't you more interested in the present?"

"I'm a historian. We're supposed to be interested in the past," Gemma explained. "And I think dead people can be very interesting. Did you know your third great-grandfather, Crevan Quinn, came to Australia on a convict ship?"

He nodded. "Most of the early settlers in Australia did. He was a thief. A pickpocket. He served his time and his parole in New South Wales and after that, he was a free man. He came up to Queensland and worked hard, bought some land and started Kerry Creek." He took a bite of his half of the sandwich. "There's a painting of him in the front parlor."

"I'd like to see that," Gemma said.

"I'll take you on a tour of the station, if you like. Although there are more interesting things to see than that old painting."

She looked over at him and noticed that he had a bit of mustard on his lower lip. Without thinking, Gemma reached out and wiped it away with her finger. But then, she wasn't sure what to do with it. "Mustard," she murmured.

He took her hand and pulled her finger to his lips, then licked the yellow blob from the tip. It was such a silly thing, but Gemma felt a flood of heat race through her body. She drew a quick breath, desperate to maintain her composure.

Cal didn't seem to be faring much better. He quickly let loose of her hand. She picked up the lemonade and took a gulp, hoping to break the tension. But the drink was more tart than she expected and it went down the wrong way. The more Gemma coughed, the worse it became and before long, her eyes were watering.

"Are you all right? Are you choking?"

He smoothed his hand over her back, gently patting. But his touch only made her more uncomfortable. She imagined his hands moving to her face, to her breasts, to her— "Oh," she groaned.

"Here, take another drink," he said, holding the glass in front of her.

She waved him off, knowing that lemonade was the last thing she needed. Was there a reason she made a fool of herself every time he came near? When she'd finally regained control, she stared up at him through her tears, her gaze fixing on his mouth. He had such a nice mouth, Gemma mused.

And then, as if the humiliation wasn't enough, she leaned forward and pressed her lips to his. The kiss took him by surprise and he drew back, a startled expression on his face. Had she made a mistake? Had she misread the attraction between them?

Gemma cleared her throat. "Sorry. I have no idea why I did that." She paused, searching for a plausible excuse. "I wanted to thank you. For everything. Helping me on the road, giving me a place to stay. Talking to me about your family. That's all."

"No worries," he murmured. Cal drew a deep breath, his lips still inches from hers. "So, what about that tour?"

His breath was warm on her mouth and Gemma knew if she leaned forward, it would happen again. And this time, it would be better, because it wouldn't be a surprise to either one of them. "Now? I'd like to get started on my research if possible. Mary said you have some old family records in your library?"

"Sure. She can show you. We'll get together later. This evening. After dinner?"

"Mary invited me to join everyone in the kitchen. You'll be there, won't you?"

He nodded.

"Then we'll go after we eat. It's a date." Oh, she hadn't meant to say that. "It's a plan," she corrected. "A good plan."

The sound of an approaching car caught Cal's attention and he turned to watch a Land Rover drive into the yard. A soft curse slipped from his lips.

"Who is that?" she asked.

"My brother, Brody." Cal slowly stood as Brody hopped out of the car and ran around to the passenger side. A woman stepped out and Brody walked with her to the back door.

"It looks like he's brought another guest," she said. "Is that his girlfriend?"

Cal forced a smile. "I have to go. But I'll see you later."

He held out his hand, then drew it back. A handshake didn't seem right now that they'd kissed, Gemma mused. But what would be a proper way to part? She stood up and pressed her hand to his chest. He stared down at her fingers as she smoothed the faded fabric of his shirt. "I'll see you later."

Cal hesitated, before nodding, then jogging down the steps. Gemma rubbed her arms, trying to banish the shiver of excitement she felt. Cal Quinn wasn't like anyone she'd ever met. She'd always dated older men—at least ten years older. Men who had been so-phisticated and highly educated, who spent their days thinking, not doing. Gemma had always assumed she'd been looking for that father figure she'd lacked in her life.

But Cal was nothing at all like her father—or like the men she'd dated. He was young and strong and unde-niably sexy. Was she willing to put aside her quest to gain a father for a chance at a different kind of lover, a man who made her heart race and her knees wobble?

Gemma sat back down and picked up her sandwich. "I'll just have to separate my personal life from my…personal life." And deal with the consequences later.

CAL OPENED THE SCREEN DOOR and stepped inside the kitchen. The scent of Mary's pot roast hung in the air and she stood at the stove, making gravy from the pan drip-pings. He looked at the clock. Dinner began in exactly five minutes. Promptness at meal times was one of the only rules that Mary enforced at the station. But Cal was dirty and sweaty from working all day and he needed time to get cleaned up before he saw Gemma again.

He'd spent the day repairing the gates in the home-stead yards where they'd driven the cattle after muster-ing. Focusing on the task had been difficult—his thoughts had been occupied with Gemma and the kiss they'd shared.

He hadn't been at all happy with his side of the en-counter. The contact had stunned him, causing him to draw away instead of pulling her into his arms. Now, the only way to fix his mistake was to kiss her again. But Cal wasn't sure whether he ought to take the lead on that or let her make the first move again.

He hung his hat next to the door and rolled up his sleeves. "How long?" he asked.

"Look at the clock, Callum Quinn. Five minutes," Mary said. "Wash your hands and take a seat."

"I just thought I'd run up and catch a quick shower. Maybe you could hold off a bit?"

Mary turned, bracing her hands on her ample hips. "You can shower after dinner. The boys will want to eat and if you're not here when I put the food down, there won't be anything left." She turned off the flame on the stove, then pulled the gravy jug from the shelf above the sink. "You look just fine. Don't worry. You could be covered in mud and you'd still be a beaut."

"I'm not worried," Cal said. "What would I be worried about? Do you think I—?"

"Of course not. Sit."

Cal reluctantly took his place at the head of the table and Mary set a beer in front of him. He took a long drink and then leaned back in his chair. After his surprising lunch with Gemma, he'd gone on to have a very strange day.

Brody had brought home a stray girl he'd found living at the jail and had offered her a job working in the stables. Though Payton Harwell didn't look as though she'd done a hard day's work in her life, the stables had been spotless when he walked through a few hours later. Either she was efficient and tireless, or she'd managed to convince one of the jackaroos to help her.

Teague had shown up shortly after Payton's arrival, staying long enough to chat up both of the ladies. But then a call from Doc Daley had sent him off on an emergency visit in his SUV.

With his competition occupied, Cal was anxious to have Gemma to himself. But he had to get through dinner first. "Maybe I should let Gemma know that dinner's ready," he said, shoving his chair back.

"She knows. She spent the afternoon in the library and just went back to the bunkhouse a few minutes ago." Mary handed him a basket full of sliced bread. "Make yourself useful. Make a pot of coffee."

The six stockmen that worked Kerry Creek arrived at the back door, a boisterous group ready for a good meal and a few cold beers. "She's a bit of alright, I'd say," Skip Thompson said as he walked inside. He tossed his hat at the hooks on the wall, but it fell to the floor.

"That she is," Jack commented. "I like long hair. And long legs. What do you think, Cal?"

"About what?" Cal filled the filter with ground coffee and closed it, then flipped the switch.

"The Yank or the Irish lass? Which do you fancy?"

"I haven't thought about it," he lied.

"Ha!" Davey Thompson cried. "A little slow off the mark there, boss? Jack here has already decided to marry the Irish girl. He wants to get to making babies straight off."

Cal's jaw clenched. "I'll warn you yobbos to mind your manners. You'll not treat these women like the girls you play with at the Spotted Dog." A knock sounded on the door and he circled the table, pulling a serviette from out of Jack's collar. "On your lap," he muttered. "And no talking with your mouth full. No cursing. Or belching. Or farting."

He found Gemma waiting on the porch, dressed in a pretty blouse and blue jeans. "There's no need to knock," he said as he opened the door for her. She'd tied her hair back in a scarf and as she passed, he fought the temptation to pull it off and let her hair fall free.

It had been a long while since he'd enjoyed the pleasures of a woman's body and the scent of her was enough to make his blood warm. Now, presented with the perfect female form, he couldn't decide how to proceed. He placed his hand at the small of her back, steering her toward his end of the table.

Cal forced himself to breathe as the warmth from her body seeped into his fingers. This was crazy. Women may have been a bit scarce lately, but he'd always been able to control his desires. Just touching her was enough to send his senses into overdrive.

"Hello," she said, smiling at the boys seated at the table. Skip suddenly stood and the rest of the stockmen followed suit in a noisy clamor. "I'm Gemma."

Cal cleared his throat. He should be making the introductions. After all, she was technically his guest. "Gemma, that's Skip Thompson, and his younger brother, Davey. This is Jack Danbury. Over there is Mick Fermoy, Eddie Franklin and Pudge Bell. And you know Mary."

He waved Pudge out of the seat next to his and pulled

out the chair for Gemma. "It's nice to meet you," she said as she sat down, sending them all a dazzling smile.

The screen door slammed and Brody stepped inside, pulling his gloves off as he crossed the kitchen. He looked around the table at the boys, all still standing uncomfortably, before resting his sights on Gemma. A slow grin spread across his face as he approached.

"I'm Gemma Moynihan," she said in a lilting Irish accent. "And you must be Brody. I can see the family resemblance."

"Gemma," Brody repeated. He glanced over at Cal, an amused expression on his face. Was it that evident, this attraction he had to Gemma? Cal felt as if he had a sign around his neck—I Fancy The Irish Girl. Well, stiff bickies. If Brody could have his fun with Payton Harwell, then Cal would enjoy Gemma's visit, as well.

"Have you met Payton?" Brody asked, smiling warmly at Gemma.

"Yes, I did," Gemma said.

"Is she coming in to eat?" he asked.

"I don't know. She was lying in her bunk when I left. She looked knackered."

"Maybe I should take her something," Brody suggested, stepping away from the table. He grabbed a plate and loaded it with beef and potatoes, covering the entire meal with a portion of Mary's gravy. After fetching a couple beers from the fridge, he headed back out the door.

"Oh, ho," Mick said with a laugh. "If Brody doesn't go back to footie, Miss Shelly might give him a job as a waitress. I reckon he'd look real fetching in the apron."

The boys found the joke hilarious and they all sat back down and began passing around the platters and bowls that Mary set in front of them. Cal held the boiled potatoes out in front of Gemma. "If you want something else, I'm sure Mary could make it for you."

Gemma met his gaze and for a moment, Cal felt as if he couldn't move. Her eyes were the most incredible shade of green. And her lips were soft and lush, a perfect bow shape. If they'd been alone, he would have kissed her right then and there.

"This is fine," she said, smiling. "In Ireland, we love our praities. And I'm so hungry, I'd eat them ten ways."

She scooped a spoonful onto her plate, then took the bowl from his hands. Her fingers brushed his, but he didn't pull away. Though it was silly to crave such innocent contact, for now it was as close as he'd get to her.

"So where did you come from in Ireland?" Mick asked.

"Dublin," she said. "I teach at University College and my mother lives there. Though the Moynihans are originally from County Clare." She paused. "And my father lives in Belfast." The last she said so softly that only Cal could hear.

"My grandparents were from Ireland," Mick commented. "They came here right after they married."

"So you're the full quid, eh?" Jack said. Cal shot him a look and Jack shrugged. "She must be smart if she teaches at university."

"I hated history in school," Skip said. "Could never remember all those dates."

"It's not just about dates," Gemma said. "It's about life. What our lives are built upon. My grandfather loved history and I'd stay with him during the summer months. He had a library full of books and I think I must have read them all. I loved the stories of the ancient Irish kings and queens."

"I sure would have studied harder if my teacher looked like you," Skip said.

Cal glanced around the table to find each of the stockmen watching Gemma intently. "You're pretty enough to be a princess," Pudge said. The rest of the boys agreed and Pudge blushed.

"The Quinns are descended from the ancient kings," she said, glancing at Cal. "I've come here to trace the history of the Australian branch of the Quinn family. I'm hoping I can convince Cal to let me dig up all the family secrets."

She was teasing him and Cal wasn't sure how to react. He barely knew her. But he did know one thing about himself—he wasn't considered a very comical fella. Among the Quinn brothers, Cal was the serious one, the guy everybody could depend upon. Brody and Teague led much more interesting lives and probably had a helluva lot more secrets to tell.

"Do you have any secrets I should know about?" Gemma asked, a coy smile playing at her lips.

"Oh, no," Davey interrupted. "Cal's life is an open book."

"I think you saw all my secrets earlier," Cal muttered. As soon as he made the comment he wanted to take it back. It was a feeble attempt at humor. It hadn't been the most proper of introductions and he probably should have just let the memory fade.

He did have a few secrets, though. He hadn't told anyone about the matchmaking service. And he'd been perving over the genealogist since he'd met her, spending most of the day trying to figure a way he might act upon his desires. *That* would go over big if he said it out loud.

"I have a secret," Davey volunteered. "And I'm not mingy about keeping it."

"Yeah," Skip said. "Davey's big secret is that he still sleeps with a teddy bear."

The rest of the jackaroos burst out laughing and Davey turned five shades of red. "I—I do not."

"I think that's nice," Gemma said. "I have a little monkey that sleeps on my bed. My grandmother gave him to me when I was young. He's made from one of my grandfather's socks and he's still one of my most precious possessions."

Davey looked around the table, a smug smile on his face. "See?"

The boys fell silent and Cal watched Gemma silently. She had a kind heart. It would have been easy to get caught up in the teasing, but she'd sensed that Davey would have been embarrassed, so she put a stop to it by siding with him.

Though he'd only known her for part of a day, Cal couldn't help but be curious about the attraction. It wasn't just physical. Yes, he thought she was beautiful. But there was more to this than just lust. Besides wanting to take her to bed, he also wanted to sit down and learn everything he could about her.

Who was she? What was her life like in Ireland? Did

she have a whole stable full of blokes just waiting to romance her or had she found a man to love? Though they weren't proper questions to ask a near stranger who was only interested in his family tree, he wanted to believe they'd move past the professional and into something much more personal the moment they were alone again. After all, she had seen him naked. That was pretty personal.

The remainder of the dinner passed in polite conversation. The boys peppered her with question after question just to keep her talking. By the end of the meal, they'd all fallen madly in love with her. When she set her serviette next to her plate and excused herself from the table, they all jumped to their feet to help with her chair.

Cal followed her out the door. Though he wanted to appear indifferent, he suspected that his preference was quite clear to everyone at the table. Was he making a fool of himself? To a casual observer, Gemma might appear to be seriously out of his league. Smart, sophisticated, beautiful. But she'd been the one to kiss him first. Maybe he did have a chance.

In truth, a part of him wanted her to finish her business and leave as quickly as possible. Her presence at Kerry Creek had upset his well-ordered life. But another part of him wanted the luxury of time—as long as it would take before he'd feel comfortable enough to touch her again, to kiss her, to make— "So, would you like that tour now?" he asked, pushing the thoughts from his head.

Gemma nodded. "Sure. I'm just going to grab my cardie from the bunkhouse and I'll be right back."

"All right," Cal said. "I'll be here. Waiting."

He watched her walk across the yard, fascinated by the gentle sway of her hips. It was nice to have a woman close at hand, to be able to enjoy looking at her whenever he chose. It may not last long, but he'd damn well enjoy it while he could.

GEMMA STEPPED BACK OUT onto the porch of the bunkhouse and closed the door quietly behind her. Payton and Brody were sharing a private moment and she'd interrupted. If she and the American girl were going to live under the same roof, they'd have to work out some kind of signal.

Cal was waiting for her in the middle of the yard. He'd grabbed his jacket and his hat and was kicking at the dirt with the toe of his boot as she approached. "Where's your cardie?" he asked.

"I couldn't go inside. Payton and Brody were…"

Cal's eyebrow shot up. "Yeah?" He shook his head. "My little brother certainly moves fast."

"Does that run in the family?"

He forced a smile, then slipped out of his jacket and draped it around her shoulders. It was still warm from his body and Gemma pulled it tight, breathing in the scent of him. Though there were plenty of handsome men in Ireland, there weren't many who spent all day long on a horse. That kind of work did something to a man's body—made it harder, leaner…sexier.

She would find a way to kiss him tonight, to shatter his cool facade. The brief kiss they'd shared earlier had been completely one-sided. But Gemma suspected that, given the opportunity, Cal was probably a pretty decent kisser.

The way she saw it, he was likely good in bed, too. She'd heard that the quiet ones were always better. A man with an ego seldom lived up to expectations. But a bloke like Cal didn't need to prove anything. No one would ever question his masculinity. After what she'd seen in the hallway, certainly not her.

"Where are we going?" she asked.

"Walkabout," he said.

"Walkabout?"

"A stroll. It's an aboriginal term. The natives wander out into the bush and search for spiritual enlightenment. But this isn't quite so serious. I'll take you to the stables first."

"Horses?"

"That's what we keep there."

Gemma had already met the three dogs that lived on Kerry Creek. They could usually be found trailing after the jackaroos who fed and cared for them. A childhood encounter with a vicious bull terrier had left her with a healthy respect for animals in general and a long scar on her ankle. And now, she preferred to stay well clear of all of them. She couldn't control another creature's behavior and Gemma didn't like anything she couldn't control.

She lagged along behind him and when he grew impatient with her pace, Cal took her hand. "I thought we were supposed to stroll," she said.

He slowed down. "You're right. So, let me tell you about the station. We have just over fifty thousand acres, which isn't big for a cattle station. There are some outfits in Queensland with a quarter million acres. We have three thousand head of cattle and about a hundred horses. There are six full-time stockmen on Kerry Creek and next month, when we start mustering, we'll hire a few more, temporarily."

"Mustering," she said.

"We gather up the cattle into a mob and drive them into the homestead yards. We brand and tag the calves and inoculate them. Count them all up. And then ship some of the cattle to market."

"To eat," she said.

"That's where hamburgers come from," Cal replied.

"I'm aware of that," Gemma said. "But I've never really looked a hamburger in the eye while it was still alive." She turned slowly. "Where are all these cattle?"

"Out there," Cal said, pointing past the collection of buildings. "Somewhere. We have to go find them when we're ready. Teague will fly over and let us know where they are."

They stopped at a long, low building. Cal stepped inside the dimly lit interior. "Come on. There's no hamburger in here."

Gemma reluctantly followed him inside. Though the stable didn't smell like a perfume factory, she didn't find the odor completely nauseating. "The horses start foaling in the fall. We bring them into the stables after we're done with the mustering. Teague likes to keep a close eye on them."

"Don't you lose a lot of animals if you just let them wander?"

"Our land is fenced and they move in groups. There

are water tanks and troughs scattered over the station. The cattle tend to stay close to water. Most of our daily work has to do with keeping the water flowing for the stock. We spend a lot of time repairing fences, too."

"What do you do when you're not working?"

"More work. The books. Driving into town for supplies or feed. There's never really time to relax." He paused. "Come on. Let's go for a ride. I'll show you the best sights on the station." He turned and grabbed a saddle from a rack across from the stalls, hefting it over his shoulder.

"I don't ride."

"Don't worry, you can ride with me."

"No," she said, more emphatically. "I've never been on a horse. To tell the truth, they scare me."

"There's nothing to be scared of," he said with a laugh. "Come on, I'll introduce you."

Gemma shifted nervously. It was hard enough with dogs and cats, but horses were another thing. They were huge and unpredictable and smelly and they had enormous teeth. And they were probably crawling with all sorts of bugs. "Couldn't we just walk? The Irish are very good at walking."

He set his saddle down, then nodded. "Are you afraid of machines?"

"What? Like chainsaws and power drills? I'm not fond of them."

"Like motorcycles? Quad bikes?"

"Oh," Gemma said, her spirits brightening. "I like motorcycles. I have a scooter I take to work in the summer. They don't have teeth."

He blinked, then shook his head. "All right, we'll take a quad bike. But tomorrow, I'm going to teach you how to ride. You can't visit a cattle station and not get on a horse."

"Oh, I'm sure I could." She stepped back and felt her foot sink into something mushy. Gemma looked down to see that she'd walked right into a pile of horse poop. "Oh, what is this? Who left this here?"

Cal laughed. "We'll also get you a proper pair of boots. Those shoes won't last a day in the dust and mud."

"I like my shoes."

"They aren't very practical."

"I didn't buy them to be practical. I bought them because they were pretty."

He stared down at them for a long moment. "I guess they are pretty. Pretty ruined."

Gemma sent him a murderous glare. "Aren't we acting the maggot?"

"Translation?"

"You're messing with me. You think it's funny I don't like horses or horse poop or dirt or dust or lizards or spiders. I'm a woman. I'm not supposed to like those things. I'm supposed to stay clean and smell good."

He arched his eyebrow. "You can always tell me to nick off. Or tell me to get knotted. Then I'll leave you alone."

"You could help me clean off my shoe," she suggested. "Give me your hand." She held on to him for balance as she pulled the slipper off and scraped it against a bale of straw. But Cal was right. The little satin flat was ruined. Gemma hopped around to get it back on her foot without touching the dirty part. But suddenly, she lost her balance and tumbled against him.

For a long moment, he held her, his gazed locked with hers. Then, with a soft curse, Cal gathered her into his arms and kissed her. This was nothing like the kiss they'd shared over lunch. This was real and powerful, filled with desire.

Gemma's fingers clutched at the front of his shirt, holding tight for fear that her knees might collapse. The quiet, aloof man had disappeared. Cal was kissing her with a hunger that was fierce and demanding. His mouth possessed hers completely, making her thoughts spin wildly out of control.

His hands roamed over her body and Gemma lost herself in the sensations that raced through her. He held tight to her hips, pulling them against his in a provocative dance. When that wasn't enough, he slipped his hand beneath her shirt and cupped her breast, rubbing his thumb over her nipple until it grew hard.

Gemma moaned, tipping her head back as he kissed her neck. She wanted to tear off all her clothes and get naked with him, to feel his body against hers, skin on skin, flesh pressed to flesh. There was too much between them.

His jacket had fallen to the floor and Cal worked at the buttons on her blouse. As each one opened, his mouth drifted lower. But his erotic exploration ended when the sound of footsteps echoed through the quiet stable.

Gemma drew back and turned in the direction of the door. She saw Teague striding toward them in the dim interior. He stopped when he caught sight of them and Gemma quickly fumbled with the buttons of her shirt. Cal pushed her behind him, offering her the barrier of his body.

"What are you doing out here?" he asked, his voice tight, his body tense.

"I'm going for a ride." Teague pulled his saddle and blanket from the rack and hauled it toward the door on the far end of the stable. "Hey there, Gemma," he said as he passed.

"Hello, Teague," she called from behind Cal's back. He grinned at her and she gave him a wave. "Nice night for a ride."

"Can't a bloke get a minute of privacy around here?" Cal muttered. He grabbed his jacket first, then Gemma's hand. "Let's go."

When they got outside, he turned to her and slipped the jacket around her shoulders. "I'm going to warn you off Teague."

"Warn me off?"

"He can be real charming," Cal said. "But I suspect he's going to meet someone. Someone he shouldn't be meeting. Another woman."

"You think I'm interested in Teague?"

"Are you?" Cal asked.

She stared at him dumbfounded. Hadn't she made it perfectly clear which Quinn she preferred? Had Teague not come along, they'd probably be having sex right now on the floor of the stable.

"Don't answer that," he said. "It was a stupid question." He bent closer and kissed her again, softly but urgently, his lips taking possession of hers until she had no choice but to surrender. When he finally drew back, Gemma tried to think rationally.

Was she really ready to do this? Though indulging in an affair with Cal might be exciting, she'd come to Kerry Creek with a task to do. Maybe it was best to focus on that and not on the way his hands moved over her body or the way his tongue invaded her mouth when he kissed her.

"I—I should probably get back to work," she said. "And it might be better to see the rest of the station in daylight."

She couldn't read his expression in the dark. Was he disappointed? "Right," he said. "Absolutely."

They walked back to the house, her arms crossed in front of her, his hands shoved in his pockets. Now that they'd acted on this attraction, it would be difficult to go back. Already, she craved the taste of his mouth and the warmth of his body.

It was clear Cal was intent on seduction. And she was powerless to refuse him. But before it happened—if it did—she needed to think it through. There were too many traps, too many mistakes to be made. And though she intended to walk away, Gemma suspected that memories of an affair with Cal might stay with her for a very long time.

3

CAL STOOD OUTSIDE THE CLOSED DOOR of the library. He'd come in for lunch expecting to see Gemma at the table. But Mary had informed him Gemma had taken a late breakfast after sleeping in and had preferred to continue working rather than eat. Four hours later, he still hadn't seen her that day.

Things had gone balls-up at Kerry Creek. The usual balance had been completely upset by the arrival of Payton and Gemma. And Cal wasn't one to appreciate chaos.

The stockmen talked of nothing else but the two women all day long, planning ways they might charm them and even challenging each other to contests of strength to see who'd sit next to them at the dinner table. It had taken the last bit of Cal's patience to keep them focused on their work that day.

In part, his foul mood had come from a lack of sleep. Cal had spent last night wide awake, pondering the mistakes he'd made with Gemma, the last one weighing heavily on his mind. When Teague had walked into the stable, so charming and confident, Cal's jealousy had bubbled over, something he hadn't wanted Gemma to witness.

He shouldn't appear too interested and yet, he needed her to know he was attracted—wildly attracted. The kiss they'd shared in the stable was proof of that. But they wouldn't find privacy in the stable. He'd just caught Brody and Payton together, the same way Teague had caught him and Gemma the night before.

Sometimes, Kerry Creek could be a lonely place. But not anymore. Everywhere he looked there were people watching him. Except for Teague. He was off in his own world, riding out last night and returning in the early morning hours, appropriating feed from Kerry Creek to take over to Hayley Fraser at her grandfather's station, Wallaroo.

His brother apparently didn't care that the family was involved in a lawsuit with Harry Fraser, a bitter fight over disputed land on the border between the two stations. Though Teague could make his own choices, his choice to spend time with Hayley irritated Cal.

Added to that was Cal's confusion over Gemma. She obviously wasn't looking forward to seeing him again. He had spent the entire day thinking about her, working out what he'd say the next time they were together. But he'd made such a botch out of the previous evening that she preferred to starve rather than face him again.

"What are you doing lurking around out here?"

He looked over to see Mary standing in the hallway, a laundry basket clutched in her arms. "I'm not lurking," Cal said.

"What, then? Are you waiting for a bus?" She nodded at the door. "It's your library, your office. You can go in if you want."

"She's in there working."

"If she's in there, why aren't you there, too?"

"I don't want to disturb her," Cal said.

"What? Is she doing brain surgery? Designing a spaceship? All she's doing is looking at musty old books and papers, Cal. Just walk in and tell her you need to get something from your desk."

Cal shook his head. "That's too obvious," he said.

"Maybe she'd like a cup of tea. Or a biscuit. You could bring her something from the kitchen."

"That's a good idea," Cal said. "I'll get her a snack. Or make her a sandwich."

"Brilliant," Mary said. "Make enough for you both so you have a reason to sit down and talk to her."

Cal nodded. "Thanks," he said.

The housekeeper shrugged. "That's what I'm here for." She paused. "On second thought, maybe she'd like a piece of cake. Try that."

Cal strode back to the kitchen. He grabbed a knife from the drawer beside the sink and cut a huge slice of chocolate cake, then dropped it on a plate. The kettle was simmering on the stove, so he made a fresh pot of tea and grabbed a pair of cups.

He held the tray out in front of him as he slowly walked back to the library. Balancing it on one hand, Cal knocked on the door, then pushed it open. Gemma looked up from the desk as he entered.

"You don't have to knock. This is your office."

Cal swallowed hard. God, she looked even more beautiful than he'd remembered. Was it possible she'd changed in the course of a single day? Or had he forgotten how lovely she was? "The door was closed. I brought you something to eat…if you're hungry. I—I thought you might want to ask me some of those questions…." He set the tray down on the desk, then busied himself pouring her a cup of tea.

"We can do that later," Gemma said. "No hurry."

"Right." He glanced down at the leather chair and thought about sitting down. But he decided to wait for an invitation. "Well, then, I'll leave you to your—"

"Aren't you going to join me?" she asked. "There are two cups here. And one very large piece of cake." She picked up the plate and held it out to him.

Gemma poured a second cup of tea, then sat back in his leather chair. She took a slow sip, watching him over the rim of the cup. Cal met her gaze, but this time he didn't allow himself to look away. If she had any doubts about his interest in her, he wanted to dispel those immediately.

"Have you found anything interesting?"

"Your great-great-great-grandfather's diaries," she said.

"Really? Where did you find them?"

"On the top shelf, behind a stack of old ledgers. He's quite an interesting man."

"I'd heard he led an interesting life," Cal said. "But I've never read the diaries." He scooped a bite of cake onto the fork and held it out to her.

"I did some research in Dublin before I flew over here. Crevan Quinn was convicted of petty theft, but he was suspected of a much more serious crime. He was accused of stealing a valuable family heirloom by Lord

Stanton Parnell, a very powerful man." She paused to eat the cake.

"Hmm. I thought he was only a pickpocket." Cal watched as Gemma licked frosting off her lower lip, imagining that he might do the task for her. Everything she did fascinated him—from the way she held a book, to the tilt of her head when she spoke, to the way her tongue moistened her lips. It all seemed designed to intensify his desire. But how could he get from cake to kissing in one simple step?

Suddenly, he realized that he didn't have a clue. His mouth went dry and he grabbed his cup of tea. "I—I should really leave you to your work." Cal stood, his tea cup clattering in the saucer.

"No. I'm finished for—"

"I've got work to do before dinner and—"

"I'd like to chat a bit longer if—"

Cal cursed softly and she stopped speaking, her expression filled with surprise at his outburst. He closed his eyes and drew in a deep breath. Then he circled the desk and pulled her out of his chair.

This time, he didn't think before kissing her. He knew exactly what he wanted and he was prepared to make it good. When his lips met hers, she sank back against the desk, clutching at the front of his shirt. Cal held on to her waist, then slid his hands over the sweet curve of her hips.

They both reached out to push the papers and books off the desk, but a wide sweep of Cal's hand sent the tray and teapot crashing onto the thick Oriental rug. Once the desk had been cleared of everything, he picked her up and sat her on the edge, then stepped between her knees.

Her hands skimmed over his shoulders and down his chest, the sensation sending a flood of warmth through his bloodstream. He'd thought so carefully about how to handle this moment, then realized he was operating on pure instinct. He didn't need to think anymore, just feel.

He buried his face in the curve of her neck and inhaled her scent. She smelled like flowers, a pure, heady scent, nothing exotic, just fresh and clean and very feminine. Why had he never noticed this about other women he'd kissed? Was it coincidence that his senses seemed more attuned to Gemma?

Cal ran his hands over her arms, reveling in the silken feel of her skin. And when she moaned softly, her breath was warm against his ear. Time had slowed, allowing Cal to savor each moment before moving on to the next. They might have gone on forever, or the rest of the night, had they not heard the knock on the library door.

Cal stepped back, pulling her up with him until they both stood behind the desk. He quickly straightened her clothes, then strode to the door and pulled it open. When he saw Mary standing in the hall, he gave her an impatient glare.

"Sorry to disturb you, but I just wanted to let Gemma know I do laundry first thing in the morning. If she has anything she wants washed, she can bring it along to breakfast."

"Thank you, Mary," Gemma called. "And the cake was wonderful."

"Glad you enjoyed it, dear."

Cal peeked out into the hall as he closed the door. "Sticky beak," he whispered. He stepped back into the room and gave Gemma an apologetic shrug. "Mary takes very good care of us all."

"Why don't your parents live on the station?" she asked.

"They live in Sydney." He slowly crossed the room to stand next to her. Reaching out, Cal took her hand, holding it up to press his palm against hers. One by one, he wove her fingers through his. "My mum left the station when I was seventeen. She couldn't take country life anymore. Four years ago, when I took over the station, my dad joined her. He missed her, so he gave up the station to be with her."

"That's so romantic," Gemma murmured, her gaze fixed on their intertwined fingers.

"Is it?" he asked. His mother knew what she was getting into when she married his father. She was aware her life would be spent on Kerry Creek. She was the one who hadn't held up her part of the bargain. "What else do you think is romantic?"

A tiny smile curled the corners of her lips. "I think you're romantic, bringing me chocolate cake and tea…even though it is spilled all over the carpet."

"Yes, but it was worth the mess," Cal said.

"Since the cake is on the floor, maybe we should go back to what we were doing?"

"Discussing Crevan Quinn?"

"No, not that," she said. She pushed up on her toes and kissed his lower lip, then ran her tongue along the crease of his mouth. "That."

"Oh, yes," he said with a slow smile. "That was nice. Are you sure you don't want to get back to work?"

"I—I think I'm done for the day," she whispered, reaching for the buttons of her blouse.

Cal couldn't help but smile. He wasn't doing too badly. They'd gotten past their initial inhibitions and moved on to playful banter. If he trusted his instincts, he'd know what to do next. Maybe these things didn't need to be learned. Maybe they were just hard-wired into a bloke's intuition.

GEMMA BRUSHED HER HAIR out of her eyes and looked up at Callum. She sat on the desk, with Cal standing between her legs, his hands cupping her face. She felt like a teenager, caught up in a crazy infatuation with a very dangerous boy. As adults, they were perfectly capable of taking off all their clothes and shagging like bunnies, but they'd spent the last half hour kissing and touching and teasing.

Gemma ran her hand over the front of his jeans, the ridge of his erection pressing against the faded fabric. He growled softly. "See what all this pashing does to me?" he murmured.

"Pashing? Is that what they call it here?"

He nodded. "What do they call it in Ireland?"

"Shifting," she said. "And you know where that leads? To sin and illegitimate babies like me."

He stepped back. "You have a—"

"Oh, no," Gemma said. "I am an illegitimate baby myself. My mother never married my father." She paused. "I know single motherhood is pretty common these days. But Ireland is still very Catholic and my mum paid a price." It was the first bit of personal information she'd revealed. Perhaps if he understood her motives, he would accept her methods.

"Do you think that makes a difference to me?"

"No," she said, shaking her head. "I just thought you might be interested."

He fixed his eyes on hers, staring at her intently. "I am. Very interested. In you."

"So tell me a secret about yourself," Gemma urged. "Something I'd be surprised to know."

"All right. But you have to promise not to laugh." Once she nodded her agreement, he continued. "I didn't kiss a girl until I was eighteen when I lost my virginity at the local whorehouse."

Gemma gasped. "Oh, my. That is interesting."

"Don't laugh," he warned.

"I'm not. I'm just amazed. You've gotten very good at kissing since then. You're kind of like a…prodigy?"

"That is the one and only time I ever visited that place. Since then, I've found legal ways to sleep with women. Although, they did legalize the knock shops in Queensland a few years back."

"So, how was it? Did they tell you what to do?"

"I knew the basics," he said. "I had done my reading. And when you live on a station all your life, you see things. It was fine. The woman was patient and didn't laugh when I fumbled around. After it was over, I was glad because I thought I wouldn't think about sex anymore."

This time Gemma did laugh. "How'd that work out for you?"

"Not well. All I did was think about sex. All the time. After I worked my way through the single women in Bilbarra, I had to head on down the road to Brisbane. But there haven't been that many women. It's kind of hard, living in the back of nowhere."

Gemma pressed her hand against his crotch. "It is hard. Very hard."

"Stop teasing. You're touching a man who hasn't been with a woman in about six months." He nuzzled her neck. "I'm excitable."

Gemma ran her hands through his hair and kissed him again. "How did we get on this subject?"

"You wanted to know a secret. I told you one."

Though she'd love nothing more than to continue the discussion, Gemma knew exactly where it would lead. If the pashing were any measure, sex with Cal would be incredible. But she still hadn't been able to rationalize her deception. Somehow, she sensed he valued honesty far more than he needed physical gratification. He'd gone six months without sex. That took a lot of self-control.

She grabbed the front of his shirt and began to button it. "Maybe we should clean up this mess. I wouldn't want Mary to think I was a bad guest."

"I'll take care of it," he said. "This is my office, so it's usually a bit of a dog's breakfast anyway."

"And I've made it…a messy dog's breakfast?"

"A dirty carpet is a small price to pay." He tugged the front of her blouse together. "I have something to show you." He took her hand and led her to the door, but Gemma yanked him to a stop.

His shirt was half-open and she hadn't finished buttoning hers. When she'd covered everything properly, she raked her hands through her hair. "All right?" she asked.

"We're just going across the hall to the parlor," he said.

"I don't want everyone knowing what we were doing in here."

He nodded toward the clean surface of the desk. "I think they're smart enough to figure it out. We weren't polishing the furniture—or maybe we were." Cal chuckled as he opened the door. They hurried across the hall and into the parlor. He led her over to the fireplace and pointed to the portrait above it. "There he is."

Gemma looked at the painting. "Who?"

"That's Crevan. The pickpocket."

Gemma gasped. "This is Crevan Quinn?" She'd walked past the portrait several times already on her way to the front door but she'd barely noticed it. She should have asked about the painting the moment she'd seen it, but her instincts for history had been dulled by her fascination with Callum.

"That's him. It was delivered the day before he died. He had it painted in Sydney. My mum always said she was glad we got our good looks from her side of the family."

Crevan's hair was white and wild and his eyes were fierce. Gemma stepped closer to examine the canvas in detail. The coat he wore was finely tailored to his form and the background was a mix of Victorian architecture and Queensland landscape.

"He is an imposing figure," she said. Her gaze fixed on Crevan's hand. How well a subject's hands were captured was always the true mark of a great painter. He clutched an ornate walking stick with a— "Oh, my God. I can't believe it."

"I know. He was a pretty ugly bugger. But I think it's just the hair and those sideburns."

It was right there in front of her, gleaming with a green fire. She glanced over at Cal, worried that he'd noticed her reaction. In the painting the Emerald of Eire was perched on the head of Crevan's walking stick. She'd found it. Just like that, the proof had dropped into her lap. But what was she going to do with it?

"It—It's an impressive portrait," she began, trying to come up with a way to ask about the jewel. If the walking stick was still around, Cal may not even realize the value of the stone embedded in the handle.

"This is why I love history," she continued. "Look at his clothing. Do you know if he sat for this portrait or was it painted from a photograph?"

Cal shrugged. "What difference does it make?"

"Well, for instance, this walking stick. Did it belong to your grandfather, or did the painter just paint it in to make your grandfather look more prosperous than he actually was? It's a lovely stick," she added, pointing toward it. "Was it passed down in the family?"

"No, I don't think so." Cal studied the portrait more carefully—too carefully for Gemma's comfort. Had he noticed the jewel? She hadn't told him about the Emerald of Eire and for now, she was going to keep that part of her story a secret.

"There must be some family heirlooms. After all, you're living in the same house he did."

"There's a lot of stuff up in the attic," Cal said. "I've always meant to go through it and sell what we didn't need and now's as good a time as ever. Maybe you'd like to help. You'd probably know if things were antiques or just old."

"There could be family documents up there, too," she said, getting excited.

Gemma felt that wonderful thrill that came when she was on the verge of a new discovery. Usually she experienced it buried deep in a musty old archive. But here she was, standing next to a man who made her body ache with desire, faced with a choice.

A knock sounded on the door and they both turned to see Mary standing in the hall. "Did we just have a weather event I missed? It looks like a cyclone hit the library."

"I'm so sorry," Gemma said. "I'll clean it up straight off."

Mary chuckled and shook her head. "No need. Dinner is ready." She pointed to Cal's chest. "Fix your shirt. You look like an unmade bed."

After she walked away, Gemma looked up at Cal, her face warm with embarrassment. "Sorry," she murmured as she reworked the buttons on his shirt. "I guess our time together isn't a secret anymore."

"No worries. Mary is very discreet," he said.

They strolled to the back of the house, their fingers intertwined. At the last moment, he pulled her into the shadows and kissed her, long and hard, leaving her breathless. It was a promise that they'd continue what they'd started in the library.

Gemma sighed softly. It was astounding how easily

she'd forgotten about the emerald. One kiss was all it took to wipe it from her thoughts completely. David Parnell was a man she didn't even know, a fantasy father that she'd built up in her mind. But Cal Quinn was a real, flesh-and-blood male.

There was a choice to be made and Gemma was beginning to question her resolve.

DINNER THAT NIGHT WAS a rowdy affair. Teague had returned and taken his customary spot at the opposite end of the table. Brody and Payton had joined them, too, adding to the excitement. The discussion had turned to the Bachelors and Spinsters ball, a wild event held in Bilbarra at the end of the month.

Both Payton and Gemma expressed an interest in attending, but Cal had to wonder if they were serious. He couldn't imagine Gemma's work taking an entire month. Though he wasn't sure what she was looking for, there were only so many books in the library. If she couldn't find what she needed in a week or two, she wasn't much of a historian.

As for Payton, she seemed quite content to stay on at Kerry Creek indefinitely. She was doing an impressive job in the stables and was keeping Brody occupied, so Cal couldn't really complain.

Cal listened to the conversation distractedly, focused instead on Gemma's hand, which rested on his thigh, hidden by the table. No one had seemed to notice, but Cal was having a difficult time breathing.

Every now and then, she'd slowly slide her palm up and then down, coming dangerously close to his crotch.

The thought of her touching him again, the way she'd done in the library, had caused a physical reaction—his erection pressed against the denim on his jeans. He was glad that Mary had made dessert, because he wouldn't be standing up anytime soon.

"It might be fun," Payton said, her interest in the ball keen. She turned to Gemma. "What do you think? When in Australia, do as the Aussies do?"

Gemma laughed. "We'd have to get something nice to wear."

"I have dresses," Payton said. "I need work clothes. I can't wear Davey's castoffs forever. Not that I don't appreciate the loan," she said, sending the jackaroo a sweet smile.

"I have to fly to Brisbane in a few days. I could take you shopping," Teague offered.

Cal sat up, bracing his elbows on the table. "Hang on there. Gemma and Payton are not going to Bachelors and Spinsters."

"We won't participate," Gemma said. "We'll just go to…observe. Think of it as sightseeing. Or anthropological research."

"If you want to see the real sights of Australia, I'll take you," Teague said. "Queensland is beautiful from the air."

"There's an idea," Cal said. "You'd be much safer in a plane piloted by our brother than at Bachelors and Spinsters."

Gemma leaned closer to him, her hand moving up his leg again. "We could go together," she murmured, the conversation going on without them. "You are a bachelor and I am a spinster."

"It's at the end of the month," Cal said. "Are you staying that long?"

Her smile faded and she shook her head. "Probably not."

Cal watched her silently as the conversation shifted to the sights the girls ought to see in Queensland. When the meal was finished, the boys scrambled to pull out Gemma's chair, but Cal waved them off and did it himself. If his intentions regarding Gemma hadn't been made clear to the boys before this, he was making them crystal clear now. He tucked her hand in his and led her out of the kitchen toward the library, leaving behind a group of dejected would-be suitors.

Cal couldn't wait until they got behind closed doors. He pulled her into his arms the moment they were out of sight of the kitchen, his hands roving freely over her body. "You were driving me mad at dinner," he whispered, pressing her back against the wall.

"That was the point," Gemma teased.

"What am I going to do about you?" He pinned her arms to her sides. "All I ever think about is kissing you." He leaned into her. "We never finished our tour of the station. You haven't seen my bedroom yet."

"No," Gemma said, shaking her head. "It wouldn't feel right."

"I want to be alone with you." He brushed a kiss across her mouth. "Someplace where we won't be interrupted." He grabbed her hand. "I know. Come on, I'm going to show you something special."

He grabbed a jacket on their way back through the

empty kitchen and slipped it over Gemma's shoulders. Then he led her toward the machine shed. The station's quad bikes were parked outside.

"Hop on," Cal said.

"I can't drive one of these things."

"I'll do the driving."

"Aren't they dangerous?"

"I'm going to drive real slow and we're not going far. Just far enough."

Gemma hiked up her skirt and straddled the bike. Then Cal got on behind her and pushed the button on the steering yoke. The machine rumbled to life and a moment later, they were headed into the outback.

Cal knew every inch of Kerry Creek, even in the dark. The quarter moon was drifting toward the horizon, providing some light to navigate by. He leaned into Gemma as he drove, feeling the warmth of her body against his. Touching her, even in such a simple way, was almost more than Cal could handle.

After months without a woman, it was nearly impossible not to think about having sex with Gemma. He could picture it in his head, every detail of her body, they way they'd react to each other, the sensation of losing himself inside of her.

And yet, he didn't want to rush this. He wanted to take his time and enjoy the foreplay. Besides, Gemma wasn't leaving anytime soon—he'd make sure of that. He knew exactly where he wanted to take her and in the distance he saw the rock, outlined by the rising moon.

The lights from the homestead had faded in the distance and Cal turned off the bike and slid off the back. He spanned Gemma's waist with his hands and lifted her off, standing her in front of him.

"What is this?" she asked.

"The big rock," Cal explained. "It's a bit of a landmark." He took her hand and led her closer. "We always came out here as kids. The rock is supposed to have some sort of magical power. At least that's what we believed."

"How did it get here?"

"I don't know. That's a question for someone who knows about history. I think the Aborigines might have smoothed the surface and rolled it here. But they haven't claimed this as a spiritual site. It was here when Crevan bought the station. There's talk that he buried a family treasure out here."

"Really?"

"We dug for it when we were kids, turned up all this dirt around the rock, but we didn't find anything."

Gemma walked over to the massive boulder and ran her hand over the smooth surface. "Is this why you brought me to see out here in the dark?"

"Look up," he said.

She did as she was told and a tiny gasp slipped from her lips. Though the view of the stars was better once the moon set, the sky was still awash with tiny specks of light. "I've never seen so many stars in my life."

"When you live in the city, the light obscures them," Cal explained.

"When I was a girl, I used to visit my grandfather in County Clare during my summer holiday. He lived just a few miles from the ocean and he'd set up his telescope on the cliffs on a clear night and spend hours identifying stars." She turned to look at him. "Mind you, it wasn't an easy thing. A clear sky on the Irish coast can be a rare thing."

"The Quinns come from County Kerry," he said. "That's why the station is named Kerry Creek."

"County Kerry is just to the north of Clare. Who knows, our families might have been neighbors back in the day." She paused. "Have you ever visited Ireland?"

"No," Cal replied. He'd never even been out of Australia. "But I'd like to go someday. Maybe I'll come and visit you."

"Oh, you should. I could show you where your ancestors came from. There are still Quinns all over County Kerry. We could find some of your cousins."

"I'd rather spend my time with you," he said. Cal wrapped his arm around her waist and pulled her close. "I want to kiss you again."

"It seems that's all we've been doing," Gemma replied.

"If you want me to stop, I will. Just say the word."

She took a ragged breath, and for a moment, he thought she might just stop him. But then, she wrapped her arms around his neck. "I can't give you a single good reason why you shouldn't."

Cal brought his mouth down on hers, her lips parting and their tongues touching. The kiss was deep and stirring and he felt himself grow hard with desire. He pulled her hips against his, the friction sending a delicious rush of sensation racing through this body.

He'd met her on the road just yesterday morning and

here they were, lost in a passion that couldn't be controlled. They didn't feel like strangers. When he touched her, she felt as familiar as any woman he'd ever known, as if she'd been meant for him all along.

He slid his hands beneath her top, anxious to touch her warm skin. Before long, they were tugging at each other's clothes. The air was chilly, but Cal didn't notice when she pushed his shirt over his shoulders.

He leaned back against the rock and closed his eyes, reveling in the sensation of her lips on his naked chest. He furrowed his hands through her hair, moaning softly as she moved to his nipple. A flood of desire consumed his body as she traced a path across his chest.

How had he ever lived without this? Cal wondered. He'd sometimes gone months between women and barely considered it a problem. But he couldn't go a few minutes without Gemma. Every waking thought was of her, her taste, her scent and the feel of her body beneath his hands.

She bent lower, kissing his belly. He wanted to stop her, aware of how close he was to the edge. But this had turned into her seduction and he was determined to enjoy it for as long as it lasted.

When she moved to unbuckle his belt, Cal held his breath. "Be careful," he warned. She slid his zipper down slowly and he winced. He was going to make a fool of himself the moment she touched him.

Cal gently grabbed her wrist. "Wait," he said. He drew a deep breath and tried to quell his need. Maybe it had been a mistake to bring her here. This is what he'd been hoping for, wishing for, ever since he'd met her. Maybe the magic of this place was part of it.

"It's all right," she said. "I want to make it happen."

She pushed his jeans over his hips, her hands smoothing over his ass. He searched for her lips again, his kiss communicating the extent of his desire. When her fingers slipped beneath the waistband of his boxers, he was already lost in a vortex of pleasure.

Cal held back for as long as he could, determined to enjoy her touch. She stroked him slowly at first, her fingers dancing over his shaft. But when she wrapped her hand around him and increased her pace, Cal knew he was lost.

His release came fast and fierce and he groaned as he felt the spasms overtake him. The intensity of it made all attempts at control vanish and he gave himself over to the wonder of her touch.

When it was finished, he opened his eyes to find her smiling at him. "What?" he murmured.

"I guess that whole celibacy thing really doesn't work."

"I wasn't celibate by choice," Cal said. "I'm geographically celibate."

"Then I'm glad I could help out."

He grabbed her, running his hand through her hair and pulling her into another kiss. "You have no idea how grateful I am."

"I'm sure you'll be able to show me."

Cal chuckled softly. Though it wasn't the seduction he had planned, it was perfect. It had brought them to a new level of intimacy, a place where they didn't need to be afraid to show their vulnerable sides. Gemma liked him for exactly who he was. That was much more than he'd ever had with a woman before.

No matter how long she stayed or what happened between them, Cal had a feeling she was about to change his life, his outlook, maybe even his dreams. And though he had always been set in his ways, this was one time when he was ready to take a chance.

4

GEMMA SAT AT THE KITCHEN TABLE, her hands wrapped around a hot cup of tea. She took a sip, then leaned back in her chair. "How long have you worked at Kerry Creek?"

Mary set the bread bowl on the table and uncovered it, tossing the cotton dish towel aside. "Let me think. Cal was seventeen when his mother left and he's nearly thirty now. So it's coming on thirteen years." She paused. "Heavens, it seems like just yesterday that I drove up to the house with my luggage in hand."

"Did you ever want a family of your own?"

Mary punched the bread down and covered it again with the cloth, then returned the bread bowl to the top of the stove. "Of course. But the right man never came along. These days, you don't need the right man. You girls have choices."

"But we still want the fairy tale," Gemma said. "We're searching for the white knight and the castle and all the happily-ever-afters."

"And what if your knight never turns up? What then?"

An image of Callum drifted through Gemma's mind, his head thrown back, his body caught in the midst of his release. He'd rescued her once, but that wasn't the only reason for her attraction. Sometimes a girl didn't need chivalry; she needed passion and excitement. "I'm going to give him a little more time."

"Yes, I think that's a splendid idea. Give him time."

It was clear that Mary wasn't talking about a generic white knight, but about Cal. And Gemma would be thrilled to allow him all the time he needed. But sooner or later, he'd begin to wonder what she was really doing at Kerry Creek. And she'd have to explain. Then, her time would be up.

"My mother raised me alone and it wasn't easy. I have a good position at the university that pays well, but I'm not sure I'd choose to have a child on my own."

"You make do with what you have and you get by," Mary said. "She did a splendid job with you."

It felt nice to be complimented for a change. Gemma's mother had never been satisfied with anything that her daughter had accomplished. Instead, she'd been obsessed with Gemma gaining her rightful place in the Parnell family, as if that were the only route to happiness.

As she observed life here at Kerry Creek, Gemma was beginning to think that money and position weren't everything. It was the connections you made with other people that determined happiness, the people you loved and those who loved you.

"Tell me about Cal's parents. Why did his mother leave?"

Mary poured herself a cup of tea and sat down at the table. "There wasn't anything else she could do. Jack Quinn was a very stubborn man and he thought the 'for-better-or-worse' part of the vows they took was written in stone. Sarah believed marriage was a work in progress. Jack never left the station, never took a vacation. Sarah wanted to see something of the world, so she went out on her own to find it. After the boys were grown, Jack realized he couldn't do without her. Luckily, Sarah still loved him."

"Is that why Cal isn't married? Because of what his parents went through?"

"Oh, there are plenty of women who'd be happy to spend their lives on Kerry Creek. But Callum's always been a bit shy and nervous around girls."

Gemma gasped. "Cal? Shy?"

"You don't think so?"

She shook her head. "No. He's quiet and perhaps a bit aloof. A man of few words. But once he warms up, he's quite charming."

"Charming," Mary repeated. "Well, I'm glad he's finally letting someone see that side of him." She took another sip of her tea. "I shouldn't tell you this, but Cal has signed himself up for a matchmaking service. To find himself a wife."

"He told you this?"

"No. He left an advert out on his nightstand and I saw it while I was making his bed. He doesn't know I've read it."

Gemma stared at Mary, wondering why she'd chosen to reveal such news. "I would think there'd be plenty of women interested in marrying him."

"Yes. I hope so." She gave Gemma a shrewd look. "If you have any thoughts in that direction, perhaps you should speak up?"

"Me?" Gemma shook her head. "No. No, I'm not interested in marriage. Nor am I cut out for life in the outback. Believe me, I would be a disaster."

"Ah, but love can change that."

"I'm not going to fall in love with Cal," Gemma said.

"Then all this kissing and foolishness doesn't mean you're gone on him?" Mary asked.

"No. We're just having a bit of fun."

"I'm not sure he would agree," Mary said. "Take care, Gemma. Beneath that hard shell is a man who leads with his heart. You can hurt him." She drew a deep breath and smiled brightly. "So, how is your work coming along? You said you were doing this genealogy for a member of the Quinn family?"

"Yes," Gemma said. It was part of the lie, but the more she got to know the people at Kerry Creek, the more difficult it had become to deceive them.

"He must be quite wealthy to pay you to come all the way over here to do research."

"Yes," Gemma repeated. "Do you have any more of those lovely biscuits you left in the library for me?" Mary took the bait and rose from the table, returning a few moments later with a cookie tin. "These are so good. What's in them?" Gemma asked.

"Almonds," she said. "And a bit of toasted coconut. They're Cal's favorite, too."

Gemma chuckled. "Stop. We may enjoy the same biscuits, but I'm not Cal's type. Trust me."

"What makes you say that?"

"I'm terrified of animals. Dogs, horses. Insects, too. Snakes, lizards. I don't like dirt or dust. I'm a city girl…" At the sound of footsteps on the porch, she stopped.

"I see what's happening. I go to work and you two ladies spend the day sipping tea and eating bickies." Cal peered through the screen door, his hat pushed back on his head. "May I join you or is this just for girls?"

"It's just for girls," Gemma shouted in a teasing voice. "Go away."

"All right, I'll stand out here all alone, hungry and thirsty and pathetic, just a hard-working bloke with no one to pity him."

Gemma rolled her eyes, then grabbed a cookie from the tin. "Thanks for the tea, Mary. I better go see to Mr. Lonely Hearts out there."

She walked to the door and stepped out onto the porch. Callum looked around to make sure no one was watching, then grabbed her and gave her a playful kiss, pinning her up against the side of the house. "Is that bickie for me?"

Gemma stuck it in his mouth. They'd become more comfortable with each other, but there were still so many things she didn't know about him. Was he really searching for a wife? And if he was, where did she fit into the scheme?

Gemma didn't mind keeping their relationship simple. There was no need for a commitment. But she couldn't help a tiny pang of jealousy, thinking about the woman who would finally win the heart of Callum Quinn. She'd be lucky to spend the rest of her nights in his bed. "What are you doing back so soon?"

"I needed a smoko," he said.

"A what?"

"A break, from work."

"Everyday I learn something new. Bickie, smoko. Last night it was pashing. What's next?"

"I have something. Come on." He took a bite of the biscuit as he led her down the steps. His horse was tied to a rail in front of the porch and he pointed to the stirrup. "Hop on up and we'll go for a ride."

"You want me to get on that horse?"

"I'll help you. Just put your foot in the stirrup."

"No," Gemma said. "I'm not going to do that. I told you, those things frighten me."

His horse suddenly turned and Gemma jumped back and screamed. The sound caused the horse to jerk and Gemma ran back onto the porch. "See. You can never tell what they're going to do. People can get killed riding horses. I've seen it on the telly. They trip and fall down right on top of you."

"Gemma, you're being irrational. We're not going to go jumping over fences or leaping across dry creeks. We'll start with a nice, slow walk."

She crossed her arms over her chest and shook her head. Her fears might be irrational, but they were her fears and he had no right to belittle them. "No. If you need to go somewhere, go. I'm not coming with you."

He stood beside his horse, his expression unreadable. She was not going to give in on this. If he wanted a woman who could ride horses and rope cattle, then he could go find one. She wasn't going to try to make herself something she wasn't.

"I have to get back to work," she murmured, turning for the door.

He was at her side in an instant, taking the steps two at a time. "Wait." Cal grabbed her arm to stop her retreat. "What's wrong?"

"Nothing," she said, trying to maintain an indifferent expression. But it wasn't nothing. It was that same old something that always seemed to get between her and the men in her life—fear. The pattern had become so common Gemma recognized it immediately. If a man tried to get too close, she'd step away emotionally, just out of reach.

"Are you angry?"

"No."

"I think you are."

"If I brought you to Dublin and asked you to stand in front of a roomful of people and talk about Irish history, would you do it?"

"No," he said.

"Because you're not comfortable with it. I do that every day and think nothing of it. You ride your horse every day and never give the skill a second thought."

"I'm sorry," he said.

Gemma took a deep breath. "I just don't see the point. It's not like I'm going to be buying a horse and riding it around Dublin. Once I go home, I'll probably never go near one again."

"When are you going home?" Cal asked.

"I don't know. Is my welcome suddenly wearing thin?"

"No," Cal said. "I was just wondering when you had to be back. Do you have the entire summer off?"

"Classes begin in early September, but I have to be back by the middle of August to prepare."

"Good. You're welcome to stay as long as you like,"

Callum said. "I enjoy having you here. For a lot of reasons, not just the—well, you know. And I'm sorry about the horse. I was just having a bit of fun."

He was right. That's what they had together—fun—and nothing more. And she was turning it into a big drama. She'd let Mary's revelation bother her. If Cal was looking for a wife, he wouldn't find a lifelong mate in her. She was a good time, a no-strings affair, a summer holiday with great sex.

The thought caused an ache in her heart. Shouldn't she want to be someone's only love? Shouldn't she be searching for that one person who made her world complete? That's what normal, emotionally healthy people did. But Gemma knew better. That kind of commitment wasn't in her nature.

"Really, I'm not angry," she said. "And you're right. My fears are irrational."

"At least come and pet him. He's a very gentle boy. Just like me."

Gemma gave them both a suspicious look, then slowly walked down the steps. "If he bites me, I'll never forgive you."

"If he bites you, you can bite me," Cal said.

Though Gemma knew what he'd meant, it still sounded more like sexual innuendo than retribution. She stood behind him, still wary. Still, she could be a good sport about this one thing. What was the harm?

He grabbed the horse's bridle and held the animal steady. "Pet his nose. He likes that."

Hesitantly, she reached out, her hand trembling slightly. "What's his name?"

"Eddie," Cal said.

Gemma ran her hand over the horse's muzzle, then pulled it away. But Eddie wanted more and he nudged her with his nose. "It's so soft," she said, stroking him again. "Like velvet."

Whenever she stopped, Eddie found a way to get his nose beneath her hand again. Gemma giggled at his clever antics. "He's a flirt."

"Hey, don't steal my girl," Cal warned, scratching the horse behind his ears.

Gemma's heart skipped. Was that how he thought of her? His girl? "Maybe you should get Eddie a girl of his own?"

"He wouldn't know what to do with her," Cal said.

"Is he gay?"

Cal laughed, reaching out to touch her face with his gloved hand. "No. He's a gelding."

"Why would you do that to him?"

"Because all stallions think about is sex. They're very difficult to control. Geldings are much more trainable. We only have one stallion on the station and he does all the work."

"I should get back to work," Gemma said.

"Me, too." He bent close and brushed a kiss across her lips. "I'll see you later?"

"You will," Gemma said.

"I know. I like that. Knowing you'll be here when I get done with my day." He hooked his foot in the stirrup and swung up into the saddle, adjusting his hat as he twisted the reins through his fingers. "Have a nice afternoon, Miss Moynihan."

With that, he wheeled his horse around and gave him a gentle kick. Eddie broke into a brisk walk, causing dust to fly up from his hooves. Gemma watched until Callum had disappeared behind the stable, then she sat down on one of the chairs that lined the back porch.

She'd known Cal for two days and already her feelings for him overwhelmed her common sense. If she couldn't control herself, she'd have no choice but to leave. Maybe that would be best.

Gemma felt a wave of frustration wash over her. Why did it have to be so complicated? Why couldn't the owner of Kerry Creek be a grumpy old man instead of a gorgeous bloke who made her heart race and her body tremble?

THE SUN HAD GONE DOWN hours ago and night had fallen on Kerry Creek Station. Cal sat on the back porch of the homestead, staring out into the yard, a bottle of beer dangling from his hand.

Before Gemma had arrived, dawn was his favorite time of day. But now, sunset meant that his work was done and he could spend the entire evening with Gemma. Unfortunately, she seemed preoccupied with her research. She'd closed herself in the library after dinner, promising that she'd be finished soon. Now, two hours later, he was still sitting alone, his mind filled with thoughts of the time they were wasting. The sooner she got her work done, the sooner she'd leave. But he couldn't think of any way to stall her progress.

She seemed to be particularly interested in Crevan Quinn. Maybe Cal could tempt her with some inside information. He hadn't been in the attic since he was a kid, but there might be something up there worth finding. And, of course, there was the legend of the buried treasure. They could spend a year digging for that.

Family legend had it that Crevan had buried a lockbox filled with gold somewhere on the station, but he'd died before he could dig it up. The story had been passed down from generation to generation, but no one had ever found a clue as to the location. With fifty thousand acres of land, finding that box was like searching for a single grain of sand on a beach.

A movement caught his eye and Cal watched as Brody emerged from the darkness, his horse at a slow walk. Considering his little brother's dislike for station work, Cal had to wonder what he was doing riding in so late at night.

"Where were you?" he asked.

"I went for a swim with Payton," Brody replied as he dismounted. "Do you have another one of those?"

Reaching down, Cal grabbled the bottle next to his chair and held it out. "You have to go fetch the next round."

Brody flopped down next to Cal and took a long drink, draining half the bottle before he paused to belch.

"Nice," Cal said. "A bit more choke and she would have started."

"Thank you," Brody muttered. He kicked his feet up on the porch railing.

"Funny how you're on your best behavior around Payton, but when she's gone you revert back to typical Brody."

"And you don't put on airs when you're with Gemma?" Brody paused. "Why aren't you with Gemma? How come you're all alone here, crying into your beer?"

"She's shut herself in the library. I can't understand what's taking her all this time. It's not like the Quinns are royalty. But she's going over every single journal and account book in there."

"What does that have to do with our family history?"

"Don't ask me," Cal said.

"She's pretty. Not as pretty as Payton, but pretty."

Oddly enough, the insult didn't sting. He was glad Brody hadn't taken a fancy to Gemma. It left the way clear for him. Still, he had to defend her honor. "I beg to differ. Gemma is much prettier."

"Payton told me she spoke with Teague today. He was talking like he'd started things up with Hayley Fraser again. And he took off in the middle of the night last night on horseback."

Callum's suspicions had been confirmed. "Shit. When I heard she was back, I wondered if he was going to see her again. What do you think she's up to?"

"You never liked her, did you?"

That was putting it mildly. He'd been trained from an early age to distrust the Frasers. Somehow, that prejudice hadn't taken with Teague, although Cal could understand why. Hayley Fraser was a hot buttered crumpet with her blond hair and her movie-star looks. "She put Teague through hell the first time they were together. He has a blind spot when it comes to her."

"Maybe that's our problem," Brody suggested.

"We've never had a blind spot when it comes to a woman. Maybe we're missing out on something."

Cal pondered the thought as he took another swallow of his beer. "Maybe." He swung his legs off the porch railing and got to his feet. He wasn't going to miss out on anything when it came to Gemma. If he felt like being with her, then he was going to sit in the library and watch her work. "I'm going to go check on Gemma. See if she needs some help." He stepped over Brody's outstretched legs and walked back inside the house, leaving his brother alone to contemplate his own romantic inadequacies.

The kitchen was dark when he entered. The sound of the telly drifted in from the parlour. Mary was wrapped up in one of her programs, lost in the fantasy of life lived in the middle of somewhere. Was that what it took for a woman to be satisfied living in the outback? A good imagination and plenty of telly?

He thought about the three women whose profiles he'd received from OutbackMates, wondering what it was that made the outback so attractive to them. He'd been honest on his questionnaire about the amount of time he spent off the station. They knew he never took a vacation. But he had mentioned that the station had a plane. He'd thought it made Kerry Creek seem more prosperous than it was. And Teague could usually be depended upon to fly his brothers wherever they wanted to go, his work permitting.

He'd have to look at those profiles again. Once Gemma left, he'd settle back into his original plan. But Cal wondered if he'd find a woman who made him feel the way Gemma did. Did lightning strike twice? Or was it simply a matter of lowering his standards?

Cal stood outside the library door, wondering whether to knock or to just walk inside. After all, it was his office, his house, his family papers. And there was no reason why she should object. Resolved, he opened the door.

The room was a mess, books scattered across the floor, old papers littering the desk. It looked worse than it had the previous evening when they'd cleared the desk for more interesting research.

He glanced around the room, but Gemma wasn't inside. Then he heard the rustle of papers from behind the desk. Cal found her sitting on the floor, intently studying a map of some sort. "Finding anything worthwhile?"

She'd been so caught up in her work that she jumped at the sound of his voice. Gemma quickly tossed the map onto a stack of papers and smiled up at him. "No," she said. "I mean, nothing that will help with the genealogy. I—I just got caught up in all the old documents. It's the historian in me."

"No worries," Cal said. "You're welcome to look through anything in here. It's all just gathering dust anyway."

Gemma struggled to her feet, then took in the condition of the room with a startled expression. "Oh, my, I didn't mean to do this. I just—well, there's no excuse for it."

"You can leave it," he said. "Everything will be here tomorrow, exactly as you've left it."

"No, I'll tidy up."

She bent down and began to pick up the papers and books lying on the floor. Cal leaned back against the edge of the desk and watched her, his arms braced behind him. He enjoyed looking at her. She was like a beautiful sunset or a wildflower. The more you stared, the less you wanted to look away.

Every detail of her body intrigued him, from the mane of auburn hair that she casually tossed over her shoulder to the delicate fingers that picked up papers from the floor. He loved her curves, her perfect breasts, her backside, the waist he could nearly span with his hands. The thought that he could find another woman just like Gemma was ridiculous. She was one of a kind.

Cal pushed away from the desk and squatted down beside her, reaching for a mess of papers to his right. He noticed they were station accounts. "This looks boring," he said.

"It does. But look. Crevan was a meticulous bookkeeper. Here, he bought a new suit of clothes for his portrait. And here's the fee he paid to have it painted. Don't you find that interesting? When he recorded this in his journal, that portrait was still just an idea. And now, over a hundred years later, it's hanging in your parlor."

Cal let the notion sink in. She was right. It was sort of interesting. He'd passed the painting nearly every day of his life and didn't think much about it. "This puts it in—"

"Context," she finished. "Do you see? Suddenly, the painting has a life of its own."

He nodded. "You really like this stuff, don't you."

"I do. It's a giant puzzle. And when all the pieces fit together, it makes the most beautiful picture. A picture into the past, something no one has seen for years and years." She paused. "But sometimes, you can't find all the pieces. That's when it's frustrating. You have to accept that things get lost over time. And what you think you might find isn't always there to discover."

Cal wasn't sure what it was, but he suddenly needed to kiss her. He slipped his hand around her nape and pulled her toward him. His lips touched hers, softly, gently. It wasn't an expression of unbridled desire, but reassurance, understanding and...

He drew back and looked down into her eyes. And affection. As much as he fought it, Cal couldn't help his feelings for her. It wasn't just about physical attraction. He truly liked Gemma. And he could come to love her.

Three days. That's all it had taken for him to fall like a stone rolled off a cliff. He was still caught in midair, dropping fast, hurtling toward— What? Would he shatter into a million pieces or would there be a soft landing below?

He pushed her back until they both tumbled to the carpet, the papers still scattered around them. His lips found hers again as he stretched out beside her. Gemma arched beneath his touch as he tugged at her blouse.

Though the kiss may have started with affection, it had quickly transformed into something entirely different. Her fingers twisted in his hair and she molded her mouth to his, challenging him to taste more deeply.

He worked at the buttons of her blouse, then moved to her jeans, then back to her blouse again. Cal wanted her naked, but he knew this wasn't the right place. When he made love to her, he wanted something more memorable than a roll on the library floor.

Unfortunately, Gemma wasn't thinking the same way. She worked at his belt until she'd managed to unbuckle it. Cal was well aware of what her touch could do to him. This time, he'd return the favor.

He grabbed her hand and pinned both her wrists above her head. A wicked smile played at her lips and she relaxed, as if she knew exactly what he had planned. He unzipped her jeans, then smoothed his hand down her belly, dipping below the denim and lace to the damp spot between her legs.

She'd made him shudder with desire and now he would do the same for her. Cal wasn't sure if it would change anything between them, but it felt right. And since Gemma had arrived, he'd learned one important lesson—to trust his instincts.

GEMMA'S BODY HAD GONE WEAK and she couldn't put a rational thought together. Instead, she surrendered to Callum's touch, a touch so intimate, so stirring, she had no choice but to relinquish control.

How had this happened so quickly? She'd been ensnared in an attraction she couldn't deny. It was so wrong, yet it felt so incredibly right. If there was an un-written code of ethics for historical researchers, she hoped there wasn't a section on taking pleasure at the hands of her research subject.

But Cal wasn't the focus of her research. He was just a bystander, a descendant of the man she'd come to investigate. What she was doing wasn't wrong. Then why did it feel that way? Was it because there was a lie hanging between them?

Cal's fingers shifted over her, his caress soft, yet purposeful. A moan slipped from her throat as she felt herself spinning toward the edge. She ought to stop this right now and confess everything. But she was afraid he'd pack up her things and send her on her way, before she'd ever know what they could have together. She didn't want him to stop.

Every touch was proof that he needed her. His kiss was restless, searching, demanding that she respond. Gemma felt completely vulnerable, as if she had no defense against his desire. She bit her bottom lip as he slipped his finger inside of her, the sensation almost too much to bear.

He took his cue from her and a heartbeat later, he began a gentle rhythm meant to drive her toward release. Gemma opened her eyes to find him staring down at her, his gaze intense. "Is this what you want?" he whispered.

"Yes," Gemma replied, a bit breathless and light-headed.

He ran his tongue along the crease of her mouth and Gemma felt the first tremors. Her body tensed and she writhed beneath Cal's hand until he found the perfect spot. And then, she was there, her body shaking in an explosion of pleasure. It seemed to go on and on, endless spasms mixed with indescribable bliss.

When it was over, he reached down to cup her cheek. "Stay with me tonight," Cal said. "I want you in my bed."

Gemma closed her eyes. She wanted nothing more than to spend the rest of the night exploring their newfound intimacy. But she was afraid of what it might mean—not to her, but to Cal. Was it just desire that drove him? Or was he looking for something more from her? She couldn't make any promises. And it was much easier to rationalize their affair when they weren't waking up together in the morning.

"Not tonight," she said. "I should go back to the bunk-house. It's getting late and you have to be up at dawn."

"I can sleep all day if I want. I'm the boss. Gemma, no one is going to say anything."

"It's not that." She reached down and fastened her jeans, then started on the buttons of her blouse. "I just don't want to get too…attached. We both know this has to end at some point and I don't want to make it more difficult."

"I don't think spending the night in my bed is going to make it any more difficult," he said softly.

There were two ways to interpret his words, Gemma thought. Either letting her go was going to be hard no matter what. Or Callum didn't plan to become emotionally invested in their affair. Oddly, both options hurt.

"You're right," he said, obviously noticing her somber mood. He got to his feet and offered her a hand. "I'll walk you back to the bunkhouse."

After he'd helped her finish dressing, Cal took her hand in his and led her through the house and out the back door. When they reached the bunkhouse, he pulled her into his embrace and kissed her.

But his kiss wasn't meant to arouse. It was full of resignation and maybe a bit of disappointment. A period at the end of a long, complicated sentence. "I'll see you tomorrow," he whispered.

Gemma stood at the bunkhouse door, watching Cal as he walked back to the house. "Well, then," she murmured. "That makes everything much clearer." A long sigh slipped from her lips and she turned and walked inside.

The interior was dark but for the light from the yard shining through the thin curtains. Payton was already asleep, curled up beneath the blankets on her bunk. Gemma flopped facedown into her bed, stifling another groan.

Gemma had enjoyed a number of serious—and sexual—relationships with men, all very unremarkable. Desire had always been stronger in the early days and then gradually faded over time until she broke it off. But what she felt for Callum was something quite extraordinary. The physical attraction between them was as palpable as an electric current racing through her body. It excited her and frightened her all at once.

She sat up and cursed softly. If there was something between them, something more than lust, she didn't want to ruin it. She needed to be honest with him, to tell him exactly why she'd come to Kerry Creek and then let the rest play out.

Gemma stood, then strode to the door. She cursed softly, then turned back to the bed. What difference did it make? It was just a small lie, nothing that would stand in the way of a physical affair.

As she walked back to her bunk, a soft knock sounded on the door. Gemma hurried across the room and opened it, peering out into the darkness. She saw Callum standing at the bottom of the steps and she slipped outside, pulling the door shut behind her. "Why did you come back?" she asked.

"I forgot to ask if you needed anything," he said. "No, that's not right. I just didn't want the night to end."

"You don't have to make silly excuses to see me or talk to me," she said.

"I wasn't—" Cal's voice trailed off. "Yeah, maybe I was. Gemma, this has all happened very quickly. It's not something I'm accustomed to."

"Nor am I," Gemma said. "It's...surprising."

"Very," he agreed. "But not unpleasant. Surprising in a good way."

"Yes. And a bit confusing."

"Are you confused? About what?"

"I came here to do a job. And I don't really like to mix my professional life with my personal one." She paused, gathering her resolve. She could tell him now. She could make him understand. "And there's something else. I—"

Gemma didn't have a chance to say any more. He took the steps two at a time, then drew her into his embrace. They came together so perfectly it took her breath away. She wanted to forget all the reasons she had refused his invitation, but she couldn't. She'd come to care about him. And with that came an overwhelming need to spare him any emotional pain. "There's something I need to tell you about my work."

"Are you working now?" he asked.

"No."

"Then we don't need to talk about it."

"But there is—"

He kissed her again, this time to silence her. How could she be faulted? She was trying to tell him, to clear up any misunderstandings before their desire was completely out of hand. But he didn't seem to care.

"Callum, I—"

"Cal," he murmured, his lips soft against hers. "No one calls me Callum except Mary. And my brothers when they think I'm acting like an arse. And my mother, when she's angry."

"Cal, I—I—" Gemma cursed inwardly. She couldn't do it. She couldn't ruin everything between them just to soothe her conscience. "I—I'm just not ready to spend the night with you. You understand, don't you?"

"Sure," he said, staring down into her eyes. "But that doesn't mean you have to go inside. We could talk. I promise, I won't ask again."

In the end, they stayed on the porch for another hour, kissing and touching, chatting softly about nothing of importance. By the time Gemma slipped back inside the bunkhouse, she was exhilarated, not exhausted.

Gemma slowly undressed, then crawled between the sheets dressed in just a T-shirt and her panties. Though Cal was a man of many contradictions, she knew he was honest and hard working, clever and self-deprecating.

He was thoughtful and a bit shy. And she knew she could trust him. He would never deliberately hurt her.

But could she say the same about herself? Whether she wanted to admit it or not, her fears about commitment had hurt a lot of men, usually when they were most vulnerable.

Tomorrow, she'd tell Cal all about the emerald. She'd explain what the emerald really meant to her relationship with her father. And then she'd be free to enjoy whatever Cal offered.

Gemma heard a rustling from the bunk on the other wall and she pushed up on her elbow and stared into the dark. "Can't sleep?"

Payton sighed deeply. "No. You can't, either?"

"No." It would be a long time before Gemma could put thoughts of Callum out of her head. She reached for the light on her headboard, then sat up, crossing her legs in front of her. "Would you care to talk?" she asked, running her hands through her hair. "I'm a good listener. All my friends tell me so."

"It's complicated," Payton replied.

Wasn't everything when it came to men? Especially the Quinns. "I can handle complicated. Is it Brody? You two seem to be...attracted."

"That's putting it mildly," Payton replied. She crawled out of bed and crossed the room, then sat down on the edge of Gemma's bunk. "Can you keep a secret?"

"Of course." Gemma had plenty of her own, so it wouldn't be difficult.

Payton lowered her voice to a whisper. "A month ago

this last Saturday, I was putting on my wedding gown in Fiji and getting ready to walk across the beach and get married."

Gemma gasped. Now that was a big secret, maybe even bigger than the secret she was keeping. "Oh, goodness. What happened?"

"I got scared and ran away." Payton frowned. "I just wasn't sure I'd found the man I wanted to spend the rest of my life with. There was just no...fire. Do you know what I mean?"

Gemma nodded. For the first time in her life, she understood how desire could burn so deep inside her that the flame never seemed to go out. "Yes," she murmured. "I know precisely what you mean."

"So I grabbed a few things and stuffed them in my bag and exchanged my honeymoon ticket for a flight to Brisbane and...disappeared into the outback."

"And here you are," Gemma said. Their stories weren't very different. They'd both landed on Kerry Creek with a boatload of baggage. Now, faced with an attraction to a Quinn brother, they were both forced to sort through it all.

Payton smiled wanely. "Yes."

"Have you called your family?"

She shook her head. "I left a message at the hotel in Fiji after I landed in Australia. I said I'd call them soon but they're going to be very angry. Not only about the embarrassment and the expense of the wedding. The gossip will be awful. I hate to even think about it now."

"What of your fiancé?"

"I can't imagine what he's thinking. I'm sure he

doesn't want anything more to do with me. Not that I want him to. I made my choice and I can live with it."

"Well, there it is, then," Gemma said, trying to put a happy face on it. "As Cal would say, no worries."

"Oh, I have plenty to worry about. Like this thing with Brody. I'm sure it's just a reaction to what I did. I was a little…repressed and now I'm testing my boundaries. The attraction will probably fade soon. But then, I'm not sure I want it to." Payton paused. "At first, I considered him just a rebound guy, but I think he might be more."

"A rebound guy?" Gemma was unfamiliar with the term, but it made a sort of sense. "I understand. But wouldn't any man who came after your fiancé be a rebound guy? So, in theory, it would be better to go out with some git after you break up so you don't waste a good bloke?"

"I suppose that would be sensible. So you think I'm wasting Brody?"

"Or perhaps, you could consider the possibility that fate has put this man in your path and the reason you ran away from your wedding is that you were really meant to be with him all along."

"No," Payton said, taken aback by Gemma's reasoning. "You think so?"

"I think it's silly to try to figure out a relationship before it's really begun. Maybe you should just let it all happen."

Payton thought about Gemma's suggestion for a long moment, then jumped to her feet. "Thank you," she said as she hurried back to her bunk. After grabbing her jacket from the bedpost, Payton headed to the door. "I'm just going to visit Brody for a few minutes. Don't wait up for me."

"I won't," Gemma called.

When the door closed behind Payton, Gemma lay back in her bunk, pulling the covers up around her chin. Good advice. Now maybe she ought to take it herself. Perhaps it was fate that had brought her here to Kerry Creek and not her search for the emerald. If she believed that, then she'd also have to believe she and Cal were meant to meet. And that whatever her motivation for coming to Australia, it didn't make a difference. It was all part of a grand, cosmic plan.

Gemma pulled her pillow up around her head and groaned. She didn't believe in fate. She'd come to Queensland for one purpose and it wasn't to fall madly in love with an Australian cattle rancher.

5

GEMMA LOOKED AT HERSELF in the small mirror above the dry sink. Though it might have served for shaving, it was impossible to judge her appearance and she wanted to look her best for this evening.

Callum had peeked in the office during lunch and told her to be ready at four. He was taking her out. Though Bilbarra was a two-hour drive, she imagined a night away from the station, away from his responsibilities and her uncertainty, might be just the thing for them both. They'd have dinner or maybe a few drinks at a pub in town.

She smoothed her hands over her dress, the prettiest choice from the small selection she'd brought along. After her shower, she'd used the last of her scented lotion to make her skin soft to the touch, suspecting he would be doing a lot of touching later. Her makeup and hair had taken an hour. And she'd even painted her toes and fingernails an enticing shade of red.

A shiver skittered though her as she thought about what might happen between them. They'd come so close over the past few days, the desire between them growing with each intimate encounter. Gemma had decided he was leaving the last move to her, allowing her to decide when they'd let passion overwhelm practicality.

"Tonight," Gemma murmured as she stared at herself. But what if he wasn't ready? He'd have to anticipate this, to have protection. He would sense this was coming, wouldn't he? If only there was a way to know for sure.

She cursed softly. Cal wasn't an idiot. And if he forgot the condoms, then he'd have to suffer the consequences. Gemma smiled. Besides, there were other things they could do that didn't involve full-on, toe-curling, mind-blowing sex.

A knock sounded on the door and she took a deep breath and hurried across the room to answer it. Cal stood on the other side, his hair damp from a shower. But he was still dressed in work clothes.

"Aren't you ready?" He frowned. "You're not planning to wear that, are you?"

Gemma glanced down at the dress. "Not nice enough? Where are we going?"

He sighed, then took her hand. "It will do. Come on, we have to leave now if we're going to get there in time."

His ute was parked in front of the bunkhouse, the engine running. Cal helped her inside and then jogged around to the driver's side. He hopped in, then reached over her and grabbed the seat belt. "You're going to need this," he said.

He threw the truck into gear, then drove out of the yard, in the opposite direction of the road. Before long, the truck was on rough terrain and Gemma was forced to hold tight to the grip above the window. They bounced over uneven ground, at times so bad that she felt as if she were on a carnival ride.

"Is this a short cut?" she asked. "Isn't Bilbarra the other direction?"

"Who said we were going to Bilbarra?" He glanced over at her. "Did you want to go to Bilbarra?"

"You said we were going out. I thought—"

"We are going out. This is out in the outback. Bilbarra is in."

"I see I've run right up against the language barrier again," she said. "And we both speak the same language."

"What were you hoping for? Drinks? Dinner? Dancing?"

"Maybe," she said.

"There'll be all of that," Cal said with a grin. "Be patient."

"Is there a nightclub out here that no one knows about?" Gemma asked.

"Yes," he said. "It's very exclusive. We'll be lucky to get in. Especially the way you're dressed."

Gemma couldn't help but laugh. Cal was usually so serious around her, so intense. But tonight he was different—relaxed and happy, as if he were anticipating a good night. He'd even managed to tease her, something he hadn't done in the past. "What has put you in such a good mood?"

He turned to her and smiled. But just as he did, the ute hit a deep rut and Gemma slammed against the door. She cried out as her shoulder throbbed with pain. Quickly, Cal pulled the truck to a stop.

"Christ, I'm sorry. I wasn't watching. Are you all right?"

"Fine," Gemma said, rubbing her arm. "It's going to be ugly in a few days, though." She looked up at him. "I bruise very easily. First it's purple, then green, then yellow. A rainbow of ugly."

Cal took her arm and examined it, his hands smoothing over her skin. "There?" he asked.

Gemma winced as she twisted in her seat. "Yes."

He bent close, slipping his fingers beneath the loose sleeve of her dress, before pressing his lips to her shoulder. "Better?"

She held her breath and he turned to her. His lips were so close and yet he hadn't made a move to kiss her. Gemma waited. "Not quite," she murmured. "Try again."

He tugged at her dress, pulling it down to expose the curve of her neck. "Here?" he asked.

"No."

Cal moved to the base of her throat. "Then here."

Gemma moaned softly. He was seducing her. Finally. And she wasn't going to stop him. They wouldn't be interrupted this time. There'd be no knock on the door or problem that needed to be solved. She reached for the buttons of her dress and unfastened the top one.

Cal drew away and reached for the next button. But to Gemma's surprise, he fastened the first. "We still have a ways to go," he said. "Are you good?"

"Yes, I'm fine," Gemma sputtered. Either he wasn't

really interested in seducing her or he had supernatural self-control. She slid across the seat and buckled her seat belt again.

He put the truck in gear. "Don't worry," he murmured. "It will be worth the wait."

Gemma wasn't sure whether he was talking about the destination or the sex. She hoped it was the latter because it was becoming nearly impossible to think of anything else. But her excitement was slightly deflated by the knowledge that she still hadn't told him about her secret. And the longer she kept it, the more difficult it would be.

Though she'd worked hard at her research over the past few days, it didn't seem to mean as much as it had back in Ireland. At home, she could think of nothing but carving out a spot for herself in her father's life, certain it would be the answer to all of her doubts. Not to mention the answer to her mother's prayers.

She'd gone through enough self-help books to recognize that her issues with both her parents had spilled over into her own life. By trying to replace her absent father, she'd found herself attracted to older men, and men who were…unavailable. Growing up with a distant mother had left Gemma with a sense of fear and an inability to commit.

Her relationship with Cal was already doomed. He lived in the middle of nowhere, on a continent half a world away from Dublin. He was looking for a woman who could help him run the station, not some silly Irish girl who was frightened of horses and hated getting dirty. Her idea of a night out included civilization, maybe a linen tablecloth and a decent glass of wine. His included bouncing around the countryside looking for God-knows-what.

The sun was beginning to go down and Gemma wondered if they'd ever find the road. Cal pulled the truck to a stop, then jumped out. He opened her door and waited. "We're here?" Gemma asked, looking around. This spot didn't seem any different than the landscape they'd passed along the way.

"We're here," he said.

Gemma stepped out of the truck. He took her hand and tucked it into the crook of his arm, then started toward a clump of trees. As they came closer, she noticed tiny glimmering lights shining through the leaves. A moment later, she saw a canvas tent and a small table set up in front of it. "Oh," she murmured as they stepped into the small bower. "It's lovely."

Cal had strung lanterns in the trees, the light wavering in the soft breeze. The camp was set beside a small pool of water, hidden from outside view. "Did you do this?" she asked.

Cal shook his head. "That tree fell over the creek and during the rainy season, all that debris piled up making a dam. The water gathers in that low spot and—"

"I meant the camp," Gemma said.

"Yes," he said. "I found this spot a few years ago. No one knows it's here. Except maybe a few thousand head of cattle. But they're not here right now." He grabbed her hand and pulled her toward the table. "I brought wine. And Mary made us dinner. In about an hour, there will be a spectacular sunset."

"And to think I was expecting a silly restaurant."

"Would that have been better?" Cal asked.

"No," she said. "This is perfect." And it was. He'd taken the time to bring all these things out into the bush, getting each lamp in place ready to light and setting the table. She walked over to the tent and peeked inside. The canvas floor was covered with a rug and he'd arranged pillows on top of an open sleeping bag. "When did you do this?"

"This morning. I figured we needed to get away. The stables are Brody's territory and the old shack is where Teague is meeting Hayley. We needed a spot of our own." He walked to the table and poured a glass of wine for her, then held it out. "It's Australian."

"Thank you," Gemma said. He poured another glass for himself, then grabbed the bottle and led her down to the small pond. They sat down on a fallen tree, staring toward the western sky as the sun sank closer to the horizon. "This land is so different from Ireland," she said. "There, everything is green. Here, everything is…"

"Ochre," he said. He bent down and ran his finger through a small spot of mud. Then he reached out for her face. Gemma drew back, but Cal smiled. "Don't worry. It's just mud."

He smeared a bit on each cheek, then did the same on his own face. "Now, you're part of it," he said. "And this land is part of you."

"What does that mean?"

"You can't leave this place. And it will never leave you."

Gemma wasn't sure about the sentiment. They both

knew her home was in Ireland. Was he really hoping she'd decide to stay? This was turning into something far more serious than she'd ever wanted. She was caught between romance and reality. Gemma had assumed that if she ever fell in love, all her choices would be simple. But with Cal, her feelings became more complicated with each passing day.

Though Gemma knew he deserved the truth about her motives, she realized that telling him would do more harm than good. Why hurt him? Why risk the chance that he'd send her away? If she found the emerald, then she'd explain herself and hope for the best. But until then, why borrow trouble?

And if there came a time when she wanted him more than her place in the Parnell family, then she should be willing to give up her search for the emerald altogether. It was just a silly jewel, an object that was no more special than the rock sitting by the edge of the pond.

"What is it?" Cal asked. "You're staring at that rock like it's about to move."

Startled out of her thoughts, she glanced up at him. "I'm fine."

"You looked troubled." He paused. "Gemma, nothing is going to happen here unless you want it to."

"I do," she said. "I want you. I have since the day you changed my tire on the road."

He brought his hands to her face, smoothing his thumbs over her mouth. Then he leaned forward and kissed her, his lips lingering over hers, tasting and then retreating and then tasting again. Gemma slipped her arms around his neck and pulled him closer, this time kissing him with a fierce urgency. They'd waited long enough.

CAL DEEPENED THE KISS, tangling his fingers in her hair as he molded her mouth to his. He thought it might be too soon, that he was rushing things. But Gemma was pliant and willing in his arms, her lips communicating her need.

He'd been thinking about this moment ever since he'd set eyes on her, yet Cal hadn't allowed himself the luxury of believing it might come to pass. But this place provided perfect isolation with nothing to distract them but each other.

The sky in the west had turned into a kaleidoscope of colors—pink and orange and violet. He'd brought her here to enjoy the sunset, but beautiful sunsets were a commonplace in the Queensland outback. Beautiful women weren't, at least not on Kerry Creek.

As he slowly undressed her, Cal took in the details of her body, all the small characteristics that he wanted to remember. Her skin was like silk beneath his calloused hands, her flesh warm and supple. When he'd finished with the last button on the front of her dress, Cal pushed it off her shoulders and it dropped to the ground.

She wore lacy underwear, a matching set, in a pale blue that he found much sexier than black. She looked as fresh as a spring flower, so sweet and natural. He'd only imagined what she might look like naked, but now his fantasies were confirmed. She had a body any man would worship, with the delicate limbs and graceful curves of a Greek goddess.

Cal drew his hand over her shoulder and down her arm, reminding himself not to rush. He might have just one night with her and he wanted to make it memorable. When she went home to Dublin, he needed to know she'd be lying alone in bed, thinking of what they'd shared.

The wind rustled in the leaves above their heads and Cal watched as Gemma carefully unbuttoned his shirt. Once she'd pushed it aside, her lips found a spot in the center of his chest and she kissed him there. He smoothed her hair back from her face as she moved to his nipple, gently teasing it until he moaned.

Satisfied, Gemma moved to the other side, slowly exploring along the way. Waves of pleasure washed over him, but it was sweet torture and he had to stop himself from taking control, from satisfying the desire that raced through his body like a wildfire.

Her fingers fumbled with the button on his jeans and Cal stepped back. Bending over, he tugged off his boots and tossed them aside, then pulled off his socks. His jeans were next and Cal skimmed them over his hips and stepped out of them, leaving him in only his boxers.

Gemma smiled, her hands dancing over his chest. "Now what?"

"Just one thing," he said. Cal took her hand and pulled her along to the water's edge. He reached down and dunked his hand in the coolness, then gently cleaned the mud off her face. "Dirt doesn't taste very good."

"Are you planning to lick my face?" Gemma asked.

"I don't know. I kind of want to leave my options open."

She wet her hands and returned the favor. "Me, too." Gemma glanced down at her toes, then winced. "Wait, I just want to rinse off my feet."

Cal laughed. He knew her dislike of dust and dirt. "Go ahead, wade in."

With mincing steps, she walked through the shallows at the edge of the creek, but the bottom was muddier than the bank and she turned back to him, frowning.

Cal walked to her and wrapped his arms around her waist. "Okay, wash them off."

Gemma fluttered her feet in the water. When her feet were clean, Cal boosted her up until he was carrying her in his arms. Her eyes went wide and she laughed and he walked away from the creek. He finally put her down inside the canvas tent, the rug soft beneath her damp feet.

"Happy?" he asked.

Wrapping her arms around his neck, she pushed up on her toes and kissed him again. "I think I am."

Her body was made for his touch. Her breath came in quick gasps as he cupped the soft flesh of her breast. Everything about this was different. He wasn't interested in just the physical sensation of sex. Cal wanted more, a way inside her heart, a way to reach her soul. He drew her down onto the rug, grateful that he'd thought to make the tent more comfortable.

"You're the most beautiful thing I've ever seen," he whispered as he stretched out beside her.

Gemma turned to face him, her hand draped over his hip. "I'm glad you brought me here."

"I've always come here alone. It's going to be difficult not to think of you here now."

"Maybe we shouldn't—"

He pressed his finger to her lips. Cal wasn't sure what this all meant and maybe he didn't really care. He wasn't worried about a boyfriend back home. He didn't want to hear why a relationship with Cal wouldn't work. None of it made a difference. "I just want these next few hours with you. Maybe the entire night. That will be enough."

She ran her fingers through his hair. "All right."

It was an understanding, Cal thought. If they didn't complicate matters, then maybe what they shared wouldn't turn bad in the end. He could let her go, watch her walk away, as long as he felt they hadn't held anything back while they were together.

Cal took her by the waist and pulled her on top of him. She wriggled, her hips moving against his, creating a delicious friction. He was already hard and ready, but in no hurry. Sliding his hands from her backside to her bra, he unhooked it as they kissed.

Without breaking contact, Gemma discarded it, then pushed up to straddle his waist. Her hair fell over her shoulders and brushed against her face. Cal wound a strand around his finger and tugged her closer. Then he sat up and buried his face against her soft breasts.

Everything he'd wanted was here. Though fate had brought them together, he had to believe it was for more than just one night. His lips found her nipple and he teased it to a peak with his tongue. The smell of her skin was like an aphrodisiac, making him dizzy with desire.

The seduction was slow and deliberate, Cal taking his

time with each inch of naked skin. He rolled her beneath him, drawing her leg up along his hip. Gemma's eyes were closed and a tiny smile curled the corners of her mouth.

He kissed a trail to her belly, then twisted his fingers through the lacy scrap of her panties. An instant later, they were gone and he found the damp spot between her legs. Gemma cried out as he began to caress her with his tongue. Her response was so sudden that at first, he thought she wanted him to stop. But then, her fingers grasped his hair, a silent invitation to go further.

Her body was his to command and he brought her close, then rescued her from the edge. Each time, she became more desperate for release and each time, he wouldn't allow it. He wanted to share it with her, to be buried deep inside of her when she finally let go.

She was ready, but Cal wasn't sure he was. Just the thought of losing himself inside of her was enough to make him come. Could he even maintain a shred of self-control, or would she drive him to the end in just a few seconds?

He rolled away from her to retrieve the condoms he'd brought along and when he returned, she was watching him. Gemma held out her hand and he placed the box in her palm. She knelt in front of him, her fingers wrapped around his shaft, her eyes glazed with passion.

Cal held his breath, her touch nearly overwhelming him. He grabbed her wrist to slow her pace and she stopped, then pushed him onto his back. He closed his eyes as she sheathed him, grateful that the barrier between them might give him more time.

Once again, she straddled him, bracing her hands on his chest as she moved above him. And then, he was inside her, her heat surrounding him. Cal grabbed her hips. "Wait," he whispered.

"I can't," she said. "Don't make me."

He loosened his grip and she began a slow, careful rhythm, rocking forward on her knees, then back until he was buried deep. Cal had never felt such exquisite pleasure before. He'd never wanted to completely possess a woman, but was instead happy to take his pleasure without any promises.

But as he drove into her, Cal realized that this was exactly what he'd sought all along, this woman with the wild auburn hair and the porcelain skin. Everything about her fascinated him and though he'd convinced himself that one night with her would be enough, he now knew that a thousands nights wouldn't come close to satisfying him.

He felt her tense and Cal opened his eyes to see Gemma dissolve into a shattering orgasm, her fingers digging into his chest and her head thrown back. It was all he could take and a moment later, Cal thrust hard and let himself surrender.

The spasms seemed to go on forever, both of them caught up in the pleasure. When she finally collapsed onto his chest, Cal was spent, his breath coming in deep gasps and his heart slamming inside his chest.

Though they might not have scored many points for stamina, the intensity had been more than enough to banish every other sexual experience from his memory. From now on, Gemma would be the standard by which all other women were judged.

Her teeth chattered and Cal hugged her tight. "Are you cold?"

"No," she said softly. "Yes, maybe."

He gently rolled her to her side, then reached out for the down sleeping bag that he'd brought along. Wrapping it around her naked body, he pulled her back into his embrace. "Better?"

"Yes." She smoothed her fingers over his still-hard shaft, sliding the condom off and tossing it aside.

"Is there anything else you want?" he asked. Her hand tightened and he groaned. "Besides that?"

Gemma bent her arm and cupped her chin in her palm, observing him through sleepy eyes. "I'm famished."

"So sex makes you hungry?"

"Ravenous," she said. "The better the sex, the more I eat."

"So, how hungry are you? A snack or an entire meal?"

"Are you asking how it was?"

Cal nodded.

"Seven-course meal. With dessert. And in case you're interested, no man has ever gone past a burger and a bag of crisps."

"A seven-course meal. This I'd like to see."

Gemma giggled. "I might embarrass myself, so be warned. And don't get between me and chocolate, because you'll be risking grave bodily injury."

"I'll be right back," he said. "Don't go anywhere, all right." He dropped a kiss on her lips, then crawled out of the tent. The sun was about to set and the sky was ablaze with color. It was a perfect evening, the air cool and the breeze clean.

Cal stretched his arms over his head, then drew a deep breath. This was why he loved the outback. Every day brought surprising changes.

GEMMA SAT IN THE CENTER of the spacious tent, Cal's sleeping bag wrapped around her naked body. Their dinner was spread out in front of her. She picked at a piece of baked chicken with her fingers. "Didn't I warn you?" she asked, holding out a morsel for Cal.

He leaned over and she placed it in his mouth. But he grabbed her hand and slowly sucked on the tip of each finger. "You did. But I wouldn't have believed it. What else don't I know about you?"

The question caused an unusual silence and she nervously began to rearrange the items on the rug in front of her. "I have many secrets," she said.

"Tell me just one."

"I'm the daughter of a British lord. A peer of the realm."

"You're royalty?" Cal asked.

"Nobility. Illegitimate nobility," she added. "That's the important qualifier. My father doesn't recognize me as his own."

"Couldn't you get one of those tests, the DNA thing?"

"My mother insisted she didn't need one. She knew for sure. I think it was because she still loved him and hoped he'd come back to her someday. She didn't want to make him angry." Gemma laughed in amazement. "Can you imagine that? It's been twenty-eight years since he walked out of her life and she's still waiting for him to return."

"Love can make people do strange things," Cal said.

She shrugged. "He has another family. Kids and a younger wife. She's only ten years older than me."

"So you see him?"

"Oh, no. Just a time or two. He gave me money for university and that was it. I guess that's more than I should have expected. Sometimes I wonder if love is made to last a lifetime. What do you think?"

"Don't ask me. My mother left the station when I was seventeen."

"That must have been hard," she said.

"Station life was hard. My father can be pretty stubborn and he never wanted to take time away. He didn't trust anyone else to manage the day-to-day business. She decided she wanted something more out of life than the drudgery and isolation."

"I'm sorry," she said.

"Don't be. They're back together and living in Sydney. My father decided she was more important to him than the station."

"And what would you do if you fell in love with someone who didn't want to live here?"

"I wouldn't fall in love with that person."

"Sometimes you can't help who you love."

"And sometimes you can," Cal said.

Gemma recognized the truth in his words. She'd spent her whole life avoiding love, trying to convince herself she could live without it. But here, with Cal, she wanted to believe it was possible. Maybe two people could find each other in this big, lonely world.

"Are you finished?" he asked, pointing to the food.

Gemma nodded. "Why, did you bring more?"

Cal laughed. "I do like a woman who enjoys a good meal."

"I do. Especially when it's made by someone else. I'm a horrible cook."

"But can you dance?" he asked. "I promised you drinks, dinner and dancing." Cal held out his hand. "I don't really dance, but I'm willing to give it a try."

"Now? We're naked."

"That will make things much more interesting." He stood, then helped her to her feet before leading her out of the tent. The lanterns still glowed from the trees, casting a soft light around the camp. He left her standing in the middle of the glade and then returned a moment later with a portable CD player.

A moment later, a soft, slow ballad drifted into the cool night air. Cal pulled the sleeping bag around them both and began to move to the music. Gemma had danced with men before, but never had it been so strangely erotic. She felt like a pagan, caught in the midst of a strange sexual rite. All of the fears and insecurities she used to have were falling away, leaving her to act on pure emotion.

His body was strong and hard against hers, their movement generating its own warmth. Gemma grabbed the sleeping bag and tossed it aside, leaving them both naked. She tipped her head back and drew a deep breath, then slowly let it go.

This was her life, this moment in time, with this man in her arms. Nothing else mattered. She'd discovered the passion that had always been lacking before and Gemma wanted to push the boundaries, to see how much more was possible.

She let her hands trail over his body as she danced, creating a provocative counterpoint to the music. Then she stepped back and continued moving, her body relaxed and sinuous. The light from the fire flickered on her skin and she imagined herself in an old pagan fertility rite, meant to lure a man into the dark world of uncontrolled desire.

Gemma felt his eyes on her body almost as if he were touching her. She ran her hands along her torso and down to her hips, then back again. Her actions instigated a moan from the other side of the fire. And when she returned to him, he was completely aroused.

Drawing her fingers over his hard shaft, she danced around him, circling, her breasts brushing against his back, her hands searching for another spot to caress. Cal kept trying to touch her, but she evaded his embrace, preferring to continue the teasing seduction.

"Are you trying to drive me mad?" he asked, yanking her against his body. "Because it's working."

"Remember this," Gemma said. "Remember how much you want me." She reached up and smoothed her hand over his eyes until he closed them. "There." She slowly stroked his shaft. "Remember how this feels."

"I don't think I could forget even if I wanted to," Cal said.

If she found the emerald, then she'd tell him the truth. And when she did, she'd bring him back to this moment, to prove that it really made no difference at all. But until the emerald was in her possession, she wouldn't allow herself any guilt over what they shared.

She realized now that she needed a lover much more than she needed a father. The past was history and nothing could be done about it. But she lived in the present. And in the present, there was only one man in her life and he was standing naked in front of her.

6

CAL HEARD THE PLANE FLY OVER shortly before dusk. He walked out of the stables and stared up into the late afternoon sky, watching as Teague circled to land.

He'd spent the day trying to stay occupied with work, but lately it had become impossible to go an entire eight hours without taking a break or two to drop in on Gemma. Yesterday, he'd come in for midmorning tea, stayed for lunch and then returned two hours early for dinner.

He'd joined Gemma in the library, working on his station accounts as she pored over stacks of old papers. He ought to feel thankful that his ancestors had maintained such meticulous records. It was the only thing keeping her on Kerry Creek.

Though they weren't always touching, it was satisfying just to be in the same room with her. He found endless pleasure in observing her, taking in the tiny details of her behavior—the way she held her pen, the single lock of hair that she constantly tucked behind her ear, the soft sigh that slipped from her lips when she put down a book or paper.

Since their evening in the outback the night before last, their relationship had changed. Cal smiled. No, it hadn't changed. It had simply begun. Now, they both acknowledged a connection, an attraction that neither one of them wanted to deny. He could touch her at will and she responded without hesitation.

Work had been pushed aside for play, and the library door locked against interruption. Yet, there was still something standing between them. The end of all this passion and desire. It hung over them like a dark cloud, a ceaseless reminder that they were just enjoying a stolen holiday from the real world.

The more he thought about it, Cal had to wonder if Gemma had a man waiting for her in Ireland. It was impossible to believe that a woman so beautiful was all alone, that her bed was empty and her desires unfulfilled.

Cal jogged down the steps and walked to his ute parked nearby. He jumped behind the wheel and before long, was turning the truck toward the landing strip. By the time he got there, the plane had already touched down and had come to a stop at the end of the dirt runway.

Tugging his hat down against the dust cloud from the propeller, Cal opened the passenger door as Teague shut down the single engine. Payton smiled at him, handing him a cluster of shopping bags as she nimbly jumped down to the ground. Cal set them at her feet, then turned to help Gemma out.

Unable to resist and seeing no reason to hide his feelings from Teague or Payton, Cal set Gemma in front of him, then gave her a quick kiss. "Welcome back," he murmured, a smile twitching at the corners of his mouth.

A pretty blush stained Gemma's cheeks as she glanced around. "Thanks."

Cal helped Teague tie the plane down, then walked with them to his ute. He saw Payton's disappointed expression as he opened the door of the vehicle and pulled the seat forward so she could climb in the back. "He took off about a half hour ago. On horseback, toward the west. I'm sure he'll be back soon."

When they got back to the homestead, Payton headed for the stables, determined to ride out to meet Brody. Teague disappeared inside the house, whispering to Cal that he needed a beer after spending so much time inside a small plane with two chatty sheilas. That left Gemma standing alone next to the ute.

He grabbed her bags. "Did you have a nice time?"

She nodded. "Payton is a lot of fun. We laughed and talked. She's a bit crazy. And we drove Teague mad, I'm sure. Had there been a parachute handy in the plane, he might have been tempted to jump out."

"What's the deal with Payton?" Cal asked, steering her toward the bunkhouse. "What's going on between her and Brody?"

"What do you mean?"

"Brody met her in jail. I'm not certain he knows anything about her, except that she's American."

"Don't worry. She's not a criminal, if that's what you're thinking." Gemma paused as they reached the steps of the bunkhouse. "We all keep a few secrets. Even you."

Cal feigned surprise. "Me? I don't have any secrets. You tell me a secret I'm keeping and I'll tell you if you're right."

She opened the door to the bunkhouse and stepped inside. "If I knew a secret about you, it wouldn't be a secret anymore, would it?" Gemma reached for one of the bags, dogging around inside. "I bought you something."

"Yeah? Something nice that you can wear and I can remove?"

She pulled a shirt from the bag. "I saw this and thought of you. Blue is your color." Holding it out in front of him, she gave it a critical eye. "Teague tried it on for me. He said you wear the same size shirt."

"It's nice," Cal said, fingering the fabric. Not what he was hoping for, but then sexy underwear wasn't the most practical gift. "But it won't hold up for work."

"It's not for work. It's for…"

"For what?"

"For dressing up. For going on a date."

"Are we going on a date?"

"No. It's for after I leave."

Cal gave her a shrewd look. Where was this conversation headed? "Am I going on a date I don't know about?"

Her gaze met his. "Mary told me about the matchmaking service," she admitted. "I know you're looking for a wife, Cal. And I just thought I might be able to give you a few pointers."

Her words caught him completely off guard. But as he considered the revelation, her reticence suddenly made sense. She'd been afraid to become too attached, knowing that the day she left Kerry Creek, he'd start the search for a lifelong mate. "No," he said. "Mary has it wrong. She saw something she shouldn't have and made a mistake. That's what comes from being a sticky beak."

"It's not true?"

"It was something I'd considered...briefly. Until you came along."

"And now you're not considering it anymore?" Gemma asked.

"Not at the moment."

"I can't stay here, Cal," Gemma said. "You understand that, don't you? I have a career in Dublin. I can't be your wife."

"Sure," Cal said, trying to appear indifferent. "Of course, I know that. I'm not asking you to stay. I just thought as long as you're here, we'd enjoy our time together. No strings. I've got plenty of time to think about the future."

"Good," Gemma said, nodding her head. "I'm glad we have that worked out."

But it wasn't worked out, Cal sensed. For some reason, she seemed quite unsettled by the subject. "A lot of fellas do it," he said. "Living in the outback, it isn't easy to meet people. And there are practical reasons for a matchmaking service."

"But, how will you know? I mean, are you willing to settle for a woman who doesn't make you...wild with desire?"

"I'm willing to admit that companionship can sometimes be more important than incredible sex. And I'm hoping for the best."

She drew a sharp breath, then nodded. "Well, dressing a bit nicer would help. What do you think of the shirt? Try it on."

"I'll try it on later," he said. This didn't feel right. He

didn't want to think about any other woman but Gemma. He didn't want to believe she'd ever leave. Sure, he was living in a fantasy world, but why not? Why couldn't he have this for as long as it lasted? When it was over, he'd find a way to get on with his life, but not until then.

She reached up and began to unbutton his shirt. "I want to see what you look like wearing it."

"Why?" Cal asked. "What difference does it make?" When his shirt was open to the waist, he hooked his finger beneath her chin and turned her gaze back to his. His lips covered hers in a long, slow kiss, perfectly calculated to make Gemma forget everything but the desire they shared.

She sighed softly, the gift forgotten as it dropped to the floor. Gemma's arms wrapped around his neck as she surrendered to the kiss. Every sensation that washed over him was pure perfection and Cal enjoyed the feel of her body beneath his hands. Why couldn't he have Gemma? Why couldn't she be the one for him? Fate had thrown them together, but it had also played a cruel trick, waiting in the shadows to snatch her away again the moment he realized he couldn't live without her.

His fingers twisted in the hem of her shirt and in one smooth motion, he pulled it over her head, barely breaking the contact between their mouths. His hand cupped the warm flesh of her breast, her nipple hard beneath the lacy bra. This was what he loved about Gemma, the softness, the sweetness that he'd never found in any other woman.

When he touched her, he felt like a man who might

be able to love, a man who might live for just one special woman. But Cal sensed that what was special about Gemma had more to do with his ever-growing feelings for her than the scarcity of women in his life.

Her fingers worked at his belt and when she'd unfastened it, she began with the button and zipper on his jeans. He held his breath as her fingers brushed against his crotch, his cock already hard and aching for release. Her hand slipped beneath the waistband of his boxers and the moment she touched him, Cal forgot all his doubts.

If he focused on the present, on the way she stroked him, then he wouldn't have to worry about the future. He could store this all away in his head, every caress, every wild sensation, so that he might recall it later, when Gemma was gone.

Cal pulled her back toward the door, then reached around and locked it. Though Payton had gone out to find Brody, he wanted to make sure they weren't interrupted. Slowly, he stripped off her clothes, item by item, tossing them aside until she was completely naked.

Her body was made for his touch. Every part of her was exactly what he needed to light his passion and to stoke his desire. "I want you," he murmured, his mouth pressed to her throat. "Only you."

Gemma tipped her head back as his fingers tangled in her hair. Another moan tore from her throat as his other hand moved to the damp spot between her legs. He was desperate to be inside of her, to feel again that sense of connection that had faded during their day apart.

It was difficult to comprehend the depth of his need. It pulsed from every cell in his body, an undeniable force that made wanting her almost painful. Was he that weak that he couldn't resist her? Or had he already given up trying?

Cal kicked off his boots, then stripped off the rest of his clothes. The bunkhouse was nearly silent. The sound of their breathing was all that could be heard, quick gasps and gentle sighs, each a reaction, a plea, an invitation.

Though it wasn't the most romantic place to make love, Cal knew he'd never step inside the south bunkhouse again without remembering what her body looked like in the dwindling light filtering through the dusty windows.

"You're the only one," he whispered as he pinned her against the wall, his fingers laced with hers. Drawing her hands over her head, he kissed her again. "You're the only one I've ever wanted."

"No," Gemma murmured.

"Yes," Cal said. "At least, give me that. Don't make me deny what I feel."

He drew her thigh up along his hip, causing his shaft to rub slowly against her sex. This was paradise right here, with Gemma. And he'd enjoy it while it lasted.

GEMMA LEANED AGAINST the stable yard fence, her arms folded over the top rail, her chin resting on her hands. The three Quinn brothers were sitting on their horses at the far side, deep in discussion. Every now and then, they looked over at the trio of women, as if trying to guess what she, Payton and Hayley Fraser were talking about.

"I know how Brody and Cal feel about me," Hayley said. "And I don't think they were too chuffed to see me turn up here."

Gemma had been living on the station for exactly a week and in honor of the Queen's birthday, Cal had decided to arrange an impromptu celebration. The campdrafting competition had already begun among the jackaroos when Teague had arrived with Hayley in tow.

She was a stunning beauty and according to Payton, a famous television star in Australia.

"Whatever is going on in their heads has nothing to do with us," Gemma said.

"Sistahs before mistahs." Hayley and Gemma both turned to stare at Payton, sending her an inquiring look. "Sisters before misters," she explained. "Girlfriends should come before boyfriends."

Gemma smiled. "Oh, yes. I completely agree."

They watched as Cal took his turn in the competition, chasing a calf around a series of obstacles. Gemma found the sight of him, bent over the neck of his horse, more than a little stimulating. He seemed so selfassured, so in control—so different from the man who'd shuddered in her arms the night before.

Since she'd returned from Brisbane, things had changed between them. Gemma wasn't sure what had caused the shift in their relationship, but they'd become more open, more honest with each other. She thought it might have begun when she admitted to knowing about the matchmaking service. Up until that point, they'd both avoided any talk of her leaving Kerry Creek.

But now, it had become an accepted fact, inevitable and unchangeable. The clock had begun ticking and they were both powerless to stop it. Gemma knew it was for the best. Her search for the emerald hadn't produced any solid clues. Her last hope was that she might find something in the attic, but Gemma was beginning to question whether she even wanted to continue.

She'd been so sure of herself when she arrived, so single-minded in her purpose that nothing could keep her from her task. In her whole life, all she'd wanted was acceptance from her father, acknowledgment that she did exist and she was his.

But the more time she spent with Cal, the more Gemma realized how her need for a father had affected all her relationships with men. Her mistrust of men in general had simmered beneath the surface, a poison, bubbling up when she began to feel emotions she was unable to explain. But that hadn't happened with Cal. She hadn't felt the need to destroy what they shared simply to maintain control over her own life. She wasn't afraid of him or of her feelings for him.

Perhaps that was because she knew it would all come to an end once she returned to Dublin. The finish had already been determined and she was biding her time until it happened. It was the simplest explanation, yet Gemma didn't believe it.

"Do you ride?" Gemma asked Hayley.

Hayley grinned, nodding. "Like the wind. What about you?"

She wasn't going to lie, even though she wanted to feel like one of the girls. "No. If they did this on bicycles I might give it a go. But horses scare the bleedin' bloomers off me. And I don't care for the way they smell, either." She sighed. "Still, I wish I knew how to ride. Cal seems to be more comfortable on a horse than he does on his feet."

"I could teach you," Payton said.

"Me, too," Hayley offered.

Gemma searched for a polite way to decline, reluctant to confess the depth of her fears. People always seemed to be suspicious of her, unable to understand how she couldn't love a cute dog or a fluffy cat—or a smelly horse. "Cal offered but I didn't want to look like a muppet in front of him, so I begged off. But as long as I'm here, I wouldn't mind trying." Though she attempted to sound enthusiastic, Gemma knew it sounded halfhearted at best.

"It's a date, then," Hayley said, turning to Payton. "You can bring her out to the shack. I'll organize a lunch and then we can ride back together."

"What do you think they're talking about?" Gemma asked, anxious to change the subject.

"Maybe they think we're plotting against them," Payton said.

Brody broke away from his brothers and rode across the stable yard, a wide grin on his handsome face. He tipped his hat as he drew his horse to a halt in front of them. "Ladies, are you having a lovely time?"

"Absolutely," Payton said, sending him a naughty smile.

"What are you doing over here all on your own?"

"Discussing our love of chaps," Gemma offered. "With or without jeans. If I might be so bold, which do you prefer?"

Brody frowned, as if the innuendo didn't register. "Would you ladies like to give it a go? I'm sure the boys would love to see you jump into the competition. And there are prizes to be had for the winners."

Payton crawled over the fence. "I'll try," she volunteered.

"Me, too," Hayley said as she started in Teague's direction.

Gemma maintained her distance on the other side of the fence. "I'm afraid I'll have to sit this one out."

"Come on," Brody insisted. "Cal will ride with you."

There would be no way to hide from her fears. She wanted to run to the bunkhouse and lock herself inside. But everyone else was participating and having a jolly time. She didn't want the stockmen to call her a wowser, the kind of person who sucked all the fun out of a party. "All right."

Reluctantly, she crawled over the fence and headed toward Cal. He slid off his horse and stood beside it. When she got close enough, he slipped his arm around her waist. "You don't have to do this," he murmured. "You don't have anything to prove."

"I know," Gemma said, her voice a bit shaky. But maybe she did want to feel as if she belonged, the way Payton and Hayley did. Maybe, if just for a little while, she'd like to believe Cal might choose her over all the other more suitable matches.

And if she'd already trusted him with her heart and

her body, then why not with her fears? She'd changed since arriving at Kerry Creek and Gemma suspected it was due to Cal. What would happen if she simply gave herself over to him, without questions or reservations. "I suppose I can try."

He bent closer and stared into her eyes. "Really? You're not scared?"

"Terrified," she said. "But I trust you."

Grinning, Cal swung into the saddle, then reached down to grab her arm. "Put your foot in the stirrup," he directed as he slid back.

Clumsily, Gemma did as she was told. He settled her in the saddle and wrapped his arm tightly around her waist. "Oh dear. This is really high. If I fall off, it's going to hurt."

"You won't fall," he said. "I won't let you." He put the reins in her hands. "Just gently tug left to go left and right to go right. It's not tricky."

Gemma nodded. In theory, it was simple enough. But this was a living, breathing creature beneath her, one with a brain of its own. What if Eddie decided he didn't want to play this little game and would rather be running across the countryside at a breakneck speed with her clinging to his back?

"Ready?" Cal asked.

"No. But the sooner this is over, the sooner I can get off this horse."

Cal called to Davey and the jackaroo released a calf from the pen. Gemma glanced over to see Payton and Brody watching them from the other side of the fence, Brody's chin resting on Payton's shoulder. Then the horse suddenly lurched forward and Gemma screamed, startled by the movement.

Cal was shouting directions in her ear but every few seconds, he seemed to want something new. First left, then right, then left again. Though Gemma understood they were trying to drive the calf around the obstacle course of barrels and posts and bales of hay, the horse didn't seem to be interested in cooperating.

After a minute of absolute chaos, Cal reached for the reins, but the stockmen watching on the sidelines shouted their disapproval.

"Drop the reins," he said.

"What?" Gemma wasn't about to let go of the only control they had over the horse. What would stop it from running directly into the fence and tossing them both to the ground? "No, I can't."

"It will be all right," Cal insisted. "I can maneuver him with my knees and feet."

Gemma let the reins slip through her fingers and almost immediately, the horse began to respond. She closed her eyes and held tight to the saddle horn with white-knuckled fingers. Her heart slammed in her chest and she could barely breathe, certain she was about to pitch headlong onto the ground in front of them.

But to her surprise, when she opened her eyes they rode easily around the turn and shooed the calf toward the pen. After it was finally over, she collapsed against Cal, gasping for breath, tears of relief swimming in her eyes.

Though the ride was terrifying, it was also exhilarating. Gemma had never been one to take risks, but now she understood the allure. She hadn't felt this alive since—well, since she and Cal had stripped naked in the bunkhouse and had their way with each other. She could see why the men at Kerry Creek spent so much time on horseback. It worked off a lot of sexual frustration.

"That wasn't so bad," Cal said as he reached down and grabbed the reins. He pulled Eddie to a stop near the gate and slid off, then reached up and grabbed Gemma's waist. She dropped lightly to the ground, but her knees collapsed beneath her and she clutched at his shirt.

"It was like one of those wild rides at an amusement park. Except the guy running it walked away from the controls and the ride was about to go right off the rails."

"I was in control of Eddie the entire time," Cal said. "Didn't you say you trusted me?" He pulled her closer, his hands sliding down to hold her hips against his.

"In most matters," she said. "It's the horse I don't trust."

"Eddie?" He turned to his mount, the horse observing them both with liquid brown eyes. "Hear that, boy?"

The horse responded to Cal's voice and he craned his neck to nuzzle Gemma's shoulder. She jumped back, a tiny scream slipping from her throat. "I think I need to go wash the horse smell off my hands." She sniffed at her palms and wrinkled her nose. "Eddie needs a bath." Gemma pressed her nose against Cal's chest. "And so do you."

"Would you like to take one with me?"

"Now?"

"Later. Tonight. After everyone goes to bed."

The offer was tempting. "The tub upstairs isn't big enough for two," she said.

"I wasn't talking about that tub. We have a hot tub. It's back by the pump house. Very private. Very…hot." He leaned forward and dropped a kiss on her lips. "I'll bring the wine and you bring…your body."

"I don't have a bathing suit," she said.

"You won't need one," Cal replied.

"Oh. I see. This isn't about getting clean."

"Meet me as soon as the boys turn in," he said. "I'll be waiting."

Gemma looked up into his eyes and saw the desire there. They had a busy day ahead of them. After the games, there'd be a barbecue and then the stockmen had insisted on a dance, deciding to take advantage of the female company while they could. Gemma had been charged with inviting both Payton and Hayley. Davey had volunteered to bring the music.

"After the dance," she said.

Cal shook his head. "I think we should just forget the dance. It's just an opportunity for every fella on this station to put his hands all over you. I don't like it."

"You don't like it because you don't want to dance," Gemma said. "You were quite good at it at our camp on the creek."

"That wasn't dancing, that was sex. And I am quite good at that. I just don't think it helps my reputation as a competent boss to be stumbling over my feet in front of my employees."

"I rode that horse. The least you can do is ask me to dance tonight."

"I'll find a way to make it up to you," he said, leaning closer, his voice soft and seductive. "I promise."

A shiver skittered down Gemma's spine as she thought about just what Cal was capable of doing to her. Maybe it was a fair trade. Five minutes on a horse for five hours of incredible pleasure. Life in the outback didn't get much better than that.

THE SUN HAD SET HOURS AGO and the sky was filled with stars, the perfect end to a perfect day. Gemma danced around the yard with Davey, the music softly drifting on the night air. Cal stood on the porch watching them both, his shoulder braced against the corner post, his arms crossed over his chest.

Payton and Brody had retired long ago, silently slipping away to Brody's room upstairs. Hayley and Teague had disappeared shortly afterward, leaving Gemma and Mary to partner with the boys. But now, Gemma was the only female at the party, one beauty among a bunch of drunk fellas.

Gemma looked over Davey's shoulder and gave Cal a little wave, a sign she was ready to leave. God, she was the most beautiful thing he'd ever seen in his life. Every day with her was a revelation, a new realization that he could live a lifetime learning all that there was to know about her.

She seemed happy on Kerry Creek, but Cal had to wonder how much longer she planned to stay. Over the past few days, he'd distracted her from her work on a number of occasions and she didn't kick up a fuss at all.

Cal suspected she'd found all she needed and was stretching out her time so that they might be together a bit longer. But the longer she stayed the more difficult it would be for him to let her go. He'd tried to remain indifferent to his feelings for her, to keep everything in perspective. He'd even pulled out the profiles he'd received from OutbackMates, hoping to convince himself that life would go on after Gemma left.

No matter how he imagined it, Cal couldn't see any way he could have a future with Gemma. Like a puzzle, he'd fit the pieces together in different angles but it always resulted in the two of them living half a world apart.

If he truly cared about her, then he should be willing to make sacrifices. But he couldn't leave Kerry Creek. This station was his life, his dream. No woman was worth giving that up, even a woman he loved. Cal was willing to spend the rest of his life alone before considering that option.

The song ended and Davey stepped back, then gave Gemma a chaste peck on the cheek. It was already past ten and everyone needed to be up again in six hours, including him. And he had at least an hour or two planned with Gemma.

"Last dance," he said to the boys. "And I'm claiming this one. I'll see you fellas in the morning."

The stockmen wandered off into the darkness and Gemma stepped into Cal's arms. She had put on her jacket against the chill of the evening and he slipped his hands beneath it, smoothing them over her backside. "I've been waiting for this all night."

"I suppose you think I'm going home with you since you're the only guy left at the dance?"

"Yeah, I was counting on it," Cal said with a chuckle.

"I don't know," Gemma said. "I'm thinking I should have taken Davey up on his offer."

Cal stopped dancing and looked down at her. "Davey propositioned you? What did he say?"

"He said I was a bit of alright and if I got bored with you, I ought to give him a chance. I told him he might be a little young for me and he told me age was a state of mind."

"Davey said that?" Cal chuckled. "Not a bad line. So are you going to consider his offer?"

"That depends upon your offer. What are you going to do for me, Cal Quinn?"

Her words were a teasing challenge, but Cal could certainly best a nineteen-year-old jackaroo when it came to seduction. He laced his fingers through hers and pulled her along toward the pump house. "I'm going to get you naked and have my way with you," he said. "I'm going to touch you in all the places you love to be touched. And I'm going to make you tremble, the way you did last night."

Gemma let go of his hand and backed away from him, tugging off her cardie and tossing it his way. "You're going to have to catch me first," she said.

With a growl, Cal ran after her. They finally came together on the far side of the pump house, a low building that housed the main well for the homestead. Cal had originally ordered the hot tub to help Brody with his rehab after his motorcycle accident. It had gone largely unused, except by the stockmen after long stretches in the saddle. But now he considered it a prudent purchase.

He pulled off the vinyl cover and a cloud of moisture rose into the cool air. Then he pulled his shirt over his head and tossed it aside. "Now you," he said, waiting for her to remove another article of clothing.

Gemma tugged off her shoe, then held it up to him. "A girl could get very bored at this pace," she said.

"Then let me move things along." He reached for her and in a flurry of movement, they tore at each other's clothes until they were both naked.

"I'm getting used to this," she said. "I might never put clothes on again."

Cal took her hand and helped her into the tub. Slowly, they sank down into the bubbling water, their bodies intertwined. "Oh, this is lovely," Gemma murmured, closing her eyes and tipping her head back. "My bum is a bit sore from that horse ride," she said. "Doesn't yours ever get sore riding all day long?"

"Why don't I do something about that." He slowly smoothed his hands over her backside, gently kneading the sweet flesh as her hips shifted against his. "When I had this installed, I never thought I'd be enjoying it with a woman. It was for Brody, after his accident."

"It's perfect," she said, pressing a kiss to his damp shoulder. "Very relaxing."

Cal ran his finger over her cheek and smiled. "Now that I have you here, I want to ask you something."

Gemma snuggled up next to him, her legs straddling his hips. "Ask away."

"I'm not sure how to put this. Is there…do you have a…someone back in Ireland? A fella? In your life?"

She pulled away from him, a frown creasing her brow. "No? Did you think I did?"

"No," Cal said. "Well, maybe. It just didn't figure."

"What do you mean?"

"You're beautiful and perfect. And you're smart and you know how to make a bloke feel real good—not in a sexual way, but…well, happy. Content. Why hasn't some guy claimed you for himself?"

"Claimed me?"

Callum sighed. "You know what I mean. I'm not the best with words, but you're smart enough to understand what I'm trying to say. Why are you still alone?"

Gemma shrugged. "I don't want to be married. I'm happy with my life the way it is." She paused. "Callum, I'm not perfect. Far from it. I have a lot of insecurities that I keep very well hidden. Don't make me out to be some extraordinary woman."

"You might not think you're perfect," Callum said. "But you're perfect for me." He reached up and ran his thumb over her bottom lip. "I want you to move into the house with me. Payton is staying in Brody's room now and there's no reason why you should be living in the bunkhouse. I have a big, comfortable bed and a door with a strong lock."

Gemma slowly drifted back to the other side of the tub. "You have all sorts of plans, don't you?"

He watched her, the underwater lights illuminating her pretty features. "It's simple, really. Either you want to be with me or you don't. I don't want to waste the time we have left." He held out his hand. "But if you do, no worries."

She studied him for a long moment, her face etched with indecision. Cal said a silent prayer, grateful she was considering his offer and hoping she'd accept. He wouldn't have any regrets about what he'd done. He'd asked and if she refused, he'd accept her decision.

But if she moved into his room, then he was going to spend every night lost in the body of this beautiful woman who had dropped into his life in the middle of a lonely Australian winter. She was a gift and he wouldn't take her for granted.

7

GEMMA AWOKE SLOWLY, AWARE FIRST of the warm, naked body lying beside her. She nuzzled her face into Cal's shoulder and sighed softly. Cal had been right. She belonged here in his room. Her bed in the bunkhouse was far too small for the two of them and his was…just right.

Though sleeping in his room did feel a bit naughty, Gemma had decided to toss aside her inhibitions and enjoy their relationship for what it was—wildly satisfying and intensely exciting. She would enjoy it while it lasted.

What in the world did she have to lose? Summer in Dublin was pleasant, but she'd spend it at the library or in her office, doing work that could be better left for another time. Here, on Kerry Creek, she had passion and desire, a man to see to her every sexual need. A girl would have to be thick as a ditch to walk away from that.

Gemma closed her eyes, smiling to herself. She was glad she hadn't told him about the emerald. She'd destroyed many relationships in the past, but she wasn't going to ruin this one. They'd been together a little more than a week. And yet, Gemma already knew what she and Cal shared was special.

The depth of her feelings for him frightened her as much as that ride on Eddie. What was she supposed to do with all this? She'd avoided even thinking of anything permanent with him. Because she knew she would go home, leaving him behind.

Strangely enough, her escape clause gave her the freedom to stay and explore this odd new emotional attachment. He was safe, yet he was oh, so dangerous at the same time.

Gemma pushed aside the bed covers and sat up, brushing her hair over her shoulder. She watched him sleep, his features relaxed, almost boyish. Her gaze drifted down, to the body that had become hers by default. Cal was a beautiful man in the physical sense of the word but her attraction to him was well beyond appreciation for a gorgeous form. She loved his heart and his humor, the way he looked at her, as if she were the most beautiful woman in the world.

Gemma reached out and ran her hand along his arm, from his shoulder to his wrist. A feeling of utter amazement washed over her as she remembered the way he'd touched her the night before. Had they really only known each other for a week? How was it possible that their bodies had become so attuned to each other?

She bent over and pressed a kiss to his chest, her hair falling around her face. Cal stirred and a moment later, his fingers touched her cheek. She turned to find him staring at her in the early morning light, a sleepy smile on his face.

"Morning," he said.

Gemma grinned. "For some of us, that might be debatable. I'm not usually awake this early."

He groaned and rolled onto his side, then pulled the pillow over his face. "Then go back to sleep. I don't have to get up for a while."

"You don't?"

"One of the benefits of being boss cocky. Besides, the boys will roll out of their bunks a bit later this morning, too, after all the beer they consumed yesterday."

Gemma snuggled against his chest, her fingers toying with the soft trail of hair that ran from his collarbone to his belly. "I had a good time yesterday," she said. "I was thinking if I stay for a while, I should probably try riding again."

He pushed up on his elbow. "Are you going to stay?"

"Maybe," she said. "I think I will. A bit longer, at least. Until the end of the month."

He ran his hand through her hair, brushing the tangled curls from her face. "That's good. That's very good." He laughed, not able to contain his delight. He grabbed her arms and pulled her up alongside him, dragging her into a long, delicious kiss. "We'll have fun," he said. "By the time mustering starts, you'll be riding as well as a jackaroo. And I think we should take some time away from the station. I can spare a few days here and there. We'll have Teague fly us somewhere interesting." He kissed her again. "You really want to learn to ride?"

"Maybe we could try riding together again, without chasing that little cow around the cattle yard?"

"That was a calf," he said.

"I know."

"And that's pretty much what mustering is. Chasing cattle around the station. But you wouldn't be up for mustering, a city girl like you. It's dirty work. I'm not sure you're cut out for it. You'd best stay in the house baking biscuits with Mary."

Gemma recognized reverse psychology when she saw it. "And you'd better get used to sleeping alone."

He growled softly, then rolled her on top of him, their naked limbs tangling in the sheets. "That's not going to happen," he said. "Sleeping arrangements are non-negotiable."

"So, what is this? What do we call it?" Gemma asked. "Is it an affair?"

"Doesn't that usually involve some form of cheating?"

"No. It can also mean a short-term arrangement. With no strings attached."

"Is that all right with you?" he asked.

Gemma didn't hesitate. "Yes," she said. "But that's all it can be. Nothing more. Agreed?"

"Agreed," Cal said. "Now, can we go back to sleep?" He twisted to see the clock on the bedside table. "I've had two hours rest and if I don't get at least four, I'm buggered for the next day."

Gemma wriggled on top of him. "But I'm not tired." She straddled his hips and sat up, moving deliberately to tease at his desire. "You were much more attentive to my needs when we weren't sleeping together. See what this has done to our relationship already? It's like my mother always told me—that old cow and milk proverb."

"What proverb is that?" Cal asked, his hands moving to her waist.

"Why sleep with the cow when you can buy the milk for free?" she whispered. Gemma leaned close and brushed a kiss across his mouth.

"I don't think that's it," he said. "But I do get your point. So, am I the cow? Or am I the milk."

"Neither." She slid down and pressed a kiss to his belly. "Where do you keep the condoms?"

Not waiting for a reply, Gemma reached over to pull out the drawer on the bedside table. She withdrew a crumpled paper and Cal quickly grabbed it from her. When she grabbed it back, she found an advert for OutbackMates. "Is this it?"

Cal groaned. "It was a silly idea. I don't know how I ever thought I'd find a woman that way." He wadded the paper into a ball and threw it across the room. "The condoms aren't in there. Since I've never had a woman in this room, there's no reason to keep them beside the bed."

"You've never had a woman in your bed?"

Cal shook his head. "You're the first. Until you got to the station, I lived like a monk." He pointed to the bookcase on the far wall. "They're behind the murder mysteries," he said.

Gemma crawled out of bed and retrieved the box, then watched him from across the room. She'd never lived with a man before, at least not for more than a few nights at a time. Was she ready for this? It went against all of her instincts, her need to protect herself from any long-term commitments. Still, if it became too much to handle, she could always move back into the bunkhouse.

"Maybe we should go back to sleep," she teased as

she walked to the side of the bed. Her gaze drifted down to his shaft, now hard and ready. "I can see you're tired."

Cal grabbed her hand and yanked her back into bed, rolling on top of her and pinning her hands at her sides. "I'm definitely not tired," he said, moving against her.

Gemma moaned softly as his shaft teased at the folds of her sex. She brought her legs up and the next time he moved, he slipped inside of her for a moment, before drawing back.

"Don't do that to me," he warned.

"It's all right," Gemma said.

"No, it's not."

Though Gemma was a good Irish Catholic girl, she didn't follow the church's edicts on birth control. The moment she'd become sexually active, she'd found a doctor to prescribe the pill and she hadn't stopped taking them since. She wouldn't make the same mistake her mother had, even though she'd been the result of that mistake. Gemma wanted control of her future and that future didn't include any unexpected babies with reluctant fathers.

"I've been safe," she said. "Have you?"

"Yes." He released a tightly held breath as she sank down on top of him.

Gemma splayed her fingers across his chest, closing her eyes as he penetrated deeper. And when he was buried inside her, she stayed still for a long moment, enjoying the warmth of him filling her.

"I've never done this before," he whispered as she began to move above him. "It feels different."

Gemma smiled. "It's nice."

His hand cupped her breast and Cal rubbed his thumb across her nipple, drawing it to a tight peak. She closed her eyes again, allowing her mind to drift, focusing on the feeling of his touch. But when his fingers found the spot where they were joined, Gemma gasped softly.

Movements that had once been slow and easy now grew faster and more determined. She rocked above him, each thrust bringing her closer to the edge. It was so simple to just let go, to lose control. But as the first spasm struck, Gemma felt a tiny sliver of fear prick at her pleasure.

Would she have the strength to walk away? Would the feelings that seemed to overwhelm her at times grow so strong that they'd be impossible to ignore? She didn't want to fall in love. Love only made a mess of people's lives.

And yet, as her orgasm slowly subsided and his began, Gemma realized she'd already allowed herself to get closer to Cal than she had with any other man. The bond between them was simple, yet incredibly strong. And breaking it might just break her heart, as well. Maybe she already loved him and she didn't even know.

CAL STOOD ON THE PORCH and watched as Brody rode off in a cloud of dust. He nodded at Teague as his brother hopped behind the wheel of his Range Rover. The screen door squeaked and Gemma stepped out, staring at him, a confused expression on her face.

"What's going on?" she asked.

"A private investigator just showed up looking for Payton. He's in the parlor right now."

"What does he want with Payton?"

"I don't know. Brody wouldn't say. He talked Teague into flying them both off the station. They're headed out to the airstrip now." He took her hand. "Come on. We better find a way to get rid of him."

When they returned to the parlor, the detective was standing near the mantel, examining the family photos displayed there. "You might as well tell me where she is," he said. "I'm going to find her sooner or later."

"Like Teague told you, she was here and then she left. Gemma knows." He gave her hand a squeeze. "Tell him."

"She was here. She lived with me in the bunkhouse. But she's not there anymore. She left."

"How long ago?"

"Days?" Gemma said. "I'm really not sure. I think it was the day after we got back from Brisbane, wasn't it?"

With a soft curse, the man picked up his hat and strode to the door. "You're not helping her." Cal made a move to follow him, but the man held up his hand. "I can find my own way out."

A few moments later, they heard the screen door slam. Gemma slowly sat down on the sofa. "What was that all about? What do you think she did that they'd send a detective looking for her? You don't think she's a criminal, do you?"

"I don't know," Cal said.

"She told me she'd run out on her wedding. Do you

think they're trying to fetch her back and make her marry the bloke? Is that legal?"

"Of course not. But this is what comes from keeping secrets. How long have you known about this wedding of hers?"

Gemma shrugged, an uneasy expression on her face. "Since last week sometime. I didn't think it was that important."

"What if she's married? What if Brody has got himself all twisted up with some deranged husband searching for his missing wife?"

"No," Gemma replied, shaking her head. "I'm sure she's not married. She would have said something about that. She ran away before the wedding took place."

"This is why I hate secrets." Cal sat down beside her and grabbed her hand. "This one little thing could ruin everything Brody has invested in this girl. I knew she was trouble from the moment she walked onto this station. I should have trusted my instinct and sent her—"

"She's not trouble," Gemma insisted. "I know Payton. She cares about Brody. She'd never hurt him. Just like I'd never hurt you."

"You're not keeping any secrets," he said. He glanced over at her only to see a pained expression cross her features. "You aren't, right?"

"Everyone has secrets," Gemma said. "There are things we keep to ourselves, things we don't allow others to see. There's nothing wrong with that."

"I think honesty is more important than anything. If you don't have that, then sooner or later, it all falls apart."

She stared at him for a long moment, then shook her head. "No. What if keeping a secret prevents you from hurting someone? Isn't that a reason to stay quiet? What if someone said something terrible about one of your brothers, something you knew would hurt them? Wouldn't you keep that secret?"

"Why are we speaking in hypothetical terms, Gemma? If you have something to tell me, just say it. Nothing will change how I feel about you."

"No," she said in an emotionless voice. "I can't. I don't want to."

Cal felt a knot of fear tighten in his gut. What was she going to say? Had she lied to him about being involved with someone else? Hell, what difference did that make either way? She was with him now, not with some nameless, faceless Irishman. "Gemma, we don't have a lot of time together. We might as well be completely honest with each other."

She watched him with suspicious eyes. "You promise not to get angry?"

"As long as you don't tell me you have a husband and three children back in Dublin."

"No," Gemma said. "No children, no husband."

"Then how can I possibly get angry."

She took a deep breath. "It's a very complicated story and I need to tell it carefully, or you won't understand. And I need you to understand." She took a deep breath. "I'm not a genealogist, Cal. I didn't come here to research your family history. There is no rich Quinn relative paying me to do this. That was just a story I told so you'd let me stay at the station."

"Why would you lie?" Cal asked.

"Because I was afraid if I told you the real reason I was here, you'd send me away." She paused. "Have you ever heard of the Emerald of Eire?"

Cal shrugged. "Sure. Everyone has heard of that."

Gemma stared at him, wide-eyed and speechless. "You know where it is, then?" she finally said.

"Ireland? Of course."

"No the Emerald of—"

"The Emerald Isle. That's Ireland. What does this have to do with anything?"

"No, you don't understand. The Emerald of Eire is an actual emerald. A huge stone. A precious jewel. It belonged to my father's family."

"I thought you didn't know your father." She was talking in riddles. Emeralds and her father and... What did any of that have to do with them?

"I don't know him. Not really. The Emerald of Eire was stolen by your ancestor, Crevan Quinn, from my ancestor, Stanton Parnell. There's a good chance Crevan brought it here to Australia. I think it might be somewhere in this house or on this station right now. I came here to get it back."

Cal shook his head. This was her secret? With her nervous preamble, he'd been expecting something more disturbing. "That's why you came here? For some old jewelry?"

"This is a huge emerald. It's worth a half million British pounds. I wanted to find it and take it back to my father. In exchange, I'd insist he recognize me as his daughter."

"That's not much of a secret," Cal said. "Why didn't

you just tell me up front what you wanted? I could have helped you look for it."

"You're just going to give me the emerald?"

"It belongs to your family, doesn't it?"

"Well, my family might have a problem proving that after all this time. And they say possession is nine-tenths of the law."

"So it might belong to the Quinns?"

"You could make a case in court. Or you could keep the jewel and sell it. Of course, an emerald that size would prompt a few questions and…" She paused. "I need that emerald, Cal. As a bargaining tool. With my fair share of the Parnell trust, I can make sure my mother lives comfortably."

"How do you know it's here?"

"The portrait," Gemma said. "It's embedded in the head of Crevan's walking stick. He had it when that portrait was painted. We'll just have to figure out where it went from there."

"And what if I do have this emerald?"

"Do you?" She held her breath and Cal could see what it was costing her to remain calm.

Of course he didn't have it. But there was another possibility, a possibility that he didn't care for in the least. "What if you find proof that Crevan sold it?"

"I don't know all the legalities," she said. "I suppose there would need to be some form of restitution. It is stolen property."

Callum knew where this was going. "I don't have a half million pounds."

"I'm sure you wouldn't owe that. But if Crevan used

the emerald to buy Kerry Creek, then there might be a problem. But that's just a guess. I don't know. I guess I didn't really think that part out very thoroughly."

He stood up, his hands clenched at his sides. This was exactly what he'd warned her about. Secrets always seemed to be more damaging the longer they were kept. And this one had the capability of turning his life upside down. "You'd better find that emerald," he warned. "Because there is no way I'd give up any part of Kerry Creek because of something that happened a hundred years ago."

"A hundred and fifty," she corrected.

Cal grabbed his hat from the end of the sofa, holding tight to his temper. "I need to get to work," he said.

"Don't worry," Gemma insisted. "I'd never let anyone take any part of the station away from you."

"You wouldn't have any say in the matter," he said. "That stone does exist. It was on that walking stick. And as long as anyone in your family remembers it, it's always going to be hanging over my family's head. You need to find it, Gemma, and then you need to take it back to Ireland."

She reached out and grabbed his arm. "I wanted to tell you earlier, but after a while, it didn't make any difference. I started to care more about you than the emerald. That's a very big step for me." The more she talked, the more distant he became. "Don't just walk out, Callum. I need you to understand. And to forgive me."

"We'll talk later," Cal said. "I'm tired and cranky. Better to leave it for another time."

As he walked out of the library, Cal pulled the door

shut behind him. He drew a deep breath and closed his eyes, cursing beneath his breath. He should have expected something like this. Her story had been suspect from the start, but he'd let his attraction to her override his common sense. And she'd been playing him all along. Maybe sleeping with him was all part of her plan, too. How far was she willing to go to get what she wanted?

And how easy would it be to forgive her? He didn't love her. Hell, he barely knew her and this incident proved his point. She was a liar. And had she found the emerald, he suspected she would have made herself a thief, as well.

He paused. Well, not exactly a thief, since technically, she'd be taking something that had been stolen from her family in the first place. Hell, he could work out the moral ramifications later. Right now, he needed hard work, exhausting work, work designed to drive thoughts of Gemma right out of his head. Once he'd done that, he could worry about what this meant to Kerry Creek.

GEMMA PEERED THROUGH bleary eyes at the journal she was reading. Over the past week, she'd gone through every last trunk in the attic, had removed every book from the shelves in the library, had searched very nook and cranny in the house. If she hadn't found any information about the emerald by now, then she was probably at a dead end.

She'd spent two days in Sydney, searching through the papers of the portrait artist, looking for clues there. After that, she'd been to the land offices in Brisbane and looked through all the deeds to the property that had been added to Kerry Creek over the years. She'd picked through expense ledgers and yellowing receipts, looking for a large infusion of cash from the sale of the stone.

"Nothing," she murmured. "There's nothing here."

In truth, she wanted to put an end to this. Since she'd told Cal the real reason for her trip to Kerry Creek, he'd become detached, maintaining a chilly reserve whenever they spoke. He'd insisted she finish her research, concerned that the emerald was a dark cloud hanging over the station.

Whenever she saw him, at meals and sometimes in passing, he'd force a smile and give her a benign greeting before finding some silly excuse not to carry on a conversation. She'd thought about sneaking up to his room in the middle of the night and forcing the issue. But she was afraid of rejection. Besides, it would be much easier for her to walk away if their relationship was beyond repair.

He seemed so tired, so spent, with dark circles smudging the skin beneath his eyes. She wanted to believe it was station business that was weighing on his mind—or the land dispute with Hayley's grandfather—or Brody and Payton's sudden departure with a private investigator on their trail.

They hadn't touched each other since she'd revealed her secret. Eight days and eight nights to be exact. She kept telling herself she was only at the station because she wanted to find the emerald—for him, not her father. But above all, Gemma was hoping they might be able to smooth over the rift between them.

How much longer could this go on? If their relationship was irreparable, then she ought to go home and save herself any more humiliation. The worst thing imaginable would be if he asked her to leave. Gemma wasn't sure she'd be able to handle that.

Funny how things had changed in her life. She was always the one who walked away from men, the one who called a swift and painless end to her romances. And now, she was hanging on for dear life, hoping that Cal would want her again.

"You're pathetic," Gemma muttered. "Grow a spine and go home."

A soft knock sounded on the door and a moment later, Mary stepped through with a tray of tea and toast. "I thought you might like something. You haven't had breakfast."

"Thank you," Gemma said. "I am hungry."

Mary set the tray down, then poured a cup of tea. "I've noticed you and Cal haven't been getting along lately. And you've been staying away from the dinner table."

"It's complicated," Gemma said. "But it's all right. I'm going to be leaving soon, so it's better our romance has…fizzled out."

Mary set the tea down in front of Gemma, then took a chair on the other side of the desk. "Cal takes his responsibilities here very seriously. And sometimes they weigh heavily on him. With Harry Fraser and this land dispute starting up again, he feels…" She paused, searching for the right word. "Threatened. He's not happy about Teague and Hayley. Brody is on the run from the private investigator who has been chasing Payton. And mustering begins in a few weeks."

"And I've just added to all his troubles."

"Yes, but not in the way you think."

"What do you mean?"

"Cal has always tried to control everything around him."

Gemma giggled. "I know how that is. I do the same thing."

"And when you walked into his life, he learned that sometimes it's just fine to forget the plans. I think he's fallen in love with you, Gemma. He just hasn't figured it out yet."

"No," Gemma said. "We're…it's just been…it's not supposed to last. We both knew that."

"Who said it's not supposed to last? If you want it to last, it will."

"But…I don't," Gemma said. The minute the words were out of her mouth, she knew they were a lie. But what did that mean? Was she really hoping that they could make this work?

"Then don't draw this out any longer than you have to," Mary said. "Leave Kerry Creek and let him get on with his life."

"Mary!" The sound of Cal's shout echoed through the house. "Mary!"

"I'm in the library," Mary called.

A few seconds later, Cal appeared at the door. "You need to come, right away. Harry Fraser just showed up in the yard and he's fallen off his horse. He's lying in the dirt outside."

Mary stood up and hurried out of the library. Cal's gaze locked with Gemma's and she stepped from behind the desk. "Did you call anyone?" she asked.

"The air ambulance is on the way. But the old man wants to get back on his horse. He can't walk. I think he's broken his leg."

Gemma grabbed his hand and hurried back through the house. When they got to the porch, she saw the stockmen gathered around Harry. He was shouting at them, waving his arm as he struggled to sit up. Mary knelt beside him, trying to calm him down.

"Did you call Hayley?" Gemma asked.

"She's somewhere with Teague, I think. They flew out a few days ago. I don't know where they went."

"See if you can find her. Call the vet he works with."

"Doc Daley," Cal said.

"He probably left a number with him. I'll help Mary."

Gemma ran down the steps and joined the housekeeper. "Boys, why don't you get back to work," she said. "Mary and I can take care of this." When they didn't move, she turned Davey around and gave him a gentle shove. "Go," she said in a low voice. "You're just making him more upset."

Slowly, the boys scattered. Gemma squatted down beside the old man. "We're going to call Hayley," she said. "Stay still. You'll be fine."

"Put me back on my damn horse," he demanded.

"No," Gemma replied in a firm voice. "I don't think you can get back on your horse right now."

"Who are you?" he asked.

"Just a visitor here," Gemma said. "My name is Gemma."

"Keep those Quinns away from me," he muttered. "They'd sooner kill me than help me."

"Why don't you tell me what hurts," she said.

"My hip." He groaned as he tried to move again. "It hurts like hell."

"Mary, why don't you get some ice and a pillow for Mr. Fraser's head. So he can lie back and relax. And can you ask Cal to take care of his horse, please?"

"Don't touch that horse," Harry warned.

"We'll just have Cal give him some water."

"Her," Harry said. "It's a mare."

"Oh. See, well, that's interesting. I don't know much about horses. In fact, I'm frightened of them. For just this reason. Is this the first time you've fallen?"

"No," Harry said. "I had a bad fall about ten years back. Broke my arm."

"I suppose it was difficult to work your station with a broken arm," Gemma commented. "How did you manage that?"

Over the next hour, Gemma kept Harry calm and alert with an endless stream of conversation. Mary went back and forth between the doctor on the phone and fetching fresh ice to put on Harry's hip.

The helicopter flew low over the homestead before it landed just beyond the house. Gemma held Harry's hand as the medics attended to him. They splinted his legs together, then carefully put him on a stretcher. As they moved him to the helicopter, she walked along beside him, keeping up a running commentary.

Cal was waiting for her when she returned to the house, standing on the porch, his expression cloudy, his mouth set in a grim line. He held out his hand as she climbed the steps. "Come with me," he said.

She followed him upstairs to his room and when he got there, Cal slammed the door behind them. He turned to her, cradled her face between his hands and kissed her. The kiss took her by surprise and she drew in a sharp breath. But then, as her mouth molded against his, Gemma sighed. They'd seemed miles apart just this morning and now, a single kiss was all it took to bring them back together again.

"I'm sorry," he murmured. "I've been such an ass."

"No," she said. "I'm the one who's sorry. It was a foolish plan for a foolish reason. I should never have come here."

"Don't say that," Cal said. "I'm glad you're here. I could never have handled Harry like that. You just kept him calm and distracted." He paused. "The last week has been sheer hell, Gemma. I've tried to stop caring about you, but I can't."

He kissed her again, his hands running over her body as if trying to make up for the week they'd lost. Before long they were tugging at each other's clothes, the passion crackling between them. When they were left in just their underwear, they tumbled onto the bed, lost in an endless kiss.

Gemma hadn't realized how much this desire had become a necessary part of her life. Touching Cal, tasting Cal, it was as natural as breathing. Even after everything that had happened, all the distance between them, Gemma felt as though they were moving toward something deeper, more lasting.

Was she fooling herself? They'd known each other for exactly eighteen days. They had everything working against them and yet, it was becoming more difficult every day to ignore the intensity of her emotions.

Gemma had protected her heart for so long, encased it in a hard shell that no one could penetrate. But then she'd come here, to Kerry Creek, and forgotten to put up her defenses. By the time she remembered, it was too late.

"No one knows I came here for the emerald," she murmured. "Just you and me. If we don't find it, sooner or later, the story will be lost to history. People will forget and Kerry Creek will be safe."

"Another secret?" he asked.

Gemma nodded. "But this is a good secret. One worth keeping."

There was a way to move into the future with Cal. But no matter how she looked at it, it would involve her staying at Kerry Creek, giving up everything in Dublin, her friends, her job, her home. The thought was overwhelming.

She didn't want to think about that now. All she wanted was to lose herself in Cal. She could sort the rest out later.

8

"ALL RIGHT. I'LL SELL YOU the land," Cal said. "I'll call our solicitor and have him draw up some sort of agreement. But the next time anything comes to a vote, you vote with me."

Cal couldn't believe what Teague had convinced him to do. After all this time arguing a land dispute with Harry Fraser, after years of fighting between the two families, Cal had just approved a peace treaty.

Though on the surface it seemed like a crazy idea, Cal had to trust that Teague knew what he was doing. Harry was in the hospital, refusing surgery for his broken hip. The prognosis was grim and Hayley was desperate to change his mind. Giving Harry the land would give him a reason to live, or so Teague claimed.

"Thank you," his brother said, smiling. "This will all turn out in the end. I promise."

Cal groaned inwardly. This was crazy, but he had to trust his brother. "I'm going to hold you to that promise. Now, get the hell out of my office. And tell Gemma she can come in."

"If it's possible, I'd like the agreement today. Before I head to Brisbane."

Cal frowned. "Today? Why today?"

"Because I need it today," Teague insisted, looking at his watch. "In the next hour or two would be good." He stood and moved to the door. "Thanks, Cal. I owe you. Free vet services for the next fifty years."

"That would about cover it," Cal muttered. "As long as you throw in ownership of the plane, too."

Callum leaned back in his chair, waiting for Gemma to return. She had poked her head in the library looking for him a few minutes ago, but excused herself when she realized he and Teague were in the midst of a serious conversation. But he needed her now, to tell him that he wasn't a gullible fool to have agreed to Teague's plans.

Odd how that all he seemed to need in life was her approval. He didn't care about anything else except Gemma. The station was still important, but it was just land and buildings, possessions that, though an integral part of his life, didn't have the capacity to make him happy. Not the way Gemma did.

Cal reached for the phone and placed a call to his solicitor. Though he carefully explained the deal he and Teague had reached, requesting a letter of agreement for the land deal, his solicitor spent five minutes arguing against it. Cal finally got a promise for an e-mail copy of the agreement, sent within the hour. That done, he turned on his computer and waited while the dial-up modem made the connection.

His e-mail account boasted five new letters, four more than he usually got in a week. He opened the mailbox, expecting to find a notification of shipping confirmation on the windmill parts he'd ordered. Instead he noticed a series of three notes from OutbackMates.

Cal opened the first to find a letter from one of the three women the service had chosen for him. Sylvie Monroe. Cursing softly, he quickly closed it. Had he misunderstood the rules? Wasn't he supposed to make the first move? Maybe these women had grown impatient waiting. After all, it had been three weeks. "Hell," he muttered. Cal already had enough to deal with and now this?

"Hi."

He glanced up to see Gemma standing at the door. She wore a pale green cotton dress that set off her eyes, eyes that he loved staring into. Cal quickly turned off his computer. "Hi."

"Mary and I baked some bickies. Chocolate chip. They're still warm. Would you like some?"

"Sure," Cal said.

"I sent some with Teague for Hayley." She took a step into the room. "Did he say how her grandfather was doing? I didn't want to press him for details."

"He has a broken hip and they want to do surgery. But he's refusing. So, Teague is taking him something that might change his mind. Quinn land."

Gemma's eyes went wide. "You're giving him the land you've been fighting over?"

Cal nodded. "Tell me I'm not losing my mind, Gemma. This seems so important to Teague. And he does have a third share in the station."

"No," Gemma said, slowly approaching the desk. "I

don't think you're crazy. It's just land. And Teague is your brother."

Cal chuckled. "Yeah. A brother who just convinced me to give away the land with the best water bore on Kerry Creek. But Teague wanted to do this for Hayley and for her grandfather."

"He loves her," Gemma said.

"Yeah, I believe he does. I think he always has, all these years. It's rather amazing if you think of it. Almost ten years apart and their feelings survived."

She circled the desk and wrapped her arms around his neck. "You're a good man, Cal." Gemma sat down on his lap, throwing her legs over the arm of his chair. "Did you notice how tidy the library is?"

He nodded. "Are you finished with your work?"

Gemma nodded, her mood turning serious. "I didn't find anything, Cal. If Crevan brought the emerald here, then he must have buried it somewhere in the outback. Because it's not in the house."

"Maybe he did bury it," Cal said. "Remember that story I told you about? The one about buried treasure on the station. You could probably ask my father. He might know more."

"Maybe when you decide to tear down a wall or pull up a floor, you'll find it hidden away. Or maybe, Crevan never had it in the first place. From everything I've read about him, he had an odd sense of humor. Maybe painting the emerald into the portrait was his idea of a joke."

"Or a clue?" Cal asked.

Gemma shook her head. "No. The emerald needs to

remain lost. It's better for you and better for me." She drew a deep breath. "And I need to get home," she added softly.

Cal leaned back in his chair. He knew this was coming, yet he hadn't decided how to handle it. His first instinct was to beg her to stay, to convince her they couldn't live without each other. But Cal knew as well as she did that begging would get them nowhere.

The feelings that had brought them this far just weren't strong enough to last forever. Sure, he wanted to believe that desire was the only thing needed for two people to fall in love. But there were many more practical considerations, as well—like living on the same bloody continent.

"When are you going to go?"

"I thought I'd stay another week, if it was all right with you," she suggested. "We haven't spent much time together lately. And I was hoping you'd teach me to ride. Unless, of course, you're too busy."

"No. Another week would be perfect," he said, relief washing over him. "I can take some time away from the station. Maybe we can see some of the sights in Queensland. We could go to the wineries at Darling Downs. Or go camping at Carnarvon. Or we could go to Brisbane and spend some time at the beach. What would you like to do?"

"I think I'd like to stay here," Gemma said. "We could go back to that spot on Kerry Creek and spend a night or two."

Cal reached out and took her hand in his, toying with her fingers. "If you're going to stay for another week, then I want you to stay with me. In my room."

She nodded. "All right. With Payton gone, the bunk-house has been a bit lonely."

It was the most he could hope for. One more week with Gemma, in his life and in his bed. He intended to make every single minute count. And after she left, he'd do his best to forget that he'd just lost the best thing that had ever happened to him.

"NOW YOU'RE RIDING," Cal called. "Just relax. See if you can move with the horse. Raise yourself up just a bit in the stirrups."

Gemma did as she was told. The horse, Tibby, was a gentle mare that Cal had chosen especially for her. Unlike the others, Tibby wasn't in foal, which made Gemma feel a bit sorry for her. She'd imagined all sorts of feelings going on in the horse's head and from the moment she touched Tibby's velvety muzzle, they'd made a connection. This was an animal she could trust.

Cal held on to a lead he'd fastened to Tibby's bridle, keeping the horse running in a wide circle around him. "Do you want to try a little faster gait?" he asked.

"No," Gemma said. "Tibby is tired."

"Don't worry. You're doing very well. Give it a try."

"All right," Gemma said, preparing herself for the fall that would soon follow. She'd nearly fallen twice already, but Cal had caught her before she hit the ground. She was counting on that again. "If I scream, you have to slow her down."

He clucked his tongue and slapped the ground with the end of the lead. Tibby responded immediately, picking up her pace. Gemma leaned forward and lifted up in the stirrups and to her surprise, she moved along with the horse's rhythm, as if they were of one mind. "I know what you mean," she called to Cal. "This is it. It's not so hard."

But a moment later, she fell out of the cadence and found herself bouncing against the saddle, each step jolting her. Cal slowed the horse to a walk. "That was good," he said.

Gemma grinned. "It was good." She leaned over and patted Tibby's neck. "Good girl." Tibby nodded her head and Gemma gently pulled her to a stop. "I think I'm going to need an hour in the hot tub. My bum is going to be sore again."

For the past week, she'd had a riding lesson every day and to her surprise, she'd managed to conquer her fears—at least some of them. She wasn't afraid of being bitten, she'd gotten used to the smell, and she'd even reconciled the distance between the top of the horse and the ground as survivable in a fall.

What she hadn't reconciled were her feelings for Cal. It had been exactly a week since she'd agreed to stay. Yet neither one of them had brought up her leaving. They both seemed content to extend the vacation, day by day, without comment or question.

But avoiding the topic of their parting wasn't doing either of them any good. It just gave them an excuse to pretend as if there were nothing standing between them. It gave them an excuse to fall more deeply in love. And that would only make it more difficult in the end.

"Again," she said. "I want to go again."

"Riding is very good exercise," he said. "Good for the thighs."

"I do love your thighs," Gemma teased. She noticed Mary approaching the stable yard and gave her a wave. "Here's Mary and she doesn't look very happy. Have we missed lunch?" Gemma stood up in the stirrups. "Mary, I'm riding!"

Mary stopped at the fence. "Gemma, you have a phone call. It's urgent. You need to come right away."

"Who is it? Is it Payton? Did the private investigator find them?"

"It's not Payton. It's your mother," Mary said, a worried expression on her face. "She says it's an emergency."

Gemma felt her heart stop. She'd called her mother a few weeks ago just to let her know where she was, giving her Cal's number to call in case of emergency. Frugal as her mother was, she'd never place a call to Australia unless something was seriously wrong.

Gemma quickly slid off the horse, stumbling as she hit the ground. She landed hard on her backside, crying out in surprise. Cal reached down and pulled her to her feet, then brushed the dirt off her jeans.

"I—I'll be right back," she said.

"I'll come with you," Cal said.

They followed Mary back to the house. She pointed to the phone, lying on the kitchen table but Cal shook his head. "She'll take it in the library," he said.

Gemma hurried through the hall, her heart slamming in her chest. She picked up the phone from the desk. "Mum? Mum, are you there?"

The connection was surprisingly clear. "Gemma.

Good. Finally. I was wondering if you'd ever come on the line. This is costing me a small fortune to call. What kind of hotel is that? Don't you have a phone in your room?"

"What's wrong?" Gemma asked. "Are you all right?"

"Oh, I'm fine, dear. I've had a bit of a cold and my elbow has been sore, but generally, I've been just fine."

"Then why are you calling?"

"Well…I have good news and I have bad. Which would you like first?"

"Mum, this isn't the time for games. You scared me half to death. Why are you calling?"

"Your father needs you," she said, her voice barely containing her excitement.

Gemma shook her head, sure she'd misunderstood. "My father?"

"I had a visit from the Parnell family solicitor yesterday evening and David's asked for you. You have to come home. He wants to see you immediately."

"Why now? After all these years?"

"He's ill, Gemma. He's had some sort of heart attack. He'll be fine, but I suppose it's caused him to think about all the mistakes he's made in the past. It seems he wants to atone for some of them."

"He should be doing that for you, Mum, not me," Gemma snapped. "You're the one who struggled to get by on nothing."

"Gemma, you need to go to him. He's your father. You need to come home right now." She paused. "Before it's too late."

"What does that mean, Mum? He's not going to die. You just said so."

"Before he changes his mind."

"About me? Let him. I don't care. I've wasted too much of my time hoping he'd finally decide to be a father to me. But I'm an adult now. It's time for me to start acting like one."

"You deserve your share of the family trust," her mother said.

"I don't want his money. It's never been about that." She closed her eyes. There had been a time when she would have rushed to David Parnell's side, thrilled that she'd been summoned and eager to do as he demanded.

But why should she give him the satisfaction now? Her father was facing his mortality, so he needed to clear his conscience by making amends for his monstrous behavior. The problem was, she didn't need his approval anymore. She'd found a man who cared about her, who respected her for exactly who she was.

"Please, Gemma. Do this for me. This is what I've been waiting for all these years. I don't think you realize how happy this would make me."

"All right," Gemma murmured. "But I'm not coming home right away. If he's not on his death bed, then he can wait a few days. Bye, Mum." Gemma hung up the phone, then buried her face in her hands. "Oh, God."

"What is it?" Cal asked.

"My father. He's ill and he wants to see me."

Cal was silent for a long time. "That's good," he finally said. "That's what you've wanted all along, right?"

"Yes," Gemma said. "No. I don't know what I want anymore." She looked at him to find concern etched across his handsome features. "I thought this is what I wanted, but now, I'd rather stay here a bit longer."

"Gemma, you have to go. He's your father."

"He's not doing this for me," she said. "He's just being selfish."

"If you don't go, you'll probably regret it. Look at Hayley. She and her grandfather had been at odds for years but she managed to work things out in the end."

"I don't even know my father, beyond a photo my mother kept and a few bits she'd clipped from the newspapers. I've met him twice in my life and both times, he couldn't wait for me to leave. Why should I give him anything he wants?"

"You shouldn't," Cal said. "I don't want you to leave. Let him die with his treatment of you on his conscience. What difference does it make?"

Gemma knew exactly what he was doing, bringing out her better intentions, knowing that in the end, she wouldn't refuse. She leaned in and kissed him, her lips communicating the trust that she'd found in him. "I'll go tomorrow."

"It's the right thing, Gemma. You'll see. And it's not like you're leaving forever."

"It isn't?" Gemma drew back and looked into his eyes. Was this some sort of proposal?

"The station will always be here. And I'll always be on the station. You can come back and visit anytime you like. Take another holiday. You're always welcome."

It was such a simple invitation, Gemma mused. The

kind of thing one would say to any houseguest. Come visit soon. You're welcome anytime. "All right," she said. "As long as you're not married. Who knows, you might find a wife next month. She wouldn't want your old lover showing up at her front door."

It was all so pleasant, this talk of her leaving. Yet inside, every word was like a stab to her heart. She didn't want to hear how easy it would be for Cal to forget her. She wanted him to get down on his knees and beg her to stay, to tell her that he couldn't live without her.

"I don't think that's going to happen," Cal said.

Gemma wanted to press him. What would he do after she left? Would he immediately resume his matrimonial search or would he pine for the Irish girl who'd shared his bed? She wrapped her arms more tightly around his neck and nuzzled her face into a spot beneath his ear.

"I think we should take a nap," she said.

Cal chuckled. "A nap? It's ten in the morning. We just got up a few hours ago."

"I need you lying next to me. With all your clothes off."

"I see. All right. Let's take a nap." He slipped his arms beneath her and stood, carrying her to the door. "I am glad we decided to stay here on the station. A nap is just the kind of adventure one should take on holiday, don't you think?"

CAL STRETCHED OUT ALONG the length of Gemma's naked body, his arm thrown over her waist, his face resting in the curve of her shoulder. He couldn't believe that by this time tomorrow, she would be gone.

It had been nearly a month, yet it seemed like just yesterday when he'd first seen her on the road trying to change her flat tire. He'd sensed that something was about to change in his life at that moment and he'd been right. He'd fallen in love—for the first time.

But would it be the last time? Would his memories of Gemma prevent him from ever inviting another woman into his life? There were so many emotions roiling inside of him. He was angry she'd been manipulated into returning to Ireland by a father she never knew. He was sad he had no choice but to let her go. And he was resigned to the fact that perhaps this was all the time they were meant to have—not even a month. But he'd shown none of these emotions to Gemma.

Callum had decided that their parting would be quiet and easy, exactly the way their relationship had been. There'd be no tears and no last-minute pleas. He'd let her walk away without a fight.

Though he'd extended an invitation for her to return to Kerry Creek, Cal knew the chances of that were slim. She'd slip back into her life in Dublin and thoughts of him would fade. Before long, he'd be just another holiday story, a man she'd met but couldn't quite remember. He pressed a kiss to her neck and sighed.

"Are you awake?" she asked.

"Umm." He kissed her again and pulled her body more tightly against his. "I can't sleep."

She turned toward him, her fingers smoothing over his face. "Neither can I."

"I want to spend every last minute with you. I can sleep in the plane on the way home."

Home. The word cut him like a knife. Her home wasn't here with him. It was in a place he'd never seen, in a country he'd never visited with people he'd never met. He felt as if he understood Gemma better than anyone, yet he knew nothing about her. "Tell me about your life," he said. "You know about mine."

"It's rather ordinary," Gemma said. "I live in a flat near the university. It's small and filled with old books that I inherited from my grandfather. My mother lives not far away, in her own flat, where I go every Monday and Thursday for dinner. When I have time off from my job, I often go to County Clare, to a small cottage that my grandparents left us. It's so pretty, set above the sea on a beautiful green hillside."

"It must be so different from life here on the station."

"It is. It's not dusty. And there are very few blowies or mozzies. It does rain much more, especially in County Clare."

"What about friends? Do you have a lot of friends?"

Gemma shook her head. "Not close friends. I never found much use for that. It's always been difficult for me to trust people." She paused. "You're my friend."

"Really?"

"I trust you, Cal. Completely. I'm not sure why. Maybe it was because of the unfamiliar surroundings. Or maybe getting away from Dublin changed my perspective."

"Besides my brothers, I really don't have any friends, either," he said. "The stockmen are my employees. Mary is like a mother to me. But I understand how you feel. There's no one that I can talk to, the way I can talk to you. I can say anything to you."

"When we first met, I thought you didn't like me. You barely said a word. I thought you could hardly wait until I left Kerry Creek."

"No. I just didn't know how to talk to you. I was nervous. I thought you were the most beautiful woman I'd ever seen in my life and I knew I'd make a fool of myself in front of you. So I just kept my mouth shut until I had something useful to say."

"Until I kissed you. Then you had plenty to say."

"Yeah, that opened the door. I reckoned if you liked me enough to kiss me, you probably would be interested in talking to me, as well."

Gemma giggled as she braced her arms over his chest and stared into his eyes. "We have had a wonderful time."

"Yes, we have," he said.

"And how will you remember it? How will you remember me?"

Cal thought about his response for a long moment. "You're like pure sunshine, all warmth and light, shining on my life for a short time. The sunshine will still be there after you leave, but it will be faded, like it's coming through a curtain."

She pushed up and kissed him, a kiss so sweet it made his heart ache. "That was beautiful."

"It was just the truth, that's all." He reached for her and drew her into another kiss, this one longer and deeper, designed to prove to them both that they couldn't live without each other.

Cal wanted to ask her to stay, to choose between her father and him, her life and his, her future and theirs.

But he knew what it was like for a woman on Kerry Creek. He'd see his mother grow more unhappy with each passing day. And he didn't want that for Gemma. If she were to come back, it would have to be her own decision, without any urging from him.

He rolled her beneath him and settled himself between her legs, slowly moving against her. He'd thought that the sex would be the most difficult thing to give up. But as they teased at each other's bodies with hands and mouths, Cal knew it was just a small part of what they'd shared.

Given the choice, he'd be happy just to have her living in the same house, the same territory, hell, even the same continent, even if it meant giving up sex for the rest of his life. It was her heart and soul he wanted to possess, not just her body.

They continued their conversation as Cal began a slow seduction, afraid that they might not have enough time to say everything that needed saying. But gradually the words turned to sighs and moans and when Cal slipped inside her, he heard her softly whisper his name.

They'd made love enough to know exactly what would please. He slowly brought her close to release, then drew her back, again and again, until Cal wasn't sure he could wait any longer. And when she tumbled over the edge unexpectedly, he let go, joining her in a perfect mingling of their pleasure.

There would never be another woman who could bring him such ecstasy. His heart, his soul and his body would always belong to Gemma, no matter where she was. And though she was walking out of his life in a few hours, Cal had to believe she'd return.

Hope was a funny thing. It could sustain a person in the most difficult of times. It could also blind a person to the realities of life. But for now, hope was all he had.

9

"THANK YOU FOR COMING, GEMMA. I know it meant a lot to him."

Gemma took her stepmother's outstretched hand and shook it, then turned and walked to the front door. A servant stood by, waiting to let her out. When the door closed behind her, Gemma let out a long sigh.

The past hour of her life had been the most bizarre experience she'd ever had. She'd arrived in Belfast a day after landing in Dublin, prepared to face her father for only the third time in her life. But this time, she had the upper hand. She didn't want anything to do with him and yet, he insisted on speaking with her.

Gemma glanced down at the packet of papers clutched in her hand. He'd drawn up documents giving her a share of the Parnell family trust. It was more money than she'd make in twenty years at the university. But unlike her college tuition, it came with no strings attached. He wanted to see her occasionally. And he wanted to know his grandchildren if there ever were any. But she was under no requirement to fulfill his wishes.

Overall, the conversation had been painfully stilted,

with long uncomfortable silences in between. It was far too late for them to enjoy anything resembling a normal relationship. And Gemma wasn't interested in trying.

"Back to the train, miss?"

Gemma smiled at the driver and nodded. "Thank you."

He held the door open and she slipped inside the car, then stared out the window at the huge manor house. With all its beautiful furnishings and expensive art, she preferred the cozy warmth of the homestead on Kerry Creek Station. That was a real home, not a museum filled with remnants of dead ancestors.

She'd left Kerry Creek nearly two days ago. A five-hour drive to Brisbane, a flight to Sydney, a stop in Singapore, a connection in London and then home to Dublin. She hadn't remembered the trip being so long and exhausting on her way to Australia.

But then, she'd been moving toward something. By coming back, she was leaving something—someone—behind. Her thoughts returned to her last moments with Cal, to the kiss he'd given her before helping her into her rental car. Gemma had waited for him to ask her to stay, anxious for the moment when he'd admit he loved her and couldn't live without her.

It hadn't come. He'd simply closed the car door and watched as she drove off. For the first two hours, she'd stop every so often at the side of the road, tempted to turn around and go back, to force him into admitting his feelings.

But then her common sense would return and she'd drive for a bit longer. With every mile that passed, it became more difficult to convince herself she was doing the right thing. Though she might love him, she couldn't make him love her.

Now, tears pressed at the corners of her eyes and she rested her head against the car window, her eyes fixed on the green countryside as it passed by. Where was her home? It certainly wasn't the Parnell country house. And her flat in Dublin didn't feel right, either. Every ounce of her longed for the rugged beauty of outback Queensland.

For a month, Kerry Creek had been her home. But it was more than just the house and land. It was the people. She'd fit in there, like a member of the family. Mary had become a second mother to her and the jackaroos like little brothers. Payton and Hayley were the sisters she'd never had.

Gemma brushed a tear from her cheek. She'd go back someday. Maybe the next summer—or winter, as it was in Australia. But would he be waiting? Or would Cal have moved on, finding a woman who was willing to be a part of his life? She took a ragged breath. Station life wasn't that bad, not when he was there to brighten her days and fill her nights with passion.

But living with him would mean a lot of sacrifices, some she'd never considered ever making for a man. Every shred of common sense told her she was exactly where she was supposed to be. So why couldn't she just accept life as it was?

If Cal had loved her, he would have told her. If he'd wanted her to stay, he would have asked. Gemma drew a deep breath and let it out slowly. Her life here in Ireland was lovely. Until she'd met Cal, it was all she'd ever dreamed it could be.

On the positive side, now she could focus on her work. She'd already decided to write a book about the Irish in Australia. There was a vibrant Irish culture alive in many parts of the country. And after learning more about Crevan and his day-to-day life, she thought she might even attempt a novel, a family saga that would begin on a prison ship and end with a present-day romance.

Gemma smiled. Writing a novel about the Quinns might be just the thing to take her mind off her troubles. She could write a better ending for herself, one where all the obstacles would disappear and she and Cal would live happily ever after. Fiction was a wonderful thing.

"Miss, are you all right?"

Gemma glanced up to see the driver watching her in the rearview mirror. "Me?" She touched her cheeks, surprised to find them wet with tears. "Yes, I'm fine. Just happy, that's all."

"Good," the driver said. "You'll be quite early for the train. Would you like to stop and do some shopping? Or maybe get a bite to eat?"

Gemma shook her head. She needed to get back to familiar surroundings. For now, it would have to be Dublin. But after a week or two with her mother, she was free to do as she pleased. And if she still felt the same way about Cal, maybe a trip back to Kerry Creek wasn't a silly idea.

She'd listen to her heart first and her common sense second. And be open to all the possibilities that the future might hold.

CAL STARED OUT AT THE HORIZON, turning his horse toward the homestead. He was hungry and dirty and he smelled pretty bad. It was time for a hot shower, a decent meal and a good long sleep in his own bed.

After Gemma had left, he'd spent just one night at home, a sleepless night wandering the station, pacing his bedroom, memories of her flooding his brain. So he'd gathered his things and ridden out just after breakfast, needing a place to think. Strangely, he ended up at the creek, at the small camp that he and Gemma had shared. For a moment, he'd regretted taking her there, upset that a visit to the spot would always bring memories of her.

But over the past two days, Cal had come to terms with what he'd had and what he'd lost. It was better to have loved and lost than never to have loved at all. Yes, it was a cliché, but he saw the truth in it. And that truth would have to get him through the next few weeks, months and years without her.

In the distance, Cal could see a pair of horses, with riders perched on them both. He came closer, expecting to find two of the stockmen from the station. But instead, he found his brothers deep in conversation. Cal pulled Eddie to a stop and looked at them both. "Are you having a party without me?"

Brody chuckled. "Where have you been?"

"I took a few days off. I needed some time to myself. When did you get back?"

"About an hour after you rode out. I was going to follow you, but then Mary told me Gemma had left, so I figured you'd want to be alone."

"I wouldn't have been great company. And I'd

reckon you haven't been a joy to live with, either, what with Payton leaving."

"You'd reckon wrong," Teague said, grinning. "Payton came back. I flew her in this morning. She wanted to surprise Brody."

Cal forced a smile. He ought to be happy for his youngest brother and he was. But the feeling was tinged with some bitterness. How wonderful would it have been to return and find that Gemma was the one Teague had brought back? "Where is she?"

"At the homestead," Brody said.

Teague pushed his hat back on his head and braced his hands on his saddle horn. "I'm glad you're back, Cal," he said. "Now that I'm running Wallaroo, I wanted to propose a deal."

"Like the one where I give up the best water bore in Queensland? Like that deal?"

"Well, I'm giving that land back. It's always been Quinn land and it's going to stay that way. Besides, it didn't quite do the trick."

Harry's death had been a shock to everyone. Cal had assumed the old man would outlive them all, just to spite the Quinns. But he'd passed shortly after surgery and had left Wallaroo to both Teague and Hayley. The arrangement hadn't been to Hayley's liking and she'd left Wallaroo the same day Gemma had left Kerry Creek.

"I'm sorry about that," Cal said. "We had our differences, but Harry was still a neighbor. How is Hayley? Have you heard from her?"

Teague shook his head. "No. I don't expect to. She was pretty angry when she left. According to the will, she has to come back within six months, so she'll have some time to cool down."

"So, you have big plans for the place?" Cal asked.

"We're going to raise horses. A small mob to start with. And we have some runs that might be good for Kerry Creek stock."

Cal blinked. First he got his land back and now an offer of grazing land. "What part of Wallaroo are you thinking about?"

Teague pointed to the northeast. "The section that runs up along the tract you gave me. We'd have to add another gate, but we could drive the cattle there after mustering and see how it works out."

"It's good land," Cal said, staring out to the horizon. "And if we have more grazing, we can increase the size of the mob. How many hectares would you want to lease?"

"As much as you want," Teague said.

They discussed terms as Teague explained his plans for the horse-breeding operation. But once again, his brother had a come up with a scheme—this one requiring that Cal give him the Kerry Creek breeding stock in return for Wallaroo grazing rights.

The horse operation had always been Teague's anyway. And it had been much more expensive than raising cattle. Really, Cal was getting the better end of the deal. Land was what he needed in order to expand the Kerry Creek operations. And land was hard to come by, while horses could be purchased almost anywhere.

"He won't go for it," Brody said to Teague. "Cal would never pay for anything that he could get for free."

"That's where you're wrong, little brother." Cal

nodded at Teague. "All right. It's a deal. I'll trade you the Kerry Creek horses for lease rights on Wallaroo."

They chatted about recent events and the women who had come and gone and in Brody's case, had come back again. Cal envied his brothers. They had choices. Both Teague and Brody had the luxury of going anywhere their women were. In fact, Brody and Payton were planning to travel to the States for Brody's tryout with an American football team. And Hayley was only a plane ride away in Sydney. But Gemma was oceans away.

"Maybe you ought to try and convince Gemma to come back," Teague suggested. "Go to Ireland. Explain to her how you feel and ask her to come home with you."

"She wouldn't want to live here," Cal said, shaking his head.

"Why not? If she loves you, she probably won't care where you live," Teague insisted. "And Brody and I can watch over the station while you're gone."

"No, I don't think so."

"What did she say when you asked her to stay?" Brody wondered.

"I didn't ask," Cal replied. "She had to go home. She didn't have a choice. Besides, I didn't want to deal with the rejection."

This started a full-on assault on Cal's stupidity when it came to women, with both Brody and Teague tossing out advice. When he'd had enough of his brothers' haranguing, he pushed his hat down on his head. "I have an idea. Follow me."

With a whoop he kicked Eddie in the flanks and the gelding raced toward the big rock. Teague and Brody followed and when they reached the spot, they climbed to the top and surveyed the land around them.

"Doesn't seem as big as it used to be, does it?" Brody commented.

Brody was right, Cal mused. They used to struggle to climb to the top and now it was quick work.

"So what do we do?" Teague asked. "I'm not sure I remember."

"We have to say it out loud," Cal replied. "One wish. The thing you want most in the world."

"How do we know it will work?" Teague asked.

"It worked for me. Remember?" Brody asked. "I wished I could be a pro footballer. And it happened."

"And I wished I could run a station like Kerry Creek," Cal said. "And I'm running Kerry Creek. I remember what you wished for. You wanted a plane."

"Or a helicopter," Brody said. "I guess you got your wish, too."

"So what makes you think it will work again?" Teague asked.

"We won't know unless we try." Cal drew a deep breath. "I wish Gemma would come back to Kerry Creek for good."

"I wish Hayley would realize I'm the only guy she will ever love."

"I wish Payton would say yes when I ask her to marry me."

Teague and Cal both stared at their little brother, stunned. Brody grinned. "You don't get anything in life unless you ask."

"Well, I guess that's it," Cal said. "We'll see if it

works. Are you riding back to Kerry Creek with us?" he asked Teague.

"I've got work to do at Wallaroo," he said. "But I'll come by tomorrow to talk about our deal."

They jumped off the rock and remounted their horses. Then Brody and Cal headed toward Kerry Creek and Teague toward Wallaroo. As they neared the station, they slowed their pace.

"You should go to her," Brody said. "Plead your case. Show her how you feel."

"No," Cal said. "I can't go to Ireland. Not now. We're going to start mustering tomorrow."

"Put it off," Brody said. "What difference will a week make, Cal? This is the rest of your life we're talking about. You're going to give that up, give up on the woman you love, just because you think it might inconvenience a few cows?"

Cal laughed. "What would I say?"

"Tell her how you feel. It's simple. It's honest. She can't fault you for that."

"Ireland?" Cal said.

"We're not talking about the moon. They do have planes that fly from Oz to Ireland. Do you know where she lives?"

"Not really. We didn't exchange addresses or phone numbers. She knows where to find me. But she did say she taught at the university in Dublin. I suppose I could go there looking for her."

"You could," Brody said.

"But I'd need a ticket. And a passport. I don't have one of those."

"You can get one in Brisbane in a day, maybe two. I don't think you'd need a visa, but we'll have to check on that, too."

Cal thought about the possibilities for a moment or two, then realized it wasn't good to think. Thinking was for fools. Action was what would win him the woman he loved. After all, what did he have to lose? If she said no, then he'd go on with his life as he'd planned. But if she said yes, then everything would change. And like Brody said, he'd never get anything in life unless he asked for it.

"All right," Cal said. "Let's figure out how this is going to happen."

CAL LOOKED UP AT THE OLD buildings of University College. This was Ireland. It was difficult to believe he'd come all this way on a whim. But now that he was here, he realized he was in the land of his ancestors. Somewhere nearby, Crevan had plied his trade as a pickpocket. And somewhere else, he'd been tried, convicted and sentenced to a life in exile.

All around him, the people spoke with a lilt that had come to be familiar to him. But was that because of Gemma or were there still some memories deep in his brain that had been passed along in his DNA? Strangely enough, he felt at home here, as if he belonged.

Cal glanced down at the map he'd purchased at the airport. There'd been some confusion on his arrival whether he'd find her at the University of Dublin or at Trinity College or at University College of Dublin which wasn't in Dublin at all. But a helpful aide at the tourist office found Gemma's name on the staff directory at University College, which was located in an area in southeast Dublin called Belfield.

He walked through the doors of the Newman Building and found the directory, searching for Gemma's name. He'd go first to her office. If he couldn't find her there, then he'd see if they'd give out her phone number. As he walked through the halls of the university, he tried to imagine Gemma working in such an atmosphere. He'd only known her at the station, where she'd set herself up in his messy library, wading through piles of books and stacks of papers.

"May I help you?"

He turned to see an older woman sitting at a desk. Cal smiled. "Do I look lost?"

She nodded. "Who have you come to see?"

"Gemma Moynihan?"

"Her office is just down the corridor and to the left. Her name is on the door. But I don't think she's in. I saw her walking over to the archives about fifteen minutes ago."

"How would I get there?"

"They're in the library. I'll call Seamus and let him know you're coming. What's your name?"

"Quinn," he said. "Callum Quinn."

"You're Australian? And with a name like Quinn, I'd say a bit Irish, too. Here for a visit?"

"Sort of," Cal said. "Which way are the archives?"

"Out through the courtyard and over to James Joyce Library. Once you're there, Seamus will help you. Enjoy your visit, Mr. Quinn."

Cal walked back outside. It seemed as though finding Gemma in Dublin was even more complicated than just getting to Ireland. There were so many places to get lost in a big city.

Cal asked directions along the way and finally found the right building, then was directed through a long series of doors and hallways until he found the archives. A student sat at the desk and watched him suspiciously as he approached. "I'm looking for Gemma Moynihan," Cal said.

"Are you a student?"

"No, a visitor. The lady over in the history building said Seamus would help me locate Gemma."

"She's inside. But you can't go in with that bag," he said, pointing to Cal's duffel. "You'll have to leave that here. Along with some identification." He gave the fellow his passport and set the bag on the floor next to his desk. "Through that door, turn left, go all the way to the end and you'll find some reading tables. I think she's back there."

The archives looked just like the library at Kerry Creek, filled with old books and boxes of papers, only a hundred times larger. He followed the directions, his footsteps echoing softly on the floor. When he turned the corner, Cal stopped.

Gemma was there, bent over a huge book, her hair tumbling down around her face, the light from a reading lamp turning it to spun copper. She reached up and tucked a strand behind her ear and he held his breath as her profile was revealed.

She didn't look different, but in these surroundings, he felt as though he didn't know her at all. He didn't recognize the clothes she wore and she'd painted her fingernails a shocking shade of pink. Had he been a fool to come so far? Drawing a deep breath, Callum took a step forward. "I would have brought tea and bickies, but I didn't have room in my bag."

Gemma jumped at the sound of his voice and turned to him with a stunned expression. Slowly, she pushed her chair back and stood, watching him the whole time as if she wasn't quite sure he was real.

"You have to say something," Cal murmured. "Please tell me I haven't made a mistake in coming."

"Oh, my God," Gemma cried. She crossed the space between them in a heartbeat and threw her arms around his neck. "What are you doing here? How did you find me?"

"It wasn't easy."

"Why are you here? Are you here to see me?"

"You're the only person I know in Dublin, so that would make sense."

"But I've barely been home a week." She pressed a frantic kiss to his lips, then drew back. "Is everything all right?"

"It is now," Cal said. "It's just about perfect."

Gemma ran her hands over his chest. He couldn't believe how much he'd missed her touch. And the effect it had on him. He covered her fingers with his. "You look beautiful," he murmured.

"So do you. Only you seem different. Out of your element." She giggled as she reached up and touched his face. "You got a haircut. And you're wearing the shirt I bought you."

"I wanted to look good."

"It's odd that you would come now," Gemma said,

turning to point to the books scattered on the table. "I've been working on finding the emerald. I think I might have missed something."

"I don't care about the emerald," Callum said.

She grabbed a paper and held it out to him. "See, I found this drawing of the emerald. It's carved with a very specific design. Crevan had probably seen this drawing in court. But this isn't exactly the same design on the emerald in the portrait." She picked up another paper. "This is what's on the portrait. I drew this. And I think Crevan drew his own, from memory, and gave it to the painter." She pulled another paper from the stack. "And then there's this—a drawing of a stone given to the British Royal Family in 1906 by a merchant named Patrick Healy. Recognize it?"

Callum nodded, his gaze shifting back and forth between the two pictures. "So you're saying the royal family has the emerald?"

"I think so," Gemma said. "It looks like Crevan didn't steal it. And I was probably right about him putting it in the portrait as a joke."

Callum smoothed his fingers over her mouth. "A joke that brought you to me. Thank God, Crevan had a sense of humor."

"Don't you understand? If I'd have found this earlier, I never would have come to Australia looking for you. I decided to do an Internet search with a description of the emerald and this came up. So it was more my incompetence than Crevan's joke that took me to Kerry Creek."

"Gemma, I don't care what brought you to me. That's history. This is now."

She nodded, turning into his touch. "Have you come for a visit, then? How long are you staying?"

"Long enough to try to convince you to come back with me," he said. "I know it's a long shot at best, but I have to try. I love you, Gemma. I wasn't sure I'd ever be able to say that to a woman. And I know, if you don't want me, there's never going to be another woman for me. I can live with that."

She opened her mouth to speak and Cal pressed his finger to her lips. "Let me say it all and then you can comment."

Wide-eyed, she nodded her agreement.

"I know the station isn't the most glamorous place to live or the most comfortable. But it's where I have to be, at least for now. But I promise you, we won't be stuck there. We can make a trip to Ireland a couple times a year and stay in your cottage by the sea. And if you want, your mother can come and live with us. There are universities in Brisbane. If you still want to teach, we'll work something out. But we can't live so far apart." Cal paused and drew a deep breath, scanning her face for a clue to her feelings.

"Is that it?" she asked.

He chuckled. "That's it. Oh, and remember, I love you."

She smiled, then ran her hands through the hair at his nape. "I love you, too, Cal."

He waited for the rest. But as seconds ticked by, he got the uneasy feeling that it wouldn't come. Tears swam in her eyes and he watched as one escaped, trick-ling down her cheek. She wasn't coming home with him. Hell, he'd done what he'd come to do. "I understand, Gemma."

"I don't think you do. I never thought I'd find someone I wanted to spend my life with. And never in a million years did I think that person would live on a cattle station in the Australian outback. But that's where you live. And that's where I'll live if it means I can be with you."

Her words stole the breath from his lungs. Cal gasped, then picked her up off her feet and hugged her hard. "Are you serious? You're not making a galah of me, are you?"

"I don't know what that is," Gemma said. "But I know I'm perfectly serious. I will hold you to your promise about coming back to Ireland, though."

He cupped her face in his hands and kissed her, her mouth soft and warm, the taste like the sweetest wine. "Maybe you should take me to meet your mother," he said. "And then we could pay a visit to that cottage. And while I'm here, I'd like to see where my ancestors came from. Oh, and the Book of Kells." He paused. "I've been reading the tourist brochures."

"We can do all of that. But first I'm taking you home to my flat. You look exhausted."

"I do?"

"Yes, utterly. I think you need a nap."

Cal grinned. "Yes, I do. That's exactly what I need."

She grabbed his hand and they walked toward the door. But Cal had already gone far too long without a kiss. He wrapped his hands around her waist and pressed her back against the shelves, taking possession of her mouth once again.

Of the three Quinn brothers, he'd thought his odds of finding love were the longest. And maybe they had been. But from the moment he'd met Gemma, Cal had known she was meant for him. They'd found each other in a big, wide world full of millions of people. And now that they were together, he intended to make sure her life was happier than she'd ever dreamed.

Epilogue

"IT'S NOT THAT HIGH," HAYLEY SAID. "Come on, then, grab my hand. I'll pull you up."

Gemma braced her hands on her waist and looked around. "Don't you find this a wee bit odd? This big rock in the middle of a flat plain. Cal brought me out here one night. It didn't look this big in the dark."

"Teague and I used to meet here all the time when we were kids. He told me it's magic. You stand on top and make a wish and your wish will come true."

Payton took Hayley's hand and scrambled to the top. "Come on, Gemma, it's not that bad."

Gemma grabbed their hands and they hoisted her up to stand next to them. She wobbled a bit, then sat down. It wasn't that hard, she thought to herself. Gemma tipped her face up to the midafternoon sun and closed her eyes, trying to imagine the Quinn brothers as kids. They probably weren't much different than they were now, just a bit smaller.

"I kissed Teague for the first time right here, on this rock," Hayley said, sitting down beside her. "I remember how surprised he was. He'd never kissed a girl before."

"Don't you think it strange that we all ended up here at the same time?" Payton asked, sitting on the other side of Gemma. "What are the chances of that? And now we're all back here, together. At least for a little while."

"Are you leaving?" Gemma asked.

"We're going to the States for Brody's tryout. And then we're going to visit my parents. After that, I'm not sure what we'll be doing...besides getting married."

"Really?" Hayley asked.

Payton nodded. "Who would have thought Brody Quinn was such a traditional guy? He wants the whole nine yards. I'd be happy with a little wedding chapel in Vegas, but that's not enough for Brody."

"Nine yards?" Hayley asked.

"The big wedding, the white dress, the huge cake. But I'm going to try to talk him into something more intimate. Maybe just our families on the beach in Fremantle."

"That sounds lovely," Gemma said. She looked at Hayley. "What about you? Are you and Teague going to have a go at marriage?"

"I suppose we ought to consider it," Hayley replied. She winced. "Since I am going to have a baby."

Gemma and Payton both gasped. "No!" Gemma said. "How could you have kept that a secret from us?"

"I wanted to wait a bit. It's been a few months, so I guess it's safe to tell. Besides, I didn't want the press to get hold of this. I wanted it to belong to us, for just a little while longer."

Payton threw her arms around Hayley and gave her

a fierce hug. "Oh, you and Teague will make beautiful babies together."

"Teague is over the moon. He can't stop talking about it. And he will not leave me alone. He's bought books and DVDs. I still have to finish out my contract with the show, but he's jumping ahead, looking for maternity hospitals. This baby can't come fast enough for his tastes."

They both turned to Gemma. "And what about you, Miss Moynihan?" Payton said. "Now that you're back on Kerry Creek, does Cal intend to make an honest woman of you?"

"He's asked. And I'm considering my answer. I love him, that much I know. And I intend to spend the rest of my life with him. Still, it would be nice to be courted for a while. In any case, I should soon put the poor man out of his misery."

"Speaking of men, look what's coming at us," Peyton said.

Gemma shaded her eyes and watched as three riders approached. "I hope they brought lunch. I'm famished."

"Help me down," Hayley said. "If Teague finds me on this rock, he's going to scold me. I can't walk to the refrigerator without him asking if it will hurt the baby."

Gemma held on to Hayley's hand as she slid to the ground, then dropped down beside her. Payton stayed on top of the rock, smiling as the boys pulled their horses to a stop. "I thought you three were working hard," she said. "Or was it hardly working?"

Brody wagged his finger at her. "You better crawl down before you fall down."

"Come and get me."

He jumped off his horse and scampered up the rock, then grabbed her around the waist and kissed her. Hayley stood beside Teague, her hand on his thigh, his fingers laced through hers.

Gemma looked up at Cal. Even covered in a layer of dust, he was still the most stunning man she'd ever seen in her life. He smiled at her, the kind of smile she'd seen the night before, after he'd made love to her. It told her everything she needed to know.

"Yes," Gemma said.

"Yes?" he asked.

She nodded. "To that question you've been waiting on. The answer is yes."

Cal jumped off his horse, grabbed her around the waist and kissed her, picking her up off the ground as their mouths met. "Yes," he said, his breath warm against her ear.

Gemma closed her eyes and held tight as he spun her around. For a moment, she was dizzy, but then he kissed her again and everything became clear. This was exactly where she belonged, in his arms, in his life. There was no longer any doubt and there never would be again.

* * * * *

Meet The Sullivans...

Over 1 million books sold worldwide!

Stay tuned for more from The Sullivans in 2014

Available from:

www.millsandboon.co.uk

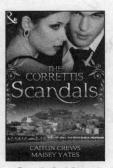

The World of Mills & Boon®

There's a Mills & Boon® series that's perfect for you. We publish ten series and, with new titles every month, you never have to wait long for your favourite to come along.

Blaze
Scorching hot, sexy reads
4 new stories every month

By Request
Relive the romance with the best of the best
9 new stories every month

Cherish™
Romance to melt the heart every time
12 new stories every month

Desire™
Passionate and dramatic love stories
8 new stories every month